LES ABEND

PAPER WINGS

WildBluePress.com

This is a work of fiction. Names, characters, businesses, places, events and incidents are either the products of the author's imagination or used in a fictitious manner. Any resemblance to actual persons, living or dead, or actual events is purely coincidental.

PAPER WINGS published by:
WILDBLUE PRESS
P.O. Box 102440
Denver, Colorado 80250

Publisher Disclaimer: Any opinions, statements of fact or fiction, descriptions, dialogue, and citations found in this book were provided by the author, and are solely those of the author. The publisher makes no claim as to their veracity or accuracy, and assumes no liability for the content.

ISBN 978-1-942266-63-1 Trade Paperback
ISBN 978-1-942266-64-8 eBook

Interior Formatting/Book Cover Design by Elijah Toten
www.totencreative.com

PAPER WINGS

CHAPTER ONE

Saturday
15:30 EDT

Tony cocked his head back and swallowed the last remaining gulp from the Budweiser can. He scrunched his face as if he had eaten a raw lemon. The beer was flat and warm. Despite the Neoprene coolie cup embroidered with a cartoon caricature of a Hooter's girl that engulfed the can, the early morning Florida sun had warmed his favorite beverage way beyond his liking. Tony jammed the empty container back into the cup holder just to the right of the shift levers on the Donzi. He wiped his mouth with the back of his left hand. With his right hand, Tony pulled back on the two throttle levers. The thirty-five-foot boat began to slow, the bow settling into the turquoise waters of the Gulf Stream.

Frank climbed up onto the deck of the Donzi. His bronze beer belly jiggled over the top of the elastic waist band of his calf-length khaki shorts. He lowered his sunglasses, straining to see any sign of a person on board the express cruiser that was floating a hundred yards in front of them.

"Do ya see anybody, Frankie?" Tony bellowed from behind the Plexiglas windscreen of the center console.

"Nope…nuthin' yet, Tony." Frank slid his feet out into a wide stance, balancing himself as waves rocked the bow. "I think the boat is one of them old thirty-foot-somethin' Sea Rays with an aft cabin. Probably '80's vintage." Frank let out a throaty belch, releasing the trapped gas from his last can of Coors Light.

The two men had known each other since elementary school in New Jersey. They had learned how to drive together. They had learned about girls together. They had got into trouble together. Nothing much had changed except for their ages. For almost fifteen years, the two men were partners in their own Fort Lauderdale construction company, a business that had flourished despite the fact neither Tony nor Frank had been educated beyond the eleventh grade. This weekend, they were escaping the wives and the kids for their annual July fishing trip to Bimini.

Halfway back from the island, Tony's eyes had captured a brief glint of the light reflected off something on the horizon. The light had come from the deck rail of the Sea Ray. The older boat was now bobbing a few feet in front of them. The white hull was chalky, dulled by years of neglect, tortured by the sun.

"Yo!…Yo! Anybody home?" Frank yelled, cupping his hands in front of his mouth. No response from the Sea Ray.

Tony called to Frank. "I'll get ya close enough to jump off, Frankie. Climb on board and see if you can find somethin'."

Frank looked back at Tony and raised a thumb in a sign of approval.

As Tony maneuvered the Donzi alongside the Sea Ray, inches from touching, Frank lurched forward, taking a small leap onto the side deck of the other boat. With his friend safely aboard, Tony pulled the gear levers aft, moving the Donzi in reverse and away from the Sea Ray.

Frank stepped down into the cockpit and underneath the faded blue canopy. He swiveled his head, scanning the entire boat from bow to stern. A beaded trail of red dots spattered a portion of the deck. A black, semiautomatic handgun that Frank recognized as a Glock, similar to what he and Tony carried with them to some of their undesirable job sites, was lying on the cockpit floor.

Reaching down, Frank picked up the Glock using two fingers pinched around the gnarled grip. He didn't know why, but suddenly realized that touching the damn gun was probably a mistake. Frank dropped the Glock back down onto the deck as quickly as he had retrieved it.

He looked at Tony and shrugged his shoulders. Tony pointed at the sliding door that led down the short stairway into the cabin. Frank nodded.

"Anybody home?" Frank called out again as he stared at the closed cabin door. He began to feel a sense of uneasiness, unable to determine why. He took a deep breath and then unlatched the door. He put a foot on the first step and peered inside the cabin and into the salon. He surveyed the entire area.

A plastic tumbler was rolling back and forth in the salon sink. Resting on its side, a half empty bottle of Bombay Sapphire gin sat on the center table. A wooden model of some type of commercial airliner was crushed on the floor like a large bug; the two miniature engines were separated from the wings. Nothing stirred. Frank took another step lower. That was as far as he got.

An overwhelming stench filled his nostrils. The stench seemed to invade every pore of his body. He began to gag. Frank turned and stepped back up into the cockpit. He slammed the sliding door shut. He stumbled toward the stern of the boat and through the transom door out onto the swim platform. He leaned forward and dropped to his knees, spewing out what remained of his mahi-mahi sandwich and the day's beer.

With confused amazement, Tony watched his wide-eyed friend scurry out of the Sea Ray cabin.

"Frankie? What the fuck? Are you all right?"

Frank raised his hand in a stop motion, a signal to give

him a moment. He retched again. Frank scooped water from the ocean and splashed it on his face. He repeated the process a few more times.

"Whatcha see, buddy?" Tony asked, an impatient tone to his voice. He jockeyed the Donzi closer to the Sea Ray. "Was it your sister naked or something?" He chuckled. "That would ruin my whole week, man."

Frank spit out some sea water, turned his head toward Tony and said, "Didn't see nothin'. It just smelled in there… worse than anything I ever known."

"No shit?"

"Yeah, no shit."

"Whad'ya think it was, man?"

"Don't know…Don't think I wanna know, Tony."

"Okay…okay." Tony pursed his lips for a moment and sighed. "Well…we can't just leave this boat out here floatin'. We'd be breaking some kinda maritime law or something. We gotta drag the damn thing in. Let's take it through the inlet and give it to the Coast Guard on the other side."

"I say fuck it."

"Yeah…I know how you feel, Frankie. But what if it was your boat?"

Frank took a deep breath and shook his head. "All right. Throw me a line and I'll cleat it to the bow." Frank put his hand on his hips and stared at Tony. He gestured back at the Sea Ray cockpit. "But I ain't gettin' back into that cabin again."

Tony nodded. He walked over to a side compartment on the Donzi and pulled out a coiled, white line. He tossed the line to Frank. Frank unwound the line as he walked to the bow of the Sea Ray. He pulled the loop end through the bottom of the cleat on the starboard side and hooked it to the prongs. He gave the line a tug and tossed the remaining length back to Tony. Tony secured the other end to a port side cleat on the transom of the Donzi. Frank shuffled his way back to the lower deck of the Sea Ray and then jumped aboard the Donzi.

Frank grunted as his flat feet plopped to the deck. "Go slow, Tony." He fed out the line attached to the Sea Ray until it was taut and the boat was about seventy-five feet behind them. The bow of the old boat waggled for a moment and then remained steady as Tony moved the throttles forward, increasing the speed.

"We're good," Frank said. He watched as the size of the wake splashing along the sides of the bow on the Sea Ray blossomed. He turned forward and took a few steps toward Tony, who was leaning against the bolster seat behind the center console. He pointed at the GPS. "Ten miles to Port Everglades. It's gonna take us friggin' forever to get there with that damn boat in tow."

Tony grinned. "Yeah, but look on the bright side. That's gonna mean less time you have to spend listenin' to the old lady bitch at you for going away this week."

"You got a point there," Frank said with a smile. "I guess there's only one thing left to do then…" Frank glanced at the white cooler that rested against the stern bulkhead. It was the size of a foot locker. He walked over to the cooler and opened the lid. He reached in with one hand and pushed cubes of ice aside. It sounded as though gravel was being moved by a metal rake. He pulled out two cans of beer and handed a Budweiser to Tony. The two men pulled their ring tops in unison. The popping sound was a familiar orchestra.

18:30 EDT

The towing of the Sea Ray proceeded without issues, at least until just before Port Everglades. As an afterthought, Tony had decided to call the Coast Guard on Channel 16 about two miles from the inlet. After a few brief exchanges, the professional voice at the other end of the radio began to develop a chill. Tony was slurring his words.

The fact that Tony had to respond on the VHF with the call sign of his boat didn't help matters. The Donzi was named "Bottoms Up." It was not the kind of attention that either man needed.

The Coast Guard officer requested a few details regarding the condition of the Sea Ray and then ordered Tony to discontinue the tow. A Coast Guard vessel would arrive shortly to resume the operation. The Donzi would be escorted to a dock at the Coast Guard station, just to the south of Port Everglades.

As if the flashing lights from the Coast Guard boat weren't enough, it would soon look like an outdoor disco a short while after Tony and Frank arrived at the dock. The Broward County Sheriff's Department became part of the production. An assembly of police boats and cop cruisers descended upon the area.

Frank knew it was going to be a long day when the pimply-faced Coast Guard officer who climbed aboard the Sea Ray exited the cabin in a rush. It was the same rush that Frank had done hours earlier. But this time something had been seen. And by the anguished look of the young officer's face, whatever was down in that cabin had to be awful.

Shit! Why couldn't they have just left the fucking boat to float out there? It would have been somebody else's fucking problem!

It didn't take long for the cops to separate Frank and Tony. Frank was brought to a room in the Coast Guard station. Tony was escorted to an aft seat on one of the sheriff's boats. Tony always wanted to see what kind of equipment the cops had on board their boats, but not this way. This way sucked.

Darkness had fallen hours ago. Tony had lost track of

time. And now a man with a brown pockmarked face was stepping off the dock and onto the sheriff's boat. He wore casual slacks and an open-collared palm tree shirt that hung over a belly that strained against the lower buttons. He smiled and introduced himself to Tony as Detective Jorge Alvarez. He held Tony's driver's license between his puffy thumb and forefinger. The driver's license had been surrendered to the Coast Guard officer just after they had docked.

"Mr. Cusmano, have you ever been in trouble with the law before?" Detective Alvarez asked.

Tony stared at his feet for a moment and then looked back at the brown-skinned man. "Uh, yeah…maybe a couple of times."

Christ! How far back are they going to go? Certainly not as far back as the dopey car heist that they pulled in their twenties.

Alvarez asked, "You've got a pending DUI conviction, isn't that right?"

"Oh, shit," Tony thought. He forgot about that one. He was almost relieved. "Yeah, Detective. I got a little stupid one night."

Alvarez nodded. He scanned the Intracoastal Waterway for a moment and then looked back at Tony. His dark eyes didn't waver. "Tell me what happened with the Sea Ray."

Tony took a deep breath. "Nothin' happened. We just found it floating about ten miles off the coast and towed it in to you guys. End of story. Shit, we thought we were doin' the right thing."

"Tell me the whole story…from the time you and Frank left for Bimini until now."

Tony sighed. He opened his mouth to protest, but no words came out. He stared back at the big detective. He shrugged his shoulders and began to tell the story from the morning they left the dock on Friday until they found the old boat today.

When Tony finished, he raised his palms in a sign of resignation and said, “That’s it. There’s nothing else.”

Alvarez stared at the deck of the sheriff’s boat for a moment. He looked up. “Tony, I want you to answer a question honestly.”

“Oh, shit, here it comes,” thought Tony.

“How do you feel about gays?”

“What?” Tony answered with an incredulous expression on his face.

“You know what I mean. Gay people. What do you think about gay people, Tony?”

“Hell, I don’t know. I don’t care.” Tony cleared his throat. “Why?”

“You ever feel like killing one…just out of principle, let’s say?”

“Fuck no. Why should I?”

“Did you ever cut up a man and throw him in a dumpster?”

Tony started to squirm on the seat. A uniformed cop on the boat shifted his stance and stared at him.

“Detective, I don’t know what the hell you’re getting at.”

“Mr. Cusmano, does the name Jonathan ring a bell?”

“No…should it?”

“Ever been to a restaurant on Los Olas Boulevard and have a heated discussion with someone…someone like the owner?”

Oh, crap. Tony had completely forgotten. Tony said, “His father and I had issues, but that was just between us. It’s been weeks since I had the argument…discussion with his dad.”

“But you did go to the son’s restaurant and threaten to cut his balls off if his father didn’t produce a decent roofing contract.”

“Who told you that?”

"Technology told me that, Mr. Cusmano."

"What does that mean?"

"We have a security video of what appears to be you in a rather animated discussion with the restaurant owner. After viewing the video, a witness recalled the threat you made."

"Do I need to call my lawyer now?"

"It depends on what you and your buddy say."

Tony let out a breath through his nose and asked, "Guess you guys found something on that boat?"

Alvarez looked at the uniformed officer. The uniformed officer shrugged his shoulders. The detective's eyes narrowed. He stared at Tony.

"A guy with a bullet through his chest, Mr. Cusmano." Alvarez paused for effect. "He was lying on the V-berth in a pool of blood."

"I'm sorry to hear that. What's it got to do with me…or the gay kid at the restaurant?"

"Well, you guys claim that you found the boat floating by itself. You've never been a choirboy, Mr. Cusmano. That's no surprise to anybody. And your last adventure now connects you with a murder, a murder of a homosexual."

"Murder!? Are you nuts? When did this happen? I've been away for the weekend!"

The detective grinned and gestured his head at Tony's Donzi, still tied up at the Coast Guard dock. "Judging by that boat, you must have a few bucks in your wallet. Fuel's not cheap these days. Maybe you had someone else get their hands dirty."

"You guys think that I'm a gay basher?" Tony's voice was developing a slight angry tone. Clenching his teeth, he asked, "So who was this guy on the boat, anyhow?"

The detective nodded at the uniform cop and then slid next to Tony on the aft seat. The two men were now separated by only inches.

Alvarez whispered into Tony's ear. "The guy was a pilot. He flew for Patriot Airlines, based in Miami. A few cops have seen him at the restaurant."

"So?"

"So…a picture was found on the cell phone of the dead pilot in the cabin of the Sea Ray. And guess what?"

Tony could feel something move to the bottom of his stomach. He braced for Alvarez's next statement.

The big man's lips held a slight upturn at the corners. "The picture is none other than the gay restaurant owner that was found in the dumpster weeks after you had words with his father."

Tony's chest started to tighten. His vision narrowed into a small swath of gray. He was fucked.

CHAPTER TWO

Friday (One day earlier)
08:15 EDT

Jim adjusted the power levers to stop the unsynchronized throbbing of the two engines on the Boeing 767. Like most pilots, he found the noise annoying. As always, his copilot was oblivious. Mike's head was lowered toward his flight bag on the right side of his seat. He seemed focused on retrieving something from the bag.

A muffled boom shook the airplane all the way into the flight controls. The electronic beep of the master caution system sounded in the cockpit. The amber caution lights were illuminated on both sides of the eyebrow panel. The EICAS alert-system screen in the center of the instrument panel annunciated the words, "AUTO PILOT DISCONNECT."

Jim sat up rigid in his seat and instinctively gripped the control yoke with his left hand. With his thumb, he clicked the red autopilot disconnect button twice. The action silenced the caution siren, extinguished the amber light, and cleared the EICAS message from the screen. Ordinarily, it was no big deal. It was not unusual for an autopilot to experience a momentary fault and cause the warnings. It was a simple matter of re-connecting one of the other three autopilots with a push of a button. But something wasn't right.

Jim continued to hand-fly the airplane at 37,000 feet, an untypical task. At high altitudes, the thin air made hand-flying a sensitive operation. Jim scanned the instrument panel for a sign of why the hairs were standing up on the back of his neck.

The sound of the electronic fire bell pierced the momentary silence. Both pilots glanced in unison at the EICAS display. The display now had the red words, "R ENGINE FIRE." The master warning lights were blinking on both sides of the eyebrow panel. The right engine fire handle glowed red. Jim stabbed a finger at the master warning light on his side. The bell went silent.

Jim's heart raced. He was not flying a simulator. It was not his annual recurrent training check ride. The drama unfolding before him was real.

"And I had high hopes that it was going to be a good day." Jim remarked, his expression stone faced. "Engine Fire/Severe Damage checklist," he commanded.

Mike leaned to his right and began to tap on the iPad that was attached to a suction cup mount against his sliding window. He searched for the appropriate electronic page of the emergency handbook. When he found the page, he pulled the iPad from its mount and held it in one hand.

In a methodical tone, Mike began to read. "Engine Fire/ Severe Damage checklist." He took a deep breath. "Auto-throttle arm switch." He paused. "Off." Mike reached over to the mode control panel in the eyebrow and moved the toggle of the auto-throttle switch down. "Off," he re-stated. Mike glanced back at the iPad. "Right thrust lever…Close…The pilot flying will retard the thrust lever to idle."

Mike nodded as he watched his captain move the correct thrust lever to the idle position.

"Close," Jim confirmed.

A chime sounded in the cockpit. Both men glanced at the overhead panel. The FWD flight attendant light was illuminated in blue. The lead flight attendant was calling.

Mike glanced at Jim. He was waiting for approval or

disapproval to answer the intercom. Jim shook his head. He sighed and said, "Let's get through the checklist first. They probably want to know why they have no galley power."

Mike nodded and began to recite more of the checklist. After he rotated the fire handle in the center console, he waited for the amber bottle discharge light to illuminate. When the light illuminated he reached down behind the center pedestal and unsnapped the intercom phone from its cradle.

Mike put the interphone to his ear and said, "Sorry, but we've been busy up here."

"Mike, it's Jackie. We've got serious problems back here."

"What's going on?"

"The right engine…when it blew up, or whatever it did…well…it threw stuff into the cabin at Row 19. We've got slices in the side of the fuselage. And…" Jackie paused for a brief moment. "I think two of the passengers in that row are…are dead. They were hit."

Mike's jaw tensed. "Are you sure, Jackie?"

"Yeah, I'm afraid so. It's not good."

"How big are the slices in the fuselage?"

"We can see daylight through them…there's a handful…maybe about three inches long for each slice."

"Shit. Thanks for the info. Do the best you can back there. We're gonna get this thing on the ground ASAP. Probably Bermuda. As soon as we get things cleaned up here in the cockpit we'll get back to you. Okay?"

"Okay." Her voice had a guarded tone.

"Have you called for medical assistance yet?"

"Yes, we did. A nurse responded." Jackie paused. "It didn't take her long to start shaking her head. I'm looking down the aisle. I think she's covering the Row 19 passengers with blankets right now."

"Thanks, Jackie."

Mike heard a click and then Jackie was no longer on the line. He reseated the interphone onto the cradle. It clacked into place. He looked at Jim.

"Two passengers may be dead. It sounds like the right engine threw shrapnel into the main cabin. There are holes in the fuselage."

Jim shook his head. His expression was somber. "This really isn't a good day."

In the very brief moment that the two pilots took to contemplate the situation, the electronic siren broke the silence. The instrument panel was now a sea of red lights. The EICAS annunciated a new message among the list of others already displayed: "CABIN ALTITUDE"

Jim reached forward and jabbed the master warning light button in the glareshield eyebrow with his index finger. The siren stopped its high-pitched wail.

Both pilots glanced at the overhead panel. Their eyes focused on the needle in the round cabin altitude gauge. The needle was moving past ten thousand feet. The adjacent cabin rate gauge was showing a 300-feet-per-minute rate of climb. On a normal day they would have felt the pressurization change in their ears. Today, more urgent matters had distracted their attention. The holes in the fuselage were allowing pressurized air to seep outside.

Jim asked, "Did I have my second cup of coffee?" He shook his head while looking at the cabin altitude needle. "We're losing the cabin," Jim stated. He glanced at Mike. "I thought that I'd never have to say this in my career, but let's get the masks on. Checklist."

If they lost the cabin completely at thirty-seven thousand feet, the pressurization issue could render both pilots useless in about fifteen seconds. Jim and Mike reached for their oxygen masks. They squeezed the opposing red tabs of the release levers. The whooshing sound of air inflating the headband cage of the masks filled the cockpit. They secured the oval cup of the mask to their faces and released the tabs. The cages encapsulated their heads.

Someone not familiar with the system would have remarked on how the two of them looked like extras in a B-grade horror movie. It was as if the creepy octopus creature from *Aliens* had attacked their faces.

"You got me?" Mike asked, keying his mic switch on the control yoke and glancing at Jim. His voice sounded muffled and nasally over the speaker.

"I'm up, Darth Vader," Jim said nodding.

Mike tried to grin, realizing that acknowledging his captain's attempt at humor would ease the tension. But the oxygen mask and his own tension prevented the recognition. Instead, Mike began to recite the depressurization checklist from memory, "O2 masks…On…100 percent."

Jim responded. "On. 100 percent."

"Communications…established."

"Established."

"Cabin altitude and rate…check"

"It's not controllable," Jim stated.

"I agree." Mike took a breath through his mask. "Passenger oxygen... On." Mike glanced at Jim and then at the overhead panel.

"Time for the rubber jungle," Jim said.

Mike reached up to the overhead panel and pushed the "Passenger O2" button. When the activation light illuminated, he nodded. He imagined the rows of yellow masks hanging from above passengers' heads like moss from a cypress tree.

"Passenger O2…on. Descent…accomplish."

Jim glanced at his altimeter and said, "We've started to drift down already because of the loss of the right engine." The altimeter pointer was moving past 36,400 feet. He tilted his head back and stared at the cabin altimeter on the overhead. The small needle indicated a cabin pressure of twelve thousand feet. "We haven't completely lost pressurization by any means. And there may be structural integrity issues considering the holes in the airplane. Would you agree that we don't need to rush downhill at the moment?"

"I'm with you, boss."

"All right." Jim glanced at the transponder on the center console. "Put the emergency code in the box. Transmit on 121.5. Give a Mayday call. Let everybody know where we are and what we're doing. Then get a hold of New York AIRINC on the HF and declare the emergency." Jim glanced at his HSI display. "We only have about one hundred miles before we're radar contact with New York Oceanic in Bermuda's airspace. I'm going to turn away from the airway now so we don't hit anybody on the way down."

The flight was in an area of the Caribbean that had no radar coverage. Airplanes were separated by assigned speeds, routes, and altitudes. Each flight reported its position via a long-distance radio frequency to a contracted service called AIRINC. The AIRINC operator entered each reporting flight into a computer database which in turn created a real-time display of airplanes. The operator also had a direct link with New York Center.

Mike nodded at Jim's instructions. He pushed the number two VHF button on his radio control panel and began to transmit. "Mayday. Mayday. Patriot Six-Three has experienced a catastrophic engine failure with a rapid depressurization. We have passenger injuries. We are a Boeing 767. Be advised that we are descending out of flight level Three-Six-Zero off airway Lima, four-six-two seventy-five miles south of PIREX intersection."

As Mike began to repeat the message, Jim reached forward on the overhead panel and snapped on the landing light switches. It was part of the emergency procedure. It made them more visible to other airplanes. He turned the control wheel to the right, banking the airplane away from the invisible airway in the sky. The triangle that depicted the airplane on their HSI map displays began to move off the magenta course line.

Jim reached to his right and pulled the speed brake lever back. He felt the familiar buffeting. He glanced at the vertical speed indicator. The needle was settling on a 3,000 feet per minute rate of descent. That rate should keep them out of trouble with the cabin altitude. And if the airplane had structural problems, it should hold together till they landed.

Had passengers really died on board his airplane? Jim's stomach tightened. He hadn't so much as scratched the paint in twenty-five years with the airline. And now this. Christ… it will be on CNN before he gets home. He glanced at his radio control panel and pushed the round PA button. The button glowed red. Jim gulped and took a deep breath. He squeezed the mic switch on his control yoke.

"Ladies and gentlemen, this is Captain Sanders. I am sorry for not making an announcement earlier. As you may have imagined, we have been working through our problems up here in the cockpit. You are probably aware that the right engine has suffered major damage. In addition, the engine pieces that entered the fuselage have caused a pressurization leak. We are in the process of descending rapidly in order to get down to a habitable altitude. The oxygen masks were deployed as a precaution. Although oxygen is not an issue, please use the masks until you are advised that we are at a safe altitude."

Jim released the mic switch for a moment and took another deep breath. He glanced at his copilot. Mike was displaying an upturned thumb. He had made contact with New York AIRINC. Jim nodded.

Jim re-keyed his mic. "Ladies and gentlemen, this airplane is perfectly capable of flying on one engine. We have no controllability issues. I am diverting the airplane to Bermuda. We anticipate arriving safely at the airport in St. George in approximately thirty minutes. As I am sure you have been doing, please follow the instructions of your flight attendants. They are experts in your safety. Thank you for your cooperation."

Jim released his mic switch and glanced out the forward windscreen for a brief moment. Nothing but pastel-blue ocean lay before them. The island of Bermuda seemed light years away. Everything that he had done in his airline career would be focused into the performance he was about to give in the next few minutes. He shook the realization from his thoughts. Who could have imagined that a simple Caribbean flight from Port of Spain in Trinidad to JFK would be his defining moment?

Through his oxygen mask Mike said, "We're good, boss. New York cleared us direct to Bermuda's runway three-zero outer marker. Descend at our discretion. No other traffic should be in our way." Mike pointed at the radio control panel on the center console. "The next frequency is in the box. They're ready for us. We'll be in radar contact soon."

"Good job," Jim said. He turned toward Mike and attempted to smile. Despite the cumbersome apparatus engulfing his face, his expression was visible. His eyes twinkled. "This is damn serious shit, isn't it?"

Mike nodded.

08:25 EDT

A glance down the aisle from the back of the airplane was all it took to realize that things weren't right. The jungle of rubber masks dangling from the overhead ceiling panels made the scene even more chaotic. Newspapers and assorted personal items littered the blue floor and the handful of empty seats. Other than an occasional sniffle from a passenger, the cabin held an eerie silence.

Jackie walked forward toward the front of the airplane. The green oxygen bottle was slung over one shoulder with the yellow strap. She took quick breaths through the mask that was cupped to her face. With the airplane in a noticeable descent, the floor angle required her to pace herself as though she was descending a steep hill. Although Jackie attempted to divert her eyes from Row 19, her efforts were futile. Row 19 was a train wreck.

Aside from the occasional disconcerting slice of sunlight that pierced through the small holes in the side of the airplane, the carnage in the seats was worse. Red was spattered everywhere in the immediate vicinity. Red was on the seatbacks. It had sprayed across the passenger service units above the seats. It had spread to the floor. It had dotted the clothes and faces of nearby passengers.

The two victims had become lifeless forms, covered with blue blankets from head to torso. Their legs flowed out from underneath the blankets in distorted positions. Jackie had helped the nurse cover them, treating the chore as a matter of course…until now. Now as she approached the victims' row, she had to fight the lump clogging her throat and the moisture seeping into her eyes. It was not the time.

An electronic chime sounded as Jackie approached the cabin class divider bulkhead. She looked at the small light that was illuminated in the ceiling near the forward galley. The pilots were calling. Jackie began to increase her pace. From a seat in first class, a hand reached up and gently gripped her wrist.

"Miss?" a scratchy voice asked.

Jackie glanced down at a man with wispy silver hair,

wearing a monogrammed shirt and a striped tie, who had pulled the oxygen cup away from his face. "Yes, sir. Can I help you?"

The man released his grip and beckoned Jackie to lean closer. Jackie knelt on one knee and tilted her head toward the man.

"Has the crew considered this to be an act of terrorism?" the silver-haired man asked, his eyes narrowing. His tone had no inflection.

Jackie sighed, trying to hide the surprise of the unexpected question. She moved her oxygen mask to the side of her face. "Uh…no, sir. Right now the crew is busy trying to handle the emergency."

"I understand, but please have them consider the possibility. Trinidad has a history of breeding terrorists. It's a documented fact."

"I appreciate your concerns, but it will not change the way the pilots treat the condition of this airplane." Jackie began to rise. "I'm sorry, but I need to answer my intercom."

The silver-haired man nodded. His face held a grim expression.

Jackie strode into the first class galley. The man's statement had given her an unsettled feeling. She unsnapped the intercom phone from its cradle and slipped the mask off her flowing brown hair. She put the phone to her ear.

"It's Jackie. Sorry for the delay."

A muffled voice from the cockpit answered. "No problem. How's things going back there?" It was the captain.

"As well as can be expected. We've got the cabin pretty well secured." Jackie cleared her throat. "It didn't take much. When the oxygen masks popped out, everyone was scared to death. This is the first time I've seen passengers actually stay in their seats when the seat belt sign is on."

"I can only imagine," Jim remarked. "Our Bermuda ETA

is about twenty minutes. We're almost level at 10,000 feet. It's safe to take off your masks. I'll advise the passengers in my next PA." Jim paused. "I don't anticipate the need for an evacuation. Unless you guys see something different, our indications are that the fire has been extinguished."

Jackie said, "There's a lot of goop dripping out around the engine. Parts of it are pretty black, but no fire."

"Good deal. Review your procedures just in case we encounter a problem. I anticipate us taxiing to the gate under our own power."

"Okay."

"And Jackie…"

"Yes?"

"Do we have injuries other than the passengers hit by the engine pieces?" Jim wasn't ready to use the word "dead." And technically, until a medical professional made a pronouncement, he couldn't.

"No, no other injuries that I know of."

"I guess we can be thankful for small favors," Jim responded.

"I guess…" Jackie replied, thinking about her last glimpse of Row 19. She paused for a moment. "Captain, I had a comment from a passenger. It's probably not important, but I thought I'd pass it along anyhow. The man didn't seem crazy, although he was intense."

"Go ahead."

"He asked if you guys had considered this whole thing an act of terrorism."

"Hmm…hadn't really had time to think about that one." Jim sighed. "I guess that's up to the accident investigators when they tear the engine apart."

"Gotcha. That's kinda what I thought."

Jim cleared his throat. "Although, it might be wise for us to advise the local authorities. They may want to detain passengers who have questionable credentials. If you observe anything suspicious, let us know. Perhaps we should have the authorities query the passenger making the remark about terrorists."

"Okay."

"Thanks, Jackie. I'll see you in Bermuda."

The intercom clicked and then went silent.

08:35 EDT

As Jim descended the airplane through ten thousand feet, he took a deep breath. The checklists were done. The flight attendants had the cabin under control. And the airplane was performing without issues. No pilot ever develops a complete comfort level operating a two-engine airliner on one engine. It's just not natural.

Had anything been forgotten? They had reached that awkward period of time between the initial rush of adrenalin and when it just became a matter of flying the airplane to its destination. The checklists were complete. The procedures for the approach had been briefed. Nothing else remained.

Jim's copilot didn't appear to be affected with the same anxiety. Although Mike had been a professional during the heat of the battle, he now appeared withdrawn and detached. Mike's stare out the windscreen was unfocused. He hadn't uttered a word since they had stowed their oxygen masks other than to respond to the instructions of the air traffic controller. The copilot was once again preoccupied with his own thoughts.

The fire bell punctured the barely noticeable white noise of air flowing through the cockpit ducts. The EICAS screen displayed an all too familiar message: "R ENGINE FIRE." This time Mike was the first to press the master warning light in order to silence the heart thumping ring of the fire bell.

"You've got to be kidding!?" Jim said with an incredulous tone. "Can't we freeze the simulator? I could have sworn I heard our check airman say, 'Nice job guys.'" He glanced down at the center pedestal. The right fire handle glowed red. He looked at Mike. "Something in the engine must have re-ignited. Maybe a greater concentration of O2 at the lower altitudes? Doesn't make sense. What's left to burn?"

Mike nodded and grasped the illuminated fire handle. He rotated the handle to the right.

"Let's hope that the last Halon bottle does the trick," Jim said. "Otherwise we're in deep doo-doo."

After taking note that the Halon discharge light was on, the two pilots lapsed into silence. Both Mike and Jim took turns glancing at the red fire handle in the center pedestal. It continued to remain illuminated. Six minutes passed.

The flight attendant call chime sounded. Because of his intense focus, Mike was momentarily startled. He snatched the intercom phone off its cradle at the back of the center pedestal and put it to his ear. He knew exactly what he was going to hear.

In an anxious tone Jackie said, "The fire is back on the right engine."

Mike didn't know quite what to say. He asked, "How bad?"

"We see flames extending out from underneath the back of the wing."

Mike grimaced and looked at Jim.

Jim didn't need to hear the other end of the conversation. He nodded and shook his head saying, "Tell her to brief for a possible evacuation. She's got about ten minutes…but tell her not to throw people onto the slides until I turn on the evac horn. The rescue guys may be able to put out the fire."

Mike nodded and repeated the instruction to Jackie. He re-seated the intercom phone and looked forward out the windscreen. The island of Bermuda was starting to appear through the scattered layer of cotton clouds. Mike glanced at his altimeter. The airplane was descending through six thousand feet.

Mike keyed the transmit button on his control wheel. "New York Center, Patriot Sixty-Three has an engine fire that will not extinguish. We may have to evacuate the airplane."

An even-toned anonymous voice replied, "We've advised Bermuda. The equipment is standing by. I'll be handing you off to the tower in one minute."

"Roger. Thanks," Mike responded.

Jim's eyes were focused on the instrument panel. His left hand was gripped around the control wheel. His right hand rested on top of the left power lever--the only one that operated a good engine. He took a deep breath. He had never evacuated an airplane before. An evacuation sometimes created more problems than the actual emergency. The slides could be a nightmare. Broken arms and legs. Cuts and bruises.

Jim clenched his teeth and glanced at the airspeed indicator. He scanned the rest of the instrument panel. The distance readout on the HSI display showed them fifteen miles from the airport.

"Flaps one," Jim commanded.

Mike slid the flap lever on the center pedestal to the one-degree notch. The needle on the round flap gauge jiggled for a moment and then moved to the appropriate position. The airplane buffeted slightly and then began to slow.

Jim glanced at the airspeed indicator again and ordered, "Flaps five."

Mike moved the flap lever to the five degree notch. The needle began to point toward the number five but then abruptly stopped. The electronic beeper blurted. A new message was displayed on the EICAS screen: "TE FLAP

ASYM."

"Shit," Jim said at a barely audible volume. "We've got a trailing edge flap asymmetry. Do you think this would be a bad time to ask for another cup of coffee?"

The latest problem was an indication that the flaps on one wing had deployed at less of an angle than they had on the other wing. The problem had the potential to create control issues rolling the wings level, but an automatic system senses the malfunction and stops all flap movement. Unfortunately, the flaps had stopped at a degree that was a far distance from the normal landing configuration.

Mike said, "I bet a part of the engine came apart into the flaps and jammed them on the right side. I'll start the checklist."

Jim nodded and said, "I've got the radio." He cleared his throat and keyed his mic switch. "New York, Patriot Sixty-Three. We've got another problem. Our flaps will only extend partially. We'll be landing at a higher speed and using more runway."

"Understood, Patriot Sixty-Three. We'll advise Bermuda again. Do you have the airport in sight?"

Jim peered above the instrument panel. The white concrete of Runway 30 was just becoming visible. He responded, "Affirm. Airport in sight."

"Patriot Sixty-Three, cleared for the visual, Runway Three-Zero. Contact the tower on one-eighteen decimal one."

"Eighteen-one. Patriot Sixty-Three. Thanks for your help."

"Good luck, sir."

"Thanks." Jim changed the frequency on his radio control panel and pushed the transfer switch to the right. "Bermuda tower, Patriot Sixty-Three on the visual for Three-Zero."

A voice with a cheery tone responded. "Roger, Patriot

Sixty-Three. Cleared to land. The equipment is standing by."

Jim responded, "Roger. Cleared to land."

Almost muttering, Mike read the checklist for the trailing edge flap asymmetry. He pressed the appropriate switches and made the appropriate responses. The checklist didn't involve much. The primary task was computing the appropriate reference bug on the airspeed indicator. They would be landing at almost one hundred eighty miles per hour, at least thirty miles per hour above the normal speed. The rollout would involve three-fourths of the runway.

08:45 EDT

Strapped into the jumpseat nearest the forward entry door, Jackie was relieved that she couldn't see the engine fire from her position. Her anxiety level was at an all-time personal high. Her energies would be better spent focusing on the possibility that her next task would be to get people off the airplane in a major hurry. She was ready.

Despite the drawn faces on the other eight flight attendants, she was confident that they would all perform. They had no choice.

During the two-minute briefing she had given, Jackie had locked eyes with each flight attendant. Not one of them had moisture in their eyes. Not one of them had shaky hands. Not one of them had the thousand-yard stare. It was as if they had pushed their own personal autopilot buttons. They would need that mindset to activate the lessons of their training.

Jackie leaned forward against the shoulder harnesses on the jumpseat. She glanced to her right and then through the galley to her left. Her attention was focused on the L1 and R1 doors. She closed her eyes for a moment and concentrated. She visualized the movement of the handles and how she would position herself. She imagined the hiss of the evacuation slides inflating. She rehearsed the commands that she would bellow to her passengers. She was certain that the other flight attendants were doing the same.

Jackie knew that the worst part of the emergency would be the long few seconds between the time the airplane touched down and the time it took to stop. And when the airplane did stop, she would have to make an immediate assessment. Would the condition of the airplane require her to initiate an evacuation on her own or would she be able to wait for the captain's command?

Jackie glanced out the round viewing port window in the forward entry door. The whitecaps were visible enough to contrast against the intense blue of the ocean. They were nearing the airport.

09:05 EDT

"One thousand," the robotic voice stated, indicating their altitude above the ground.

"Checklist complete. Cleared to land," Mike announced.

The copilot raised his head and looked out the windscreen at Bermuda. The large white stripes of the airport's Runway 30 filled the view. It was a welcome sight.

Mike glanced at his captain. The man's face was pure focus. Although Jim's left hand was firmly attached to the control wheel and the right hand to the operating power lever, there was a relaxed fluency to his subtle movements. It was a fluency born of years manipulating the same machine over thousands of hours.

Jim made a quick crosscheck of his instrument panel. He peered out the windscreen at the runway. He glanced down at the center console. The right fire handle still glowed an ominous red. Although it was impossible to see the engine from the cockpit, he visualized orange flames and black smoke.

"Five hundred," stated the unemotional male voice of the automatic altitude call-out.

"Sinking at eight hundred. On speed," Mike called out.

The eyes of both pilots danced between their instrument panels and the outside. Fire trucks and emergency vehicles were visible on the parallel taxi to the north. The flashing lights accented the urgency of the situation. It felt as if the whole world awaited their arrival.

CHAPTER THREE

Friday
09:05 EDT

Hart Lindy perched himself at the end of the exercise bench and then lay down with a pair of dumbbells poised on each side of his chest. When he was flat on his back he sucked in a deep breath and began to push the weights upward. Before he had completely extended his arms, an image on the flat screen TV caught his attention. Hart exhaled, the escaping air from his lungs emitting a sound like a deflating air mattress. He allowed the dumbbells to descend back to his chest in a controlled motion. He rose back to an upright position and released his grip.

The rubber-coated weights dropped to the padded floor with a muffled thud. The gym was quiet except for the clang of a barbell being re-racked on a nearby bench press machine.

As Hart stared at the TV mounted high in the corner of the room, he felt his stomach start to tighten. CNN was broadcasting a disturbing video. The video footage was of a large airplane landing on a runway. The aft portion of the airplane's right engine was engulfed in flames. The airplane was a Boeing 767. A large furled American flag was painted on the tail. The flag was the recognizable logo for Patriot Airlines. Patriot Airlines was Hart's employer. He took a deep breath. This wasn't good.

Although the image was slightly erratic, the detail was sufficient. The picture was being filmed from a camera that must have been located at the far end of the runway. The angle was almost head-on from slightly above. The upper right hand corner of the TV screen displayed the printed words, "LIVE." The video feed had to be coming from a news helicopter.

The 767's main gear trucks were only a handful of feet from the concrete. Hart gritted his teeth. The closed-caption words rolled across the bottom of the TV screen. The captions frustrated Hart. The words moved at a snail's pace.

A wisp of white smoke blossomed from underneath the tires as the airplane touched down. The smoke dissipated like the after-effects of a magician's trick. The nose of the 767 lowered toward the ground. Emergency vehicles of all sizes began to chase the airplane, lights flashing. In a few moments, the image of the bulky airliner filled the screen. All movement stopped.

Hart held his breath. Would he see the white tentacles of the slide rafts deploy from the doors? If smoke from the engine had not infiltrated the bleed system, the cabin should still be habitable. Hart slid his hands to his hips and shifted his weight to the other foot. His muscles tensed. He crossed his fingers. He stared into the darkened windows of the cockpit. Don't rush, Captain. Wait.

A steady stream of foamy, white spray flowed from a fire truck and onto the fiery orange glow of the right engine. Black smoke rose above the top of the fuselage and then disappeared. The white stream stopped. Water and foam dripped around the entire perimeter of the gaping engine nacelle. The only colors that remained were black and grey. The glow of orange was no longer visible. No flames. A short burst of spray was directed back into the engine.

A man wearing a bulky silver jumpsuit appeared in front of the nose. The man focused his attention on the cockpit. He held a portable radio to one ear. The man dropped the radio to his side and held up a gloved hand. He positioned his fingers to form an awkward OK sign. Emergency vehicles began to roll away from the airplane.

A blocky, blue tug with painted red, white, and blue stars banded along its sides positioned itself in front of the nose. Two men were seated on the tug. The man in the passenger seat stepped to the pavement. The man scurried to the nosewheel and began to connect a tow bar. A few moments later, the man walked out from underneath the nose and gestured a thumbs-up at the tug driver. The 767 lumbered forward.

Cool! No evacuation. No injuries. Good deal. But what the hell happened…? Hart read the captions. "*Bermuda. Airplane departed Port of Spain, Trinidad...175 passengers... possibly two fatalities.*" Two fatalities…? Shit! How…?

Hart reached to his hip for the cell phone that was normally clipped to his waist band. It wasn't there. Damn! The phone was in his truck. He looked at the dumbbells that he had dropped to the floor. Should he…? Hart hesitated. If he didn't finish his workout now, he would never finish it. Exercise would help him think straight.

As the pilots union safety investigation chairman, Hart's phone would be ringing all day. How many beers had he knocked back when he relented and finally let Sam volunteer him for the position? PAPA had other qualified people. He didn't really have the time.

With the chemotherapy and radiation treatments intensifying, his father needed Hart more and more. No matter how many times Dad had claimed that he was managing just fine, Hart began to notice a creeping deterioration. The family airport, Dad's livelihood, was taking incremental steps backwards. Bills not being paid. Hangar customers leaving because of leaks and decay. The maintenance shop sitting idle more frequently. The little paved strip out in the boonies of upstate New York had become a burden even before Dad got sick. The place squeaked out barely enough of a profit to pay for groceries.

But Dad was emphatic about Hart accepting the chairman position. It was important work. And Hart had the credentials and the qualifications. The fact that the president of the pilots union considered Hart a valuable asset was an honor. Besides, giving back was a quality that his father insisted upon.

Giving back to what though? Hart grunted to himself. The majority of his contemporaries did nothing. They criticized and bitched, complaining about the ineffectiveness of their leadership. But at the end of the day they went home to their families and collected their paychecks, never once volunteering to assist in union business.

For some, PAPA had become an acronym for necessary evil. The Patriot Airlines Pilots Association had been unable to conclude a contract settlement with the company for the last four years of negotiations. The National Mediation Board hadn't helped to advance the process either. It was the same old crap. Politics. Infighting. Contentious management. Employee morale at all-time lows.

None of that mattered. Hart had volunteered for the assignment. He had made a commitment. Plain and simple. The Bermuda event he had just witnessed on TV was now on his watch. Well…only if the British government granted the NTSB authority to conduct the investigation. They had no reason not to. Bermuda had limited resources. And the airplane was registered in the U.S. to a U.S. airline. The government wouldn't want to spend time and effort on an accident that probably didn't involve British citizens.

Hart twisted his neck from side to side until he felt a satisfying crack. He could feel the tension starting to build. He looked away from the TV.

The twenty-something kid with the tattoos obliterating his arms strutted into the free weight room. He grunted his usual unintelligible greeting to Hart. Hart nodded. The brief interruption took Hart away from his thoughts.

It was time to work up a good sweat. He took a couple of steps toward the flat bench, bent down, and then gripped a dumbbell in each hand.

09:30 EDT

Jim sighed and looked at Mike. They had just been towed to a gate stand. The airplane's nose faced the pastel orange terminal building as though it had been scheduled to arrive like any other Patriot Airlines flight. Despite the circumstances, the two pilots remained professional. They completed the parking checklist as they had done thousands of times before.

"I hope this is really Bermuda, because if it's not, then we have other problems," Jim said with a wry smile. "I guess it's time to face the music." He rotated the clasp of his seat-belt harness and began to rise. Jim extended a hand toward his copilot. "Thanks for the help. Couldn't have done it without you."

"Nice job, boss."

"Thanks, Mike. If you don't mind, I'd rather not have to do this again."

As Jim slid away from his seat, he glanced out the left side window. Ground personnel were scurrying about the ramp area. One of the fire trucks that had responded on the runway was parked a few yards away. Portable air stairs were being driven to the forward entry door.

"The welcoming committee is about to board. I hope our agents have organized a game plan for the passengers that go beyond ten-dollar meal vouchers," Jim remarked.

"We'll see...," Mike said with a doubtful tone.

Jim opened the cockpit door, stepped down, and walked out to the space between the forward galley and the entry door. He surveyed the cabin. To his surprise, many people were still seated. Expressions varied from wide eyes to weariness. Many just stared.

And then amidst a few long seconds of awkward silence, a handful of passengers began to clap. Initially the sound was random and unorganized. But within a few moments the entire airplane became a symphony of applause.

Jim's face felt flush. He nodded with a reluctant smile. Jim turned back toward the cockpit and motioned for Mike to step forward. Mike shook his head and remained within the safety of the flight deck, his trim physique framed by the door opening. Jim glanced to the left and locked eyes with Jackie, standing only a foot away. As she attempted to form a smile, water began to fill her eyes. Jim clasped her shoulder.

The awkwardness was soon broken up by a familiar whooshing sound. The forward entry door was being opened by the agents outside. Jim was grateful for the interruption. When the door locked into its upward position, a small crowd of people in various uniforms, suits, and IDs flowed onto the airplane.

A young man in a crisp, tan suit spoke first. "Nice job, Captain. We can only imagine other outcomes."

"Thanks, but two fatalities are enough."

"I understand, sir." The young suit paused for a moment. "In that regard, we will need your passengers to remain seated in order for our medical examiner to make a determination of death. And then we will have to remove the deceased."

Jim felt a surge of blood and adrenalin flow into his veins. He peered over the head of the young man. He exchanged glances with the two uniformed Patriot Airlines gate agents standing behind the man. He recognized them from some of his flights that they had worked over the years. The agents shrugged their shoulders.

"And who might I have the pleasure of talking with?" Jim asked.

The young man looked down at the blue carpet and then shuffled his feet. He smiled at Jim and said, "Michael Brown, assistant airport authority manager."

"Mr. Brown...," Jim clenched his teeth for a moment and tried to grin, "...these passengers have not only been through hell they have lived it. Forcing them to remain on the airplane while your M.E. verifies the carnage seems counterproductive...especially if you want cooperation from these folks."

"I'm sorry, Captain. But it's procedure."

It was the first time that the melodic island accent of Bahamas residents sounded abrasive to Jim.

"I see. Well, I have procedures too." Jim clasped his hands behind the small of his back and rocked on his heels. "One of my procedures is not to torture passengers unnecessarily. So...your choice is either to allow them to deplane in an orderly fashion to a safe area of your choosing in the terminal, or...they can deplane right now onto the ramp willy-nilly style. I'm certain that neither your boss nor your Customs officials would enjoy the chaos."

The assistant airport manager opened his mouth to speak, but Jim halted his comments with a raised index finger. One of the gate agents nodded at Jim. On cue, she took a few steps toward the forward bulkhead and unsnapped an intercom handset from its cradle. She pressed the PA button. Her voice amplified itself throughout the cabin. Passengers began to sigh in response to the agent's deplaning instructions. They gathered their belongings from the overhead bins and from underneath seats. They shuffled into the aisles, anxious to exit the bad B-movie in which they had unwillingly become actors.

The young suit shook his head. He stepped back onto the landing of the portable air stairs to await the parade of passengers. An older man with nappy graying temples and a crisp, open-collar shirt stood beside the assistant airport manager. Jim could only assume that the gentleman was the M.E.

With carry-on bags gripped in their hands or strapped across their shoulders, the passengers began to deplane. Some nodded. Some shook Jim's hands. Some offered words of thanks. Some wiped tears from their eyes with the back of their hands. Some just inhaled the fresh sea air that flowed into the cabin.

As the last passenger walked out the door, Jim gestured his head toward the young Mr. Brown, inviting him back inside the airplane. The older man with the graying hair accompanied him. The older man nodded at Jim and followed the assistant airport manager down the right side aisle toward Row 19.

Jim felt compelled to assess the damage also. He *was* the captain after all. And passengers had died on *his* flight. Jim drew in a deep breath and began to walk down the aisle. The images of Row 19 would haunt him long past his retirement.

09:45 EDT

The whop-whop sound of helicopter blades beating the air overhead was distracting. Mike pressed the End button on his cell phone, terminating the call. Fortunately, the conversation was brief. The noise would have made further reception impossible anyhow.

Mike had taken the opportunity to assess the damage outside the airplane. He peered up from his position on the ramp. A royal blue Jet Ranger hovered less than a hundred feet above the airplane. The insignia of a local TV station was circled on the side. Mike could see the figure of a man seated sideways inside an open door. The man's legs were slung just over the skids. A video camera was perched on one shoulder.

The thought of displaying a lone middle finger in the direction of the helicopter was a brief consideration. Instead, Mike opted for a quick salute. That would make a nice video clip for the networks. His family would enjoy the vision of him standing by the airplane that he had heroically helped to land. Well…maybe.

Mike had dropped a bombshell the night before he left on the trip. Despite the frustrating hormonal mood swings of his two teenage daughters, they had taken the news better than anticipated. His wife was another story. She had reacted with anger and bitterness. It didn't matter. Their relationship had been drifting apart for years. Now she knew why. But the why wasn't what she had expected. Frankly, it wasn't what Mike would have expected either.

Mike exhaled in a slow and deliberate fashion. He wiped the thoughts from his head. For the moment, he had more immediate concerns. He continued his pace around the front of the nosewheel and over to the right side of the fuselage.

When Mike looked at the right wing, he stopped in his tracks. He hadn't prepared himself for the scene. He felt his eyes grow wide and his mouth open. Holy shit! Except for the basic shape, the big GE engine barely resembled the same power plant that he had seen during his preflight walk-around inspection in Port of Spain.

The inlet was a black hole of soot. It oozed fire retardant spray. The symmetrical mosaic of crafted titanium fan blades was an obliterated mess. The scattered few blades that remained were twisted and contorted. Most of the blades were broken like shards of a sliding glass window. It was as if a rock had been thrown at a smiling row of teeth.

The inboard side of the engine cowl was split and shattered. The composite material was sliced and fractured. Pieces of compressor blades and assorted engine parts must have blasted through and then pierced the fuselage where the passengers were killed.

Mike's brain was having difficulty absorbing the catastrophic damage. His eyes were downloading visual information faster than the images could be processed. He narrowed his focus and scanned the impact area of the fuselage. The impact area was just forward of the wing root. It was peppered with dents and slices. The aluminum was warped in places, wrinkled in others. It was a miracle that they had been able to maintain pressurization at all.

As Mike continued to stare, he was oblivious to the smattering of airport personnel that were doing the same. Fingers pointed in various directions. Heads shook. Feet shuffled.

"Not much you can say, except, 'Holy shit!'" a strained voice said over the noise of the APU and the helicopter.

Mike turned to see Jim standing behind him. The captain was peering directly into the inlet of the deformed right engine. Jim's tie was drawn tight. His white uniform shirt had barely a wrinkle. His hat was perched on his head in perfect alignment.

Jim said, "It could have been worse." He gestured his head at the damaged area of the fuselage. "Boeing knows how to build an airplane."

10:00 EDT

The armored car drove through the perimeter gate and toward the Patriot Airlines 767. Although the unexpected stop would add another half-hour to his route, the driver didn't mind. He loved airplanes. He loved the St. George airport. He would make the pick-up from the cargo hold and take the opportunity to chat with his airline friends. Expecting the usual nods and greetings as he approached the ramp, he soon realized that today would be anything but routine.

Instead of the typical baggage cart vehicles and fuel trucks, the 767 was engulfed by fire trucks, official airport cars, and police units. The sooty, black mess of one engine told most of the story.

Shit! What the hell!? And how was he going to get anywhere near the airplane? He slowed the armored car to a crawl. He recognized the smiling white teeth of Patriot Airline's crew chief. The crew chief didn't have much of a smile today. The driver waved at him through the windshield. The crew chief nodded and motioned him forward toward an open cargo compartment.

The driver maneuvered the car in position, backing toward the open cargo door in the fuselage. He parked and stepped out onto the ramp. He exchanged greetings with the crew chief. The driver gestured his head at the deformed engine.

"Engine exploded," the crew chief yelled above the noise. "Stuff went through the cabin, mon. Two people dead." The crew chief sighed and shook his head. "Fucking mess, mon."

With a sympathetic nod, the driver acknowledged the explanation. He surveyed the scene again and then turned his attention toward the cargo compartment. He peered in.

The crew chief pointed at a box wrapped in clear plastic about the size of a small file cabinet and said, "I tink dat's your pick-up, mon."

"Tanks," the driver said as he walked over to the rear of the armored car. He swung open the double doors and then turned toward the cargo compartment of the airplane. He slid the wrapped box across the floor of the compartment and into his arms. He wrestled the box into the back of the armored car and closed the heavy doors with two thwacks.

Somebody always had a reason to move money. A bank. A business. A rich guy. He never really knew the reasons. It was better not to know. At least that's what his boss always told him. It didn't matter. He shrugged inwardly and handed a clipboard to the crew chief. The crew chief signed the release form attached to the clipboard and handed it back. The two men shook hands. The driver climbed back into the armored car. He put the car in gear and rolled away from the airplane as slowly as he had arrived.

CHAPTER FOUR

Friday
10:15 EDT

Kim opened the glass door of the vice principal's office. She shifted the straps of her knapsack to the other shoulder and walked with a reluctant gait toward the secretary who sat behind the tall counter. The thirty-something secretary had big hair and big boobs. Mom said that the boobs were probably as fake as the silvery blond hair. It was all the more reason why Kim hated a trip to see the VP.

As Kim approached, the secretary looked up from her computer screen. She smiled, rolled her chair backwards, and rose to her feet. On most occasions, Kim got an eyebrow raise at best. Depending upon the severity of her visit, Kim would get advice on her mascara or maybe her inappropriate attire. And then she would be escorted into the vice principal's office for a dose of discipline on whatever crime she had committed.

Usually the crime was a knee assault to some boy's groin. Boys just seemed to like Kim; unfortunately, not the right ones. Rather than offer a coy and giggly "No" to their inappropriate touching like the other girls, Kim just drew her knee back and fired. Problem solved. Unfortunately, the boys fabricated their own stories.

Gutless little wimps! The frequency of these occurrences was such that her credibility was suspect no matter how logical her explanation. It wasn't her fault that somebody gave her a Victoria's Secrets figure and then stuffed it inside a seventeen-year-old body.

Despite the trips to the office, Kim had a feeling that the VP found her explanations reasonable and simply wanted an excuse to visit. No discipline of any consequence was ever administered anyhow. Well...maybe a study hall or two. And everybody knew that the VP was a rug-muncher. Why else would she want Kim in the office? Besides, the boys never got a visit to the VP's office. They always ended up with the principal. And Mr. O'Malley didn't waste time chatting. He handed out a three-day suspension at the blink of an eye.

The secretary walked around the counter and grasped Kim's wrist with a gentle touch. Her head was cocked to one side, her smile soft and congenial. Her voice was bordering on a whisper.

"Kim, honey. Ms. Abbott would like to see you. Your sister is already in the office." With Vanna White-poise, the secretary motioned her up-turned palm toward the half-opened door.

My sister? Shit! This is gonna be cool. My little sister never does anything wrong. "A+ Ashley" in the VP's office? Hmm…this might be worth the visit.

As Kim swung the door open, Ms. Abbott stood up from behind her desk. The VP was wearing her standard Hillary Clinton pantsuit. If only her hair wasn't so butch short, she might actually be considered pretty.

Ms. Abbott pointed at the open chair beside Ashley and said, "Kim. Please. Sit down." Noticing the wary look, the vice principal smiled and added, "It's okay. You're not in trouble, Kim."

This is really weird, Kim thought, glancing at her sister. Ashley was twirling a finger into a lock of her long, brown hair. Her sister tried to smile a greeting, but her lips never quite made it past a mild grimace. Ashley shifted her weight and squirmed to the other side of the seat.

Maybe this was about the news that Dad sprung on us the other night. That was something. Holy crap! Mom freaked out. It wasn't that much of a surprise to Kim. Hadn't Mom seen the signs? The weird phone calls? The late nights? Dad not coming home from his trips until the next day…

Please don't make this a counseling session. My parents haven't been talking like a married couple for years. I can't remember the last time they kissed. Hell, they rarely even slept in the same bed. Dad's announcement was a blessing. I don't need counseling for this crap. Maybe Mom does…

"There's no real easy way to break the news to you two ladies," Ms. Abbott said, jolting Kim out of her train of thought. "I guess the best way is to tell you the truth." She paused.

"Oh, shit…here it comes," Kim muttered under her breath.

Ms. Abbott leaned forward. The springs of her padded office chair squeaked. "Did you say something, young lady?"

"Uh…no, ma'am. Nothing." Kim lowered her chin and shifted her gaze to the platform Uggs on her feet.

Ms. Abbott glanced at Kim for a brief moment and then cleared her throat. "Anyhow…it seems that your dad was a hero today. He helped to land an airplane that was on fire. The airplane diverted to Bermuda. He is safe and so are the passengers…well, two people were killed. Apparently one of the engines blew up. That's all the information we have."

"Cool!" Kim exclaimed. "If Dad's okay, does this mean we get to visit Bermuda?"

"Are you sure my dad wasn't hurt?" Ashley asked with wide eyes.

Always the angel! Kim glowered at her sister and rolled her eyes. In response, Ashley stuck out the tip of her tongue.

"I'm positive he wasn't hurt, hon." Ms. Abbott said.

She peeled a pink message form from the top of a pad and scanned the note. "Your mom called about fifteen minutes ago. Because your dad has made the news, she is concerned that the local TV stations will try and interview you guys. She wants you to stay put for the moment. She is leaving work early. She'll pick you up here at school. She'll call when she's on her way."

TV cameras? National news? Way cool. Kim had only been on TV once…for like ten seconds. And that was for some stupid girls soccer thing. Now she would have a chance to actually say something. If her mom let her say something…probably not.

The VP continued. "So…I'm going to have you ladies wait here for the moment. And then Mr. Washington, our security officer, will escort you out the building to the back parking lot. Okay?"

Ashley and Kim nodded.

Ms. Abbott said, "I have to leave the office for a little while." She looked at Kim with a sly smile. "I have to find more students to torture. In the meantime you can use my desk to finish any homework that you might have. If you're not here when I return, please give my regards to your dad when he gets home."

The VP rose from her chair and gently patted both Ashley and Kim on the shoulder as she left the office.

Kim turned to face her sister. She gave Ashley a playful punch to the shoulder and said, "Awesome! We're going to be celebrities, Sis!"

10:25 EDT

Rod was perched on the corner of his desk. He looked away from the TV screen that sat on an end table in the corner. He stared out the window of his office at the 777 parked at the gate below. The jet bridge that was mated to the forward entry door was now moving away from the airplane. The red rotating beacon light on top of the fuselage was illuminated, an indication that the airplane was about to begin its pushback. He twisted his wrist to check the time on his Breitling watch.

The watch was an anniversary gift. His wife felt that Patriot Airlines' new Miami chief pilot should have a watch that was reflective of his status. He wasn't fond of watches with big faces, but his wife had spent almost every bit of her schoolteacher's monthly paycheck to buy it for him. He smiled for a brief moment. What a difference from his first marriage…

The 777 was the morning departure to London. Good. It was on time for once. As the big jet began to roll backward, Rod sighed. He brushed his salt and pepper hair away from his tan forehead. His tan was a result of the weekend's efforts on the golf course. He hadn't played well, nor had anybody else for that matter. The tournament was an airline-sponsored charity to benefit breast cancer research. The only event that was taken seriously by the players was the Scotch tasting at the clubhouse.

Rod patted the TV remote control into the palm of his other hand as if the device was a ball in a baseball mitt. He had grown weary of pressing the channel button. None of the network news stations had definitive information on the accident or his crew. He should have known better.

The chief pilot stared at the mess scattered across his desk. He hadn't moved one piece of paper since the telephone call when he had got the news a half-hour ago. He felt himself begin to grind his teeth. Patience was not one of his better virtues.

The console phone on the desk warbled a ring. Rod slid off the corner to his feet and turned to look. A green light was illuminated. It was his direct line. Finally! Maybe he'd get some real information. He yanked the receiver off the cradle.

"Rod Moretti."

"Captain Moretti, how the hell are you?" The voice on the other end of the line didn't wait for a response. "You haven't drunk all of the management Kool-Aid yet, have you?"

"Only half. And I pour Grey Goose into the other half. Who the hell is this?"

"Sammy. Who'd you think?"

"Wow. Sam Mason! How do I deserve the pleasure of a phone call from the union president?" Rod paused. "Wait… don't tell me…let me guess." He smiled. "You guys want me to ask the company for a full-time masseuse in the crew lounges?"

"How did you know?"

"I'm psychic that way."

"Psychotic don't you mean? I've seen you fly an airplane."

"Don't judge me when I'm not sober."

"Sorry."

Rod sighed, and said, "Sam, I don't know what to tell you. I've got all my intel about the accident from CNN. I'll probably be the last to know."

Sam cleared his throat. His tone became serious. "In fact, I've got news for you."

"That figures."

"Don't take it personal. It seems that the crew actually followed the accident checklist on our little laminated cards that we have the guys attach behind their ID badges. As per the checklist, the captain called PAPA headquarters about an hour ago."

"No sense in the captain talking to his supervisor. I certainly don't give a shit about their well-being. "

“Like I said, don’t take it personal. They’re doing the right things. And remember…you decided to put on the black hat, buddy.”

“It’s only a black hat to the 2 percent of the seniority list that wants attention for the wrong reasons. I still have this stupid notion that I can make a difference.” Rod sighed. “Is my crew okay?”

“For the most part. My understanding is that physically they are fine. A brief conversation with the copilot seems to reflect some stress issues. That’s to be expected. We’re sending two trained critical incident stress management pilots from our peer support group on the next flight from JFK to Bermuda. PAPA’s accident investigation Go-Team is assembling as we speak. So far, we haven’t got confirmation from the NTSB regarding its authority to conduct the investigation. I think they’re waiting for approval from Bermuda via the State Department. They must not see a problem because the investigator-in-charge, the IIC, has already been assigned. I think the company is getting their usual suspects together also. They promised to let us know who the players are on their Go-Team.”

“It sounds like the ball is rolling,” Rod said.

“Well…” Sam’s voice trailed off for a moment. “Yeah… pretty much.”

“What’s wrong, Sammy.”

“It appears that Bermuda’s version of our U.S. Airport Authority is dragging their feet for the moment.”

“Really? You know why?”

Sam released a quick snort and said, “It seems that our captain exercised his captain’s authority.”

“How so?”

“Apparently he wasn’t happy with the request from some airport manager-type for the passengers to remain on board until their M.E. officially pronounced the two fatalities as deceased." Sam let out a brief chuckle. "Our captain, in so many words, told this manager guy to get fucked. The captain initiated the deplaning process on his own authority."

"Good for him."

"We're all on the same page, but it's delaying the process."

"I'll make a call."

"I was hoping you would say that," Sam replied.

"Anything else?"

"How about making sure that our peer support guys and the Go-Team are allowed travel passes with Class-1 status from their home bases to Bermuda?"

"Done. Just give me a list of names. Is that it?"

"For now, thanks. I love you, man."

"I love you, too, Sam. Just do me a favor and keep me up to date…even if it's off the record. Sooner or later, I'll be in the loop. As a chief, I'll have to talk to the crew when they return."

"Do you want off-the-record stuff now?"

"Of course."

"I'm not on speaker phone, am I?"

"Nope. Go ahead."

"GE engines don't just come apart without warning. The captain said that there was no indication of any problem prior to the shit hitting the fan. He's been on the Seven-Six for a hundred years. He's had one precautionary shutdown in over ten thousand hours of flying the airplane. And that was because of a low oil pressure EICAS message verified by the oil gauge display."

Rod glanced at the muted images on the TV screen and asked, "No high temps? No vibration indications? No power fluctuations? Nothing?"

"Nothing." Sam drew in a deep breath. "You do know that Trinidad is a nice place to harbor terrorists?"

"Careful. Let's not go there yet."

"That's what accident investigation is for."

"How about that gremlin creature from the *Twilight Zone* movie? Anybody thought of that idea?"

"That's a good theory. Maybe you should participate with the company's Go-Team instead of waiting in your office to give the standard fifty lashes to the guys calling in sick."

"We don't give lashes anymore. It's messy and inhumane. We use electroshock therapy."

"Excellent. Things have improved already since you got the chief job a month ago."

"Don't mention it." Rod sighed and said, "I looked at the crew list. I don't really know the captain other than to just say 'Hi'. Is Jim a ...?"

Sam interrupted. "I know what you're thinking. Jim's a straight arrow. Former Air Force F-16 jockey. Gulf War vet. Plays well with others. All of that stuff. You probably wouldn't have seen him in your office until the day he signed his retirement paperwork."

"Gotcha. Thanks, man."

Sam added, "By the way, Hart Lindy will be in charge. He'll have official NTSB status as the union's Go-Team party coordinator. He's our accident investigation chairman as you probably know."

Rod winced at the sound of Hart's name. A few moments of silence passed.

"Yeah, sounds fine," Rod acknowledged. "I'm sure he knows what he's doing."

"You'll be getting a call from the Miami domicile reps soon. Have a good one, buddy."

Rod heard a click in his ear. He set the phone back down onto the console cradle.

"An airplane accident with fatalities and Hart Lindy. Great. This can only get better…" Rod muttered.

10:45 EDT

Hart had just laid his open bag on the corner of the bed to start packing when his cell phone began to chirp. The chirp was the selected ring for an unknown caller. Other than at the gym, his cell phone hadn't spent much time away from his ear for the last hour. Hart glanced at the digits displayed on the caller ID. Where was that area code from? He had seen it before. Hart stared at the number for a moment. He remembered. Washington, D.C. Hart pressed the green Talk button.

"Hey, it's Hart."

"Is this Captain Lindy?" a female voice with a hint of a Hispanic accent asked.

"Yes, it is. Who's calling?"

"I'm Julia, the secretary for NTSB investigator-in-charge, Maureen Blackford. Could you hold please while I put the IIC through?"

"Yeah, sure," Hart replied as he walked into his closet, the cell phone pressed against an ear. He surveyed the array of shirts hanging in a meticulous row, all of them facing in exactly the same direction. What would be appropriate attire for Bermuda?

"Captain Lindy?" a calm voice inquired.

"This is he."

"It's Maureen Blackford. Remember?"

Hart thought for a moment. No images were rushing into his head. He probably should know.

Maureen added, "It's all right. It's been a while. San Juan. Flight 57. Coming back yet?"

Flight 57...? Hart looked at the floor and shuffled his feet. Maureen Blackford? Oh, yeah. His mind flashed an image of a tall woman with an intense expression on her face. The tall woman was wearing a pair of khaki pants with a blue polo shirt. A circular NTSB insignia patch was sewn above a breast pocket.

"I'm sorry, Maureen. I remember now. You were chairing the procedures committee, right?"

"Yup, you got it."

"Yeah. I was assigned to the systems committee. We never really crossed paths too often," Hart said. An uneasiness that hadn't surfaced from his memory was making Hart feel unsettled. He couldn't put a finger on it.

"Well, it looks like we will be working together again. I understand that PAPA has designated you as the party coordinator."

"That's true. A friend of mine had the lapse in judgment to promote me past my level of competence. And the sad thing is, it's a volunteer position. At least my friend gets paid."

"The government did the same for me."

Both Hart and Maureen Blackford chuckled.

Maureen said, "Bermuda has given us the green light to begin the investigation."

"Good. Glad to hear it."

"Me too." Maureen paused. "If you would, please have a roster available that lists your party members to present at the organizational meeting."

"I will. In fact, I can offer you resumes. They all have appropriate backgrounds for their appropriate investigative committees."

"I'm sure. If your people are anything like your guys at the Flight 57 accident, we'll be in good shape."

"Thanks. The great aspect to this accident is that not only do we have surviving crew and surviving passengers, we have an intact airplane." He added, "Just let us know the agenda and where you folks are going to set up your command center and we'll do the same. My group should be on scene by tonight sometime."

"We'll have the information available in a few hours. How about I have my secretary email you?"

"Works for me, Maureen."

"See you soon."

Hart's cell phone went silent as the call disconnected. He stared at the iPhone for a moment as if the device could explain his uncomfortable feelings. He dismissed his thoughts and turned his attention to the wardrobe in his closet. He glanced at his stack of shorts. Well...he *was* going to Bermuda. Nah…maybe for the bar at the end of the day, but not for the investigation. He certainly wasn't going to wear a pair of those geeky, calf-high, ankle socks.

He ran a thumb over the top of his shirts. Maureen Blackford? Now it was coming back. She had first introduced herself at the NTSB Command Center that was set up at a banquet room of the Caribe Hilton in San Juan. Most of the faces involved with the investigation of Flight 57 were grim, but Maureen's eyes sparkled with excitement. It was bothersome. Not so much that she was enthusiastic, but that her attitude seemed contrary to someone immersed in a tragedy.

When the CVR transcripts of the last few minutes of airborne dialogue were made available to the investigation, a checklist omission by the flight crew had been discovered. When the checklist item was discussed at a progress meeting with the other committees, Maureen minimized the omission as a contributing cause of the crash. But her murmured discussions with the IIC at the podium indicated otherwise. And so did the press briefing that followed.

When the press briefings were aired, the synopsis discussed by the IIC seemed to be leading in the direction of pilot error. Maureen could always be seen on camera, strategically located at just the right spot in the background. She wore her best professional smile, nodding at the appropriate moments.

The pilot-error theory was treated by the PAPA investigation team as if the Kennedy assassination's Grassy Knoll was being revisited. When the Heineken started to disappear from the ice-laden cooler in the party coordinator's room, the adjectives used to describe Maureen Blackford were not for public consumption. It took several reminders over several days for the party coordinator to impress upon the team that their responsibility as third-party participants was to help find a cause for the crash and not to defend any one person or any one theory. Their main objective was to assist the NTSB in determining the cause to prevent the same accident from ever happening again.

But there was one more aspect to his uneasiness toward Maureen Blackford. His brain had conveniently stored the information away until just now. Flight 57 had been a horrific scene. The devastation to the small section of old San Juan where the Airbus 320 impacted had been instantly transformed into a war zone. Blackened buildings. Airplane fragments. Clothes scattered among the tops of coconut palms. Body parts. And the all-consuming charred smell. The smell hadn't left his nostrils for months after the investigation.

Hart had needed an escape. He had teased the hotel bar manager with his best lines and his best smile late into the night. She had followed him to his room. Before Hart could slip his key card into the slot, the bar manager had slipped a wet tongue into his mouth. At just the right moment, Maureen Blackford had trotted down the hallway. She had simply nodded, a barely perceptible grin etched on her face.

And now it would be Hart's responsibility to keep the investigation team focused on the main objective. He gnashed his teeth. It would also be his responsibility to keep opinions of the new IIC from influencing the course of the investigation. Great…

CHAPTER FIVE

Friday
12:05 EDT

Chris DeFazio took a big gulp from his beer mug and glanced at the blond-haired guy sitting at the other end of the bar. Crap! What the hell was he doing in this place!? A frickin' gay joint! If the guys at the VFW saw him now, it would be over. If only this job wasn't paying so damn well…

He dropped an elbow over his hip and felt the hard plastic handle of the H & K hidden beneath his tropical shirt. Chris had just called his contact. Now that he finally had tracked the guy down at the bar, he'd have to find out just how much the light-in-the-loafers dude really knew.

This job wasn't as much of an adrenalin rush as Iraq, but it was better than selling car insurance to assholes at his brother's office. That sucked. Every time the phone would ring and the light would blink on his desk phone, he would cringe. In the worst way, he wanted to be back in-country shooting ragheads with his buddies. Nobody understood. They just thought that he was crazy.

That touchy-feely shrink at the VA had told him to join a support group that dealt with PTSD. Post-traumatic stress disorder? Shit! What did that shrink know about PTSD? The shrink's only lifetime trauma was probably an increase in the greens fees at the country club! Bet the shrink had never seen a Humvee do barrel rolls after getting whacked by an IED…and then seen the guys you just had breakfast with get burned to a crisp like the bacon they had eaten. Worse yet, you couldn't do anything to help except watch.

When that buddy from his old unit met him at Houston's Restaurant on the Intracoastal in Pompano Beach with a job proposal, Chris jumped at the chance. His buddy had introduced him to the slick-haired dude. If that gleaming white forty-something-foot Tiara docked at the restaurant was any indication, the slick-haired dude had some cash. The two chicks sprawled out on the bow wearing thong bikinis and new tits weren't cheap either.

It wasn't the money that the slick-haired dude offered so much as it would be like living on the edge again. And the stuff he would be asked to do wasn't anything he hadn't already seen in the Army. Just like Iraq, he'd still be dealing with bad guys. And he'd be doing somebody a favor--ridding the world of idiots one asshole at a time. Well, maybe he'd just bust a few heads.

Chris looked up at the TV screen that was mounted over the wine glass rack on the other side of the bar. The caption on the bottom of the screen read, "Breaking News." The local TV station was flashing video footage of an airplane landing on some island. One of the airplane's engines was on fire. The video switched to a newscaster standing in front of a tropical-colored building. The screen changed to photographs of the airplane and the engine damage. Passengers climbed down the mobile stairs that were mated to the side of the airplane. Two gurneys with black body bags were being rolled toward an ambulance.

"What's that all about?" Chris wondered. He peered back over at the tall, blond guy still perched on a bar stool. The guy had slid forward on the stool. His focus was intent on the TV screen. He was in a trance. His elbows were planted on the bar while his hands cupped his chin. He was shaking his head with an almost imperceptible motion.

"Something's up," Chris thought. He gestured at the skinny bartender with the close-cropped burnt-orange hair and said, "Dude, can you turn up the sound?"

The bartender nodded and reached behind him to the side of the cash register. He grabbed the remote control and aimed the device at the TV.

Chris listened to the dark-skinned newscaster with the long legs babble about airplane crap. It was obvious that she was making stuff up just to fill time. Shit! *He* knew more about airplanes than the dopey reporter. But one thing she said caught his attention.

The airplane had departed Port of Spain, Trinidad. Isn't that where his damn pilot was supposed to have flown on his layover? And then he was flying to JFK on his second day... as in today? What the hell would he be doing in Bermuda? Chris tilted an ear toward the bar TV.

It didn't take long for him to hear what he was hoping not to hear. The names of the captain and the copilot were announced. Two separate photographs of the crew were on the screen. The captain was dressed in his uniform, two boys in their teens and what appeared to be his wife with their yellow Lab flanking him.

The copilot's photograph pictured him in a T-shirt, casually slouched in a chaise lounge by a pool. Yup, it was him. Crap! Now what? His task yesterday was to follow this copilot dude and make sure that the guy reported for his trip to Port of Spain. Chris even went so far as to pass through airport security in order to observe at the departure gate.

An old high school buddy from the army worked for TSA. He had allowed Chris to transit via the law enforcement entrance at the far end of the MIA terminal. He had watched the copilot walk onto the jet bridge with the captain. And then Chris had waited at the gate until the airplane had pushed back.

Of all the fucking luck! The airplane had an emergency! Shit! The guys in New York would be pissed.

Chris's iPhone vibrated in his pants. He slid the phone out of his pocket and looked at the caller ID. It was the slick-haired guy. Chris pressed the Talk button and put the phone to his ear. He blocked the bar noise by pressing a finger to his other ear.

"Yo," Chris said into the phone.

The flat voice at the other end of the line said, "We're on this. Stay with the faggot. See what you can find out…and then do what you have to do. And then get the fuck out of there. We're probably going to need you for something else in a few hours."

"Roger," Chris responded in the same flat tone. The call disconnected. He shoved the phone back into his pocket and glanced up at the bar TV. The local news was airing a video clip of the latest recruit for the Miami Dolphins. The rookie linebacker was practicing with the team.

"They need me for something else?" he muttered to himself. What the hell did that mean? Chris was not fond of surprises. The military had trained him to always be prepared. How could he prepare if he didn't know the mission?

With a tilt of his head, Chris shot a brief look at the tall guy. The tall guy was staring at his half empty glass. He was slumped, a despondent expression on his face.

"This could be interesting," Chris thought. What approach should he take? He'd probably have to pull the sympathy card, like he sometimes did when he was on the prowl with the ladies. Only he'd have to add a gay twist to the act. He was out of his element.

Chris sighed. He took a slow sip of his beer. He could do this. He gripped the handle of his mug and slid it off the bar. Chris began a slow shuffle toward the tall, blond guy.

12:10 EDT

It wasn't until she heard the sharp honk that Robin realized that the traffic light had turned green. The light had probably been green for a while. The face of the driver in the annoying German yuppie car behind her was contorted with frustration.

"Big deal. Chill out, buddy," Robin muttered. She had been in a self-induced trance. She took her foot off the brake and pressed on the gas pedal of the Prius. The little car began to roll forward at an unimpressive pace. The German car behind swerved to the left lane and accelerated past her at an unnecessarily high rate of speed.

"Idiot!" Robin blurted.

South Florida was full of idiots. Maybe it was time to leave. Maybe it was time to go back home to Indiana and be with the rest of her family. Hell, after last night's announcement from Mike, she had nothing holding her to Florida. She didn't like the idea of having to pick up a snow shovel again, but it beat the coldness of her Fort Lauderdale neighborhood. Unfortunately, it would be a hard sell to the girls…especially Kim. Kim was anchored to her teenage friends.

And now this drama with Mike's flight; just what they needed to complicate their relationship. Shit! Would she have to travel to Bermuda? Why should she care now?

Robin slowed at the stop sign and rolled through the intersection with a right turn. The white concrete of the girls' high school came into view at the end of the street. The sprawling building contrasted against the row of organized palm trees that defined the entrance. The building resembled a prison more than it did a school. Considering the tattoos, piercings, and other assorted gangland dress of some students, the institutional architecture was almost appropriate.

As Robin drove past the side of the school, she scanned the area. The usual assortment of cars and school buses cluttered the front parking lot. No blinking lights. No TV crews. No satellite antennas with telescoping poles. Nothing. Good deal. The media hadn't connected all the dots yet.

And then Robin turned the corner toward the back parking lot. The serenity at the front of the building was a sharp contrast to what she began to see at the back of the building.

Chaos was in full progress. On the sidewalk that bordered the rear portion of the school, a man with a nametag pinned to his tan blazer was lying face up. A large dark stain on the sidewalk surrounded the upper part of his body. The man wasn't moving. A handful of adults, one of them in a pastel-blue uniform dress holding a stethoscope, huddled around the prone man. Heads were shaking. Many were beginning to look away.

A mass of peering students were perched on the steps of the rear exit to the building. They were being gently held back by the upheld hands of two male teachers. The shrieking wail of a siren grew louder in the distance.

"Oh, shit!" Robin exclaimed. She steered the Prius between two white lines on the pavement and parked the car. Still staring at the unnerving scene twenty yards in front, she unbuckled her seat belt, pulled the key from the ignition, and stepped out of the car. She stood in place, knowing that she had no useful contribution to offer. She felt immediate sorrow for the victim's family. It would no doubt be the worst day of their lives.

Robin surveyed the trauma. Was this a shooting or a knife fight? At her daughters' high school, no less! This was not the education that she was promised by the real estate agent ten years ago when they had been house hunting. More sirens screamed in the distance. The police were probably only moments away. Crap! If only she had left the damn office earlier. Now she would have to wait until the dust settled to retrieve her girls. The selfish thought gave her a twinge of guilt.

A woman who had been part of the huddle surrounding the man on the sidewalk rose to her feet. She wore a dark pants suit. Robin recognized her. It was Tracey Abbott, the vice principal. Robin had seen the inside of Tracey's office almost as often as her daughter Kim. Their discussions were long and lively. The vice principal had a genuine concern for her daughter.

The two women had become friends, often shopping at the local malls together. She had kept their friendship a secret from Kim. Kim's status among her circle of rebellious teenage girls would suffer a tremendous blow if they knew that the vice principal and her mom were pals.

Tracey Abbott turned her head and took a few steps away from the horrific scene. She caught a glimpse of Robin standing by her car. Tracey's eyes grew wide. Her complexion began to pale. The vice principal hesitated for a brief moment and then began a slow gait toward Robin. Robin was uncomfortable with the look in Tracey's eyes.

Police cruisers and an EMT van screeched into the back parking lot.

As Tracey approached, Robin shut the car door. She leaned against the driver's side window. An unmarked police car, its blue light flashing on the dashboard, appeared from around the corner. It parked at an awkward angle near the commotion on the sidewalk.

"Hi, Robin," Tracey said with a guarded tone. She held out her hand to shake. It was their standard greeting when on school grounds.

"Hey," Robin said as she shook Tracey's hand. She gestured at the activity on the sidewalk. The paramedics were opening the rear doors of the EMT van. "Not a good day."

"No, it's awful." Tracey looked at the ground for a brief moment and then back at Robin. "That was Mr. Washington. He was our security guard. Retired Miami cop. He was shot."

"How? By whom?"

"Not really sure at the moment." Tracey bit her lip and stared into Robin's eyes. "It gets worse, Robin"

"What do you mean?"

Tracey cleared her throat. "There was an abduction. That's why the security guard was shot." She paused. "At least that's what we think."

"Abduction? Who was abducted?"

Tracey's eyes began to water. She took a long breath. She began to move her lips. Words weren't making it past her vocal chords.

Robin didn't have to hear. The anguished expression on the vice principal's face gave away the answer. She gasped.

"Please tell me it isn't true," Robin whispered.

Tracey was paralyzed. She lowered her head and stared at the ground.

"Both of my girls?" Robin asked, a pleading tone in her voice.

Tracey nodded with her head still lowered toward the pavement.

12:15 EDT

The white Escalade motored through the intersection of U.S. 1 on Sunrise Boulevard. The blonde behind the wheel glanced at the speedometer. The indicator pointed directly at forty mph. At that speed, she would not attract unwanted attention from law enforcement. The car's blackened windows concealed the precious cargo strapped in the two rear seats.

"Where are you taking us?" Ashley asked, trying to hide a sniffle.

The driver shifted her bare white shoulders against the seat but remained silent. Her flowing blond hair swung across the back of the headrest like a pendulum.

"They'll find us, you know. It won't take long," Ashley continued.

Kim turned toward her sister and glared. She shook her head and rolled her eyes. She said, "Ash, shut up. You're not helping."

Tears began to fill Ashley's eyes. She turned away from Kim and stared out the window.

An impulsive thought crossed Kim's mind. She focused her gaze on the hair draped over the headrest. Should she? Kim looked into the rear view mirror that reflected the sculpted face of the driver. Her long eyelashes outlined her piercing green eyes. The eyes were focused on the road ahead. Why not?

Kim lunged forward and pulled down on the blond hair. Surprisingly, the driver protested with only a muffled groan. She resisted Kim's tug, holding her head just level enough to see through the windshield.

With clenched teeth, the driver said, "You have two choices, young lady. You can let go now or I can use the gun again…this time to shoot your sister." The black barrel of a handgun began to make an appearance over the center console of the Escalade. Ashley began to sniffle.

Kim yelled, "If you went to this much trouble in order to kidnap us, we're too valuable to shoot!"

"Do you want to call my bluff?" The driver said with a sinister tone.

Kim looked at Ashley. Streams of tears were running down her pink cheeks. Kim took a deep breath and then released her grip on the long blond hair.

"Good choice, young lady," the driver said. Her reflection in the rearview mirror revealed a coy smile. She shook her head and brushed her hair with the fingers of her free hand. The movement was more an act of defiance then it was a grooming attempt.

They continued in silence until the driver made a series of turns that ended in the back parking lot of a four-story office building. Numerous windows of the office building held banner-size signs with the red words "For Lease." The lot was empty except for a battered dumpster and a black Audi A6 parked in-between two faded white lines. The Audi's windows were tinted the same dark shade as the Escalade.

The blonde rolled the Escalade to a stop next to the Audi. She unbuckled her seat belt and pulled the key from the ignition. She turned to face the girls.

"Get out!" the blonde ordered. "You're going for another ride. She gestured at the Audi and pointed the gun at the side of the car nearest to Ashley. "Go out that door. Open the rear door of the Audi and get in."

The two sisters turned to face each other. Anxious expressions were etched on both of their faces. They remained still for a few moments.

Almost on cue, the muffled voices of the Jonas Brothers reverberated into the Escalade. The tinny sound was the ringtone coming from the cell phone that was wedged into a pocket of Kim's jeans. Kim's eyes widened. She stared at the blonde.

The blonde's eyes narrowed. She glared at Kim. "You're full of little surprises." She reached out a hand, palm facing up and her fingers beckoning. "Give me the cell phone, you little brat!"

Kim crossed her arms.

"Now!" commanded the blonde.

With a reluctant sigh, Kim shoved a hand into her pocket and slid out her iPhone. She slapped it against the blonde's upturned palm. The blonde curled her red fingernails around the phone and turned to face Ashley. "Give me your phone too, little sister."

Ashley said, "Don't have one yet. Can't have one until I'm Kim's age."

"You'd better not be lying, girlfriend."

Ashley shook her head and unbuckled her seat belt. With a brief sniffle, she opened her door and slid her feet out to the pavement. She took a step toward the Audi still parked a couple of feet from the Escalade. Ashley hesitated for a second and then with a tenuous motion reached for the rear door handle. Kim followed, keeping a watchful eye on the blonde and her gun. With the door of the Audi open, the girls slid across the back seat.

A throaty female voice from the driver's seat ordered, "Close it now!"

Kim reached for the armrest and slammed the door shut. She looked ahead at the woman in the driver's seat. This woman had long, fiery red hair. It was tied in a ponytail with a sparkling silver clasp. The woman turned to glance at Kim and Ashley. Her orange tan accented the high cheekbones of her freckled face.

The passenger door opened and the blonde from the Escalade slithered into the seat. Her fashionably tattered, skin-tight jeans contrasted with the plush interior of the car. The bra under her sheer, pink tank top did nothing to hide the outline of her breasts. She swung her long legs over the transom of the door. The clunky spikes of her high heel shoes clicked against the metal as she shifted her body inside.

"Welcome, ladies," the redhead said. If you cooperate with our instructions, everything will be okay. We might even have a little fun. If you choose to be difficult, life will not be pleasant." The redhead moved her stare from Kim to Ashley. "Understood?"

Both girls offered reluctant nods. The blonde opened the glove compartment of the Audi and reached inside. She pulled out two eye masks, the type used to block out light when sleeping. She turned in her seat and dangled the masks in front of Kim and Ashley.

"Put these on, little darlings! It'll be more fun if you don't know where you are."

Kim and Ashley exchanged fearful glances. With a brief moment of hesitation, they reached for the masks and slid them over their faces. They fussed with the elastic bands as they adjusted them behind their heads.

"And no peeking, you little brats! I'll know!"

The driver smiled and looked at the blonde as she swung the passenger door closed.

"You look especially slutty today, love."

The blonde grinned and said, "Thanks. It means a lot coming from you." The two women chuckled. The blonde gestured at the parked Escalade. "It's all set. Can I be the naughty one?"

"You can, but wait till we get at least a block away," the redhead said as she moved the gearshift into Drive.

As the four drove away from the office parking lot, the blonde reached into her purse and pulled out a keychain-size remote control device, one that would normally be used as a garage door opener. Once they had traveled a few hundred feet, the blonde turned in her seat and pointed the remote control at the Escalade they had left behind. She pressed a button.

A few brief seconds passed. A sharp crack, followed by a whoosh filled their ears. The Escalade was almost completely engulfed in orange flames. Thick black smoke began to belch high above the burning car. The redhead slowly increased the speed of the Audi, moving away from the scene.

"Holy shit!" Kim quietly exclaimed.

The blonde said, "I never did like that car anyhow. Too big." She glanced at the redhead. "Did you like it?"

The redhead said, "Didn't like the color. Everybody has a frickin' white Cadillac in Fort Lauderdale." She paused. "Whose car was it anyhow?"

"Don't know, really. It was only around for a couple of days. I think Ted had one of his creepy dudes steal it off a dealer's lot."

"Well…good luck to the cops. They'll have a hard time finding prints now."

The redhead zigged and zagged around side roads and then turned south onto Bayview Drive. A few minutes passed in silence. They turned east onto a side street. Within a few moments they rolled onto the tan pavers of a circular driveway. The driveway was attached to an expansive two-story home that was surrounded by a meticulously manicured lawn accented by every species of local palm.

As the redhead inched the Audi forward toward the house, a wood-stained garage door began to open. When the door had almost risen to its maximum height, the Audi rolled into the garage. The floor was glossed with a paint that made it appear wet. A fire-engine red, low profile sports car was parked on the other side. The garage door began to close behind them.

The blonde turned in her seat toward Ashley and Kim saying, "Okay, ladies, time to move again. Get out of the car." She turned to face the two blindfolded teenagers. "And be careful opening the door! Ted will take away our bikini allowance if you ding the Ferrari."

Kim muttered under her breath, "Yay. We got kidnapped by Thelma and Louise."

Ashley jabbed Kim in the thigh with a loosely clutched

fist. She grimaced and then slowly opened the car door.

The blonde stared at Kim for a moment and said, "I don't know what you said, girl. But I can tell that you're a little smart-ass. You don't want to push it with either one of us. Do I make myself clear?"

Kim nodded, resisting the urge to display a middle finger.

Once the two girls were out of the Audi, the two women pushed and prodded Ashley and Kim through a side door and into the house. Though they couldn't see it yet, they had entered a sprawling living room that flowed from the granite counter top of an immaculate elevated kitchen, out sliding glass doors, across a glistening aqua-blue swimming pool, and onto a gleaming white concrete dock. A white Tiara was tied up alongside the round wooden pilings anchored to the dock. The ripples of the water's surface reflected off the hull of the sedan-bridge boat. The ends of the black lines tied to the boat's cleats were curled into flat concentric circles on the dock.

The blonde walked over to one of the sliding glass doors and pulled it open. She smiled at Kim and Ashley.

The blonde said, "Now it's time for the fun part of the trip. You can take your blindfolds off." When the girls slid the masks off their eyes, blinking as the sudden bright light of the sun invaded their pupils, the blonde gestured her head at the Tiara and ordered, "Get on board, ladies." She sighed and chuckled quietly. "Too bad you forgot your bikinis." The blonde looked at Kim and scanned her body. "With that figure, you could fill out one of Amber's little numbers quite nicely. Want to borrow one, girlfriend?"

Kim rolled her eyes and said, "Thanks, but I'm not in a swimsuit mood today. I think I'd rather be in math class taking a pop quiz."

"Such attitude." The blonde's expression went cold. "We'll have to change that."

The blonde walked out the door onto the pool deck and turned toward the boat. Ashley and Kim felt a nudge on their shoulders from behind. Amber, the redhead, was pushing them outside.

"Your yacht awaits," Amber said. "Don't keep the captain waiting."

The blonde had removed her high heels and had climbed onboard. She plopped down onto the helm chair and twisted the ignition key to one of the engines. The motor sputtered for a brief moment and then warbled to life with a throaty rumble. As Kim and Ashley stepped over the side gunnels and onto the deck, the blonde started the other engine.

Amber began untying the lines from the dock cleats. When the boat was free, Amber jumped onto the deck.

The blonde turned toward Amber and asked, "Ready?"

"Ready," Amber replied.

Kim watched as the concrete dock began to slide past. The boat glided forward out into the middle of the neighborhood canal. The Intracoastal Waterway lay a few hundred yards ahead.

"Damn! If only her girlfriends could see her now!" Kim thought. Wait… she could text a picture. Instinctively she reached for the iPhone in her front pocket. She fumbled in her jeans and felt nothing. This trip was really going to suck.

CHAPTER SIX

Friday
12:30 EDT

His introduction to the tall gay dude wasn't as painful as Chris had anticipated. Other than a veneer of sarcasm, conversation was surprisingly easy with Jonathan. A couple of wine spritzers later, the discussion got even easier. And, as an added bonus, the bartender with the spiky orange hair hadn't been charging Chris's tab for Jonathan's drinks. Must be a gay custom or...?

Chris raised an eyebrow and looked at his new friend, asking, "Hey, Jonathan, are you a regular at this joint?"

"You might say that. Why do ask?"

"Just curious. It's my first time here, and I rarely see a bartender buy a round for a new customer in this town.

"I own this joint," Jonathan said with a smirk, emphasizing the word "joint."

"Kinda' thought so. Makes sense."

"What gave it away?"

Chris thought for a moment. If he were dealing with a chick, now would be an opportunity to throw out a compliment. He said, "Just your comfort level. You have an air of authority about you. Kinda like my sergeants when I was on active duty in-country."

Jonathan smiled. The corner of his mouth turned upwards with a hint of slyness.

Chris continued, "It's a good quality. It gave us grunts

confidence that the guy in charge knew what he was doing… and that he wasn't going to get our ass shot off."

"I think I understand." Jonathan stared at his glass for a moment and then looked back at Chris. "Thanks for doing what you did over there, protecting our freedoms and all. You've probably heard the same bullshit before, but I do mean it."

"It's okay. You can never hear it enough. Although sometimes I think it's just over-compensating for the Vietnam guys. We treated them like shit."

"Could be some truth in that statement," Jonathan said, sipping from his wine glass.

Chris grabbed the handle of his beer mug and threw back a big gulp of amber liquid. With a muffled thud, he set his drink back down on the over-shellacked bar.

Jonathan snorted. He scanned Chris's biceps, and asked, "So, soldier guy, is the Army how you got so big?"

Chris could feel the blood surge in his cheeks. He was embarrassed but not because of the reasons the fag may have thought.

Jonathan chuckled and said, "Aha! You're a shy one…"

"Yeah, always have been a little self-conscious." Chris was feeling queasy in the middle of his stomach. He needed to move away from this pickup game without having the guy lose interest. It was time to get on with the mission. "Hey, you never did say why you seemed so upset at the TV news a little while ago?"

"It's a long story."

"It's my day off. I got time."

Jonathan's sly smile reappeared. "I'll tell you the long version only if you promise to stick around until after I help my girls get the dinner prep-work done." "Girls" was said with a sarcastic inflection and a wink.

"It's a deal," Chris responded with his best imitation of

a coy grin. Girls? He hadn't seen a female body in the place since he first walked through the door.

Jonathan rotated his seat to the side and slid off the barstool. His movement was cautious. The wine spritzers had taken their toll on his equilibrium. As he stood up, he squeezed a bicep on Chris's arm and grinned.

Jonathan said, "Like a rock, big guy." He turned and walked toward the swinging kitchen door. "See you in a few. Don't drink the bar out of Budweiser before the end of Happy Hour, please."

"Promise," Chris said. He agonized over maintaining a smile for another second longer. "Shit," he muttered under his breath.

12:35 EDT

The round, brown man rolled up the white sleeves of his wrinkled Ralph Lauren shirt. He was seated in the corner chair of the vice principal's office. Sweat had caused some of the material over the man's portly stomach to adhere tightly against the undershirt beneath. He snapped open a small, spiral bound notebook to a blank page and pulled out a pen that was clipped to the top cover. He raised the pen to his mouth, clenching it lightly in his teeth. He pulled the pen from his lips and pointed it casually at the vice principal, seated behind her wood veneer desk.

The brown man said, "Uh…Ms.…Ms.…"

"Abbott. Tracey Abbott, Detective Alvarez."

"Yes, ma'am. I'm sorry." Detective Jorge Alvarez took in a deep breath. "Ms. Abbott, tell me again where you were when the incident occurred?"

Tracey shifted in her seat and said, "In the gym. I was discussing a new exercise program that had been suggested by our phys ed teacher."

"Okay. But you had left the two Townsend sisters unsupervised in this office, correct?"

"Yes. I gave them the opportunity to complete homework assignments while they waited. My secretary was directly outside the door. And Mr. Washington had been given instructions on escorting the sisters to the back parking lot when Robin…I mean, Mrs. Townsend, called en route."

The detective raised an eyebrow and glanced at Robin who was seated in one of the chairs directly in front of the desk. He looked at the vice principal and asked, "Are you two ladies friends?"

Tracey smiled and glanced at Robin. "Yes, Detective. Mrs. Townsend and I have socialized together. Is that a punishable offense?"

Robin's expression remained solemn. She stared at the small area of carpet between Tracey's desk and her feet.

"No, of course it's not punishable," Alvarez said. He couldn't quite rid himself of his first impression of the VP. The short hair and square stride offered the possibility that Tracey Abbott was a lesbian. He didn't get the lesbian vibe from Mrs. Townsend. Would the two women hang out together regardless? Did it matter?

Alvarez added, "It's always helpful to establish relationships no matter how insignificant they may appear."

"I understand," Tracey said with a nod.

The detective scribbled a few words in his notebook and then tapped the open page with his pen. He looked up at Tracey and began to speak but was interrupted. A uniformed police officer had stepped past the half-opened door and was standing inside the office.

"Uh…Detective…can we release the body to the coroner now?" the officer asked.

"I assume CSI has finished with their magic shi…" Alvarez glanced at Robin and Tracey, wincing at the four-letter word that almost came out of his mouth, "…their magic show, I mean?"

"Yes, sir. CSI is done for now." The officer's expression remained neutral.

"Okay, good." Alvarez paused. "Any word on the security camera footage?"

"The principal is assisting, but he's not familiar with the system. If an incident occurred in the past that required a review, the school security officer handled the request. The principal has contacted the vendor that installed the system."

"I assume a sense of urgency has been conveyed?"

"I believe so, sir."

Alvarez said, "Thanks, Tom."

The uniformed cop nodded and walked out of the office.

Tracey Abbott raised her eyebrows and asked, "Detective, don't you guys normally operate with a partner?"

Alvarez expression became drawn. He replied, "Budget issues, Ms. Abbott."

"I see," Tracey said with a nod.

Alvarez sighed. "Well, Ms. Abbott, that answer is not totally honest. I lost my partner of four years as a result of a shooting in Pompano Beach last month. He was off duty and attempted to break up a fight in a Walmart parking lot. Unfortunately, the fight was the result of a crack deal that was not progressing as planned. My partner was shot with his own weapon."

"That's awful, Detective. I'm sorry."

Robin looked up from her gaze at the floor with sad eyes and said, "I'm sorry. This can be a very cruel world."

Alvarez nodded and continued. "The sad part is that my partner was buying baby formula for an abused mother. We had arrested the boyfriend a few days prior after he attempted to stab her with a serrated, fish-cleaning knife." The detective offered a weary smile. "My partner was a good man, wanted to save the world. Anyhow, I wasn't quite ready to work with somebody new. I've been doing this for almost ten years, so my boss didn't fight me on not having a partner…at least for the moment. And it helped my boss with his budget."

Alvarez cleared his throat and slid a hand through his hair. He looked at Robin. She was impassive, chewing a fingernail.

"Mrs. Townsend, could you think of any reason that someone would want to abduct your daughters?"

Robin released a long breath and said, "No. I can't." Her eyes narrowed. "Do you think that whoever took my girls might be a sex offender?"

"Don't think so, ma'am. I can't see a pervert having the patience to wait in a school parking lot in the middle of the day, hoping that two students would walk outside. I'm not involved with the sex crimes division, but my understanding is that sexual predators aren't normally armed. Hopefully the security tape will give us more answers."

Robin nodded.

"Are you sure that somebody in your family might not have enemies seeking retribution? Business acquaintances? Neighbors? Bad kids?"

"Nothing comes to the top of my head, Detective."

"How about finances? I'm sorry to ask the question, but do you have a bank account that might draw some attention?"

Robin offered a nervous chuckle and said, "My husband is an airline pilot, not a banker. We owe everybody."

"Well…okay. A bad debt maybe?"

"Does last month's cable bill count?" Robin asked with a smirk.

"Who handles the finances?"

Robin glanced at her wedding ring and looked back at Alvarez. "Mike does the big stuff. Mortgages. Investments. Things like that. Before he got hired with the airline, he had a background in finance. Mostly college courses. A few low-level corporate accounting positions."

"All right. Well, if you think of something unusual, let me know," Alvarez said.

Robin nodded. She thought of telling the detective about the bombshell Mike had dropped last night, but what difference would it make really? And why give the subject a chance to become public knowledge, especially with all the media coverage about Mike's emergency landing…and now the girls' abduction.

Robin glanced out the window and looked back at Alvarez. "Mike holds a national position with PAPA, the pilots union. He's the secretary/treasurer." She sighed. "It takes time away from us and the girls, but I've never heard him discuss anything out of the ordinary. The job is supposed to be prestigious. It looks boring to me. Miles of paperwork and financial statements. He's always going to meetings at headquarters in Miami. Contract negotiations with the company have dragged on for years. That's the only thing that he really gets wound up about."

Alvarez asked, "Has he received any strange phone calls recently?"

"They're all strange phone calls, Detective," Robin said, shaking her head and shrugging her shoulders. "Anything related to union work usually comes through his cell phone. I don't field any messages. The iPhone is glued to his ear. I've got to admire the dedication of the other union officers. But they must not have a life when they're not flying. The part of the conversation that I hear sounds like the guy at the other end is bitching and whining about something. Mike responds to them more like a therapist than a finance guy."

"Hmm…,"Alvarez said as he scribbled more words into his notebook. "Okay, I've got some of the picture. Everything helps." He cleared his throat. "More law enforcement departments may become involved with this case, including the FBI. It depends upon the direction that the abductors take. I will assure you that we will leave no stone unturned in pursuit of your daughters and their captors."

"Thanks," Robin said at a volume barely above a whisper.

"What concerns me is that the whole mess seems to have occurred within hours of your husband's airline emergency. I don't like coincidences." Alvarez tapped the pen to his chin and asked, "Do your daughters have cell phones?"

Robin sighed and said, "Kim has an iPhone."

"And your other daughter?"

"No. Both girls were promised phones when they reached the age of seventeen. Ashley is only fifteen." Robin raised her eyebrows. "Why do you ask, Detective?"

"We may be able to track their location via the cell phone signal."

Robin nodded and said, "Kim is like her father. That thing is surgically attached."

Alvarez said, "If we can still receive a signal, it will be a tremendous help. All I need is the number."

"You mean like the program, Find My iPhone?"

"Yes, only we'll use a more sophisticated type of tracking."

Robin leaned over Tracey's desk and scooped up a small pad of pink sticky notes. She grabbed one of the pens standing in a tall coffee mug and scribbled Kim's phone number onto the sticky note pad. She peeled off the top piece and handed it to Alvarez.

Alvarez nodded and said, "In the meantime, it would be best if you went home and tried to relax. Call family or friends to help get you through this. Can I have one of our officers drive you?"

"No, Detective. I'll drive myself. I'll be fine. I have to break the news to my husband anyhow. I'm sure with the emergency landing that he's going to have more than enough to fill his plate."

Alvarez nodded and reached into his jacket pocket. He pulled out a business card and handed one to Robin and one to Tracey. "My cell is listed also. Call me with anything." He stood up, took a step toward Robin, and reached out to shake her hand. "We'll be in touch, Mrs. Townsend." He turned toward Tracey seated at the desk. "Thank you for your time, Ms. Abbott."

Tracey nodded.

As Alvarez exited the vice principal's office into the school corridor, he met up with the uniformed cop who had earlier requested the release of the security officer's body to the coroner.

The cop asked, "Find out anything useful, Detective?"

"It's what I didn't find out that's useful, Tom."

"How do you mean?"

"Is this school part of your normal patrol?"

"Yeah, for the most part. Why?"

"Have you had any dealings with the security officer?"

"Just the usual stuff. Delinquent kids. Vandalism. Fights."

"Did he seem like a stand-up guy?"

"Retired cop. Just got divorced. He's a little bitter. The usual pissed-off attitude. Drives an older Lexus. Seen him in the local gin mills. Always seems to have a friend or two around. Mostly cops."

"Something isn't right," Alvarez said scratching his temple. "Even an idiot like me can figure out that the abduction is not a coincidence. The airline pilot father has an emergency landing in Bermuda, and his daughters are snatched from their school within hours of the event?" Alvarez slowed his pace for a moment. "How did the perp or perps know that the kids were being released from school early? Did our bitter, retired cop have a hand in this thing?"

"Good question," the uniformed cop replied. "You're thinking that maybe he was shot because he would be an information liability later?"

"It's possible," Alvarez said. "I've also got other ideas…"

12:45 EDT

Hart rolled to a stop in the driveway and parked his truck in front of his girlfriend's home, an old-style Florida ranch house. The tangerine stucco paint was a refreshing change from the drab colors of the surrounding neighborhood. He got out of the truck and walked past the long windows that led to the front door. He glanced at his reflection, making an assessment of his appearance. Khaki pants with cuffs. Good. Pin-striped, slightly tropical short-sleeve shirt. Not bad. Casual braided belt. Cinch it up one more notch? Probably not. Was that a hint of flab protruding over his waistband? Couldn't be. More gray hair or was that just the effect of the sunlight? He sighed. Hart tapped on the door and then walked into the house toward the kitchen.

Cathy was using her favorite knife to chop a colorful array of vegetables on a wooden cutting board. Blond hair cascaded over her shoulders. She looked up from her chopping and smiled. It was the same sexy smile that had captivated Hart years ago.

Hart flashed through an image of Cathy wearing only the apron. His eyes scanned Cathy's hourglass figure. He chuckled.

"What's so funny?" Cathy asked, the big knife poised over a red pepper.

"Oh, nothing really," Hart said with a grin.

"Yeah, right. I've known you way too long. Nothing is something."

"Well, okay. It's that 'Don't-fondle-the-cook' apron that

you're wearing. It's turning me on in a weird way."

"You're full of crap." Cathy pierced the red pepper with the knife and began to cut the vegetable into thin slices. She grinned. "So…you're going to leave me and my salad tonight? Notwithstanding the fact that you could be spending a wonderful evening with my neighbors…the ones that own your favorite dog that barks at the wind?"

"It's not a dog. Real dogs aren't able to fit into tote bags. It's a rodent." Hart rolled his eyes and smiled. "Tell me again…why are you having your neighbors over for dinner?"

"Remember when they watered my plants while we were skiing in Park City? And they checked on your boat."

"Oh...yeah. I remember. Didn't they kill the cactus by over-watering it? Who kills a cactus? That takes talent."

"Details. It was the thought that counted."

"You're right. I also forgot that he didn't check to see that the shore power attached to the boat had tripped. The bilge pumps operated on the batteries until they died. Guess I should be thankful for small favors that the boat didn't actually sink."

"Just more details, Hart."

"Aside from the rodent dog thing, the husband's conversation usually starts with a riveting weather report and then goes directly to how I can better manage my 401(k)."

"He's a financial planner, Hart. Not everybody can be a daring and dashing airline pilot," Cathy said with a smirk. "And it couldn't hurt to consider some of his financial advice considering your abilities to spend money."

"Funny. Well, enjoy them without me. I'll take a rain check."

Cathy put the knife down and looked at Hart. Her eyes softened. "This isn't going to be like the last one is it?"

"No, Cath. It's not. Only two fatalities. We've got a live flight crew. An intact airplane. And no nasty crash site. I'm the party coordinator this time. Being the boss means I can delegate. I don't have to focus on the ugly stuff."

"Give me a break. I know you," Cathy said, shaking her head.

The sound of Hart's cell phone playing the theme song to the original *Airport* movie rang at his side.

Cathy rolled her eyes and said, "Get the phone. I'm sure it has something to do with the accident. Promise me that you'll schedule the surgery to remove that Bluetooth headset thingy from your ear as soon as you come back from Bermuda."

Hart smiled and looked at the display screen. "Unknown caller." He had been getting a lot of these all day long. Had the circumstances been different, he would have let the call go to voice mail. He put the headset in his ear.

"It's Hart Lindy."

"Captain Lindy?"

"Yes. How may I help you?"

"The investigation of Flight 63…you're the PAPA party coordinator, right?"

"Who is this please?"

"It's not important. Just listen." The barely audible voice had a commanding tone. Hart detected a hint of an accent. He couldn't place it. "Be careful with the investigation. You are in dangerous territory. People who have a different regard for human life could destroy you and your team."

"Are you threatening me?"

"No, Captain. I'm only offering you a warning."

Hart gritted his teeth and said, "It sounds like a threat."

"Take it any way you would prefer. But you're out of your league. Even your own government authorities won't be able to assist."

"I plan on doing my job, making sure the investigation of this accident is conducted fairly and accurately along with the NTSB."

"You're living in a fairy tale, Captain Lindy. Take a good look at that pretty woman in front of you." The voice transformed into a throaty whisper. "She's worth seeing again, isn't she? Don't jeopardize her happiness with something inconsequential."

Hart glanced at Cathy and then focused on the orange of the Mexican tile floor. "What are you saying?"

"You've been warned. Good luck, Captain."

The phone went silent. Hart pulled the headset out of his ear and stared at the display.

Cathy had resumed her preparation on the cutting board. She glanced at Hart and then back at the counter. "Everything okay?"

"Uh…yeah, everything is fine."

"I didn't like the tone of the conversation. Who was that?"

Hart said quickly, "Oh just some anonymous overzealous moron that thinks he knows more about the accident than the experts." He snorted. "Probably just one of our pilots that contributes nothing but to bitch. We hear from those kinds of guys all the time."

Cathy nodded, looking unconvinced.

Hart peered out the kitchen windows. Was the caller staring at them with a pair of binoculars? The only movement was from the coconut palms that lined the opposite side of the street. They jittered with the breeze.

Cathy said, "Please come back without injuries, physical or otherwise." She sighed. Her eyes narrowed. "And come back without another phone number on your contact list. I hate having you tell me that it's a wrong number in the middle of the night."

Hart grimaced as he smiled. "Ouch, that hurts." He picked up a piece of shredded chicken from the cutting board and popped it in his mouth. "Don't worry. The girls in Bermuda are too expensive. They're looking for investment banker types, not poor airline pilots. And the other women are blissfully involved with their honeymoons."

"Not funny."

"I'm sorry," Hart replied. "You know that I've been a good boy."

Hart thought of his mother. The trail of boyfriends during and after her marriage to Hart's father could have filled a hotel suite. His mother had just recently returned from rehab after her second DUI and her second divorce.

Hart walked behind the kitchen counter and grabbed Cathy around the waist. He twisted her toward him. They stared into each other's eyes for a long few seconds. And then Hart drew them into a tight embrace. Their lips melted together.

12:55 EDT

Rod glanced at the desk phone. The flashing green light and warbling tone indicated that the call was the office intercom. Rod picked up the handset and put it to his ear.

"Rod, it's Donna. You need to pick up Line 1. It's the crew schedule M.O.D."

"This can't be good," Rod said.

Calls from the crew schedule manager on duty usually concerned a pilot who had missed a trip, or had some issue that could potentially turn into a discipline problem, or...

Donna said, "No, it's not good. That's why they're calling you. More shit has just hit the fan."

"Great. Do I get paid extra for this?"

"Not as far as I know, but you do get Princess parking."

Rod aimed a finger at Line 1. "I've got it, Donna." He pressed the button.

"Rod Moretti. What can I do for you, crew schedule?"

"Captain Moretti, this is Misty Adams. I'm the M.O.D. We just got a call from a Robin Townsend. I believe that is First Officer Townsend's wife. Apparently crew schedule was her only point of contact in an attempt to reach her husband. She didn't know any other way. Considering the circumstances, I thought it best to call you."

"Thanks, Ms. Adams. You did the right thing."

"Understandably, she sounded very distraught."

"I'm sure she is. I'll handle this. I'll call First Officer Townsend in Bermuda right away."

Misty Adams cleared her throat and said, "The emergency landing is not really the concern."

"What do you mean?"

"I'm getting this information second-hand through the crew scheduler that got the original call…but it appears that the first officer's daughters were abducted this afternoon at their high school."

"What?"

"Yes, sir. I know. It gets worse. The security officer escorting the two girls was shot and killed during the abduction."

Rod listened to the M.O.D. as she conveyed the remainder of the story. Unbelievable! How was he going to break the news? It didn't matter. He had to get the man home, NTSB investigation or not. He'd make the call to Bermuda, but…

Hart Lindy should be informed regarding the development with the copilot's family. He didn't like it much, but it was the right thing to do. Hart's group would be better prepared to deal with this crisis. Plus, the pilots union would have more influence…at least for the moment.

"Shit." Rod muttered under his breath. He had hoped his new position would avoid contact with Hart. How many years had it been now? How many years had they been friends?

His falling out with Hart had been almost as disappointing as his divorce.

It wasn't important now. His priority was to a pilot at his base who was about to enter crisis mode.

CHAPTER SEVEN

Friday
13:10 EDT

The traffic on I-95 was beginning to clump into fast and slow sections. Rush hour and its ensuing South Florida madness were in the early stages. Hart noticed that his grip on the steering wheel had tightened. If he were lucky, the highway wouldn't turn into a scene from "Mad Max" before he got to the employee parking lot at MIA. Maybe he should have taken the turnpike…

As the traffic slowed to a crawl near the Griffin Road exit, Hart reached for his iPhone. Gliding his thumb across the home key, he selected the program that contained the latest audio book download. The book was a series detective thriller--his adult pacifier. The baritone words of the narrator filled the speakers. He sighed.

Traffic began to once again resume a more frantic pace. Hart glanced at his speedometer. The flow of cars had now reached sixty mph. Not bad. Maybe a few more sticky spots and he would be home free.

Hart peered into his rearview mirror. A lunatic driving a black Mercedes with over-tinted windows was swerving in and out of lanes. How much faster did the schmuck think that he was going to get there ahead of everyone else? The Mercedes accelerated past Hart on the right, coming within what appeared to be only a foot from his door.

"Moron!" Hart uttered out loud.

The Mercedes darted to the left across two lanes of traffic and then unexpectedly began to slow. The car was now only a few yards ahead. The right rear window began to roll down, leaving a gap of about six inches.

A black rifle barrel slid its way into the gap. The business end of the rifle pointed directly toward Hart's line of sight. Time began to move in a series of snapshots as if the scene ahead of Hart was an old, animated flip-book cartoon.

"Really...? You can't be serious," Hart muttered. Instinctively, he ducked behind his dashboard while still maintaining a grip on the lower part of the steering wheel. Hart hoped he could keep control of the truck without hitting another car.

The sound of muffled thumps reverberated inside the cab. He felt a handful of faint vibrations. No crack of a gunshot. No shattered glass. What the hell?

Hart peered to his left. The view through his driver's side window and rear passenger window were obliterated by a line of quarter-size red dots. Each dot had spattered outward in the form of a mini explosion. Hart heard the shriek of tires and the increasing rpm of a high-performance car. He sat up and watched as the Mercedes accelerated away in a flash of gleaming black.

As his heart rate and adrenalin rush began to dissipate, Hart took a deep breath. He slid his foot back onto the gas pedal and surveyed the mess on his windows. He shook his head. He had been the victim of a paintball attack.

"You've got to be kidding?" Hart said out loud. Other drivers were passing him, glancing and pointing. Some had serious expressions. Others were smirking. "Great. Thanks for your concern, folks. No, really. I'm okay. Idiots!"

Hart glanced at a grinning twenty-something guy who was driving a jelly bean-shaped Toyota. The chassis of the car was low enough to the ground that it appeared to be sweeping the pavement. The Toyota spit out a series of crackling pops through its chromed barrel muffler. The twenty-something guy was wearing a baseball cap turned backwards. His seat was slid far enough rearward that he might as well have been sitting in the back of the car. The kid nodded his head with an exaggerated motion, acknowledging the paintball attack with a smirk.

"I've got to reconsider that log cabin in Wyoming. The black bears out there have more compassion than these South Florida maniacs." Hart said through his closed window.

The narrator of the detective novel continued to drone through the truck's speakers. Hart reached for his phone, pressed the audio book exit button, and ended the narration. He couldn't focus. The silence was more soothing. Should he call 911? Probably. Hart divided his attention between the highway and his phone. He began to press the number buttons but was startled by the vibration as his phone began to ring.

Hart glanced at the display. It read, "Unknown caller."

"Of course," Hart thought. He pulled the Bluetooth headset from his shirt pocket, pressed the answer button, and wiggled the device into his ear.

"It's Hart."

"Captain Lindy, that little paintball episode was a warning. Perhaps you'll take me seriously now. The next time the rounds could be real."

Hart could feel another surge of adrenalin as his heart began to thump. He exhaled and said, "Nice. Couldn't you have at least met my deductible with the damage?"

"You've been warned, Captain."

"Your little paintball stunt attracted a lot of attention. Is that really helpful?"

"It does not matter to us as long as our mission is accomplished."

"And what exactly is your mission?"

"It is not your concern."

Hart frowned and said, "Good talking with you, dude. I've got an investigation to help organize. Thanks for the warning. I'll make sure to let the appropriate authorities know your concerns. Have a great day."

Hart pressed the End button. He shook his head. Should he or shouldn't he call the cops? Other than a frustrating act of vandalism, nothing had really happened. But he was threatened…again. Were the rest of his investigative team members at risk? He couldn't take the chance. He picked up his phone and began to press the buttons for 911.

The end of this day would require a very cool beer in a very tall glass.

13:15 EDT

As the Tiara motored up the Intracoastal Waterway, Kim and Ashley peered out the porthole windows. Arms folded across their chests, they were seated opposite each other on the salon couches down below. The door that separated the cockpit from the cabin had been locked from the outside. The girls were trapped--prisoners in a luxury yacht.

"I bet they have Cokes or something," Kim said, gesturing at the three-quarter-size refrigerator.

"I'm not thirsty," Ashley replied. She glanced out a porthole. "Where do you think we are?"

"I'm pretty sure that we turned south. Thought I saw us go under the Commercial Street Bridge."

Ashley's lower lip protruded. She looked at the refrigerator. "All right…I'll have something. Doesn't matter what it is."

Kim nodded, slid off the couch, and opened the refrigerator door. She surveyed the shelves. Every rack was jammed with either a food item or a beverage. Sliced sandwich meats. Cold chicken. Pasta salads. Coke. Sprite. Beer. Wine.

Kim reached in and grabbed two Cokes. She shook her head and looked at Ashley. "They packed all sorts of crap in here."

"That's good. We won't starve."

"Ash, you don't get it." Kim handed a Coke to her sister and pulled back the tab on her can. It popped and hissed.

"Wha' d'ya mean?"

"Think about it, sis." Kim pointed at the open refrigerator. "When does Dad ever load up with food on the boat unless we're headed out somewhere for more than a day or two?"

Ashley stared at her sister for a moment, lowered her head, and said, "Oh…"

"Yeah…exactly." Kim took a sip from her Coke and swallowed with a gurgle. "They plan on keeping us for a while.

"How long?"

"I'm not a mind reader, sis." Kim gestured out past the tinted cockpit door. "I'm sure that Thelma and Louise out there have never sold Girl Scout cookies. I don't think they give a rat's ass. We're being ransomed for something. And I think it has to do with Dad."

"Ransomed? Why? Mom's always complaining that we don't have enough money."

Kim said, "Well, maybe Dad isn't telling us everything."

Ashley rested her elbows on her thighs and cupped her chin. She shook her head. "Make me a sandwich. I'm too hungry to think."

Kim sighed. "Why not? Nothing else to do." She reached into the refrigerator and began to pull out the wrapped plastic bags of sliced meats marked with the Publix grocery store logo. She flung the bags on the salon counter.

Ashley swiveled on the couch and peered out a starboard side porthole. The bow of a sleek center console boat slid into view. The boat was gliding its way past them. Ashley's eyes widened. She recognized the distinctive green lettering on the side of the boat. It read: "SHERIFF."

"Kim!" Ashley shouted in a high-pitched whisper.

"What, Ash?"

The younger sister pointed at the Marine Patrol boat.

"Shit!" Kim said spitting out the word. "Well…don't just point. Yell."

Tentative at first, the girls began to shriek. "Hey! Help us! Help!"

Kim began to slap her hands on the inside of the hull. The decorative padding of the sidewalls muffled her efforts. Ashley soon followed with her own random slapping.

The sisters stared out the porthole windows as they continued their unorganized symphony of noise. They waited for the uniformed officers to draw their weapons and order their crazy female captors to shut down the yacht. The guns, however, remained at the officers' sides. The cops smiled and waved.

What the hell? Kim stopped slapping. She raised an index finger at Ashley, signaling her sister to stop also. A deep throaty noise was reverberating through the upper deck and down to the salon. It took only a moment to realize the source. Very expensive Sony speakers were emitting a high fidelity bass tone in synchronization to a deafening Pearl Jam song. Their cries for help had been drowned out by the on-deck entertainment system.

Kim scampered up the three steps that led to the cockpit and peered through the tinted glass door. Crap! Of course! The bitch that called herself Amber had shed herself of every piece of clothing except for a red, string bikini that didn't even have enough material to be used as a dish towel. At the aft end of the cockpit deck, Amber was artfully swaying to the music. The only object missing from her impromptu dancing act was a chrome pole.

"We got screwed by fake tits and fucking Pearl Jam, Ash," Kim said shaking her head. "Pearl Jam! That crap is so old even Grandpa knows the words!" Kim turned away from the cockpit door and sat down on the upper step. "Remind me not to smile at the Marine Patrol anymore. They're not as cute as I thought," she grumbled.

Ashley glanced out a porthole and said, "I can't see the Marine Patrol anymore."

The rumbling bass sound above their heads stopped, replaced by the soft thudding of footsteps. Behind Kim's back, a metallic clack signaled that the latch was being slid open. Kim jumped off the steps and back into the main area of the cabin.

Amber ducked her head as she walked down the steps into the salon. Her feet were bare, her toenails glossed with jet black polish. Her bikini-clad body was now covered by a man's long cotton dress shirt. Amber's right hand clenched a semiautomatic handgun. She directed the open barrel at Kim.

"You think you're smart don't you, you little shit?" Amber said, sneering at Kim.

Kim slithered next to Ashley, now sitting cross-legged on the couch. Kim kept silent, drawing her lips tight.

Amber shifted the aim of the gun at Ashley. She looked at Kim and said, "Okay, big sister, you want to live with the fact that you were responsible for the bullet in your little sister's head?" Amber stared at Kim, waiting for a response. Kim stared back but her lips remained closed. "I know what you're thinking, smart-ass. You're thinking that you guys are too valuable." Amber glared. "Well, you're only half right. I just need one of you."

Kim brought her arms across her chest.

"I suggest that you reconsider that fact before you attempt another little escape," Amber said, emphasizing every word. She scanned the salon and gestured at the unopened sandwich meat bags on the counter. "Good, I see that you little princesses were being resourceful. Make yourselves something to eat. Don't expect me and my blond-haired girlfriend to be your bitches."

Kim glared.

Amber smirked and said, "Remember, Big Brother is always watching…and listening." She shrugged her shoulders and twirled on her toes. Amber climbed up the steps and out the cabin door. The door snapped closed and the latch thwacked into place.

The girls remained silent for one long minute. With glistening eyes, Kim slid off the couch and walked over to the counter. She began to unwrap a plastic sandwich bag. She drew in a long breath. Being brave was getting harder.

Kim cleared her throat and said, "They've thought of everything. Somewhere hidden in the salon they rigged a video camera and microphone."

"We're going to be okay, Kim. I just know it. Mom and Dad won't let anything happen to us," Ashley said from across the salon with the same glistening eyes.

Kim nodded and said, "You'd better be right, Ash."

13:45 EDT

TSA at the employee checkpoint was especially annoying. Of all days, he had been randomly selected for the standard security screening rather than being allowed to use the authorized flight crew member access point. Hart expressed his appreciation for having to remove his shoes and his belt with an unabashed rolling of the eyes. When he questioned the agent that motioned him forward through the magnetometer arch, the cryptic answer was simply that he was not in uniform. The fact that the terrorism risk increased when he was not wearing pilot garb despite his ID credentials, made no rational sense. Knowing that pressing the issue for a logical explanation was futile, Hart simply shook his head and collected his belongings at the end of the X-ray belt. TSA was just doing their job.

Hart walked into the concourse and scanned the departure video screen. His gate was miles away. He glanced at the array of people standing on the escalator that led upstairs to the terminal's air train. Forget it. He wasn't in the mood to merge with crowds on a jammed train. He had time to walk. He could use the exercise.

Unfortunately, the brief relaxation that he achieved during his fast-paced stride dissipated as he approached the boarding area. He stiffened.

Standing among the scattered crowd of passengers and lounge chairs, the recognizable barrel-chested profile of Rod Moretti was unmistakable. Rod's salt-and-pepper hair contrasted with his pale blue shirt and striped tie. Why the hell was he here now? The chief pilot turned toward Hart, nodding with a perfunctory smile.

Rod reached out a hand and said, "Captain Lindy, how are you?"

Hart grasped Rod's hand and replied, "Not bad, Captain Moretti. What brings you out of the Batcave today? Surely you're not here to give me a goodbye kiss."

"Hadn't thought of that. But then people will talk." Both men grinned awkwardly. Rod took a deep breath and shifted his stance to the other leg. "Listen…got a call from Sammy. He told me that you were the guy for this investigation. I saw that you had listed for this Bermuda departure." Rod gestured his head at the gate podium. "Anyhow, we have a crisis brewing with the first officer. I wanted you to be aware of it."

"You mean Mike Townsend?"

Rod nodded and said, "It may interfere with your investigation."

Hart crossed his arms in front of his chest and asked, "Okay…what's up?"

As Rod explained the circumstances behind the abduction of the first officer's daughters, Hart remained motionless.

When the chief pilot finished, Hart looked at the floor and shuffled his feet. "The poor guy must be freaking out. Have you given him the news?" Hart asked.

"Not yet. I was just about to when I noticed that you were taking this flight. A few extra minutes won't change things. I wanted you to be aware of the situation first."

"Thanks."

"Don't mention it."

"I'll figure something out regarding his testimony with the NTSB," Hart said. "I may have to run interference with the IIC, but I'll deal with that later. The important thing is that we get him home ASAP…hopefully, the first flight in the morning."

"I agree," Rod said.

A brief moment of static crackled over the PA speakers. With a Latin accent, the agent at the gate announced a short list of stand-by passengers. Hart heard his name. He looked at Rod and motioned toward the gate.

"Let me get my boarding pass, and I'll be right back," Hart said.

As Hart walked down an aisle of chairs toward the gate agent, a thin man with curly, jet black hair and a day's growth of dark beard stubble rose from his seat. He stared at Hart as he walked past. With a wary eye, Hart stared back. A prickly uncomfortable feeling entered his gut. He continued his walk to the gate agent.

With his boarding pass in hand, Hart strode back toward Rod. His eyes swept the crowd. The thin guy had disappeared. Had he boarded the flight or just walked away? Paranoia. Great. Just what Hart needed.

"You didn't happen to see a creepy looking thin guy pass your way, did you?" Hart asked.

"It's Miami. When don't you see a creepy thin guy?" Rod remarked.

"You're right." Hart sighed. "But let's just say I woke up in a parallel universe this morning."

"Bad beer from last night?"

"Technically, no beer is a bad beer."

"Got me on that one." Rod raised his eyebrows. "What then?"

Hart explained the threatening phone calls and the paintball assault while driving on I-95.

Rod said, "You must have really pissed somebody off."

Hart smirked for an instant and then his expression became serious. "Somebody wants this investigation to go away. Whoever it is has inside information. And they have help from some unfriendly people."

"I can make some calls," Rod said.

"I've already started that ball rolling." Hart cleared his throat. "Are you still friends with that cop in Lauderdale?"

"Yeah, we play golf and have a beer every once in a while. His youngest son keeps saying that when he grows up, he wants to be an airline pilot. Of course, I tell him that he can't do both."

Hart and Rod chuckled for a moment.

"How can my cop buddy help?" Rod asked.

"With Cathy," Hart said.

An uncomfortable silence passed.

Hart said, "The guy at the other end of the threatening

phone call seemed to have knowledge of our relationship. Can you have your cop buddy find a way to keep an eye on her while I'm gone? But I don't want her to know. She already suspects that something isn't quite normal with this event in Bermuda."

Rod's eyes softened. His mind flashed to a sailing trip in the British Virgin Islands. He thought of Hart trying to keep his balance on the pitching trampoline deck of the catamaran they had leased for the week. Hart was attempting to deliver a tray of cocktail glasses overflowing with a frozen liquid concoction. Cathy and his ex-wife beamed with glee.

"Of course," Rod said.

"Thanks."

Rod nodded and said, "I'd appreciate any information regarding the investigation that you feel comfortable passing my way without risking PAPA's third-party status with the NTSB."

"Will do. We've got the organizational meeting tomorrow morning and if all goes well, the field investigation will begin later. I'll see where we stand after a day or two and I'll let you know."

"That would be great. E-mail or call."

"I am sure you are aware that the company has its own investigation team," Hart stated. "They have the same third-party status. Aren't you supposed to be wearing *their* hat now that you're on the dark side?"

"In the end we wear the same hat." Rod grinned. "But let's just say that the dark side isn't always prompt with their information. Besides, my primary concern is our pilots."

Hart said, "Got it." He held out his hand.

The two men shook and then walked away in opposite directions.

"Well…that didn't go too bad," Hart muttered to himself. He joined the line of passengers flowing into the barrier strap corridor that led to the jet bridge. He took a deep breath and exhaled slowly. On to the next crisis…

CHAPTER EIGHT

Friday
13:55 EDT

The clattering of dishware and glasses blended into the sound of steel drum music being pumped through speakers deftly camouflaged by the local foliage. The occasional deep-throated laugh or high-pitched giggle contrasted with the murmur of normal conversation. Wicker-bladed ceiling fans rotated in slow rhythmic circles above white linen cloth tables. The corners of the tablecloths flapped gently with the breeze from outside.

A haphazard line of T-shirt clad tourists grazed at the buffet island in the hotel restaurant. The tourists grinned and shoveled mounds of food onto white china plates. If it weren't for the circumstances, the lunchtime scene would have been the routine of a typical sixteen-hour Bermuda layover. But not today.

Mike and Jim had found a table in the corner of the dining room nearest the open partition that led to the hotel gardens. They shuffled bits of food around on their almost empty plates. They sipped iced tea from tall, thin glasses. Periodically, one of them would look up from his plate and focus on some small aspect of the surroundings.

Jim reached for the napkin on his lap. He wiped the corners of his mouth. In a soft tone he said, "Still can't understand why the damn thing threw itself into pieces."

Mike reached for a lone black olive and popped it in

his mouth. He chewed for a moment. He looked toward the garden and said, “It’s an old airplane. It’s an old engine. Sometimes shit just comes apart for no reason.”

“I suppose. But there was no warning. No high temps. No vibration.”

“This fucking airline is always trying to cut corners. Who knows what corner was cut where? Maybe stuff is getting pencil-whipped. Or maybe we’re buying cheap parts from the Chinese. Wouldn’t surprise me.”

“Hope you’re not right, Mike.”

“Sorry. I know. I’m singing an old song. I gave up a captain’s bid and 25 percent of my paycheck to keep us away from the bankruptcy precipice. Now we’re hearing rumors about it again. And I’ve been wearing three stripes for almost twenty years.”

Jim nodded. He took a gulp from his glass of iced tea. “Hope that the NTSB interview isn’t painful. I’d like to get out of this paradise by tomorrow.”

Mike snorted and said, “I’m with you on that idea. Paradise or not, this place isn’t exactly cheap. I’m not holding my breath for the company to pick up the cocktail tab.”

“Gotta say, though, this island has class. The prices seem to keep the body-piercing, tattoo crowd away.”

Mike nodded with a smirk and said, “People actually wear jackets and ties…even on the airplane…in coach no less.”

A buxom waitress stopped in front of the table. She smiled and began to collect the empty dishes. She stacked them neatly in the crook of her arm. She twirled and walked away.

Jim sighed. He looked at his copilot and asked, “Terrorism?”

“Anything is possible.”

“But why not just blow up the whole damn airplane?”

"Maybe it was a failed attempt," Mike replied.

"Could be." Jim crossed his arms over his chest. The printed tropical flowers on his shirt bunched together over his stomach. "Hopefully the investigation will find answers."

"Hopefully," Mike said. He stared off into space. Both pilots lapsed into a comfortable silence.

The sound of tapping footsteps took Jim and Mike away from their thoughts. A twenty-something man wearing a gold nametag over the breast pocket of a crisp, white shirt was approaching. The man was holding a cordless phone. He stopped in front of the table, his eyes darting between the two pilots.

The man queried, "Mr. Townsend?"

"That's me," Mike said, raising his eyebrows.

"Phone call for you, sir." The island cadence of the man's voice made the statement sound elegant. He handed the phone to Mike.

"Excuse me, Jim." Mike pulled the napkin from his lap and stood up. With a tentative stride, he walked away from the table.

The man with the nametag nodded and trotted toward the hotel front desk.

Mike stared at the phone for a brief moment and then put it to his ear. "It's Mike," he said.

"Hi, Mike. It's Rod Moretti." Five seconds of silence passed. "Your new chief in Miami, Mike."

"Uh...sorry, Captain Moretti. It's been a long day."

"I understand." Rod cleared his throat. "How are you holding up, sir?"

"Just fine."

A seagull swooped across a table of dirty plates. The bird snapped up a half-eaten bun and flew away toward the beach.

Mike said, "Jim and I are trying to wind down from this morning's adrenalin rush. We're on our third martini, and it's only lunchtime. Do you think it would be okay if we swapped with the New York crew and flew the afternoon departure to JFK? I don't think our blood-alcohol content would really make much of a difference."

Rod tried to chuckle. He said, "Guess you haven't lost your sense of humor." He drew in a deep breath that was audible in the phone. "I'm afraid that I've got some serious news. There is no real easy way to tell you."

"Go ahead, Captain Moretti. I'm listening."

Rod began to give Mike the details of the abduction of his daughters. As Rod conveyed the information, Mike backed up against a wooden column. He closed his eyes and rested the back of his head against the hard surface. His eyes grew moist. This wasn't happening…

Somewhere within the confines of his brain, in the far distance, Mike heard the voice of the chief pilot offer to help in any way that he could. He heard something about a flight that he could return home on in the morning. He would be given Class-1 pass status. And then he heard himself say "Thank you." And then, click.

Mike dropped the phone to his side and walked as if in a trance back to the table. He bit his lip for a moment and then looked at Jim. Mike stood rigid. He detailed the crisis involving his daughters in factual terms as if the methodical handling of the airplane emergency and the abduction were equal in magnitude.

Jim stood up from the table and clasped Mike's shoulder for a brief awkward moment. He offered to help in any way that he could. He promised to check on Mike later in the day. He insisted on paying the lunch tab.

Mike nodded and strode away from the dining area. He stopped at the front desk and dropped the cordless phone on the counter. He mumbled a "thank you" to the clerk. He walked slowly back to his room and opened the door.

He sat down on the corner of the bed and dropped his head into cupped hands. He sat unmoving for a few long minutes and then looked up. He rubbed his eyes and stared out the window. He scanned the multicolored boats moored in the bay. The tranquility of the scene clashed with the thoughts in his head. His temples throbbed.

He had to get home. Finding his daughters was paramount...at all costs.

14:10 EDT

From a far corner of the boarding lounge, the three men greeted Hart, shaking his hand and smiling. They offered small snippets about the latest from their lives at home and their lives at the airline. They bantered in typical fashion, dry pilot humor permeating the conversation. The men were comfortable with each other. Having worked together on other events, the team had bonded through past history.

Hart shifted his feet out to a wider stance and clasped his hands behind his back. He glanced at the line of passengers streaming past toward the jet bridge. Some of the passengers stared, curious as to the purpose of the small gaggle of men wearing airline ID tags around their necks. Hart interrupted the discussion and said, "Gentlemen, if I could have your attention for a moment."

The team members finished their separate conversations and looked at Hart.

"First of all, my apologies. As you are aware, as a result of low standards, our union leadership decided to put me in charge. That being said, I will be relying on your superior expertise." Hart cleared his throat. "It's obvious you guys have no life and no judgment skills, otherwise you wouldn't have agreed to participate in this investigation." Hart's expression became solemn. "You guys are part of the 10 percent that does 99 percent of the work for this union. Thank you for coming."

The three men nodded and grinned.

Hart gestured at the line of boarding passengers. "This is neither the time nor the place, but let's just say some interesting dynamics have come into play outside of the actual field investigation. I'll discuss this and the ground rules in my room tonight when you guys have an appropriate beverage in your hand."

The team members' grins widened at the thought of free cocktails.

Hart gestured toward the open jet bridge door. "Bermuda, anyone?"

The men collected their rolling bags and laptop cases. One by one, they merged with the rest of the boarding passengers.

Don Patterson, the systems investigator, knew more about a Boeing 767 than Boeing did. His mechanical background included an airframe and power plant license, an inspector's authorization, and an electrical engineering degree from Purdue University. He had single-handedly helped Patriot Airlines rewrite the electrical section of the operating manual. Don had found glaring errors in switch functionality that had gone undiscovered. He had been a captain with the airline for almost fifteen years.

Hart snickered to himself as he watched Don shuffle toward the airplane. If Don could only ditch those knit shirts with the damn alligator…

Matt Mattson, the power plant team member, was equally as qualified. In his first life, he had helped Pratt & Whitney design a turbine section for the first generation of highly fuel-efficient jet engines. After a couple of years he decided that he'd rather fly jet engines than design them. Still enjoying hands-on work, he got involved with rebuilding old radial engines, mostly for a new breed of billionaire aviation enthusiasts who collected WWII vintage bombers and fighters. His two-car garage became his shop. But his wife evicted him after he relocated her BMW outside. A sympathetic friend offered a hangar at the local airport. Matt's oil-speckled topsiders were a reflection of his priorities.

Ron Stephens walked past Hart while pushing his glasses higher on the bridge of a very short nose. A pair of khaki pants and a slightly wrinkled dress shirt with two pens clipped to the pocket gave Ron the appearance of a corporate accountant. In addition to his day job as a 737 copilot, Ron was actually a bona fide member of the Florida Bar Association. Many of his cases involved contract law. He had a photographic memory for anything nauseatingly dry. He was the expert for the operational procedures part of the investigation. Ron was the guy you wanted on your side in a Trivial Pursuit game.

It wasn't long before the shuffle of passengers shoving bags into overhead compartments and plopping into seats was complete. Soon after, Hart felt the gradual motion of the airplane pushing back from the gate. He stared outside the window, focusing on nothing in particular. Fatigue from the events of the day had made its way into his head. When the airplane lurched into the sky, he pushed the recline button on his seat. He closed his eyes.

It wasn't until Hart felt the buffeting of the spoilers on the wings being extended that he realized he had dozed. They were nearing Bermuda. Hart stretched his legs under the seat in front of him and twisted his neck until he heard that satisfying crack. He peered above the rows of seats and watched the flight attendants scurry through the aisle collecting passenger trash into blue, plastic garbage bags.

Eight rows ahead, a passenger turned in his seat, placing an empty soda can into a plastic bag. Was that the thin, creepy guy? Or was he just starting to lose his mind? Hart noted the seat number.

14:25 EDT

"Are you going to play hard to get?" Jonathan asked. He took another sip of merlot from his long-stemmed wine glass.

"Whad'ya mean?" Chris asked. His stomach felt queasy again. He knew exactly what Jonathan meant.

"Well…you're pacing around my living room like a mountain lion. Thanks for admiring the artwork, but my prints aren't really all that interesting."

"Sorry. I've never been able to sit still for very long." Chris gripped his Corona bottle tighter.

Jonathan smirked and said, "You sat still long enough to eat my lasagna special at the restaurant."

Chris forced a contrived grin. "Yeah, well…food is different."

"Okay, then. Pretend I'm a piece of New York strip. Come sit down." Jonathan patted the cushion next to him on the cracked leather couch.

The evening had turned into a perverse cat and mouse game. It had long ago gone from a challenge to a serious annoyance. Chris needed to end the madness sooner rather than later. He wasn't sure he could last another minute in the two-bedroom townhouse on Los Olas. He had the information he needed anyhow. The faggot finally confessed over the last glass of merlot. The news wasn't going to make his slick-haired boss happy. For that matter, it wasn't making Chris happy either. Somehow, he would be held responsible.

With a coy smile, Chris said, "I gotta go to the bathroom. I'm thinking about a shower."

Jonathan grinned and said, "Really? Good idea." He

lifted his glass off the sculpted dolphin coffee table and took a gulp of wine. "Use the shower in the master bath. Towels are in the cabinet opposite the sink. Get started without me. I've got some dishes to clean."

"Okay," Chris replied in a low tone of voice. He walked away from the expansive living room and down a mosaic tiled corridor to the master bedroom. He could feel each individual heartbeat thumping in his chest. Think Iraq, he told himself. This is war.

Chris walked directly into the bathroom and shut the door behind him. He glanced at the shower. It was the cavernous step-in type with large bell-shaped showerheads on opposite ends that adjusted the spray pattern.

Perfect. Glancing at a tall cabinet, Chris opened a door. Towels were carefully rolled, stacked as though they had come directly from the department store display at Macy's. Chris removed the thickest towel that he could find.

With a twist of the handle, Chris turned the spray to its maximum flow. Steam started to permeate the bathroom, reducing visibility and fogging the mirrors. He drew in a deep breath and exhaled with a slow and deliberate effort. He waited for the sound of footsteps.

Although it seemed like an hour, only minutes passed before Chris heard the padding of Jonathan's bare feet. The bathroom door swung open.

Jonathan cooed. "Wow! Very cool. You do like it hot and steamy!"

In one fluid motion, Chris stepped out from behind the open bathroom door. The mist made his target just a tall silhouette. Chris lunged. He grabbed Jonathan's shoulders and thrust him into the shower.

"Hey! I like it rough too, but this fucking hurts!" Jonathan half shrieked.

Pushing Jonathan against a corner, water streaming over

his clothes, Chris raised the towel that concealed the barrel of his H & K semiautomatic. As trained, he squeezed the trigger with a painfully slow movement. A loud crack echoed in the bathroom.

One hollow-point bullet exploded shrapnel inside the cavern of Jonathan's skull. Red splattered against the smooth tiled shower wall and onto the sliding glass door. An inky river of dark red began to flow into the drain. Jonathan's eyes were locked in a stare that focused on nothing. His knees buckled. His body slid down the corner of the shower stall until it hit the tile floor and crumpled into an unrecognizable pile.

Chris surveyed the damage he had inflicted, his eyes unblinking. The shine of his bald head was streamed with rivulets of water from the shower. It was time to clean up his mess. This would be his most difficult and dangerous chore.

When Jonathan didn't show up back at the restaurant the next day, sooner or later someone would call the cops. But that would take time. Chris would have a head start. He had clipped the wiring of the security cameras, so his description would only come from eyewitnesses, if there were any.

Before the panic button was really pressed, a victim had to be found. And the victim would be concealed in a dumpster. Chris hoped garbage pickup day was sooner rather than later. Well…regardless, it solved the problem…at least for a while.

The old adrenalin rush was back. Cool.

CHAPTER NINE

Friday
14:30 EDT

Todd O'Malley peered over Detective Alvarez's shoulder. The two men were watching blotchy images on the screen of the principal's laptop. After spending almost two hours with tech support, the principal had finally unlocked the secret to reviewing the high school's security camera footage. He had invited the detective to sit in his office chair.

Alvarez grinned and said, "Don't know why you spent all that time on the phone with tech support. This school is full of little eggheads that could dance circles around us on the damn computer."

"Believe me, Detective. I thought of that." O'Malley sighed. "The rumors on this tragedy have made the rounds. I didn't think it necessary to add more fuel to the fire. The most popular story among my student body is that one of our…" The principal paused and scratched his chin. "Hmm…how should I say this? One of our most qualified candidates for Fed U ordered the hit on our security guard."

Alvarez looked away from the computer screen and said, "You're right. Computer assistance from a student was just a passing thought." The detective turned his attention back to the security footage.

An image of a female student and a male student meeting in the back parking lot a half-hour prior to the abduction appeared on the screen. The two figures stood next to a low riding, vintage BMW. A wadded up roll of green was exchanged between the two students. A clear, plastic sandwich bag containing a leafy substance was passed next.

The two students smiled at each other, embraced, and then kissed. The male student opened a rear door of the car. With suspiciously awkward expressions, the two students slid inside the BMW and closed the door.

Alvarez slid his finger on the mouse pad. He moved the cursor over to the pause selection. The action stopped.

The principal leaned forward, moving closer to the laptop screen. He said, "That explains the new blue jeans and tennis shoes every month…and the boy's stunning 2.0 grade point average. The little bastard was telling me that he was helping his dad with the plumbing business. Should have known that he was dealing pot."

Alvarez said, "Don't feel bad. He's not a good businessman. It looks like he's discounting his product for sexual favors."

"Ironic that the kid's worst subject is math?"

Alvarez shook his head and smirked. He said, "As painful as it may be, I'm going to watch the remaining footage." He pointed at the screen. "Those horny kids may be my best witnesses to a crime."

The principal nodded. "I'll check with my secretary and make sure that the two lovebirds are still in the building."

As O'Malley began to walk out of the office, Alvarez moved the cursor over the "Play" selector and clicked. He leaned back in the chair. He scanned the footage as the parking lot scene progressed. This was going to be painful.

By the time Alvarez reached the moment in time where the action started, the fast forward button had become his friend. He slid the cursor over the Pause selector and began to advance the video forward one frame at a time. Clicking away, Alvarez watched as the two Townsend sisters walked to the curb with the security guard.

A white Escalade drove a sweeping arc around the parking lot. The bulky SUV stopped along the sidewalk. A discussion ensued for less than fifteen seconds. A hand with red nail polish emerged through the driver's side window holding what appeared to be a semiautomatic. Nail polish? A female perp? No kidding…

Alvarez continued to click away on the Forward button. A puff of smoke. The security guard fell awkwardly to the ground. The two sisters stared at the man crumpled on the sidewalk. They abruptly turned their attention to the driver's side window. Sheer terror was written on their faces. The younger girl opened the rear door of the Escalade. Both girls jumped into the car. The Escalade accelerated to the end of the parking lot and out the driveway exit.

The detective glanced at the upper corner of the laptop screen. The elapsed time indicated that the entire episode had taken thirty-two seconds. Amazing. This was a well-planned and well-executed event.

Alvarez clicked on the Reverse arrow until the image on the screen displayed the rear view of the Escalade. He moved the cursor over the Zoom selection. He enlarged the SUV until the view was adequate enough to read the license plate number. He wrote the numbers and letters down on his notepad. It was a long shot. Judging by the professionalism exhibited, the odds were great that the plate number would lead him nowhere. He would probably have better luck with the two students in the BMW. Fortunately for Alvarez, the kids had picked the wrong day for sex, drugs, and rock and roll.

The detective reached into a front pocket and pulled out his cell phone. He began to tap away with a text message to his new patrol officer friend. The patrol officer dealt with license plate crap almost every day. He would send Tom the number. In addition, Tom had promised to do a little more unofficial snooping with regard to the school security guard's background.

O'Malley stepped back into the office. He sat down in the chair on the other side of his desk and faced Alvarez.

The principal asked, "How's the Academy Award docudrama going?"

"Not quite riveting, but definitely interesting," Alvarez replied.

"Glad to hear it." The principal glanced around the room. "Never really saw my office from this perspective. I can see why the kids find it intimidating from this side." He paused. "Speaking of which, my young porno stars are still in school. What's the verdict?"

"Yup, I need them. They remained in the vehicle until at least fifteen minutes after the dust settled. Can you bring them to me ASAP?"

Alvarez's cell phone began to chirp. The detective glanced at the caller ID. The patrol cop was calling.

The principal rose from his chair and said, "I'll have them here in a few minutes."

"Thanks," replied Alvarez. As he watched the principal walk out of the office, he pressed the talk button on his phone. "Hey, Tom. Thanks for getting back to me so quick."

Although the conversation was frustrating, the information Tom provided helped tie up loose ends. First, John Washington, the security guard, appeared to have nothing dark in his background. The only blemish on his record after twenty-four years on the job was a complaint filed by a Miami Beach woman who claimed he was verbally abusive when he arrested her for public intoxication. Reading between the lines, the woman was probably a neighborhood drunk. The only reason it remained in the file was likely due some political affiliation the woman had with a local council member.

Washington had no unusual transactions in his bank accounts other than a large sum paid to his ex-wife. The sum was most likely attributable to an alimony settlement. And phone records for the past couple of months indicated nothing out of the ordinary. For the moment, it seemed like a dead end.

As for the license plate number, it *had* been registered to a Cadillac owner…but not the owner of a Cadillac Escalade. The license plate belonged to the owner of an Eldorado. Up until a week ago, the Eldorado had been driven once a month by an eighty-eight-year-old woman with failing eyesight. The woman's children had convinced their mom it was time to give up driving. The car was in showroom condition. The original dealer gladly agreed to buy it back at a heavily discounted price. The transaction was still in progress.

Apparently, a white Escalade had been on display on the lot of the same dealer. The Escalade was reported stolen twenty-four hours ago. In addition, the Eldorado license plate mysteriously turned up missing, the dealer thinking that it had been misplaced during the purchase transition. Late in the morning, a VIN number was traced to the stolen Escalade. Unfortunately, only a shell remained of the vehicle.

The fire department had responded to a car fire in an isolated parking lot of an empty Fort Lauderdale office building. The veteran firefighters thought it suspicious, skeptical that spontaneous combustion was the culprit despite the vivid imagination and enthusiasm of the rookies. The scene was contained early, allowing the rookies an opportunity to ply their skills in a relatively nonthreatening environment.

No evidence of human remains was found in the smoldering mass of metal. However, the charred remnants of a cell phone were recovered in the glove box. The crime lab people were doing their best to determine ownership. The Find My iPhone app was unable to locate a signal. The last confirmed location of the phone was within a two-mile radius of the school. Not very helpful.

Alvarez would check out the scene regardless. Hopefully, the abduction guys were working on their end of the investigation. The FBI had been called but enough resources were available between Dade and Broward Counties that the feds may not have to become directly involved. Time would tell.

The principal strode back into the office. He closed the door behind him and sat on the corner of the desk. He smiled at Alvarez.

"I've got your witnesses. Do you want to question them in my presence?"

"Absolutely. Why should I have all the fun?" Alvarez closed the lid of the laptop. He looked at the principal. "Have you told them the reason for this visit?"

"Nope. I've learned that it's better to keep them in suspense for a little while. I know it's like mental water-boarding, but fear of the unknown has an interesting effect."

"That's awful, Mr. O'Malley." Alvarez grinned. "Ever thought of being a cop?"

The principal smiled and said, "Shall I let them in?"

"Please," Alvarez said as he stood up from the desk. He walked over to a wooden chair in the corner of the office and turned it backwards. He sat down and straddled the seat.

The principal resumed his position at his desk. He pressed the intercom button of his console phone.

"Please have Sandra and Jason come into my office."

"They're on the way, Mr. O'Malley," the secretary replied.

With a tentative swing, the door opened. The two students shuffled over to the chairs placed in front of the principal's desk. They sat without uttering a word as if the entire scene was a familiar dance. The secretary closed the door with a quiet thud.

The principal gestured at Alvarez and said, "This is Detective Alvarez. He has been investigating today's abduction of the Townsend sisters and the murder of Mr. Washington. I know the whole thing has been tough on everybody, but you two may be able to help."

Sandra's eyes focused on the floor. She fidgeted with the dangling red feather of a large hoop earring. Jason bit his lip and brought his arms across his chest. He wore a T-shirt with an orange Harley Davidson emblem in the center. A barbed-wire tattoo ran across an anemic bicep.

Jason said, "We didn't see nothing. We were inside."

Alvarez cleared his throat and asked, "Inside where?"

"We were both in study hall, dude."

"Are you sure about that?"

Jason squirmed in the chair and replied, "Yeah, man." His tone was defensive.

Alvarez glanced at the principal and pointed at the laptop. He said, "What if I told you that Mr. O'Malley over there has video footage of you guys making out in the parking lot just before the crime?"

"Bullshit!" Jason spit out the word.

"Really? Well…okay." Alvarez nodded at the principal. The principal began to open the laptop.

Jason glanced at the desk and said, "I want a lawyer."

"Listen, young man. This is not a script from *Law and Order*. All I want is your explanation."

"What's in it for me?"

"That's actually a good question, Jason. But don't be such a narcissist." Alvarez gestured his head at Sandra. "Ask what's in it for *both* of you."

Jason rolled his eyes.

"Okay, what's in it for us," Sandra asked with a mousy voice.

"Glad you asked, young lady." Alvarez smiled. "It's simple. You guys consummated a drug deal on school property." Alvarez looked at Jason. "Drug dealing on school property gets a lot of jail time. Also, I'm willing to bet that you're at least eighteen, my friend." Alvarez switched his focus to Sandra. "And since the young lady is a sophomore, I'll just assume she is a minor. Your little romp in the back seat would technically be classified as rape. That's a biggie. And just for fun, I'll throw in truancy."

Jason and Sandra lowered their eyes and browsed the carpet.

Alvarez said, "Soo…I won't charge you guys with all that ugly stuff for now, if you tell me exactly what you saw."

"Are you going to make a deal with Ms. Abbott, too?" Jason asked.

Alvarez raised his eyebrows and asked, "The vice principal? Why would you ask that?"

Jason leaned back in his chair. A smug expression appeared on his face. He said, "She was outside in the parking lot at the same time, man."

O'Malley interrupted and said, "Of course she was. We were all out there. We were trying to help poor Mr. Washington."

Alvarez held up an index finger, indicating that he wanted the principal to stop talking. The principal nodded, removed his eyeglasses, and put one end of the frames in his mouth.

Jason said, "Ms. Abbott was already outside before all that shit happened. She was standing in the corner by the gym exit door." The principal winced and shook his head at Jason when the boy uttered the four-letter word.

"What was Ms. Abbott doing?" Alvarez asked.

If the kid was telling the truth, Alvarez had missed

seeing the vice principal's image on the security video. And he knew why. After gaining an intimate knowledge of the school's camera locations, he was certain that the gym exit was outside of electronic view. Interesting.

Jason said, "Dunno what Ms. Abbott was doing. She was talking to some ugly skinny guy. The guy didn't look like he had shaved in a day or two. Seen the dude before. I saw him hand Ms. Abbott an envelope. That was it."

"How many times have you seen the skinny guy?"

"Maybe five, six times."

"Did the discussion seem heated?"

Jason crossed his legs and said, "You mean like an argument?" The detective nodded. "Nope, wouldn't say that. They both looked serious. No smiling."

Alvarez said, "Okay you two. Take me through what you saw with the shooting and the abduction. Tell me every little detail even if you think it's not important."

A few minutes later, Jason and Sandra completed their fragmented description of the crime scene. The kids discussed the event as though the drama was just another cop episode on TV. The shooting of the security guard barely raised an eyebrow. A trip to the food court in the mall would have evoked more emotion.

One tidbit of information from Jason was helpful. He indicated that the driver of the Escalade was a blonde. Although he couldn't be more specific about her appearance Jason was quite certain that she was a "hottie."

Had the circumstances been different, Alvarez would have chuckled at the comment.

When Jason and Sandra were excused to the waiting area--or the holding pen, as O'Malley liked to call it--Alvarez stood up and walked over to the principal.

"Thanks for all of your time, Mr. O'Malley. I made a thumb drive copy of that security footage. Don't think the camera angle will show the exit that Jason described, but the skinny guy may be visible at a time earlier than I reviewed. I'm guessing that he came from the parking lot via his own car. I might be able to zoom in on a license plate." Alvarez rubbed his chin. "Ever seen this skinny guy?"

"Nope. Sorry. Not a clue," the principal replied.

"Do me a favor. Keep the information about Ms. Abbott between you and me."

"No problem," the principal replied.

Alvarez pointed a finger toward the waiting area and asked, "You going to throw the book at those two?"

The principal smiled and clasped his hands behind his neck. "Not sure yet…but I'm not going to be as easy on them as you were. I'm thinking about parental involvement. Sometimes that's worse than jail."

"Well, if he doesn't straighten his act out, chances are good we'll eventually do business with Jason. It might only be a matter of time. Good luck, Mr. O'Malley."

"I think you'll need more luck than I will, Detective."

The two men shook hands.

Alvarez walked out of the office. He might have to skip the sports bar with the guys tonight…and probably dinner at home with his wife and three boys.

16:35 EDT

Once Hart had descended the portable stairs and stepped onto the ramp in Bermuda, he walked over to the gate agent standing by the steps. The agent was talking into a portable radio. The flexible antenna of the radio jiggled as she spoke. Hart recognized her from the occasional trips that he had flown to the island.

As Hart waited for the agent to finish her business, he scanned the scattered line of passengers walking into the terminal building. He still couldn't find the creepy, thin guy.

The agent completed her conversation and released the transmit button. The agent smiled. She asked, "How have you been, Captain?"

Hart replied, "Great. Can't complain. Nobody listens at this airline anyhow. How about you? Everything okay?" He smiled.

"No complaints either, Captain," the agent said with a melodic accent.

Hart exchanged pleasantries for a minute or two. As the members of his investigation team reached the bottom of the boarding steps, he introduced them. Each man nodded a greeting to the agent.

The agent said, "Heard you guys were coming. Some of your folks are already at the hotel. The accident crew is there. I think the two that said they were CISM peer support volunteers, critical incident stress management types, came in earlier."

"Good," Hart responded.

The agent turned and gestured away from the terminal building. "The accident airplane is parked over there on the north side of the runway."

"Yeah, I saw it as we taxied by." The 767 was a sooty, black mess. "Any chance somebody could take us over there after we clear Customs?"

"I'd be glad to have one of our ramp guys drive you." The agent watched a gaggle of passengers descend the air stairs. She looked back at Hart. "I'm not sure how close to the airplane that you boys are going to get, though."

"Why is that? Is the NTSB restricting access?"

"No…not the NTSB."

Hart raised his eyebrows and asked, "The Airport Authority? I heard a rumor that the captain didn't quite endear himself to the assistant manager."

The agent grinned. “Well, yes…this is true. A few feathers got ruffled.” She sighed. “That situation was rectified with a phone call from your chief pilot in Miami. Our station manager here also helped to soothe the troubled spirits.”

“Glad to hear it.” Hart crossed his arms. “Then who is restricting access?”

“Your FBI.”

“Really?”

“Yes, Captain. They’re considering the airplane evidence in a crime scene.”

The investigation team shuffled their feet and muttered among themselves. Hart scanned their faces and said, “Look guys, I know it sucks but the FBI is within their rights.” He gestured his head across the runway at the airplane. “Let’s take a cruise over there anyhow.”

Hart turned toward the agent and said, “One more thing, if you don’t mind.” He pulled a business card out from his pocket and handed it to her. “I wrote down a seat number on the back. It’s probably nothing…but the guy with this seat assignment made the hairs stand up on the back of my neck. Some not-so-nice-people have made my day a little interesting...and not in a good way.”

“No problem, Captain. I’ll check him out and let you know.”

“Thanks. I appreciate it.”

The four men gathered their bags, and walked toward the thinning line of passengers entering the terminal building. Within ten minutes, the investigation team had processed through Customs.

The company van arrived within a few minutes. The driver recognized many of the pilot faces. He shook hands with the team as they shuffled in through the open sliding door. As soon as Hart plopped into the passenger seat next to the driver, they drove out the airport exit and away from the terminal.

A few twists and turns later, they stopped in front of a gate on the north side of the runway. The van driver slid an ID card over an electronic reader. The gate clanked itself open, moving in a slow jerky motion to the side. They rolled past the gate and onto the ramp.

The hulk of the Patriot Airlines 767 became visible as the van pulled forward. A stanchion barrier of yellow caution tape surrounded the airliner. Bright orange cones were strategically placed around the footprint of the airplane. The blackened right side of the fuselage contrasted with the white concrete of an immaculate ramp.

Lacking was the sound of screaming forced air from the APU or the whine of a hydraulic pump. An eerie quiet prevailed. If the airplane were a living/breathing creature it seemed as if it was begging for attention.

A dark Jeep Wrangler with its doors removed was parked underneath the tail. As the team's van approached, a stocky man stepped out onto the concrete. The man wore a black Tommy Bahama shirt with a printed pattern of bright orange, bird-of-paradise flowers. At the bottom of a pair of white, cuffed trousers were a pair of penny loafers, socks not included.

In traffic cop fashion, the stocky man held out the palm of his hand, signaling the van driver to stop. With his fingers, the man gripped a thin wallet that had been flipped open. The wallet displayed ID credentials and a badge. The metal of the badge reflected an occasional glint of sun. In the man's other hand was an unlit cigar. He brought the cigar to his mouth and clenched it with his teeth.

Hart asked, "FBI, maybe? Who wears tropical flowered shirts anymore? What happened to the dark suits?"

"Do you think if I gave him a hug he would smile?" Don asked.

"He has a gun, Don. A hug isn't a good idea. I'll use my charm. If that doesn't work, you're in."

"Have it your way, boss," Don said with a sarcastic grin.

Hart took in a quick breath and exhaled. "Let's see how this goes." He adjusted the strap that held the airline ID tag around his neck, ensuring that the photo side was visible. He opened his door and stepped out onto the ramp.

The FBI man pulled the cigar from his teeth. In a nasally voice he said, "Sorry, no access to this area."

Hart walked over to the FBI agent and extended his hand. The agent surveyed Hart for a moment and then shook.

The stocky man smiled and said, "I'm Special Agent Ryan Fredricks."

"Pleasure to meet you, sir. My name is Hart Lindy. I'm the party coordinator for the Patriot Airlines Pilots Association." He turned and pointed at the van. "My investigation team along with the other parties will be working with the NTSB."

"The NTSB? Never heard of them." The FBI man grinned.

"Aren't you supposed to be driving a dark-blue Ford Taurus? And why aren't you wearing a thin tie with a black suit and the no-nonsense expression?"

"The movies and TV have given us a bad rap. We're trying to change our image to a more updated version."

"It may take a while to grow on people."

"We've also changed our motto to, "We're not happy until you're not happy." Special Agent Fredricks cleared his throat. "And in that regard, I'm not allowing anybody near this airplane for the moment."

"I think you guys are stealing the FAA's motto by the way," Hart said with a smirk. "Do you mind telling me why we can't conduct a preliminary walk-around? We promise not to touch."

"I've already explained that to the NTSB."

"Would you humor me with an explanation? The organizational meeting isn't until tomorrow morning. The NTSB didn't make us aware of access issues." Hart folded his arms across his chest.

The FBI man rocked a thumb back behind him in the direction of the airplane. "We are considering this a crime scene."

"Okay. Based on what evidence?"

"Good question. Actually, I'm surprised that you, of all people, would ask."

"I beg your pardon?"

"Aren't you the same Captain Lindy that experienced a multitude of threatening little events today?"

Hart said, "Word travels fast."

"Our Miami field office got your report through the Dade County P.D. and forwarded it on to me."

"I appreciate that."

"Well…your experience today concerns us. It adds another element to this investigation."

The FBI man pulled a lighter from a trouser pocket. He flicked the lighter and moved the orange flame in a circular motion around the cigar. He placed the cigar between puckered lips and began to puff. Smoke billowed from his mouth.

Hart sighed. "Is there physical evidence that indicates this incident was caused by something extraneous to mechanical causes?"

Agent Fredricks looked away for a moment and then said, "Extraneous? That's a big word, Captain Lindy. I'm just a government employee. We try to keep our syllables at two per word. But that being said, we have our suspicions."

"But no preliminary investigation on the airplane itself has been conducted?"

"Nope."

"Do you have resources here in Bermuda that would assist an investigation involving aircraft mechanics and procedures, more specifically, resources involving a Boeing 767?"

"Nope."

"Forgive me, Special Agent Fredricks, but aren't we all on the same page?"

Ryan Fredricks smiled, took a puff of his cigar, and said, "Well…let's just say that we're on the same chapter."

"Look, in the end, all of us would like to find the cause of the emergency and determine why two people died."

"Agreed…but not until I release the airplane."

"Wouldn't it be in your best interest to allow aviation experts the opportunity to assist?"

Agent Fredricks crossed his arms in front of his chest. He said, "Captain Lindy, I kind of like you. But right now you're starting to annoy me. I'm sorry, but you just can't play with your airplane today."

Inside the van, Don, Matt, and Ron smirked. The conversation wasn't quite audible, but the stiff body language spoke volumes about the discussion.

In his Southern drawl, Don said, "I think our boss is losing his charm." Don chuckled. "You guys want to start pooling cash for bail money just in case it gets ugly?"

The rest of the team, including the driver, snickered.

Back at the airplane, Hart sighed and said, "All right, Special Agent Fredricks. I got the message. We'll stay out of the way." Hart grit his teeth and grinned. "If I buy you a cocktail at the hotel tonight, will you change your mind?"

The FBI man smiled and said, "Call me Ryan, please. And that offer seems like a thinly veiled bribe. I'm a government official. I was hoping for something more substantial than a cocktail. Regardless, access to your airplane probably won't happen until tomorrow."

Hart nodded and said, “On other subjects, along the lines of nefarious activities, I got bad vibes from a passenger that flew inbound on our deadhead flight. I asked our gate agent to reference this guy’s seat number for an ID check.”

“I’ll confer with the agent and check it out. Anything in particular about this passenger that concerned you?”

“If I was non-politically correct, it would seem the gentleman had a Middle Eastern origin to his physical characteristics. But we don’t profile, of course.” Hart glanced at the pavement for a moment. “The man had an uncomfortable air about him. Perhaps it’s my pilot, post-9/11 paranoia.”

“Understood,” the FBI man stated.

Hart extended his hand. The men shook, and then Hart strode back to the van. Hart opened the door and plopped into his seat. He stared out the windshield and offered a casual salute to Special Agent Fredricks. Fredricks nodded.

“I either made a new friend or a new enemy. I’m just not sure. The man certainly doesn’t fit the FBI mold,” Hart stated.

Don said, “For a second or two we weren’t sure whether he was going to shoot you or arrest you.”

The team broke into a chorus of subdued laughter.

17:30 EDT

Hart heard two loud thwacks on his hotel room door. He pulled the toothbrush out of his mouth and rinsed it quickly under the faucet. He drew a towel across his face and then tossed it on the granite sink counter. Hart walked to the door and opened it.

“Took you long enough to get to the door,” said the man with the wire broom moustache who stood in the hallway. The moustache grinned at Hart and stepped past him into the room. "Are you getting slow in your old age or were you just adding a little more mascara to your eyelashes?"

Hart smiled and watched his friend, Jerome Jordan, strut into the suite. He was wearing a black, skull and crossbones T-shirt that exclaimed, "Give up your booty!" His khaki shorts were frayed at the bottom edges. Although Jerome shared the last name of the legendary basketball player, life had dealt him a cruel irony. His stature reached all of five-foot-seven. But what he lacked in height, he made up in pure energy.

It was still hard to imagine Jerome sitting in the left seat of a 777. And not just because he was vertically challenged, but because his demeanor and appearance were more appropriate to a college football coach on vacation than an airline pilot. That being said, he took the insults concerning his height in stride.

Their former fraternity brothers had been relentless in harassing Jerome. When the two had begun the pledge process, Hart and Jerome shared a bond of mutual empathy, Jerome for his height and Hart for his odd name.

The last name, Lindy, although coincidental, was a proud reminder of the aviation legend that had flown the Spirit of St. Louis across the North Atlantic. In Lindbergh's honor, Hart's dad had argued for his son to have the first name of Charles. But Hart's mom did not share the same passion for aviation. She was less than enthusiastic about being constantly reminded of a long dead hero. Acquiescing to her husband's unrelenting love of all things airplane, she offered a compromise. Women aviation heroes should be represented also. Amelia, if it was a girl and Hart if it was a boy. Problem solved.

Unfortunately, time took its toll on his parents' relationship. Airplanes were the center of all that was wrong with Deloris Lindy's life. The small, country airport that was their sole source of income did not meet her pre-marital expectations of being able to drive a new Cadillac every year. Hart's dad seemed more committed to the airport than the marriage. Deloris Lindy sought commitments elsewhere. Before Hart had gone off to college, he had memories of his mom rolling into the garage at the same time the morning school bus was rolling to a stop in front of the driveway.

Jerome scanned Hart's hotel room. Bleached wicker furniture and tropical paintings with picturesque ocean scenes were scattered about. A ceiling fan painted with tropical flowers circulated above a glass coffee table in the center of the room. The view out the sliding glass door opened to the bay.

With a sarcastic snarl, Jerome said, "I guess you have to be a big deal party coordinator to rate a suite on the PAPA expense account."

Jerome held out his hand and shook Hart's with a firm grip.

"I'll be glad to swap with you, Captain Jordan." Hart swept his arm in a wide arc. "But since this side of my suite will become the command center, I'd thought you'd enjoy some privacy in your own place. I know how cranky you can get."

"Likely story." Jerome grinned.

"How are you anyhow?"

"Never better. Living the dream with this almost-bankrupt airline just like you."

"Wife? Kids?"

"They always seem to be home when I walk through the door," Jerome said shaking his head. "They're just not smart people."

Hart asked, "Aren't you going to be sending the oldest to college?"

"Yeah, can you believe it? I told him that college was

overrated. After all, look what happened to his dad." Jerome shuffled his feet. "Princeton for crying out loud. The kid got a full ride to play soccer."

"Glad to hear it. He deserves it. He worked hard in high school."

Hart pointed at the couch against the wall. Jerome dropped onto one of the cushions. Hart sat on a reclining chair opposite his friend. For a few more minutes, the two men discussed random subjects. Wife. Cathy. Airline. Goals. Ambitions. Vacations. Friends.

When the conversation turned to the investigation, Hart said, "I need to make use of your charm."

"That's asking a lot."

Hart explained the predicament involved with the copilot of Flight 63. He also described the events of the day, including the creepy, thin guy. Throughout the narration, Jerome's eyes remained wide. He barely took a breath.

Hart said, "Before the other guys get here for my pre-cocktail briefing, I need you to conduct his investigation interview. It will be your best opportunity before First Officer Townsend leaves on the morning departure to Miami."

"What d'ya mean he's leaving? He'll be a great witness. Really? Have you told the NTSB?"

"Nope. I don't want to take the chance that they delay him here. The IIC is Maureen Blackford. I think she likes to dot the i's and cross the t's twice. I'm going to beg for forgiveness rather than ask permission. Just make sure that you record the interview."

"Why me?"

"Because you're on the witness committee, remember?"

"I'm not just another pretty face?"

Hart looked at his friend's pockmarked, puffy cheeks and grinned. "Let me know how it goes. The rest of us will either be up here in my suite or at dinner."

"I always miss the fun." Jerome rose from the couch. "How's Dad?"

"The chemo has got him feeling like crap. But you know him. The word 'whine' is not in his vocabulary. He's still working at the airport every day. It keeps him alive. When this investigation is over, I'm due for a visit."

Jerome said, "Well, send him my best. And when you get up there, why don't you see if you can find our Super Cub. You've been talking about it for the last hundred years."

"It's gone. I don't think it's based at Dad's airport anymore. A guy that's a CEO for some dot-com company owns it."

"Figures. What happened to the days that airline captains owned all the toys? Maybe you can buy it back."

"Maybe," Hart sighed.

Jerome sighed and said, "Before we all got caught up in this airline career, the three of us had a lot of fun in that airplane. We did have fun, remember?"

Hart nodded. He, Jerome, and Rod were flight instructors back in those days. The three were inseparable. They flew the Super Cub in and out of grass fields. Windows open. Never getting higher than 500 feet. The girls they took up for rides sooner or later ended up at one of their perpetual parties or in their bedrooms or both. He loved that airplane. But then Don, their retired airline pilot mentor and owner, sold it. Hart had grieved as though he had lost a brother.

Jerome said, "And, sorry, but I have to ask. Have you and our boy that went to the dark side mended fences yet?"

"As a matter of fact, Captain Moretti and I had a civilized conversation about this investigation just before I left Miami."

"Civilized?" Jerome shook his head. "I guess you guys haven't come to terms."

"No. I guess not."

"What's it gonna take?"

"Probably a lot of alcohol."

"Well, that's a start." Jerome shrugged his shoulders.

Hart said, "We'll see. I've got other fish to fry at the moment." He stared at Jerome's T-shirt. "On other subjects, there is no doubt that you're a chick magnet with that ensemble you're wearing but would you consider a little different attire for the interview with the copilot?"

Jerome grinned and patted his chest over the skull and crossbones on his T-shirt. He asked, "Do you mean this isn't professional enough?"

"Get out of here. I've got important things to do...like put ice in the cooler."

The two men smiled. Jerome stood up and walked over to the door. He turned the knob and began to hum the shark's theme from *Jaws* as he disappeared into the corridor.

CHAPTER TEN

Friday
18:05 EDT

Despite Hart's best intentions to keep his initial briefing alcohol-free, he was unable to prevent access to the cooler in his room. He had only himself to blame. The cooler was too visible. Only a matter of minutes passed before each team member held a frosty bottle in his hand. With a sinister grin, Don had snapped the cap off the top of a bottle and handed it to Hart. If you can't beat 'em…

The briefing had progressed with limited questions. NTSB committee assignments were confirmed. The known facts surrounding the event were explained. The objective and rules of conduct were discussed. And the threatening events that Hart experienced were brought to light in addition to the current status of the investigation in regard to the FBI's jurisdiction. He advised his team to be extra cautious.

Jerome returned from his interview with Mike Townsend in ample time before the briefing was complete. His entrance was received with the usual repertoire of short-people jokes. The references to his nonexistent basketball career soon followed. As always, Jerome reveled in the attention. His pained expressions were a thin veil for his pure enjoyment of the camaraderie.

Once Hart realized that no further constructive discussion would ensue, he began to herd the team out of his room. It was time for dinner. With limited resistance, the room emptied.

The team headed in the direction of the hotel restaurant. Hart followed.

The five men were ushered by the hostess to a large table near the outside. As they passed the bar, Hart caught a glimpse of a familiar face. Maureen Blackford was seated on a tall stool between two men with short, close-cropped hair. Her fitted jeans enhanced the shape of her long legs. She was engaged in conversation with the two men. She was smiling, the expression accenting her sculpted jaw line.

Maureen looked away from the bar and saw Hart approaching. She nodded and continued to smile.

"Maureen," Hart said, extending his hand. The close-cropped-hair guys swiveled on their stools. Maureen reached for Hart's hand and shook it. The grip was firm.

"Hart. Glad to see that you made it. How are things?"

"Things are good." Hart leaned against an empty spot on the bar. "My understanding is that hotel space is limited. I guess we'll be sharing room service with the U.S. government."

Maureen smiled and said, "We promise not to order the same pizza."

"Good. Because if you've seen my guys, they're not the type to take a lack of pepperoni lightly." Hart gestured at the table where the four pilots were beginning to sit down. Maureen turned to survey the table. She nodded in the team's direction.

Maureen introduced the two men with her. As Hart had guessed, they were part of the NTSB Go-Team. One of the men didn't look old enough to have ever experienced a razor. They exchanged pleasantries.

Maureen reached for her martini glass. It was filled with a pink, slushy liquid. She said, "So I hear that you made the acquaintance of Special Agent Fredricks."

Hart chuckled and said, "He has an interesting fashion

sense for an FBI guy."

"You'll warm up to him." Maureen took a dainty sip of her drink. "Or not..."

"Well…now that we're all dressed up with no place to go, what's the chance that the FBI will release the airplane so we can do our job?"

"Good question," Maureen said. She slid her glass back onto the bar. "As eager as you guys are to begin, let me deal with the FBI. It's my job anyhow. I'm hoping that we'll have access tomorrow after the organizational meeting." Her lips formed a coy smile. "I'm sure that Special Agent Fredricks will see the light. He's not about to initiate an investigation on his own. He can't tell a Boeing 767 from a Cessna 172. But please…don't piss him off any more than you already have."

"I promise," Hart said with a smirk.

"Good," Maureen replied. She directed her attention at the two Go-Team members sitting at the bar. "Would you excuse me for a moment, gentlemen? I have something to discuss with Captain Lindy."

The men nodded. Maureen slid off her stool and moved away from the bar. She gestured her head toward a corner of the dining room. Hart followed, trying unsuccessfully not to focus on the sway of Maureen's hips. He glanced over at the table where his team was seated. They grinned at him with leering eyes.

Jerome pantomimed an eating motion with a fork. He was asking Hart whether he would be joining them for dinner. Hart nodded, raised five fingers, and mouthed the words, "five minutes." Jerome nodded.

Maureen turned to face Hart and said, "Listen, I have a small, personal matter to discuss." She scanned the bar and the dining room. "There are too many eyes. This is not the place." Maureen pursed her lips. "Would you come see me after dinner, please? Room 23034."

Hart raised his eyebrows and said, "Yes, Madame IIC. If you wish." His tone was cautious.

"It's a professional issue, Captain." Maureen glanced around the room again, catching furtive glances from Hart's team. "And now, I would appreciate it very much if you would give me your best deadly, serious expression…like I had just told you where Jimmy Hoffa is buried. And then walk away to your table."

"I already know where Jimmy Hoffa is buried, but thanks," Hart said narrowing his eyes. He did his best to maintain a grim expression. Hart nodded at Maureen and then strode toward his team.

The four pilots offered unconvincing expressions of nonchalance as Hart sat down on the chair at the head of the table. Jerome began to smirk. The other team members stared at Hart but said nothing.

Hart shook his head and said, "You guys are pathetic. A group of high school seniors at the prom would be more discreet." He attempted to disguise a smile with a frown and then gestured toward the NTSB members at the bar. "My business with Ms. Blackford? Logistics. That's all." He scanned the table. "Where's my beer, please?"

Jerome replied, "I ordered you a Shirley Temple with two cherries." He pushed a Pilsner glass full of amber liquid toward Hart. Hart grinned and took a sip.

"Maureen Blackford believes that the FBI will allow us access to the airplane later in the morning. The organizational meeting is at eight o'clock," Hart said.

A few questions were asked and then separate conversations resumed. Menus were reviewed and then collected. Orders were taken. The usual amount of island time passed. And then dinner arrived in a flurry of plates. Glasses were raised. Toasts were made to a variety of people and events. The meals were consumed as though no one had eaten that week.

The bill arrived. It was promptly passed to Hart. As though choreographed, the team members immediately rose from their seats. They grinned and thanked Hart in patronizing tones, well-aware that dinner would be added to PAPA's expense account. With a shake of his head, Hart pulled the MasterCard from his wallet.

When Hart finished signing the receipt, he glanced around the dining room. It was empty except for a small table occupied by a white-haired couple. They sat opposite each other, staring into each other's eyes. Wine glasses clinked. The couple laughed.

Hart sighed. The couple were probably celebrating their fiftieth wedding anniversary. It was Bermuda after all; probably a good bet they had honeymooned on the island. Hart's parents had honeymooned in Bermuda. It was difficult to imagine. He had too many memories as a kid hiding in his room to escape the fury of angry words and slamming doors. Hart erased the thoughts from his head and rose from the table. He strode down the corridor toward the hotel rooms.

When he reached room 23034, Hart stopped. He looked down the hall in both directions. He hesitated for a moment and then knocked. The door opened halfway. Maureen Blackford peeked through the open space. She wore the same jeans but had removed the flowing red blouse that had been covering a string-strap tank top underneath. The tank top clung tightly to her hourglass figure. Maureen's lips were drawn tight.

"Come in, please, Captain Lindy," Maureen said softly.

"Thanks," Hart replied. He took a few steps into the room while Maureen closed the door.

Maureen smiled and motioned for Hart to take a seat on one of the lounge chairs. Hart slithered cautiously into the chair. Maureen remained standing and asked, "Do you think it says anything about a person in how they knock?"

"Perhaps," Hart replied with a curious expression. "I guess it depends upon the circumstance." Hart looked at the door for a brief moment and then at his watch. "In my case, the fact that Mickey's hands are now both close to the 12, I thought it best not to disturb the neighborhood with an especially long and loud knock."

"I'll buy that," Maureen said with a quick smile. "But under normal circumstances, how would you have knocked?"

Hart brushed an imaginary piece of lint off his jeans. He said, "Well…hadn't really thought about that one, but I would define myself as a three-time knocker in rapid succession. Probably with a solid bump.

"Thought so. That would be my knock also. Sign of confidence, wouldn't you say?"

"I'll buy that," Hart replied. He crossed his legs and cleared his throat. "Can't say that I've ever had a philosophical discussion on door knocking." Hart squirmed in his chair. "Certainly door knocking isn't the reason for this private meeting?"

Maureen took a step closer. "Professionalism is the reason I asked you to come see me."

"Professionalism?" Hart asked raising his eyebrows.

"Yup. Professionalism in our relationship. Me as the IIC. You as the pilots union party coordinator."

"Okay," Hart replied. He uncrossed his leg and shifted his weight in the chair.

"You do remember Flight 57 in San Juan?" Hart nodded. "Might you remember an escapade with a little barmaid at your hotel room door?"

Hart had a vision of red lips intertwined with his while being gently molested by a tall, lanky Latin brunette, all before she took a step into his hotel room. He had worked his charm at the bar for a while, never expecting her to make an appearance. "Uh, yeah…actually she was not just a barmaid, she was the bar manager." Hart took a deep breath. "Look, I understand. I'll keep my conduct professional. I'm sorry you had to witness that moment. I hadn't intended it to be an event for public consumption."

Maureen sat down on the armrest of Hart's chair. Hart didn't move, attempting to hide his discomfort. He felt awkward.

"I'm okay with that. I just thought you had better taste."

"No comment. It wasn't Ms. Right. It was Ms. Right Now." Hart tried to grin.

"If truth be told, I was turned on. And when I learned that you were a party coordinator for this investigation, I felt both reluctance and excitement."

"Uh…I don't get it."

"Hey, let's face it. You weren't fond of me at the Flight 57 investigation. Your words were cordial, but your eyes said something completely opposite."

"That's not fair," Hart said as he squirmed.

"Be honest. Haven't you felt the sexual tension between us?"

"Well…"

Hart felt a thump in his chest. This doesn't happen.

"Look. I might be one of only a handful of women in this business, but I didn't get my job because I slept around with the boss. I got my position because I am confident. I can assess a situation and make a reasonable decision within a relatively short period of time. In that respect, I'm thinking that if we release that tension now, we can go beyond it into our professional roles. Otherwise we'll be distracted from the task at hand."

With a graceful twist, Maureen dropped herself from the arm of the chair and into Hart's lap. She wrapped an arm around his neck. She stared into his eyes and then moved her lips toward him. Hart relaxed his mouth and felt the moisture of her tongue slither over his. Without taking a breath, they kissed for a long while.

Maureen drew her head back and smiled. Her eyes sparkled in the dim light. Hart caressed her dark hair and then moved a hand over the small of her back. With the other hand he glided his fingers over her shoulders, down her slender arm, and over the cup of her breasts.

As he held Maureen in his arms, Hart rose from the chair. He began to carry her toward the king-size bed.

Hart said, "Professionalism? Really?" He grinned. "I've never considered sleeping with someone an act of professionalism."

"You haven't tried it yet," Maureen whispered.

23:55 EDT

Initially, Jim had been resistant to speak with the two CISM guys from the union. What the hell was "critical incident stress management" anyway? Wasn't that for wimps that couldn't handle a little pressure? He flew F-16s in the Gulf War. Bad people tried to shoot him out of the sky. The emergency he dealt with today was nothing.

If they really wanted to help mitigate the aftereffects of the event, Jim suggested that they focus their energy on Mike. Mike's situation was far more serious. They agreed and indicated that Mike was already a priority. In fact, Jim's participation would be of great assistance when the two had an opportunity to debrief the event together.

Out of respect for his colleagues, Jim had invited them into his room. After all, they had volunteered to come to Bermuda specifically for just such a purpose. At first, Jim was reluctant to discuss the circumstances of the emergency on his plane. But their relaxed demeanor promoted conversation. And before Jim realized it, he had covered almost every detail.

They listened to his bad jokes and his dry sense of humor. And they also listened to a self-critique of his performance. Somewhere in his mind he felt that he could have achieved a higher standard…or that maybe better vigilance could have prevented the entire event. The two CISM guys had told him that his reaction was normal, dismissing his self-deprecation as typical.

When the two union guys had left, Jim felt a surprising sense of relief for having unburdened himself. For the moment, he needed something to numb his brain. He pressed the power button on the TV remote. The screen crackled to life. As he surfed, CNN caught his attention. Video of the emergency landing was being replayed.

This was the first time he had actually seen the entire footage. The blazing right side of the airplane was an amazing sight. From the cockpit, none of this had been visible. It was just as well. The impersonal nature of flashing lights, electronic bells and messages kept the reality of the drama from view. In simple terms, the cockpit warnings focused him on matter-of-fact problem-solving.

Now that it was over, the serious nature of the entire event began to sink in. Jim shook off the feeling. Why dwell? It served no purpose. But then after watching the spectacular video in which he was the star, why not at least commemorate his success with a photo of the dramatic image of the airplane landing. A trophy picture. He chuckled. The all-about-me wall in his office could certainly use something other than his plaques and squadron photos.

A knock on the door interrupted Jim's thoughts. Still gazing at the last seconds of the images on the TV screen, he walked toward the door. He heard two more knocks.

A voice on the other side said, “Room service.”

Jim rolled his eyes. He twisted the door handle saying, “Didn’t order anything.”

Without warning, the heavy wooden door slammed open into the room. A flash of silver metal struck Jim hard on the temple. He struggled to maintain his balance, teetering toward the low dresser against the wall. The door thudded closed. Jim caught a quick glance of the object that hit him as it clanked to the floor. It was a room service plate cover. What the hell was happening?

Jim felt a sharp pain in his abdomen. Something slammed him solid in his gut. He doubled over, falling toward the tile floor. Jim’s head struck the corner of the TV frame as he fell. He felt a warm trickle on his forehead. His focus narrowed. The world became grey.

As his jaw smacked the tile, Jim heard a voice come from some unknown direction in the room. The voice was hollow with a heavy accent.

“This is another message for Captain Lindy. He doesn’t seem to be paying attention.”

Jim heard footsteps shuffle around his head. He watched as the toe of a black shoe rocketed in a blur against his side. He felt a searing pain. Instinctively, he covered his head with his hands. He heard the footsteps travel away and then the sound of the doorknob clacking open. The door slammed shut. Silence.

Time lost all perspective. He wasn’t sure how long he remained motionless or whether he had even remained conscious. Jim began to drag himself across the floor. He reached for the phone on the dresser. He pulled on the cord. The console crashed to the floor with a crack. Jim picked up the receiver and pressed the “O” button. A voice that sounded distant and faint answered.

“I need emergency medical help now,” Jim coughed into

the phone.

His vision began to blur. And then he was enveloped by blackness.

CHAPTER ELEVEN

Saturday
05:30 EDT

The drugs the hospital intern had prescribed were starting to lose their effectiveness. Rather than searing pain, Jim was beginning to sense a dull ache. The ache had migrated to almost every pore of his body. He pushed with his arms, attempting to move his upper torso higher against the inclined hospital bed.

"Captain, please. Do not strain yourself, mon. It's too early yet," a lilting female voice from somewhere within the room scolded.

Jim scanned his arms. They were covered with tubes and bandages. He could feel the gauze on his forehead and around his side. He glanced out the small window by his bed. The glow of an occasional car headlight from the street nearby was all that was visible.

Jim asked, "What time is it please?"

The voice replied, "5:30, Captain."

"Is it morning?"

"Yes, Captain."

"Can I have a martini? Two olives and a splash of vermouth, please."

"How about a little shot of morphine instead, mon?"

"That's not what I had in mind, but it will have to do."

The voice walked over to his bed. As he had guessed, the voice belonged to a nurse. She was thin with short, black hair that was flecked with gray streaks. The nurse smiled and reached for a button lying by Jim's side. The button was attached to an unidentified wire cord. She handed it to Jim.

The nurse said, "Here's your martini, Captain. Press the button when your pain requires a cocktail."

"Great. How soon before I have to attend a rehab clinic for drug addiction?"

"Probably tomorrow. All of you pilots think the same way. I haven't created any drug addicts in this hospital yet." The nurse pressed the button. "You'll feel better in a minute, mon."

"This is Bermuda. There are no drug addicts on this island," Jim said, making a feeble attempt at a grin. He felt fortunate that his injuries weren't inflicted while on one of his other less medically sophisticated layovers. He shuddered at the thought.

The nurse began to walk from the room. Abruptly she stopped and turned. She asked, "This is probably against my better judgment, but are you feeling up to visitors?"

"What visitors?" Jim asked.

"You have quite a list actually."

"Really?"

"For starters, an officer from the Bermuda Police Service, the FBI, and some pilots from your airline."

"Who are the pilots?"

"I'm a nurse, Captain, not a hotel concierge."

"Are they all here now?"

"The officer has been here most of the night."

Jim said, "Okay, send him in, please. What about my airline guys?"

"Apparently the airline people didn't find out about your assault until very late last night, but my understanding is that they are on their way."

"Can you have them sent up when they arrive?"

"Would you like me to carry their luggage also?" The nurse sneered.

"That won't be necessary," Jim said with a smirk. He added, "I think you and I could be an item, don't you think?"

The nurse glowered with a grin. "Be careful, Captain. I have access to a lot of needles and other sharp objects."

The nurse strutted out of the room. Jim heard her murmur to somebody nearby. A large portly man walked into the room. The man wore the black and white uniform of an inspector. He introduced himself to Jim.

A discussion ensued about the forced entry of Jim's assailant into his hotel room. Jim became frustrated with his own lack of clear details. He couldn't determine whether the whole mess was a blur as a result of the assault, as a result of his injuries, or a result of his pain medicine. His only concrete recollection of the event was of the room service knock on the door. The inspector listened with narrowed eyes and tight lips. He left the room with a perfunctory nod, wishing Jim the best for his recovery.

Jim couldn't help but feel unsettled. Guilt crept into his thinking. Couldn't he have defended himself better? Or perhaps, been wary enough not to have opened the door in the first place?

While Jim became lost in his thoughts, three figures stepped into the room. Jim recognized two of the faces as the CISM guys that he had met earlier the previous evening. They exchanged greetings and surveyed the extent of Jim's injuries.

The third man introduced himself as Jerome Jordan. He explained his position with the PAPA investigation team. Jerome's cheerful demeanor took Jim away from his dark place. Although he indicated that Jim's account of Flight 63 was vital to the investigation, his convalescence would take priority. When he was ready, Jerome and the NTSB would discuss the details of the emergency.

Jim had stiffened at the suggestion that his ability to articulate was considered impaired. But when the pain returned, he resigned himself to Jerome's assessment of his condition. Jerome said that, no matter the intimate details, his decisions had saved lives. End of story.

Jerome excused himself to attend the NTSB meeting. The CISM pilots remained in the room for a while longer. Jim appreciated the support and the camaraderie. And sometime in the afternoon, his wife would arrive. He was surprised at how much he missed her smile. He could really use it now…

08:05 EDT

The hotel banquet room murmured with the sound of voices in various stages of conversation. An occasional chuckle. A subdued laugh. A stifled cough.

Round tables covered with blue linen cloths were distributed throughout the room. Pitchers of water sat on top of the tables. A podium was positioned in front. Members of various third parties circulated throughout the room, mingling with NTSB Go-Team investigators. The FAA, the airline, the flight attendants, the engine manufacturer, the airplane manufacturer, and the pilots were all in attendance. Lanyards attached to laminated ID tags with the NTSB logo were draped around the necks of the participants.

Hart scanned the room. Although time had blurred people's names, some of the faces were familiar. The faces brought back memories of Flight 57. Some of those memories involved grim expressions and thousand-yard stares. Hart was certain that age wasn't the only reason for the appearance of new lines and creases on the foreheads of those faces.

The sound of a water glass clinking grew louder and

louder. Within a few moments, the electronically amplified voice of Maureen Blackford rose above the din. Maureen requested that the participants take their seats.

Introductions were made. Chairmen and chairwomen of the various NTSB Go-Team committees rose as they were recognized by the IIC. Gratitude was extended to all of the third-party participants for their attendance. The rules of engagement were clarified. The seriousness and value of each committee member's contribution was reinforced.

And as with all accident investigations, confidentiality was emphasized. Any details released to an outside source were to be approved only by the NTSB. If the policy were violated, the offender's third-party status would be in jeopardy.

Maureen finished her briefing and then glanced at her wristwatch. She announced, "The FBI is allowing us the opportunity for a leisurely coffee break after this meeting. We will be given access to the airplane at ten o'clock." She paused and looked at the man standing to her right. "Please give Special Agent Fredricks your attention."

As Maureen took a few steps away from the lectern, Ryan Fredricks moved forward. He adjusted the microphone. The flexible stand creaked. His ensemble consisted of an unbuttoned, sailfish-adorned, Guy Harvey shirt draped over a black T-shirt, revealing the white letters "F-B-I."

Special Agent Fredricks tapped the microphone and said, "Ladies and gentlemen, thanks for coming. I appreciate your understanding in our delay." He chuckled. "Isn't that something you folks say all the time?" He scanned the room. Only a handful of people were smiling, mostly as a courtesy. "Sorry, consider my career as a stand-up comic over. I promise not to quit my day job." A few guarded chuckles were heard.

"Moving on… We are releasing the airplane into your

hands because it will be a more efficient use of investigation skills. You are the experts in this arena. However, it is important for you folks to understand that we are still considering the possibility that a crime was committed. We are not ruling out terrorism. In that regard, we ask that you tread carefully. In other words, if you find something suspicious during the course of the investigation, please advise us immediately. I am sure nobody has to be reminded that they are working in sensitive territory."

The FBI man glanced at Hart. Hart nodded with a grim expression.

"In that regard, some of you may not be aware of last night's rather serious development." Ryan scanned the faces in the banquet room. All eyes were focused in his direction. He continued. "The captain of Flight 63 was assaulted in his room at approximately 00:05 hours."

Ryan waited for the handful of suppressed gasps to subside.

"He is in serious but stable condition. Despite the captain's willingness to provide information, his description of the assailant was virtually nonexistent due to the surprise nature of the encounter. We are confident that this was a planned attack. The perpetrator's instruction to the captain was to convey a warning to PAPA party coordinator Captain Lindy that the investigation should be discontinued."

Scattered whispering was heard. People shifted positions in their chairs. Eyes glanced about the room.

"We are working with local law enforcement on this assault. In addition, we are following a different lead that was provided by Captain Lindy." Ryan cleared his throat. "Please also be aware that we have detained some of the passengers from Flight 63. Let's just say that they have questionable backgrounds. As a matter of fact, one of these individuals was a former member of the no-fly list."

A few tables broke out in hushed conversations.

The FBI man waved a dismissive hand. He said, "Look, I know you all have apprehensions. My job is to investigate crime against the United States…and to keep you safe. You will find increased security measures at the hotel and at the airplane. Although it will seem tedious at times, please cooperate with these measures. They are being implemented for your protection. Please also help us do our jobs by exercising extreme vigilance. Trust me; we are looking at every aspect of this event. Thank you for your time this morning."

Ryan stepped away from the lectern. He nodded at Maureen and then walked out a side door at a brisk pace. A small sea of hands rose. Maureen leaned into the microphone and began to acknowledge questions from various participants. Within fifteen minutes, she officially dismissed the organizational meeting.

Hart rose from his chair and walked over to Jerome, who was seated a couple of tables away. Jerome was grinning. All eyes from his table were focused in his direction. Judging by his friend's body language, Jerome was about to deliver a punch line for one of his off-color jokes. Hart never understood why only Jerome could get away with such antics, especially with strangers. The group around the table began to chuckle. Had the circumstances been more jovial, a belly laugh would have been included.

When Jerome saw Hart, he excused himself and stood up from the table.

"What's up, boss?" Jerome asked.

Hart gestured at Maureen still standing next to the podium and said, "Time to face the music about First Officer Townsend's departure."

"And you want me at your side just in case she shoots laser beams out her eyes?"

"Exactly."

Jerome smiled. "Let's get my NTSB witness committee chairman involved also." He motioned at a young guy just starting to rise from the table. The young guy had short, close-cropped hair. He was the same Go-Team member that Hart had met at the bar last night. Hart remembered his name to be Chad from some suburb outside of Boston.

As the three approached, Maureen was just completing a conversation with a tall man that Hart recognized to be the Boeing representative. She held up an index finger for them to wait. Maureen ended her conversation with a handshake. The Boeing man walked away. She turned to face Jerome, Hart, and Chad. Hart introduced Jerome.

"Gentlemen, what can I do for you?" Maureen asked.

"Madame IIC, I've got a confession to make," Hart said with a solemn tone.

Maureen's eyes widened. She said, "I'm listening."

"I'm taking full responsibility."

"I don't like the sound of this."

Hart glanced at Chad and then back at Maureen. He said, "I authorized the copilot of Flight 63 to take the early morning departure back to his base in Miami. He's no longer available on site."

Maureen's eyes narrowed. Hart couldn't be certain whether she was staring or glaring at him.

"I'm sorry, but extraordinary circumstances were involved. That being said…" Hart gestured his head at Jerome, "…my witness committee member already conducted an interview. The interview was recorded."

A few seconds of icy silence passed. Maureen said, "Well, at least the captain is available."

Jerome took a deep breath and said, "Actually, Madame IIC, he's not."

"Please explain," Maureen replied. She clenched her

teeth.

"The captain has been prescribed heavy doses of pain medication for his injuries. Although he is cooperative, his faculties are not reliable at the moment."

"Are you telling me that even though we have been fortunate enough to have surviving cockpit crew members neither one is available?"

"I'm afraid that's true," Jerome said. He shuffled his feet.

Maureen looked at Chad and Jerome. She said, "Gentlemen, if you will excuse us, Captain Lindy and I need to discuss the date of his execution."

The two men nodded. They began to slither away toward the back of the banquet room where a large silver carafe of coffee had been placed on a table. Jerome smirked when he walked around Hart. In mock fear, he bit the fingernails of one hand.

When the remaining crowd started to gravitate toward the back of the room, Maureen put her hands on her hips and said to Hart, "You spent most of the night in my bed. Might you have considered informing the IIC of this decision?"

"Sorry, I was a little preoccupied with Madame IIC's thong panties."

Hart explained the circumstances surrounding the personal crisis that Mike Townsend was facing at home. Maureen's eyes widened but she remained tight-lipped. She sighed.

"How am I supposed to handle this?"

"Meaning?"

"I'm not overly concerned about cockpit crew input. We can obtain most of the information from the cockpit voice recorder and the digital flight data recorder…something we will be doing anyhow."

"Okay, I figured the CVR and the DFDR would be a priority today," Hart said.

"My issue is the procedures breach you made."

"My suggestion?"

"I probably shouldn't listen to this," Maureen grunted. "But go ahead."

"At the end-of-the-day progress meeting, admonish me publically."

"Are you serious?"

"Absolutely," Hart said. He smiled. "I was wrong. Make me an example."

Maureen ran a few fingers through her hair. She said, "So, why *did* you let him leave?"

"I couldn't be certain that you would release him."

"Do you think that I drink blood?"

"Do I have to answer that?"

Maureen fought a grin. "I'll take your discipline suggestion under advisement, Captain Lindy. In the meantime, watch your step."

"I will, Madame IIC."

Hart nodded at Maureen and walked toward the crowd huddled around the coffee in the back of the room. He thought of Cathy. He envisioned her rubbing her tiny nose the way she always did when she was about to express her displeasure with Hart. What had he got himself into now?

10:05 EDT

Although Mike was met by the chief pilot and offered a ride home, he politely declined. He needed the time it took to drive between Miami Airport and Fort Lauderdale to think without interruption. He thanked Rod Moretti for his concern and walked outside the terminal. He waited for the next bus to the employee parking lot.

Turning his iPhone on had been a mistake. He had purposely delayed pressing the power button until he was in his car. The amount of voice mail, text, and e-mail messages was overwhelming. He was tempted to delete everything. None of the messages would amount to anything more than sympathy. And if any one of them was consequential enough to require a response, that individual would contact him again. Nothing really mattered except for his daughters anyhow.

And when the gate agent in Bermuda had informed him that his captain had been the victim of a vicious assault the night before, Mike felt a greater sense of urgency.

As Mike became more immersed in thought, the late morning traffic on I-95 transformed into a blur. The road signs and billboards may as well have been printed in Japanese. None of the words formed intelligible communication. It wasn't long before all sense of time disappeared.

When Mike turned from McNab Road onto his neighborhood street, it took only a glimpse for him to discover that his house had been transformed into a circus. The local news stations had parked their vans on the street just barely off his lawn. The satellite dish of each van was extended to above rooftop level. Other unidentified cars were parked on the grass. The driveway was crammed worse than the back section of a used car lot. Some of the vehicles he recognized as belonging to Robin's friends. A handful of police cruisers and unmarked cars added an element of surrealism to the scene.

And then, of course, his oldest daughter's prized possession sat off to the side of the garage. On the day Kim had passed her driver's test and had maintained a 3.0 grade point average, despite the protests of Robin, Mike surprised her with a brand-new, bright-yellow VW Bug.

The smile on his daughter's face and the twinkle in her bright eyes was worth every cent the silly little car cost. But the moment was bittersweet. A hug and a happy tear later,

Kim drove away. She would return not as a little girl but as a young woman. Remembering that moment, Mike stared at the yellow Beetle. It sat in the driveway, headlights looking like a forlorn pair of eyes.

Two uniform patrol officers that were leaning against the trunk of a cruiser stood up as Mike approached. Mike considered driving away and waiting elsewhere but he knew it was inevitable that he get involved. He just had no interest in dealing with anybody but his wife.

Mike pressed the button for the driver's side window. When the window slid down he asked, "Any chance there might be room for the owner of this house to park?"

The cops looked at Mike, noticing the epaulets on his uniform shirt.

The taller cop said, "I'm sorry, Mr. Townsend. It got a little out of control here. Believe it or not, it was worse earlier. You can leave your car right where you are behind us. Leave the keys in the ignition. We'll valet park for you, sir. And please allow us to escort you into your house so you can avoid the cameras."

"Can I trust you guys with a twelve-year-old Mercedes that's in bad need of a new exhaust system?"

The cops smiled. The shorter man opened the door. Mike slid out of the driver's seat and slung his uniform jacket over his shoulder.

Mike asked, "Anything new?"

The shorter cop replied, "Can't say for sure. We've been outside in your driveway most of the morning. It would be best if you got the information from the detective inside."

The cops began to walk on either side of Mike. The sliding door of a TV van opened. The cops increased the pace to a brisk walk. From the corner of his eye, Mike spotted a man with a jacket and tie and a microphone. The man began to shout questions. Before Mike had an opportunity to respond, he was gently guided through the front door.

Almost every available seating space in the living room was occupied. Neighbors. Friends. Strangers. Uniformed cops. Uniformed pilots. Faces began to turn in Mike's direction. Individually, all eyes acknowledged his entrance.

A glance into the kitchen revealed a sink and counter overrun by bowls, dishes, and glasses. Two of Robin's tennis friends had begun to clean the disarray. They nodded at Mike with sober smiles.

From the hallway, Robin walked toward him. The whites of her eyes were pink. Dark circles were starting to work their way toward the surface of her skin. She attempted a smile but only got her lips just past a frown. Tentatively, she put her arms around Mike.

"Guess I missed a party last night," Mike said. He drew in a deep breath and squeezed his wife. "How are you holding up?"

"Okay for the most part. Fortunately, I haven't had a lot of time to dwell. I've been kept occupied," Robin said.

Mike looked above his wife's head and scanned the house full of people. He said, "Good. I'm glad." He gently released Robin and took a step back.

Robin said, "I'll introduce you to Detective Alvarez. I'm sure you have questions for him. And I know he has questions for you."

Mike nodded at Robin. The word "detective" made him wince. An uneasy apprehension crept into his psyche. Mike walked into the center of the living room and greeted the unexpected guests. Introductions were made. Thanks and appreciation was given. Encouragement and support was received. Once the crowd became comfortable with Mike's emotional status, the stiffness dissipated. People began to have subdued conversations among themselves.

Having experienced such situations on numerous

occasions, Detective Alvarez had blended himself into a small corner of the house. Now that the awkward moment had passed, the detective walked toward Mike. He extended a hand. When the introduction was complete, Alvarez gestured toward a dining room away from the main group of people. The two men walked together and then sat down at a large oval table.

"How is Bermuda this time of year?" the detective asked.

"Despite the circumstances, not bad."

"I understand," Alvarez said, resignation in his tone.

"What can you tell me about my daughters, Detective Alvarez?" Mike planted his elbows on the table and rested his chin on top of his clasped hands.

"We're following some leads, Mr. Townsend. But honestly, we don't have much."

The detective discussed the security tape and the two student witnesses. He mentioned the Escalade and that it had been found in a vacant office parking lot burned to the ground. Initial reaction from the fire department investigators on scene indicated that arson was most likely involved. Alvarez suspected that Mike's daughters were transferred to another vehicle. Unfortunately, no security video was available from the empty office building.

Mike lowered his head and said, "I was hoping for better news, Detective."

"Believe me, we all were. But not one of us is even close to giving up hope. Every law enforcement agency has received a bulletin about the abduction. The media has been on our side. All the scheduled news broadcasts have included the story. And we have an active Amber Alert in progress."

Mike looked up and stared unfocused at a sunset painting on the wall.

Alvarez said, "I was hoping that you could help with some information."

"Anything," Mike said. He smoothed a wrinkle on the tablecloth with his thumb.

"This whole event is too coincidental for me."

"How so?"

"The fact that you were involved with an emergency landing…and within a very short period of time, your daughters were taken."

"I thought about that myself."

"Mr. Townsend, I know that this is a tough time…but is there something you're not telling me?"

He stared at the detective and said, "No, Detective. I have nothing to tell you."

"Forgive my drama, sir, but your daughters' lives may be in the balance here. I'll find out in the end if you have withheld pertinent information."

"I don't need threats right now, Detective."

"It wasn't a threat, Mr. Townsend. It was simply a promise."

Mike slowly rose from his chair at the table. Realizing that any further questioning would be futile, Alvarez stood also. Both men offered each other polite smiles. They shook hands. Alvarez reached into a shirt pocket and handed his business card to Mike.

"If you do think of anything, Mr. Townsend, I'm only a phone call away…anytime of the day or night."

"Thank you for your efforts, Detective Alvarez. I am grateful."

The two men walked back into the living room. Much of the crowd had begun to funnel out the front door. A few minutes and a few handshakes and hugs later, the house was empty. Only the uniformed cops remained. They stood guard in the driveway. The quiet inside of the house was deafening. Mike longed for the sound of giggling voices to emerge from a bedroom or a bathroom.

Robin seemed to sense the same. She took a few steps toward her husband. Her eyes began to cloud with tears. She reached for his hand and then pulled away.

Mike took a deep breath and said, "Robin, it's okay. We're on the same page with this. Just because I have become honest with myself, doesn't mean that we can't comfort each other."

"Why did you live this lie for so long?"

"I'm sorry. I don't have an answer for you."

"You brought our girls into this mess."

"It wasn't my intention, Robin."

"Maybe you should have thought of that a long time ago."

"Maybe we should focus on how best to get them back."

"I don't think you understand the pain, Mike."

"I don't think you understand the internal conflict I have been dealing with most of our marriage…and my career." Mike shook his head. He gestured his hands at himself. "Are you aware that my profession does not exactly welcome this…lifestyle, despite the liberal claims in the media?"

"That's self-centered and narcissistic."

"Is this argument going to get our girls home?"

A long minute of silence passed between Mike and Robin. They both stared out through the sliding glass doors at the water in the canal. Their boat rocked against the dock in a slow rhythmic motion. The scene seemed to take the sting out of the emotional rollercoaster they were riding.

Mike said, "Let's get through this crisis first. Then we can confront the issue between us. Please?"

A stream of tears streaked down Robin's cheek. She nodded and said, "The news channels showed the video of your landing in Bermuda. It looked like an awful fire. I'm glad you're okay."

"Thanks," Mike said with a tiny smile.

Robin walked away toward their bedroom. Mike leaned against the wall and rubbed his forehead. He knew what he had to do next. He just had to succeed.

10:30 EDT

Although Hart had expressed a desire to remain at the command center, aka his room, the team insisted that his presence on site was necessary…at least for an initial perspective. The group had a valid argument. If he were to coordinate assignments, an overview of the investigation would help him delegate duties.

Hart's resistance was being guided by the mistakes made at the investigation of Flight 57. The PAPA party coordinator at that time had been unprepared for the chaos. In reality, nobody had been prepared. Hart recalled one especially bad day of the investigation.

At the crash site in San Juan, the NTSB had directed the construction equipment volunteers to move mangled pieces of the wreckage into various piles. Once the piles were established, the recovery workers requested that available Go-Team members identify the parts of the airplane that might be needed in the investigation. Remaining parts were to be discarded. Fragments of airplane pieces were scattered across the two blocks of the impact site. Seats. Landing gear. Fuselage scraps. Luggage. Torn magazines.

Although the lifeless forms of passengers had been removed, reminders of the human devastation were still embedded in the rubble. Firefighters were seen cradling personal effects in gloved hands to the staging tent where a police officer would tag each item. Watches. Rings. Wallets. Bracelets.

PAPA's party coordinator had been on scene every day. He had witnessed the routine. On this particular occasion he had been asked by the firefighters to help determine the significance of twisted airplane metal amidst a large pile. He donned the hooded coveralls of a Tyvec suit and waded into the mess. After a few minutes he received a tap on the shoulder. The firefighters politely offered to take a deformed piece of metal from his grip. At first he declined but then realized that he had dragged the captain's control wheel out of the pile. He stared at it for a moment and then understood. Parts of the captain had adhered to the mechanism. With an anguished look, he walked away. He sat on the tailgate of a pickup truck for a half-hour without uttering a word.

Hart didn't want to repeat the performance. Fortunately, the devastation of Flight 63 was a mere fraction of the horror at Flight 57.

The Flight 63 team shuffled out of the van with the eagerness of high school seniors on a field trip. They separated into their appropriate committees at the appropriate staging areas of the airplane. Hart trailed behind, taking a few moments to survey the 767. At a slow pace, he began a walk from underneath the horizontal stabilizer on the right side.

The evidence of fire and explosion made its first appearance just below the aft-most entry door. Black, oily soot streaked rearward along the fuselage. Scattered dents and hatch marks interrupted the otherwise streamlined body of the 180-foot airliner.

As Hart continued his methodical advance, various people crisscrossed in front of him. They stopped in different positions around the airplane, some of them taking a moment to scribble notes on a clipboard. A small gaggle of investigators pointed and nodded at the prominent diagonal slices in the aluminum skin just below the passenger windows forward of the wing's leading edge. Hart didn't need an explanation. It was the obvious point of entry for the engine shrapnel.

The slices looked as though a mischievous teenager had treated the fuselage like an empty beer can, plunging the pointy end of a giant Ginsu knife into the metal. Hart shuddered at the thought two passengers' lives had ended near those slices. Their only mistake that day was to have accepted that seat assignment.

Crouching slightly, Hart scanned the underside of the right wing behind the engine. Thick, black soot. More slices. Jagged sections of cut or bent aluminum. When the engine tore itself apart, it peppered everything in the immediate vicinity with its innards.

Except for the basic shape, from the rear looking forward, the GE power plant barely resembled a piece of machinery that had once provided sixty-one thousand pounds of thrust. From within, the engine was mangled and twisted. Only fragments of the turbine blades remained. Whatever pieces had come loose, they traveled with destructive malice through the entire engine.

Walking around the footprint of the right wing starting from the trailing edge and around the wingtip down the leading edge, Hart made his way to the front of the engine. Hart nodded at his team member, Matt Mattson. Matt and the other party members were studying the engine from different angles, arms folded across their chest, pensive expressions on their faces. One man would break from the group and point at an area. The rest would shuffle over to his position, conferring about the new observation.

Hart peered into the front of the engine. As expected, charcoal dust covered the inlet. Some of the fire retardant goop that was sprayed by the rescue unit remained. Many of the compressor blades had been deformed into Twizzler shapes or were just plain missing. Hart shook his head at the chaotic damage.

Taking a few steps back away from the inlet, Hart had a thought. He motioned for Matt to join him. Matt excused himself and strode away from the group.

"What's up, boss?" Matt asked.

"I'm sure that you guys are going down this road, but I just want to make sure."

"Go ahead."

Hart clasped his hands behind his back and rocked on the balls of his feet. He gestured his head at the engine. "This thing has as much damage in the back as it does up here at the fan blades. That means that whatever destroyed this piece of GE technology began at the inlet, destroying everything in its path on the way out the back end. If that's the case, wouldn't the origin of this mess have to be foreign to the engine…like a big bird or something?"

"Maybe."

"Okay. Maybe… Well, these guys were in cruise configuration at a flight level...three-seven-'O' is my understanding. You and I have both heard the unverified stories of Canadian geese--or whatever--flying at ridiculous altitudes, but really? A frozen piece of blue water from the toilet of the International Space Station is more likely."

"Can't disagree with you," Matt said with a grin.

"Okay, then what?"

"Something came apart internally. That's why we're scratching our heads. We've got company mechanics inbound that just arrived from Miami. They're on the passenger side of the airport now. They'll be pulling the engine off this thing and taking it apart."

Hart asked, "Matt, can you explain how an internal malfunction from behind the fan blades could send parts and pieces forward. Wouldn't the destruction occur rearward?"

"Logically, yes…but we're not sure."

"Fair enough. I'll let you do your thing." Hart smirked.

"Remember…you guys were the ones that wanted me to pop out here to the field investigation. I was perfectly satisfied with my loneliness at the command center."

Matt smiled. Hart began to walk away, but a glint of sun reflecting off something from within the engine inlet caught his attention. Hart strode forward and leaned over the soot-encrusted cowl. Matt moved next to him. Hart pointed at a small, not quite rectangular fragment that was lodged between two broken fan blades.

"Doesn't look like it belongs up at the front end," Hart said.

"Maybe not," Matt said, staring at the fragment. "We'll check it out, boss."

Nodding, Hart walked toward the nose of the airplane. He turned to face aft. The view offered a broader perspective of the damage. Such an enormous piece of machinery. But even a tiny mechanical issue could make it a dysfunctional nightmare. That's why airplane manufacturers built redundant systems and that's why pilots were trained for almost every conceivable contingency.

Hart sighed and glanced back at the right engine. A crowd had formed in front of the inlet. A man with "NTSB" printed on the back of his windbreaker was hopping inside the cowl. It was one of the close-cropped hair guys, this time the engine committee chairman, Frank. Interesting. Apparently Hart had gotten their attention. Cool.

Ducking underneath the airplane just behind the nosewheel, Hart walked toward the portable air stairs. The air stairs had been positioned against the left side. He began to climb the steps. Once on the top landing, he walked through the L1 door and down the left side aisle.

Except for the hanging jungle of oxygen masks from the PSU units, the cabin contained the standard mess seen at the end of a typical long-range international flight. Blankets strewn about the floors and the seats. Newspaper sections and magazines scattered across the aisle. Crumbs and food portions smeared underneath seats and open tray tables.

As Hart approached the fatal row, he nodded at the committee members standing across the other aisle. They moved around the seats like marbles in a maze. Some were sketching rough diagrams while others were simply absorbing the scene.

The obvious investigation activity notwithstanding, the sense that something tragic had occurred was palatable, a concept that was difficult to explain to the uninitiated. Perhaps that was why hushed tones were spoken.

Hart moved closer to the row of the two fatalities. The seats were stained in dark red. The floor beneath the seats and in the immediate vicinity contained similar blotchy stains. Other seats were speckled with varied sizes of crimson dots. Some of the upholstery had been ripped and torn. Puffy pieces of foam material billowed out from the fabric.

A glance at the inner wall of the cabin told Hart that the difference between life and death was measured in fractions of an inch. The scattered slices where engine pieces had pierced the fuselage skin were allowing thin bands of sunlight to penetrate. It was amazing that the airplane had been able to maintain pressurization for as long as the copilot had reported.

Old airplane disaster movies depicted passengers being sucked outside through even the smallest of holes--a sensationalized piece of fiction. Depending upon severity, the real story was that a fuselage hole was a simple pressurization problem. If the problem couldn't be mitigated by the automatic systems, the crew had to take action in the form of an emergency descent. End of story.

Staring at the headrest of the outermost fatal seat, Hart noticed a scrap of metal protruding from within a portion of the escaping foam. He shuffled across the row of middle seats between him and the opposite side of the airplane. Hart moved behind the headrest and studied the piece of metal. He glanced around the cabin. The other investigators were gathered in an awkward circle, involved in an impromptu discussion. Hart pulled the darkened metal from the headrest and rolled it around in his fingers.

A turbine or compressor blade fragment? Nope. It didn't have the appropriate shape let alone the appropriate material. It certainly had to have come from the engine. What the hell was it? Hart cautiously stabbed at the headrest again, squirreling his finger around in the foam. To his surprise, he discovered two more pieces similar in characteristics. He rattled the pieces together and then clenched them tightly in his fist.

Retracing his path, Hart exited the airplane. He marched down the air stairs and walked around the front of the nosewheel back over to the right side. Hart slowed his pace. The engine committee members were standing in a loosely organized semicircle around the front of a familiar Jeep underneath the wing's leading edge.

Special Agent Fredricks was leaning against the hood. He was waving an arm at the right engine while speaking in an authoritative tone. Maureen Blackford had arrived and was positioned behind the line of men, listening intently to the FBI man.

This didn't look good. Hart felt the urge to slither away to another part of the investigation, but Matt Mattson beckoned him over to the group. Hart clenched his teeth and walked toward the crowd. Ryan Fredricks discontinued his discussion.

"Ah, Captain Lindy. Thanks for joining us," Ryan said. His tone was slightly patronizing. He grinned. "It appears that we have discovered a potentially interesting bit of evidence.

Evidence that may indicate a crime was committed. And apparently, we owe you some gratitude for bringing it to the attention of the investigation team."

"Uh...would you clarify for me, Special Agent Fredricks?" Hart asked, raising his eyebrows.

"Absolutely, Captain. The item you noticed may very well be a fragment from a cell phone battery."

"No shit?"

"No shit, Captain Lindy."

"What now?"

"That's what we were discussing, actually. I'm thinking of shutting down this investigation to the NTSB."

"Why?"

"It's looking more like a crime scene."

Hart puffed out a deep breath and asked, "May I speak with you and Ms. Blackford for a moment?"

The FBI man nodded. He motioned for Hart and Maureen to step forward toward his Jeep. The line of team members scattered toward the right engine.

"Look, Ryan, I respect your position," Hart said. He shuffled his feet. "You've got great resources here. Let us do our job. I promise we can conduct this investigation to the benefit of the FBI. I'm sure Ms. Blackford would agree." Hart glanced at Maureen. She nodded. "People died on this airplane. It's important that their families know the how and the why. It doesn't matter from our standpoint that the cause appears at the moment to be nefarious. Let us find out for certain."

"Don't go to my emotional side, Captain. I pay my therapist for that." The FBI agent grinned. "You're annoying me a little again. I'll keep this production in NTSB hands for now, but don't screw it up." Ryan snickered and added, "I have a gun."

Hart nodded with a smirk.

The FBI man walked to the driver's side of his Jeep, sat down, and started the car. He offered a cursory wave to Hart and Maureen. As he drove by, he shouted in Arnold Schwarzenegger style, "I'll be bock!"

When Ryan exited through the ramp gate, Maureen shook her head and said, "Nice save, Captain Lindy. I'm impressed." She gave Hart a coy grin, turned and walked away toward the portable air stairs.

Shrugging his shoulders, Hart trotted toward the engine investigation team. He explained that that the FBI had decided to allow the NTSB to continue the investigation. With varying degrees of emphasis, the men expressed their relief.

Hart looked at Frank and said, "Open your hand, Mr. Chairman." Frank raised his eyebrows and presented his palm. Hart dropped the pieces of metal shrapnel that he had found in the cabin seat into his hand. "Maybe you guys can figure out where in the engine these pieces came from. They were embedded in the headrest of the window seat fatality. I don't think they're compressor or turbine blades."

"Thanks," Frank said. "You may be right."

"Well, gentlemen, apparently I've done enough damage for the day. I'm going back to where I belong…the command center. I'll see you all at the progress meeting."

12:30 EDT

The lunchtime crowd at Shooter's was in its early stages of activity. A small armada of boats was beginning to circle in front of the long dock. The dock guys were scampering about, tying up boats and directing the rafting process. Fenders were being slung over the sides. Lines were being fastened to cleats. A festive mood was punctuated by the enhancement of the tan, bikini-clad women perched on bow decks and brightly colored upholstered seats.

The addition of a forty-five-foot Tiara among the lines of rafted boats was barely noticed. A long-legged blonde and a slinky redhead emerged from the cockpit, receiving the typical leering glances from the drooling throng of men dispersed about the pool area. They paused before taking the next sip from their half-empty Budweiser cans.

The two women were familiar faces…at least to the attendees of the weekend hot bod contest. Their current employer had recruited them directly from the weekend parade of high heels and thongs that strutted across the pool walkway every Saturday and Sunday afternoon. Making the rounds of the R-rated South Florida bathing suit circuit, the beer-soaked men had been a regular part of Amber and Serena's world until a chisel-faced dark-haired man offered them the opportunity to be his personal assistants for an obscene amount of money. And if an occasional romp to a king-size bed was required, that was okay…as long as it didn't involve anything overly kinky.

As the two women waited for Chris, they felt drawn to the party atmosphere that had been their life. Unfortunately, they had work to do. The two pain-in-the-ass high school girls locked in the Tiara's salon were a serious liability. They needed to leave the dock ASAP.

A deep, scratchy voice from behind them said, "Didn't know that the hottest chicks in Lauderdale knew how to drive a boat."

Amber and Serena turned to see a bulky figure with a bald head climb awkwardly over the rail of the express cruiser that was tied alongside them. They smiled at Chris.

Serena said, "Hey, we've got college degrees, big man. Can't you tell that we're putting all that brainpower to good use?"

"Absolutely. But I'd rather see you put those tight asses

to good use instead," Chris said with a sneer.

"You're a pig like the rest of them," Amber said with a grin.

"Thanks, babe," Chris replied with a smile as he jumped onto the boat. His Sperry Topsiders slapped the deck with a pronounced thud. He swiveled on his heels and scooped Serena into a thick arm. He squeezed and gave her an audible kiss on one of her high cheekbones. Chris took a step toward Amber and wrapped both arms around her tiny waist. He hugged and rocked backward, lifting the redhead off her bare feet. He smacked Amber on her glossy lips and then lowered her back to the deck.

"You're late, Mr. Clean," Amber said.

"Last night's job went into overtime," Chris said. He thought of yesterday's infiltration into the gay world. He shuddered. At least he had ended the day on a high note.

"Likely excuse," Amber cooed.

Chris asked, "How's the babysitting going?"

"Not bad," Amber said. "The older sister has more balls than some guys I know. She got a little out of line, but nothing that a little threat from our friends at Smith & Wesson couldn't handle."

"Can't wait to meet them," Chris said with a smirk.

Serena said, "There will be plenty of time for introductions. Let's get out of here before we attract attention."

"You two should have thought of that before you shook that booty in those bikinis."

Serena smiled and bellowed, "Get the bow line, swine!"

"Aye, aye, Captain Blighness," Chris bellowed, saluting.

CHAPTER TWELVE

Saturday
17:30 EDT

Although never officially assigned, the Go-Team participants returned to the same seats they had occupied in the morning, a familiar habit. Conversation in the hotel banquet room buzzed. The atmosphere pulsed with a demeanor more conducive to the original intent of a room designed for festivity. Voices were less subdued and more animated. People's stances were less awkward and more limber. Frowns were less frequent and smiles more abundant.

From the podium, Maureen Blackford called the end-of-the-day progress meeting to order. Voices slowly diminished from a normal tone, to a murmur, and then to complete silence. Reading from a yellow legal pad, the IIC briefed a summary of events. With her briefing complete, she slid the eyeglasses off her nose and held them between her fingers. She twirled them in a slow circle.

Maureen pointed at the chairman of the systems committee. A tall, lanky man in his mid-forties stood and faced the seated crowd. He cleared his throat and began to explain the investigation progress of his team.

"Coordination with DFDR information will confirm the engine fire and its effect on other aircraft systems. It appears that the preliminary finding, without DFDR and CVR input, indicates that the flight crew responded appropriately to multiple emergencies."

The systems chairman paused for a brief moment. He locked eyes with Maureen and said, "The DFDR will most likely substantiate that a cause external to the right engine initiated its destruction."

Maureen raised an eyebrow and asked, "Can you elaborate?"

"Uhh…well…EICAS data that has been downloaded and a one-hundred-hour history of engine parameters logged through the airline's maintenance system offer no evidence that any adverse issues were developing to cause a catastrophic failure."

"Okay, what then?" Maureen asked with a mildly impatient tone.

"We are considering that a high probability exists a source not related to the engine caused an explosion."

"I see…" Maureen glanced at the lectern and grabbed it by the outside edges. "Are you basing this theory on anything related to the information that will be presented by one of the other committees?"

With a solemn tone, the tall, lanky man said, "No, ma'am."

"Okay. Thank you." Maureen turned toward another table. "Witness committee? Chad Levine?"

Chad stood. His knit shirt fit tightly across his chest. The NTSB emblem protruded outward. As he clutched a clipboard, his biceps stretched the elastic band of his short sleeves.

"Ms. Blackford, the witness committee has focused its attention on those passengers that indicated they had direct visual and/or aural exposure to the event. Since the airline immediately arranged for alternate travel routing, our contact with most of them has occurred via phone conversations. We have coordinated with the FBI in regard to the questioning of suspicious passengers." Chad Levine gestured his head at Ryan seated at the table. "Special Agent Fredricks has additional information once my briefing is complete."

Chad continued. "The common denominator seems to be a very sudden event. An explosion of sorts. And a pronounced, one-time vibration that felt as though the airplane made contact with an airborne object; a speed bump in the sky is how one woman described it. In addition, the typical smoke and fire scenario was part of most stories. The passengers seated behind the engine in the aft cabin added credibility to this fact. The flight attendants confirmed many of the passenger accounts. All of this, of course, could be attributed to an engine coming apart internally…but I'll leave the specifics to my colleagues on the other committees."

"As was discussed at the organizational meeting this morning, the captain and the first officer are not available. Although their input will be of great assistance, the CVR is our best source for crew participation. That being said," the committee chairman nodded at Jerome, "our Patriot Airlines Pilots Association member conducted a recorded interview of the first officer, Mike Townsend. The interview gave us a detailed perspective of the event. The conversation has been transcribed."

Chad Levine scanned the banquet room and said, "That's all we have for now. Special Agent Fredricks?"

As Ryan rose from his seat, he pulled the soggy stub of an unlit cigar from his lips. His jumping sailfish shirt hung unbuttoned at his sides. The black T-shirt underneath didn't hide the bulge that rested on top of his belt.

Ryan said, "Let's not beat around the bush here. We all know where this is going. You folks can dot your i's and cross your t's using the appropriate NTSB procedures, but as far as I'm concerned, we're involved with a criminal investigation."

A few sighs were heard. A handful of eyes rolled.

"Look, I apologize for my abrupt social skills. Please understand that I appreciate your expertise. You folks will be invaluable in building our case." Ryan took in a deep breath and exhaled. "Let's talk about what the FBI has discovered thus far." He looked around the room. "First, we detained two passengers with questionable backgrounds. One of these passengers possessed a valid Trinidad passport. He has some criminal history, but mostly robbery arrests- nothing that indicated a connection with an organized group.

"The other detained passenger was born in Saudi Arabia but possessed a British passport. His business card lists him as a computer software marketing director for a London-based company. We've checked with our British counterparts and it appears that the company is legitimate, but…his frequent visits to a mosque that has bred Al-Qaeda soldiers have got people's attention. Although he hasn't made the no-fly list roster yet, that possibility may become a reality in the not too distant future. We are currently working with the Trinidad authorities to verify his activities over the last several weeks."

"Thanks to Captain Lindy, we are tracking another individual who arrived from Miami on the same flight as the pilot investigation team. It turns out that this individual must have been traveling under an alias. His seat assignment matched a passport ID, but a database search tied the name to a very recently deceased U.S. citizen. We believe this individual returned to the States via a flight to JFK. His movements are being tracked. He may have been involved in the assault on Flight 63's captain."

Seats clattered with the sound of people shifting their position. A murmured conversation began among one of the tables.

The FBI man said, "That's all I have for now, folks. Please communicate any pertinent information that you discover to your committee chairman or myself. And remember, the information discussed is confidential. Please don't even discuss this with your significant others. Thanks." Ryan nodded at Maureen as he plopped down onto his chair.

Separately, the committee chairmen from the airframe group and the cabin group stood and discussed their portion of the investigation. Their briefings were predictable and short in duration by virtue of the fact that most of the investigators from other teams had already taken the opportunity to tour the destruction inside the cabin. And when it came to the airframe structure, that mess was visible to everybody.

Without looking up from her notes, Maureen called for the chairman of the engine committee. She added, "I saved the busiest committee for last."

Frank rose from his chair. His movements were stiff and awkward. He conveyed a tangible nervousness. He raised a battered clipboard to his line of sight.

"As many of you may already know, our unofficial findings of the right side GE CF6 'dash' 80 engine indicate a catastrophic event occurred internally. We have found no evidence of foreign object damage. And as mentioned by the systems committee, historic analysis shows no signs of irregular operation."

The engine committee chairman wiped his brow with the back of a hand. He continued. "The destruction of numerous fan blades, compressor blades, and turbine blades accounted for the instantaneous engine failure." He dropped the clipboard to his side and looked at the IIC. "A fragment of a cell phone battery was found lodged against a stator vane. The battery's position suggested that it had been ejected forward from within the engine. Additionally, shrapnel material that was discovered embedded in the seat of the window fatality had its origins from the accessory drive area. When the mechanics remove the engine from..."

With a solemn expression, Maureen interrupted. "I think that we're all following you. Can you cut to the chase?"

Frank nodded. He cleared his throat, shuffled his feet, and looked at the floor. He began to open his mouth, but was interrupted again, this time by Matt Mattson.

Matt began to rise from his seat. He glanced at his committee chairman and asked, "May I?"

With a relieved expression, Frank nodded.

Matt said, "Thank you." He turned to look at Maureen. "Ms. Blackford, it appears that a device was detonated in very close proximity to the IDG. It was most likely activated remotely via a cell phone or sat phone. End of story."

The room was enveloped by the sound of whispering. All eyes focused on the IIC at the podium.

Rubbing her forehead with one hand, Maureen asked, "You're telling us that an external explosion near the integrated drive generator blew the engine apart as opposed to an explosion that originated from the engine itself?"

"We believe so," Matt said. "At the moment, we can find no other logical explanation."

"Thank you, sir. I appreciate your candor."

Matt nodded at both Maureen and the committee chairman. In a slow movement, he slid back onto his chair. He searched the back of the room and found Hart seated at a table near the back wall. Hart displayed a thumbs-up. Matt nodded with a somber expression.

As Maureen emphasized the need to continue following NTSB policy and procedure despite the preliminary findings, Hart contemplated the speech to his team at the command center. The investigation was taking an interesting turn.

A familiar voice from behind Hart's shoulder interrupted his thoughts. "Captain Lindy, I need to talk with you."

Hart turned to find Ryan Fredricks crouching on one knee behind him. Ryan gestured toward the exit door at the corner of the banquet room. Hart scanned the room and then slithered away, following the FBI man out the door.

When the two men were in the corridor, Ryan said, "Come with me to my room, Captain." Sensing a quip from Hart, Ryan added, "Don't get any ideas, fly boy. Pilots aren't my type. You guys have bigger egos than the CIA guys."

Hart grinned and said, "I promise not to kiss and tell."

Ryan shook his head and rolled his eyes. In silence, the two men walked down the adjacent hallway and into Ryan's ground level room. When the door clacked closed, the FBI agent slid the chain into place. He walked over to the bleached wicker desk resting against the far wall and sat down. Ryan pressed the power button on his Mac laptop. He made a few adjustments and stood up. He motioned for Hart to be seated.

Hart looked at the laptop screen as he sat down. A low quality color video of a Patriot Airlines 767 mated to a jet bridge was displayed. The vantage point of the camera appeared to be directed from roof level toward the nose of the airplane. The entire airliner, except for a portion around the left wing was visible.

"Do you recognize the airplane?" Ryan asked.

Hart studied the frozen scene for a moment. He read the N-number printed on the nosewheel door. Hart nodded.

Ryan said, "It's the accident airplane. It's the accident airplane approximately one hour prior to gate departure."

"Okay," Hart acknowledged.

"This is the security video. I'm not going to say a word. I want you to watch. I would like your professional pilot opinion on what you see."

"This isn't a musical, is it? I hate musicals," Hart chided, masking an uncomfortable feeling in the pit of his stomach."

"No, it's worse than a musical," Ryan responded dryly. He moved the cursor over the play selection and clicked.

Ryan reached into his shirt pocket and pulled out two cigars in cellophane wrappers. “Cigar?”

Hart raised his eyebrows and said, “Really? In the room? The hotel staff must love you.” Hart reached for a cigar, unwrapped it, and brought it to his lips. “Thanks.”

“Everybody tolerates a man with a gun and a badge,” Ryan said. He flicked his lighter underneath the end of Hart’s cigar.

As the room began to haze with white smoke, Hart focused on the security video. A few seconds passed, and then a pilot with three stripes on his epaulets emerged from the side jet bridge door. The pilot walked down the grated stairs to the ramp. Hart understood the familiar scene. It was the copilot. He was beginning the walk-around inspection.

The copilot walked in front of the nose of the 767. He paused for a moment and then in a methodical pattern continued his tour, following the footprint perimeter of the wide-body airplane. The copilot paused every few feet to peer at the next section of the 767, a typical procedure. A handful of minutes later, the copilot reached the outboard side of the right engine. He stopped. In one fluid motion, Hart watched as the copilot pressed the latches of the IDG access panel, opened the door and just as quickly closed it.

Hart felt his chest pound. He could feel his adrenalin level rise. The image of the copilot continuing to plod around the airplane remained on the screen. It didn’t matter. Hart’s vision was unfocused. His mind raced. Shit! This couldn’t be…

Like a train that had been traveling at high speed suddenly stopping at a station, the video froze. Hart hadn’t noticed that the FBI man had leaned over his shoulder and paused the action.

“You saw it didn’t you?”

Regaining his composure, Hart asked, “Saw what?”

"Don't screw with me, Hart. The IDG access panel. That's part of the reason I was out at the airplane this afternoon. Your team told me what it was. Flight 63's copilot opened it."

"Yeah, and…"

"Is that normal procedure for a preflight inspection?"

"Not every pilot inspects that area. No, it's not a requirement."

"I looked into your background at the airline. You were a check airman on the 767. Did you instruct your guys and gals to open that panel?"

"No, I didn't…but other check airman might have."

"Look, don't bullshit me. My understanding is that the access panel is a maintenance function."

Folding his arms across his chest, Hart looked at Ryan and said, "What do you want me to say?"

"Okay, I had a feeling it was going to play out this way." Ryan took a puff of his cigar. He directed the smoke toward the floor. "I like your sorry ass, Captain Lindy. And I respect you for trying to protect one of your own. But this is how it's going to work." Ryan grinned. "I'm going to give you forty-eight hours. If you give me a better explanation, I'll back away from your copilot as a suspect." He took another long puff on his cigar. "But if you withhold information from me, I'll shoot you as promised and then have you arrested for interfering with a federal investigation. Clear?"

"What happened to the new and improved FBI?" Hart asked with a sly smile.

"Don't press your luck when you're on my good side, Captain."

Ryan walked over to a dresser and grabbed the bottle of Dewars that had been sitting on top. He twisted open the cap and poured the caramel liquid into two separate plastic water cups. He handed a cup to Hart.

"Cheers, my friend," Ryan said as he tapped his cup to Hart's. "Here's to crime fighters and pilots everywhere."

20:05 EDT

The foggy numbness in Mike's head was attributable to fatigue. The evening's two glasses of merlot had virtually no effect other than to act as a mild tranquilizer. He had once again been unsuccessful at a nap. The bed had served only as a relief from the exertion of pacing. Regardless of his energy level, it was important that Mike focus. He had formulated a plan.

A glance out his kitchen window offered a positive sign. All but one news station van had departed the neighborhood. And only one patrol car was parked in the driveway. Mike took a sip of coffee. He would have to make a rapid exit.

Peeking into the master bedroom, a place he hadn't occupied for months, Mike caught a glimpse of Robin. She was sprawled across the king-size bed, her face almost completely buried in an overstuffed pillow. He was amazed that she was asleep. She must be exhausted, he thought.

He sighed and walked quietly down the hallway out the French doors to the dock. He carried a small duffle bag. He could feel the weight of the .45 caliber Glock at the bottom underneath his extra clothes. He hoped not to employ its use.

Mike walked at a brisk pace toward the boat. The thirty-six-foot Sea Ray express cruiser creaked as it rocked against the pilings. The white hull was dull and chalky. He felt a twinge of guilt. He had bought the boat before Ashley was born. It had been part of the family. Fishing. Overnights. Vacations. Restaurant hopping.

But now that the girls had grown older, other interests took precedence. Neglect had taken its toll. For the past two years, Mike's primary activity with the boat was only to start the two cranky, gas-guzzling engines. His hope now was that they wouldn't fail him.

He sat down on the railing at the aft end of the boat and swung his feet inside onto the deck. He shuffled to the cockpit, pumped the left throttle, and turned the left ignition key. The engine thumped and whined, finally uttering a throaty warble as it came to life. White smoke blossomed from the exhaust, curling up over the transom. The right engine offered the same resistance, sputtering as its rpm increased to idle.

"Yes!" Mike whispered to himself. He clenched a fist and shook it at the deck underneath where the engines lived.

He jumped off the boat and untied the lines, leaving them scattered on the dock. He jumped back on the boat, hopped onto the cockpit bench seat, and pushed both transmission levers forward. Within moments, Mike and the Sea Ray were motoring down his neighborhood canal toward the Intracoastal.

With the boat steering straight ahead, Mike dug into his pocket and slid out his iPhone. He slid his finger across the screen and tapped the Sprint Family Locator icon.

Mike had used the tracking program more as a safety net then a snitching tool…although he did eventually admit to Robin that the program was useful in verifying his oldest daughter's location. He had caught her in a typical teenage lie just last week. Kim claimed to have been visiting her girlfriend. The tracking program had proved that she was located two neighborhoods in the opposite direction…at her boyfriend's home.

Not wanting to reveal the source of his information, Mike smiled when Kim walked through the front door. He asked how his daughter's day had gone with the girlfriend. She averted his eyes and simply said, "Fine." Mike chuckled to himself. He conveyed the story to Robin later that evening. Robin had grinned and then no longer expressed resistance to Mike's cyberspying.

Like most kids, Kim was a savvy iPhone user. She knew how to temporarily disable the Find My iPhone app. Mike caught on to her wisdom on a handful of occasions when her phone location disappeared off the grid. The Sprint program did the trick.

And now Mike would be using the program to rescue his daughters. Involving the cops would make things complicated. The chilling phone call he had received in Bermuda was motivation enough. It was a page right from the script of a bad TV movie. But he wasn't going to take a chance.

He had turned on his iPad last night and found a cell phone signal…but it wasn't Kim's. The signal was from Ashley's phone. That fact disturbed him. Why hadn't he found Kim's signal also? Her phone was always at her side. Was she okay? He had kept the phone purchase for Ashley a secret from Robin. Mike had given it to her before the agreed-upon birthday. But Ashley was an A-student…and her maturity level often exceeded those of girls ten years older. She deserved the phone.

The signal location was curious, indicating that the girls were not on land. If the location was accurate, it appeared the phone was located just offshore from Fort Lauderdale. Initially, the location made no sense. But then Mike understood. That rich chisel-jawed bastard was probably using that flashy Tiara to abduct the girls. He had met the arrogant prick and his boat months prior.

The Tiara had been tied up against the dock during the Shooter's hot bod contest. The day was sizzling enough to distort the air above the pool deck into visible shimmers. The asshole was sitting shirtless, sandwiched between three or four overly tanned thong-bikini-clad women. The bikinis did little to hide the finest in Florida plastic surgery.

When he saw Mike approach, the chiseled-jaw guy dismissed the bikini girls with a wave of his hand. The two men sat alone underneath an umbrella that hovered over the top of a round, plastic table. The conversation with Mike was condescending and brief. Mike left with a bad taste in his mouth.

The memory of the bastard's pristine boat and his pompous attitude had remained. Mike clenched his jaw. Nothing mattered now except for bringing his daughters home safely. He had narrowed their location. They were about a mile off the beach, opposite the Oakland Street Bridge.

But first Mike would pick up Jonathan near Los Olas. He would need his partner's help…and his encouragement.

20:25 EDT

Writing reports was an activity that Hart would just as soon leave to secretaries and college freshmen. When the phone rang in his room, he was glad for the distraction. He yanked the handset off the cradle with zest.

"Hart Lindy."

"Hey, Hart. It's Anne at PAPA headquarters." Her voice held her typical cheery tone but it was uncharacteristically guarded.

"I know I haven't screwed up an expense report because I'm yet to file one. To what do I owe this pleasure…and after business hours nonetheless? "

"Well…I'm not sure that you're going to consider it a pleasure after you hear what I have to say."

"It's okay. I've had my second adult beverage."

"Do you know anything about the law firm of Horton and Carty?"

"Don't think so. Should I?" Hart asked.

Anne said, "If you recall, the board of directors passed a resolution last month to conduct monthly internal audits of union expense disbursements. It's part of the belt-tightening initiative. I started an informal audit yesterday. I found something curious."

"Does it involve my group?"

"Not from an expense perspective." Anne took a breath. "It may relate to your investigation."

"You've got my attention," Hart said.

"Apparently, a number of wire transfers in various amounts have been going to Horton and Carty. The transfers have flowed in that direction for almost a year. Interestingly enough, the transfers seem to have been disbursed within a couple of days after a deposit for the same amount. Sometimes the transfers are multiples of the total deposit, unequally divided."

Anne cleared her throat and continued. "The law firm has an office in New York and in Port of Spain, Trinidad. The money leaving PAPA headquarters has been going to Trinidad. The firm will be providing legal counsel in anticipation of potential bankruptcy proceedings with the airline. The board of directors approved a retainer expense."

Hart said, "Interesting…but other than the fact that Flight 63 departed Port of Spain, how does this relate to our investigation?"

"The wire transfers were authorized by our secretary/treasurer."

"Mike Townsend? The copilot on Flight 63?" Hart asked.

"None other."

"Nobody else noticed these wire transfers until now? How can that be? What happened to membership transparency?"

"The secretary/treasurer is responsible for monitoring all transactions and expenses."

"Great system. Only one person is in charge. I think

the by-laws need to be rewritten." Hart exhaled a deep breath. "But you indicated that the wire transfers were of equal amounts to the deposits. If it's embezzlement, that's a strange technique."

"My thoughts exactly," the union secretary said.

"Have you provided this information to anyone else, Anne?" Hart asked.

"Not just yet."

"What's the chance that you could keep this under your hat for a little while? I need to sort out some details with this investigation."

Anne said, "I can give you another couple of days. The official audit has to be submitted in time for the special board of directors meeting."

"Thanks, that's all I should need."

"Hart, one last thing."

"I'm not sitting down, so go easy," Hart said with a sigh.

"The last deposit to our PAPA account was made within a week of the accident. It was about $5 million, the largest this year. The next wire transfers out of the account went to the Horton and Carty Law Firm. As you probably guessed, the disbursements occurred within a few days. They totaled $5 million, almost to the penny."

"This just keeps getting better. Five million? Seems to me that's above and beyond a retainer…even for a New York law firm." Hart thought for a moment. "Any idea how much of this particular account has made its way down to Port of Spain?"

"I'm crunching the numbers now. But I'd guess close to $35 million."

"Nice," Hart said.

"Yeah, I thought you would be impressed."

"Anne, I appreciate the call. I'll be in touch."

"My pleasure," Anne said.

Hart heard a click on the line. He replaced the handset in the cradle and shook his head. The vision of Mike Townsend opening the jet engine's IDG access panel ran through his head.

"This is not good," Hart muttered to himself.

CHAPTER THIRTEEN

Saturday
21:30 EDT

She looked through the bedroom window out at the empty dock. The moon wasn't quite full, but its silver luminescence was enough to shower the canal side of the backyard with a white glow.

Robin remembered sultry summer nights on the boat gazing at a similar scene. Kim and Ashley were barely out of diapers. Robin and Mike would wrap them with blankets on the bench seats that surrounded the cockpit, a place they loved almost as much as the bow. When the giggling stopped, the girls would fall fast asleep. Robin and Mike shared the day's stories and their dreams over a bottle of cheap merlot.

Had she been living a lie with the man she loved all this time? Where were the fucking signs? Was it something she had done…or something she hadn't done? And where the hell was he anyhow?

The boat was gone. In the middle of this crisis, he had decided to go for a cruise. Great. She wasn't that surprised. The boat had always been Mike's therapy. The last time he had taken it out for any length of time was when the airline had negotiated with the union for a 25 percent pay cut… among other things…to avoid bankruptcy. He was thinking of the mortgage and the MasterCard bill, and all the other debts that were barely being paid. And he was thinking of the tuition when he sent the girls to college. That was almost a year ago.

But Mike had never stayed out past dark. She hadn't heard his departure from the dock. Even through closed windows, the rumble of those old engines was unmistakable. She must have finally passed out. Before Mike had arrived home, despite her exhaustion, insomnia had been winning the battle over sleep. This time she'd had enough. The little blue pills came out of the medicine cabinet.

Still a little groggy, Robin shuffled from the bedroom hallway into the kitchen. She brewed some tea. She took a slow sip and peered out the kitchen window. A patrol car was parked in the driveway. Through the glow of the dashboard lights inside the car, she could see the silhouette of the officer in the driver's seat. One lonely TV news station van was perched on the other side of the street.

The crowd of strangers outside the house was gone. The blinding blue police lights no longer reflected off the side of the garage doors. Other than the occasional bark of a neighborhood dog, all was quiet. It appeared that the world was losing interest in the disappearance of her daughters and her hero husband who helped land a fiery airplane.

Robin shook her head and set her mug down on the counter with a thwack. Some of the tea splashed over the rim and onto the tile surface.

"Screw him!" Robin said out loud to the kitchen refrigerator. "I'm not dealing with this alone!" She took a few strides to the other end of the kitchen island and grabbed her purse. Robin fished her hand inside the purse and retrieved her cell phone. She pushed a speed dial button and waited. She pressed the phone hard against her ear.

The ringing continued until Robin heard Mike's voice-mail message. She cringed. She hated the rhythm of his DJ-like greeting. It sounded condescending and shallow.

She waited for the beep and then said, "This isn't the

time for a boat cruise. Where the hell are you? Call me back if it's not too much trouble."

Robin mashed the End button with her thumb and tossed the cell phone onto the kitchen counter. It clacked as it slid. He was ignoring her calls. Bastard!

Maybe something was actually wrong. Should she contact the detective? Robin stared at her cell phone again. Why the hell not? She pulled the cop's business card out from beneath the magnet on the refrigerator and entered the number into her phone. She pressed the Send button. A number of rings later, Robin prepared to leave a message. But a familiar voice finally answered.

"Alvarez here," the voice said. The detective's speech was distorted. He was chewing and talking.

"Detective Alvarez, this is Robin Townsend. I hope it's not a bad time."

The sound of clattering silverware wafted from the background.

"No, not at all," he said with a squishy snap as he chewed his last bite. "Your call might get me out of doing the dishes."

Robin took a deep breath and said, "I may be overreacting, but Mike…well…he disappeared on our boat. I had taken some sleeping pills. I was probably comatose because I didn't hear him start the engines…and he's…he's not answering his cell phone. I woke up about an hour ago."

"Mrs. Townsend, you did the right thing. Are you still at home?"

"Yes."

"Stay there, please. I'll be right over."

The phone went silent. Robin glanced at the phone's background display of last year's family Christmas portrait. Mike's smile in the photo now appeared forced. The screen displayed "Disconnected." She felt her eyes begin to fill with tears. She gritted her teeth knowing that beyond the emotion, another bout of stinging and burning was next. Her eyes had drained out more tears than she thought humanly possible. Why couldn't she wake up from this nightmare?

Having the need to focus on accomplishing some type of task, Robin reached for the mountainous stack of mail at the end of the kitchen counter. She began to sort the envelopes of junk mail into a pile. The chore was brainless, but somehow it soothed her anxiety.

A few minutes later, as Robin scooped envelopes into the tall trash can, a pair of headlights appeared in the driveway next to the patrol car. The lampposts outside bathed the nondescript sedan in yellow light. The driver's side door opened, and the round shape of Detective Alvarez stepped onto the dark pavement. He walked around the front bumper toward the patrol car.

21:55 EDT

The uniformed cop in the patrol car emerged from the darkness. He greeted Alvarez with a warm smile. The two men shook hands.

"Sorry, Detective. I must have been in transit to replace the last uniform that was on duty here at the Townsend house. I missed Mr. Townsend's exit," the uniformed cop said.

"No big deal, Tom. I've got Marine Patrol on the lookout. We'll find him. I just want to know what the hell he's up to in the damn boat."

Tom nodded and said, "Understood."

Alvarez folded his arms across his chest and leaned back against his car. He asked, "So…your phone call got me curious. What you got?"

"I did some snooping around at the high school. Got some of the kids to talk. They're reliable types. A-students. Lacrosse team. Baseball team." Tom slapped a mosquito that had landed on his forearm. “Anyhow…our vice principal is just not adding up.”

“Tracey Abbott? How so?”

“She’s got a girlfriend.”

“That doesn’t surprise me,” Alvarez responded.

“I know…I know. Being a lesbian is underwhelming info in this town, but there’s more to the story.”

“Well, it does beg the question on an ulterior motive regarding her relationship with Mrs. Townsend. I don’t get the impression that the pilot’s wife swings that direction.”

“That’s part of my story, because the VP didn’t begin a relationship with Mrs. Townsend until about a month ago.”

Alvarez sighed, swatted at an airborne mosquito, and said, “Tom, I spent the other day scouring the security video. I’ve got two student witnesses to the homicide abduction. Unbeknownst to them, they were stars of their own parking lot porn film. The two students offered Tracey Abbott as another witness. Apparently, at some point prior to all hell breaking loose, she was receiving something in an envelope by the corner of the building hidden from the cameras. According to one of the porn stars, she had been receiving these envelopes on a few prior occasions.”

“Interesting,” Tom said, smoothing his wavy brown hair with his hand.

“Last night I missed my wife’s Cuban pork roast.” Alvarez patted his protruding belly. “Instead of adding more shape to my figure, my eyes were bleeding at the office. I was looking at security footage. I’m trying to find the car that belonged to this unshaven, skinny guy that made the delivery to the vice principal.”

“Don’t damage your retinas anymore. Betcha the skinny guy drove a black Mercedes,” Tom said with a smile.

Alvarez narrowed his eyes and said, “I’m listening.”

“That’s the reason I brought the girlfriend thing up.

The kids that I talked to would open the back gym door for fresh air while they practiced. At the end of the day they had occasionally seen Tracey Abbott climb into the back seat of a black Mercedes. She would throw a big lip lock on a redhead that was already sitting in the back."

"Wait…let me guess. The driver of the Mercedes was an unshaven, skinny guy," Alvarez said, shaking his head.

"That's why you're the detective."

"I'll be damned. Nice work, Tom. Maybe I can have you out of that uniform soon."

"Maybe. Not sure homicide is my gig though."

"It grows on you," Alvarez said with a smirk. "Anyhow… I've been looking at the wrong time frame to try and find a license plate. I never considered going beyond normal school hours."

"Let me know when you get a good plate number. I'll run it."

Alvarez nodded. He looked at the front entrance of the Townsend house and said, "Duty calls inside. Maybe Ms. Townsend has more information than she admits." The detective reached out his hand and shook with the uniformed cop. "Thanks for your help, Tom." Alvarez began to walk away.

Tom smiled and said, "Keep me in the loop, Detective, if you don't mind. Writing speeding tickets for my high school seniors is what I live for, but a change of pace is always welcome."

"Will do, Tom," Alvarez said, waving a raised hand.

22:55 EDT

Staring unfocused at the black water of the canal, Mike took a bite of his mahi-mahi sandwich. Even though the meal was one of his favorites, it was cold and tasteless. The waitress at the Southport Raw Bar had made her rounds through the clutter of outside tables at least three times to check on his status. On each occasion, Mike's plate showed no evidence of activity. His brain was preoccupied, drifting in a haze of confusion.

Southport Raw Bar was his refuge. Familiar surroundings. Familiar faces. He was incapable of any form of decision process other than to drive a boat and consume food. In a robotic trance he had tied up the Sea Ray at the restaurant an hour ago. He couldn't stay where he had been on the New River, or anywhere near Los Olas Boulevard. Mike needed time to breathe, to consider his options. He never envisioned the horror he had found at Jonathan's place.

After escaping from home, Mike had motored up the New River. He was excited at having located his daughters via the GPS program. The prospect that he would be able to recruit Jonathan for the rescue was even more encouraging. And even more so, he would have Jonathan's attention for the remainder of his plan. Despite the setback with his daughters, the plan would still prove successful.

Mike had tied up at an open spot along the city dock. Ignoring the tourist circus of Riverwalk, he strode directly toward Jonathan's restaurant on Los Olas Boulevard. When Mike turned the corner from the side street, the usual flow of sunburned, T-shirted people was interrupted by a barrage of green and white Broward Sheriff's Office patrol cars and motorcycles. The police activity surrounded almost the entire block of the restaurant.

A small platoon of BSO cops and plainclothes men with short haircuts bustled around the entrance. A sinking feeling began to envelope Mike's stomach. Where was Jonathan?

A crowd of curiosity seekers had formed, eyes wide, darting their focus around the outside of the restaurant. With cautious steps, Mike walked over to the crowd. He blended into the mass of people from behind. He listened to the murmured conversation.

Never showed up for work. Gay basher. Questioning employees. Body recovered in a dumpster. Pieces.

After a few minutes of eavesdropping, Mike's anxiety level began to peak. He dreaded asking the obvious question, but it was unavoidable. He tapped a white-haired woman on the shoulder. She turned.

"Who was it? Do you know?" Mike asked in a strained whisper.

The woman shrugged her shoulders and said, "I think it was the owner of this place." She pointed at the open door of the restaurant. "He was shot in his own townhouse down the street. The cops are questioning the staff."

It took only a moment for Mike's vision to narrow. The world became gray. He leaned against the post of a street sign, hoping it would support him while his knees resumed their normal function in keeping him upright. He turned away from the crowd.

Maybe the information was inaccurate. How would anybody really know unless they were cops? The thought gave him enough comfort to regain his composure. Perhaps a visit to Jonathan's townhouse would prove the information wrong. Mike slithered away from the madness at the restaurant and walked west on Los Olas.

It wasn't long before Mike's hopes began to shatter. A similar scene to the restaurant was unfolding a few blocks away. More BSO uniforms. More patrol cars. Yellow police tape. And this time the non-uniform types were wearing latex gloves.

As he slowed his pace to a crawl, Mike peered up six levels to the top floor and Jonathan's kitchen windows. A silhouette of figures seemed to be moving back and forth within the townhouse. Mike stopped at the corner. It was pointless to continue any further. The cops were obviously conducting an investigation. His worst fears were confirmed. Mike took a few steps toward a newly painted park bench. He sat down and dropped his head into cupped hands.

Unaware of how much time had passed, Mike rose from the park bench. In a mind-numbing fog of thoughts, he walked back to the boat still docked on the New River. As much as he wanted to just sit and try to further absorb the situation, he had to maintain the momentum. Inaction would render him useless. He had to move forward. And soon, the cops would connect him to Jonathan. But where would he go?

Surprisingly enough, his stomach was protesting with periodic rumbling. Mike hadn't eaten since chomping on a stale bagel at breakfast time. Food would help him think. Southport Raw Bar was the only idea that made its way into his limited decision process. The restaurant was a local's hangout, a frequent boat stop for Mike and the girls. Kim and Ashley loved the conch fritters. The girls treated the fritters like an exotic delicacy. And the place was hidden at the end of a long canal. It made perfect sense.

Before he left the dock on the New River, Mike stepped down below into the salon. He needed a drink to take the edge off his nerves. He grabbed a plastic tumbler from the cabinet above the sink. He scooped up a handful of ice from a small Playmate cooler and dumped it into the tumbler. Mike pulled out a bottle of gin and poured the clear liquid into the glass. He closed his eyes and took a few sips.

And now, as Mike took the last couple of bites of his sandwich at Southport Raw Bar, the low visibility in his mind began to clear. He had only one decision to make. It was simple. He would find his girls and return them home safe and sound. And then he would face the consequences of his actions.

Mike slid the iPhone out from his pocket. He drew in a deep breath. He began to type a text message. Mike stared at his words for a moment. Satisfied, he pressed the Send button. Hopefully the message would reach both Kim and Ashley in time.

Picking a french fry off his plate, Mike took a small bite. He stared at his Sea Ray. The wake of a center console boat that had just left the adjacent slip lapped against the hull of the express cruiser. The rub rails creaked against the wooden piling of the dock. Mike sighed. It was time to go.

He reached into his pocket and pulled out a few bills. He shoved the money into the check wallet that the waitress had dropped off over an hour ago. Mike rose from the table and walked a few steps down to the dock. He climbed into the boat and started the engines. He untied the lines from the pilings and then resumed his position at the helm seat. He slid both transmission levers into forward gear.

As he turned the boat south on the Intracoastal, Mike gazed upward at the night sky. The moon was glowing like the sun. The glow would be helpful and a handicap at the same time. The silvery brightness would assist in his navigation out the Port Everglades inlet and in his ability to locate the boat where his daughters were held hostage. But the natural illumination would make his arrival easier to detect. It didn't matter. Somehow he would make it work.

Sunday

00:05 EDT

He glanced at the digital alarm clock on the nightstand next to the bed. The blue numbers glowed "12:05." Hart sighed and clicked the power button on the remote. The color images on the flat screen TV faded to black. He had been watching a mindless romantic comedy. The name of the movie escaped him. He didn't care. Hart was using the TV as a sedative, hoping that his most recent yawn was a positive sign for sleep.

He closed his eyes. Seconds later he heard tapping. Was it his door? Couldn't be… It was too late. The tapping started again, slightly louder than the first time. Crap! The sound *was* at his door. Hart slid off the bed and reached for a pair of jeans he had tossed over the back of a chair. He pulled the jeans on, took a step toward the door, and then stopped.

Remembering the beating that Flight 63's captain took last night, Hart didn't want to be the second victim. He scanned the room for an impromptu weapon. His eyes found an iron on the top shelf of the closet. He walked over to the shelf, grabbed the iron, and wrapped the cord around his wrist.

With cautious steps, Hart moved to the door. He peered through the viewing port. The hallway was empty. Only the closed door of the room opposite him could be seen. Should he investigate? His curiosity was getting the best of him. Hart tightened his grip on the handle of the iron. He took a step backward and opened the door. He raised his weapon to shoulder height. He braced for a human form to rush toward him. Nothing…

What the hell…? He waited. Still nothing. Hart took a deep breath and began to close the door. He heard a faint shuffle. He moved his feet to a wide stance and drew back with the iron as though he was about to swing a baseball bat one-handed. The figure of a woman appeared in the opening at the threshold.

"Nice," Maureen Blackford said as she moved her gaze from Hart's bare chest to the iron in his hand. "I love a half-dressed man who gets the wrinkles out in the middle of the night. I would have brought a few of my blouses over had I known."

With a heavy sigh, Hart released the tension in his muscles. He shook his head and said, "Shit, Maureen. I thought I was going to have to wrestle the same nasty guy that our captain had to deal with last night."

"Sorry. My bad." Maureen said with a coy smile. Her perfectly aligned white teeth sparkled even in the dim light. "Are you going to let me in…or do you need to take a nitroglycerin pill?"

"Maybe not nitroglycerin, but a martini might help. Come in."

Hart shuffled his bare feet backward and closed the door behind Maureen as she glided into the room. He dropped the iron on the dresser. Maureen leaned against the end of the couch. Her form-fitted jeans followed the curve of her hips. The jeans contrasted with the T-shirt that hung loosely off her shoulders. The shirt did nothing to hide the soft shape of her breasts beneath. A bra was absent.

Hart surveyed Maureen, making no attempt to disguise his focus. He smirked and asked, "I assume this visit concerns the investigation?"

"You *are* an asshole," Maureen murmured.

She slithered over to Hart and wrapped her arms around his neck. She pulled him toward her, meeting his lips. She enveloped his mouth with hers. She moaned in quiet gasps. Hart squeezed Maureen closer. He reached his hands behind her waist and pulled the T-shirt up and over her head.

With a dreamy smile, Maureen moved a hand between their fused bodies and over Hart's zipper. With a gentle tug, she pulled the zipper lower. She slid her fingers into Hart's jeans and began to caress his hardening penis.

Hart smiled and whispered, "I thought we had checked off the sexual tension square. Are you still tense?"

Maureen grinned, "Not only am I very tense, but I need

to punish you for your procedural improprieties."

"I thought my admonishment at the progress meeting was my punishment."

"I work differently than other government employees," Maureen said as she pushed Hart toward the bed."

Hart chuckled and then allowed Maureen to give him a shove onto the mattress. She slithered on top of him. Hart reached into her jeans, feeling her soft bottom. He began to gently pry her pants lower. Maureen moaned. Their bodies writhed together, their lips intertwined.

When the phone rang, the sound initially melted into the passion of the moment as if part of a dream. It took a couple of rings for Hart to comprehend that the intrusive sound was a reality. He grunted and lay still. Maureen slowed the undulating motion of her hips, her hair flowing across Hart's chest.

Maureen sighed and said, "Really? Now?"

Hart shook his head and said, "Sorry. At this hour…and the way things have been going…my guess is that it's not somebody about to tell me that my lottery numbers hit."

With a groan, Maureen rolled to Hart's side. She allowed him enough room to stretch over her and reach the phone by the nightstand.

Fumbling, Hart put the receiver to his ear and said, "Hart Lindy."

The familiar voice at the other end of the line said, "Sorry to call so late."

"Cathy? Are you okay?"

Hart glanced at Maureen with raised eyebrows. Maureen offered a look of resignation and then buried her head in a pillow.

"I'm okay now. I just wanted you to be aware of something," Cathy said, her voice indicating strain. "How's your investigation going?"

"Let's just say that it's been interesting." Hart took in a breath. "Forget that. What's up with you?"

"Well…it's over now, but today was a little scary."

"Okay. I'm listening."

"I was running around all day. And almost everywhere I went, the same creepy guy was in the immediate vicinity. Winn Dixie. Macy's. The gas station. I know he was watching me." Cathy paused for a moment. "When I got home, this freak parked his yuppie Mercedes at the end of the driveway."

Hart cringed and asked, "Did he try anything, Cath?"

"No…no. He just stared for a few seconds and then rolled down his window. The freak grinned at me like he was taking off my skirt with his eyes. I was thinking that I shouldn't have showed that much leg for just running errands around town. And then I got up the courage to ask him what he wanted."

"And…?"

"He said that he wanted nothing except to give me a warning." Cathy's voice cracked slightly.

Almost certain of the answer, Hart drew in a deep breath and asked, "What was the warning?"

"For you to leave the investigation in Bermuda alone… or…or…bad things would happen to us."

"I'm sorry, Cath."

"It's not your fault."

"Well, in a way it is." Hart glanced at Maureen. She had rolled to her side and was looking at him with the one piercing, brown eye that wasn't covered by her cascading hair. "I didn't want to give you cause for concern, but I did receive a threatening phone call en route to the airport." Hart thought it best to leave out the paintball episode on I-95.

Cathy asked, "Did the phone call involve me?"

"Indirectly. But I didn't take it seriously."

"It's okay."

Hart began to feel a twinge of guilt rise in his chest. He said, "It's not okay, Cath. I have an FBI connection here in Bermuda. I could have been more proactive and had the agent make the appropriate phone calls." Hart had a momentary spike of resentment. Why hadn't Fredricks taken the initiative? After all, the man had already been aware of the I-95 incident. And what happened to Rod's cop friend who was supposed to keep an eye on Cathy? Were the two of them out golfing again? He'd deal with that later.

"Hart, I'm okay. I called the cops. They'll be keeping an eye on me and the house for a while."

"Good." Hart rubbed his forehead and stared at the ceiling, deliberately trying to avoid eye contact with Maureen. "Cath, what did the guy look like?"

"I gave the cops a description. I couldn't see much through the guy's open car window. He was driving a black Mercedes with overly tinted windows. He looked skinny. Unshaven. Some kind of accent."

Shit! The prick was supposed to have flown to New York from Bermuda according to Fredricks. How did the bastard end up back in Miami? Fucking FBI! Are they doing their jobs?

Cathy asked, "Hart, are you still there?" She paused. "Hart…you are alone aren't you?"

Hart closed his eyes and shook his head. It took only seconds for him to reply, but he knew it was probably too long. "Yes, Cath. I'm alone."

"Okay."

Hart said, "Our work here in Bermuda is mostly done. The IIC is conducting an early morning press briefing. I should be able to take the morning flight back to Miami."

"Give me a call when you get back," Cathy said, a sullen quality creeping into her voice.

"Will do."

"Love you."

Cringing, Hart said, "Good night, hon."

The line was silent for a moment. Hart could hear Cathy's breathing. And then he heard a click.

Maureen had raised herself up on her forearms, her round breasts exposed. She took the phone from Hart and placed it back on the cradle.

Hart looked into Maureen's eyes and said, "I'm a jerk."

"That may be true," Maureen said with a coy grin. "But at least the acknowledgement indicates that you have a conscience."

"Maybe…"

Maureen rolled to her side and moved a hand over Hart's chest and down to his midsection. Hart felt himself throb. She rotated her body on top of Hart and began to nibble on his ear.

CHAPTER FOURTEEN

Sunday
02:05 EDT

The moon's reflection shimmered on the water. Aside from the rhythmic roll of the swells, the Atlantic Ocean was almost a sheet of glass. Had he not been focused on the mission, Mike might have shut the engines down, drifted with the current, and then simply gazed at the twinkling night sky.

Instead, Mike was dividing his attention on both the view directly in front of the bow and on his iPhone. He was studying the icon of Ashley's cell phone location. The icon had remained stationary. The satellite view of the family locator map had positioned his daughters approximately two miles offshore. It appeared that the boat with his girls was anchored somewhere halfway between the extension of Oakland Boulevard and Commercial Boulevard.

Mike was moving the Sea Ray at a painfully slow speed. At such a low rpm, the muffled exhaust that escaped just above the water line created a warbling sound as the boat rose and fell with the waves. He didn't want to miss spotting the Tiara, nor did he want to alert his daughters' captors of his approach any earlier than he had to. In that regard, Mike had shut off all exterior and interior lights.

The water lapping against the hull would have been calming if his stress level hadn't already peaked. Mike felt his grip on the chrome wheel of the helm tighten. Clammy moisture from his palms was beginning to seep out onto the metal. If he had been flying the 767, he would have silently criticized himself. A relaxed touch in an airplane always produced better results.

As Mike scanned the darkness ahead of the bow, a silhouette in the distance caught his attention. Another boat? Was it *the* boat? Or was it just anxiety flirting with his mind? Mike squinted. Was that a red nav light? Couldn't be… Wouldn't the maniacs that abducted his daughters want to be as stealthy as he was?

A glance at the locator program and then a quick study of the boat's GPS display indicated that whatever floated out there corresponded with the position. But how could he be certain? What if it was just a group of buddies on a late night fishing excursion? Mike thought for a moment. Idiot! Turn on the radar. The return should be able to verify the relationship of his visual sighting with the spot on the locator map.

Mike reached forward and pressed the radar power button. The screen was mounted upright on the far corner of the instrument panel. The old monochrome display began to bathe the cockpit with a dull, green light. When a long minute passed, a steady sweep began to trace across the screen. Only three sweeps had cycled before Mike began to focus on two small pinpoints of green.

Two? Shit! Which return was the right one? They were both within a half-mile of each other. It was a 50/50 chance. Mike stared at the locator map. He had to take a gamble. Mike turned the wheel, aiming the Sea Ray at the nearest speck of green illuminated on the radar display. He reached into the duffle bag and slid the Glock out onto an empty spot by the throttle levers. He reached forward and pressed the power button on the radar display until the screen went black. He peered forward through the windscreen and out toward the rolling water into the night. The silhouette of the boat that he had sighted earlier reappeared. Mike's heart began to thump.

An agonizing few minutes passed. Soon, Mike was within close enough proximity to discern the hull characteristics of the boat. Yes! It was a sedan bridge. He had to be careful with his approach. The calm winds would allow the boat to swing in a wide angle. Assuming the anchor line was attached to the bow, he didn't want to snag it in his props.

With a quick jerk, Mike moved the throttles to idle and then the transmission levers to neutral. The Sea Ray glided forward, moving in a course that would slowly parallel the sedan bridge. The cabin of the other boat was dark except for the eerie orange glow of the instrument panel lights.

Just above the hiss and rumble of his engines, Mike heard voices. The voices seemed to be originating from the deck at the bow. As the Sea Ray neared the stern of the sedan bridge, Mike reached for the Glock. He gripped the weapon tightly in his right hand, being careful to keep his finger away from the trigger.

"Hey!" a voice shouted from the deck of the sedan bridge.

Mike stepped from underneath the bimini top and moved his feet to a wide stance. He aimed the automatic weapon at two dark figures. One of the figures seemed to be scampering along the inside of the starboard rail, moving aft toward the cockpit of the boat. As the moonlight illuminated more of the scene, Mike could see that the person moving toward the cockpit was clutching a beach towel around their body.

"What do you want, asshole?" the male voice asked, a slight insecurity inflection in his tone.

The figure attached to the voice reached down for something on the deck. Mike tensed. Should he squeeze the trigger? The figure grabbed at a small lump. A pair of shorts? The figure began to struggle, balancing on the deck in an awkward dance. The figure was trying to pull the shorts up. He tugged at the zipper as Mike drew closer with the Sea

Ray.

Still aiming the Glock and now moving his finger over the trigger, he glanced at the emblem attached to the side of the sedan bridge. The emblem read, "Silverton."

Shit! It wasn't the Tiara!

Shaking his head, Mike ducked back under the bimini top. He dropped the automatic weapon to his side. He had just interrupted a couple trying to screw under the stars. He stepped over to the helm and pushed the transmission levers into forward gear. Crap!

From the Silverton, Mike heard, "Dumb-ass! Learn how to drive a boat! You almost killed us!"

The man's outburst was probably the understatement of his entire life. Mike took a deep breath, hoping that he could slow his heart rate. He had almost shot an innocent man.

When he had put some distance between the Silverton and the Sea Ray, Mike brought the transmission levers to idle. The boat slowed, rocking with the motion of the waves. He removed his hands from the wheel and massaged his temples. He took a few more deep breaths and thought for a moment.

Mike pressed the power button of the radar. He stared at the display. The other green pinpoint reappeared. According to the range, the other boat was about a quarter-mile ahead and slightly to the right. It just had to be the Tiara…

After smearing the sweat from his palms on his jeans, Mike reached forward and once again pushed the transmission levers into forward gear. He sighed and stared ahead into the darkness. With the same technique as he employed on the airplane, he began a systematic scan of the horizon. A few anxious minutes later, the moonlit shape of another sedan bridge boat appeared. Mike felt his heart rise into his throat.

Using the strategy from the previous encounter, Mike motored to gliding distance. He slid the transmission levers into neutral and turned the helm wheel to steer the Sea Ray alongside. Within moments, he recognized the Tiara. This time he wouldn't need to see the logo emblem. He grabbed the Glock off the instrument panel. Mike stepped out from underneath the bimini top and extended his arms, the automatic weapon poised firmly in his hands.

A yellow dome light splashed the cockpit deck of the Tiara with a dim glow. The light flowed over two human forms that were standing toward the aft end of the cockpit deck. Judging by the hourglass shapes and the long hair, the human forms were female. Should he pull the trigger…on women? If it meant saving his daughters...

From a place in his throat that he didn't recognize, Mike shouted, "Do not move! I have a weapon aimed at your heads!" The women on board the Tiara remained stationary. No response. The Sea Ray glided closer. "I want to see Kim and Ashley on the deck!"

No movement. No reply.

"Now!" Mike yelled.

A muffled voice screamed from within the cabin of the Tiara. "Dad!? Dad! Is that you?"

In an instant, the cockpit of Mike's Sea Ray exploded with the illumination of intense white light. Mike's vision was overwhelmed by the glare. He squinted and instinctively attempted to cover his eyes by holding a cupped hand against his forehead. Where was the source of his blindness? He heard a cackle of laughter. His mind raced. He squeezed the trigger of the Glock. The sound of the shot crackled.

A wispy female voice from the Tiara, yelled, "Shit! It burns! I think I've been hit!" A groan. A stifled thump. The glaring white light disappeared as quickly as it had appeared. And then a heavy thump. Mike's deck shook. What was that?

Someone from the Tiara must have jumped on board his boat because in an instant, Mike felt the heel of two palms shove him backward with a crushing blow. The impact pushed air from his lungs. The force threw him onto the deck of the Sea Ray. Whatever air remained completely escaped as his back and head were pounded against the hard surface. The Glock fell away from his grip. The gun slid across the deck.

As Mike coughed and gasped for a breath, the hulking outline of a large man took shape before him. The man reached down and grabbed the center of Mike's T-shirt. He twisted the thin fabric into a knot and then pulled, forcing Mike onto his feet. In a futile attempt, Mike resisted. Most of his energy had escaped with his abrupt fall to the deck. His efforts had no effect other than to further enrage the large man. The man's arms were made of steel.

"You shot one of my girls, faggot!" The hulking man spit from his lips.

Mike wheezed, "I just want my daughters!"

"You fucked up, faggot! Did you forget who you were dealing with?"

"I'll get what you want. I just need time," Mike said, taking gasping breaths.

"You should have thought of that before you took your little airline trip."

A raspy female voice from the Tiara yelled, "Chris…it's not looking good for Amber! I don't think she's breathing!"

Mike felt the grip of the muscular man relax on his T-shirt. The man reached down for the Glock that was still lying on the deck. He clenched the gun in one beefy hand and pointed it at Mike's temple.

Glaring, the muscular man spoke in a loud, commanding voice. "Come over here and get on board this piece of shit boat, Serena. You watch this fudge-packer. I'll jump back over and check out Amber."

A cold voice from the Tiara responded, "I'm coming."

In a few moments, tan slender legs slid over the rail of the Sea Ray. A tall blonde took a few steps toward the monstrous bald man holding the gun aimed at Mike. The bald man passed the Glock to the blonde without taking his eyes off Mike. The blonde took a wide stance and aimed the gun with a two-handed grip.

"Take him below decks for now, Serena," the man snarled. Get the information out of him. I'll let this barge drift for now. There's no sense in rafting it alongside…at least for the moment." He gestured at the cockpit. "Do you think you can figure out how to steer this thing back to the Tiara?"

Serena nodded and rolled her eyes. Both of them knew she could maneuver almost any boat.

As the man climbed back aboard the Tiara, the blonde pointed the gun at the sliding door that led down to the Sea Ray's salon. Mike took a deep breath and limped over to the salon door. He opened it and descended the two steps into the darkened room. A throbbing pain encompassing his back and sides restricted his movement to a cautious pace.

"Move, asshole!" the blonde sneered. She prodded Mike with the barrel of the gun. Mike took a few small steps into the cabin. He steadied himself by leaning on the salon table. As the blonde climbed down the steps, she commanded, "Go sit on the V-berth!"

Mike hobbled toward the bow. He grimaced as he hoisted himself up and onto the mattress of the V-berth using his shoulders. He turned and sat facing the blonde with his legs dangling over the side of the raised platform.

As he stared into the woman's steely eyes, Mike tried to focus. He was losing an important battle. Actually, he was not only losing the battle, he was losing the war. He had been fighting the war his whole life; it had been his own personal conflict. He had not been honest with himself. He had not been honest with his family. He deserved to die.

How ironic that the stunning woman aiming the gun at Mike's head was the perfect opposite of his true desires. He had forced himself to believe that he was attracted to such beauty, but he felt nothing. Instead of accepting his true feelings, Mike had pursued the traditional American dream. He married. He had children. Robin was right. He *had* lived a lie.

And now the two people that mattered most might have to pay for his mistake. The only hope was that his contingency plan would not fail.

02:35 EDT

Kim whispered, "I can't hear anything. He's probably still on our Sea Ray."

Ashley nodded and bit her lip. She watched her sister peek out through the glass of the locked cabin door. She asked, "Is the bald guy out there?"

Kim said, "I think so. It looks like Super Shrek is kneeling over the red-haired chick." Kim moved her face closer to the glass. "The red-haired chick isn't moving."

"Kim, I've got something to tell you," Ashley whispered.

Kim continued to peer out through the glass door. "Is it important? Can it wait?"

"No."

Turning to face her little sister, Kim said, "Oh for Christ's sake, Ash, what the hell? Is this really the time for true confessions?"

"I got a text message about an hour ago."

"You got a what…?"

"I got a text message…a text message from Dad."

"Ash, you don't even have a cell…" Kim's voice trailed off. Her eyes widened. "When did you get a cell phone? Dad said that you weren't getting one for another year."

"I was supposed to keep it a secret. Dad felt guilty that he had bought you the VW. He thought I was responsible enough. My grades were really good. It doesn't matter."

Kim said with narrowing eyes, "You little bitch…so why did you wait until now to tell me? We could have been calling or texting to tell people where we are."

Ashley waved her hand around the boat and said, "They have cameras and microphones hidden down here. Remember?"

"Yeah, you're right." Kim glanced back outside for a brief moment.

"Do you think they're monitoring us now?" Ashley asked.

Kim said, "No. Super Shrek is still occupied. I heard the blond slut say that she was jumping onto the Sea Ray. The red-haired slut is unconscious...or something. I think Dad shot her." Kim slid off the salon steps and walked over to Ashley still seated on the couch. "Show me the text, sis."

Squeezing a hand into her blue jeans pocket, Ashley pulled out her iPhone. She tapped the screen and handed the phone to Kim. Kim began to read.

"*I am coming. Know where you girls are. If anything goes wrong, you must try and escape. They will try to hurt you. Use the defensive tactics I taught you. You will be OK. Love u always. Dad.*"

With a solemn nod, Kim gave the iPhone back to Ashley. Ashley slid the phone back into her pocket.

"But how did he find us if you couldn't call Dad…or text him?" Kim asked with raised eyebrows.

"Really? Are you serious?"

Kim's eyes widened. "Tell me, brat!"

"You've never heard of the Find My iPhone app?"

With a sigh, Kim said, "I'm not an idiot. Of course."

She raised her palms with an incredulous expression. “But I turned the app off on my phone.”

Ashley sighed and said, “Ever hear of parental authority?”

“Out with it, Ash! We don’t have time for twenty questions.”

“Sprint has its own program, Family Locator or something.”

Kim shook her head and rolled her eyes. “No wonder Dad would have that sly look when I’d come home from Justin’s house. He knew that I wasn’t doing homework with Nina.”

“And Mom…you told her that you were at study hall even though you and your girlfriends were slurping iced lattes at the mall.”

The two girls lapsed into a long minute of silence.

In one fluid motion, Kim tilted her head back, shook it, and then dropped her face into her hands.

“What?” Ashley asked.

Talking through her hands, Kim said, “We’re idiots.” She raised her head abruptly and looked at Ashley. “If Selma and Louise…and Shrek get what they want from Dad, whatever the hell that is, we’re no longer useful to them.”

“What are you saying?”

“I’m saying that we have to find a way to get the hell out of here before the maniacs get rid of us!”

Ashley’s upper lip began to quiver. Her eyes began to well up. She took in a deep breath and sat up straight, fighting the emotions that were about to escape. “What do we do? We’re locked down here like a couple of witches about to be burned at the stake.”

“Exactly. That’s why we have to wait.”

“Wait for what?”

Kim gestured her head up toward the salon door and outside. “For the crazy people to come down and get us.”

"Then what? Are we going to yank on Super Shrek's little finger till he cries?"

"I've got a plan."

06:05 EDT

"Ladies and gentlemen, please take your seats!" Maureen Blackford said, bellowing through the array of microphones bearing the names of various news agencies attached to the lectern. She surveyed the hotel banquet room, offering an impatient sigh as the accident investigators shuffled into their seats.

In front of the tables, crouching men and women scurried about. Shutters clicked. Lights flashed. Cell phones were held in the air. Electrical wires crisscrossed the rug.

A dull murmur persisted. Then, after a moment or two, the room fell silent except for the occasional squeak of a table or chair.

Maureen slid a pair of black-framed glasses onto the bridge of her nose, glanced at a yellow legal pad, and said, "First, I would like to begin by thanking not only my NTSB team but all of the participants in the investigation of Patriot Airlines Flight 63. This task would have been daunting without each and everyone's contribution." She scanned the tables. "It is important to remember that our purpose is to find reasons for such catastrophes so that they never occur again. We owe it not only to the families that lost loved ones, but also to the traveling public. The traveling public depends upon the professionals that maintain the standards in keeping air travel the safest form of transportation in the world."

Clearing her throat, Maureen said, "I would like to welcome members of the media to the conclusion of this field investigation." She gestured an upturned hand toward the back of the banquet hall.

Shutters clicked again. The back wall was filled with standing men and women wearing ID tags and news agency logos. Their faces displayed a diverse group of expressions from anxiousness to impatience to boredom.

Maureen continued. "The conclusion of the field investigation does not conclude the entire investigation. The process continues, utilizing all the data that has been obtained on site. I am gratified by the thoroughness demonstrated from each and every party member of the investigation team. Because of their thoroughness, we will be able to determine a conclusive cause for the damage to the airplane and the resulting fatalities."

Hart leaned back in his chair and exchanged glances with Ryan Fredricks. The FBI man offered a solemn look. He drummed his fingers on the tablecloth and shifted uncomfortably in his seat. Earlier, Hart had chided Ryan for his uncharacteristic wardrobe of a blazer and open-collar, buttoned-down shirt. Ryan had responded with a dour expression and a roll of his eyes.

"In that regard…" Maureen paused for effect, "…as of this moment, it appears the cause of the engine fire was the result of a detonation occurring outside of the main structure of the right engine, just inside the cowl. This caused the internal destruction of the engine, which resulted in turbine and compressor blade fragments breaching the fuselage of the airplane. The metal fragments became shrapnel, causing the death of two passengers. Under normal circumstances, jet engines are designed to contain their internal parts in the unlikely event severe damage occurs."

"A preliminary review of the cockpit voice recorder indicates the crew followed emergency procedures and protocols in the manner for which they were trained." She scanned the room. "In other words, their performance was exemplary despite the circumstance of multiple emergency events."

The media people in the back of the room shuffled on their feet. Eyebrows were raised. A handful of pens were brought to notepads.

"Translation?" Maureen asked, pausing for effect. "A device foreign to the engine was remotely detonated, causing the damage. We have evidence that the device may have been activated by a cell phone or satellite phone. In other words, Patriot Airlines Flight 63 was sabotaged."

The banquet hall began to rumble with a steady crescendo of hushed voices. Hands started to rise in the air. The people from the back wall advanced forward a step at a time.

"I'll take questions in just a moment, but first…" Maureen's voice trailed off as she watched Ryan rise from his chair and stride toward the podium. "It appears FBI Special Agent Fredricks would like the opportunity to speak." Maureen frowned, her expression mildly incredulous. She gave Ryan an almost imperceptible glare and slid to the side, allowing him access to the microphones.

Ryan took a deep breath and said, "Ladies and gentlemen, I echo Ms. Blackford's sentiments. The FBI is grateful for the expertise provided by the investigation participants." Ryan tugged on the sides of his blazer, adjusting the jacket's position around his collar. "This should come as no surprise, but as of this moment, the investigation is no longer under the jurisdiction of the NTSB. The FBI is now treating the event as a criminal act."

The back of the banquet hall erupted in a cacophony of voices. Once again, hands were raised. The words "Special Agent" were uttered loudly in inquisitive tones. The newspeople exchanged perplexed expressions. Cell phones were raised to ears. Pens scribbled on pads. Laptops and iPads were opened.

The investigative team members remained seated at their

respective tables. Some squirmed in their seats. Most had impassive faces, an indication that the FBI man's statement was already a matter-of-fact assumption. Others looked amused by the reaction of the press.

Rising above the din, a voice with a distinctive British accent resonated from the back of the room. The voice identified itself as being from CNN and asked, "Is this event being considered an act of terrorism?"

A momentary hush flowed into the banquet hall.

Ryan Fredricks gritted his teeth. He looked at Maureen Blackford and shrugged his shoulders. Maureen responded with a nod and a smirk that indicated the crowd's reaction was no longer her problem.

"Terrorism? At this time we are not ruling anything out," Ryan stated.

The CNN voice asked, "Do you have a suspect or suspects…or anybody claiming credit?"

"The investigation is ongoing. I can't say at this moment."

Another voice shouted, "Special Agent Fredricks, is it true that the captain of Flight 63 has been hospitalized as a result of an assault in his hotel room?"

"Yes. Fortunately, the captain's injuries are not life-threatening. That investigation is also in progress."

The same voice asked, "And it is also our understanding that the copilot's daughters were abducted within hours of Flight 63's emergency landing here in Bermuda?"

Ryan took a breath through his nose and said, "Yes, that is a correct statement."

The CNN voice inquired, "Has it been determined that the captain's assault and the abduction of the copilot's daughters may be related? It seems like an awful coincidence, even to us in the media." The CNN man grinned, an attempt at self-deprecating charm.

"Everything is being considered," Ryan replied.

More questions were shouted. The noise became an almost unintelligible din of singular origin.

Amid the chaos of voices, Ryan's stern voice announced, "Ladies and gentlemen, please! When we have definitive information, we will pass it on to you. We are in the preliminary stages of a criminal investigation that is dynamic with many moving parts. Please give us time to do our jobs. Thank you!" Ryan looked at the sea of faces staring in his direction. "That's all I have."

The FBI man walked away from the lectern and out a side door. A roar of questions continued.

Maureen resumed her stance on the podium in front of the lectern and said, "Thank you all for coming. This concludes the NTSB's field investigation report." Maureen glanced at Hart and shook her head. The NTSB IIC exited through the same door as Ryan, leaving the banquet hall in a commotion of babble.

Hart felt compelled to follow her, but resisted the urge. Now was not the time, especially with the world's attention focused on the latest developments. At this point, it was best if Hart focused his own attention on strategy outside of the accident investigation. But he couldn't tell his team. He didn't want them implicated if his plan unraveled.

As Hart rose from his chair at the table, his cell phone chattered against the change in his pocket. He surveyed the room and noticed a small cadre of reporters advancing toward his position. He glanced at the caller ID. It was the president of PAPA. Hart caught the attention of Jerome, seated at an adjacent table, and gestured in the direction of the advancing reporters. Jerome nodded, walked toward the approaching crowd, and watched Hart escape out the side door.

Hart pressed the Talk button and said, "Sammy, you don't waste any time. The press conference is barely over. You didn't even give me the opportunity to be molested by a flock of media people. I might have missed my debut on *Anderson Cooper*."

"Anderson Cooper can wait." Sam sighed and asked, "So what's your take on this?"

"Well, it's definitely sabotage. Terrorism? Hmmm… maybe."

Sam said, "I understand that you've had some interesting experiences of your own."

"Yeah…creepy stuff. That's why I won't rule out terrorism just yet."

"What aren't you telling me?"

Hart sighed and said, "Sam, you're going to have to trust me on this. It's better that you don't know everything for the moment." Hart peered down the hallway. A reporter he recognized was walking toward him at a slow gait. Hart turned away into a narrow corridor and opened the door to a room labeled, "Housekeeping storage." The dark storage room held a stale, musty odor that intensified as he shut the door behind him.

Hart whispered, "Listen, I'll be glad to send you all the info on the nuts and bolts of the accident investigation but we need to leave it there."

"Okay. I understand. But don't hurt yourself. Love you… well, in a man-crush kind of way."

"I love you too, Sammy. Thanks. Oh…can you keep me on paid union leave for at least another three days?"

"Not a problem. I'll make it happen. Talk to you soon."

As the phone displayed, "Call ended," Hart cracked the door open just enough to view the immediate vicinity. No one was nearby. He exited the storage room in a quiet rush and headed in the direction of his hotel suite.

Hart thought, "I'm doing cloak and dagger stuff. Really?" He was beginning to feel like an actor in a bad spy movie.

CHAPTER FIFTEEN

Sunday
06:15 EDT

Ashley and Kim huddled together on the acrylic steps of the Tiara's salon. They peered through the tinted glass door outside into the boat's cockpit. The nearly rising sun bathed the area with a dim glow. From the girls' vantage point, activity was minimal. Occasionally, the big, bald guy would stomp past their line of sight, but that was all they could discern.

A far corner of the cockpit had a dark smear on the deck. The smear was probably blood from where Amber had fallen. But the slinky redhead was nowhere in sight. The implications of the dark smear sent a collective chill down their spines.

And for a long time now, no sign of their dad was evident. Earlier they had heard some scuffling outside accompanied by raised voices. The Tiara's deck above their heads had thumped with footsteps. For a while, through the portals of the salon, they could see the old Sea Ray bobbing alongside. But now the girls saw only open ocean. Where had the boat gone?

Turning away from the scene outside, Ashley started to ask, "What do you think happened to…?"

Kim interrupted, "I don't know. Dad's gotta be okay. He just has to be…" Her voice dissipated into a whisper.

The sisters remained silent for a few moments. As they

sat, the sound of shuffling feet grew louder. The shuffling feet were accompanied by a metallic scraping noise. Kim peered out onto the deck and leaned closer to the salon door.

Kim gasped and whispered, "O-M-G, Ash!"

Ashley turned to look outside. She was about to ask the reason for Kim's exclamation but the scene she witnessed was all the answer needed.

The big bald guy was carrying a limp Amber in his thick arms. His T-shirt and Amber's blouse were speckled with blotches of red. Most of Amber's torso was wrapped with a heavy aluminum chain, the links tightly bound. In a free hand, the bald guy was dragging a large Danforth anchor that was attached to the chain.

"We're not really seeing this, are we?" Ashley asked with the intonation of a faint whimper.

"We need an erase button," Kim said with a shudder.

Mesmerized, the sisters stared outside. They watched, both knowing the outcome while simultaneously hoping that something other than the obvious would occur.

The bald guy leveraged his leg over one of the stainless steel transom doors that led to the swim platform. He kicked, forcing the door to swing open. He shuffled out onto the swim platform and swiveled his head from side to side as if someone would actually witness his activity this far offshore. Satisfied, he lowered Amber's lifeless body into the water. Slowly rising to his feet, his expression, distorted by the dim light, was a mixture of somberness and anger. The bald guy shook his head, stepped through the transom, and back into the cockpit.

Ashley grabbed Kim's wrist and pulled her off the salon steps toward the dining table in the center of the cabin. They stopped and turned, staring back through the sliding glass door, perhaps hoping that the horror from outside would vanish. The girls shook their heads, tears filling their eyes.

"What's next?" Kim whispered.

06:20 EDT

Mike sat uncomfortably on the Sea Ray's V-berth. He had propped his arms behind him in an attempt to support his upper body. His fingers were pressed tightly into the bedspread that covered the thin mattress. He grimaced periodically, clenching his teeth when the occasional needles of sharp pain pulsed through his body. The back of Mike's head and his ribs had taken a nasty blow when the monster of a bald guy had knocked him down with linebacker force.

The woman the bald guy called Serena had relaxed her wide stance. She had also released her two-handed, tactical grip on the Glock. The gun was now in one hand, resting against her hip, leveled at Mike.

With a quick jerk of her head, Serena flipped away a few strands of blond hair that were covering an eye. Her jaw stiffened. She snorted and said, "You're in a tough spot, Mr. Pilot."

Mike looked up at Serena for a brief moment and then slowly lowered his gaze, moving his eyes in an unfocused stare at the mottled carpet.

"You do understand that you're in a lose/lose situation?" Serena asked, not expecting an answer. She shook her head in disgust. "Let me explain it to you. It's real simple. First, you probably killed Amber. That makes the bald refrigerator and me really, really pissed. He's not a nice person when he's pissed. Second, we need access to what you left in Bermuda. Withhold that access, and we'll end the life of your little daughters…and we'll let you watch."

Mike snapped his head up and glared at Serena. He snarled and asked, "If I give you the information, who's to say we won't all be murdered anyhow?"

"Do you want to gamble with your daughters' lives?"

Still staring at the blonde, Mike took a deep breath. A minute passed in silence. He turned toward Serena and gestured toward the galley. "Open the drawer to the right of the sink. There should be a pen and paper inside. I'll write down a user name and password along with an online website. Your boss will know what to do with it."

Serena glowered with a nod. She took a step toward the galley sink and opened the drawer. She peered inside, shuffled an assortment of junk, and pulled out a pen and a piece of scrap paper.

Shoving the pen and scrap piece at Mike, she said, "The information better prove correct. I don't have to remind you of the consequences."

As he reached for the items in the woman's hand, Mike developed a sense of clarity. His vision lost its myopic focus; his view broadened beyond the small space he occupied. The sound of each breath and the water lapping against the hull increased in volume. He could smell his own perspiration, the sweet smell of his captor's perfumed shampoo, and the boat's saltwater mustiness. His pain disappeared, replaced by the adrenalin beginning to surge through his veins. His body stiffened. If his expression had been submissive moments ago, it was no longer apparent.

Mike lunged with lightning speed. In the blink of an eye, he grasped Serena's slender wrist and yanked her toward him. His other hand pried the pen from her fingers. He gripped the pen and jabbed it with vicious force into her abdomen, applying an upward thrust.

The blonde's face reflected searing pain. Her eyes widened. With a look of incredulity, she stared down at the hand that was pushing a pen hard into her gut. As Mike followed her gaze, he noted with some irony that the logo of Patriot Airlines was emblazoned on the pen.

With her lips drawn and her face becoming expressionless, Serena tightened her fingers around the Glock. In a robotic motion, she raised the barrel of the gun and squeezed the trigger.

A deafening noise filled the small area of the boat's salon. Time froze. Mike's mouth opened but he could say nothing. He winced in agony. He lowered his chin and stared at the darkening stain on his chest. His eyes widened and then became unfocused. He collapsed backward onto the V-berth.

As an expanding pool of red oozed out onto the mattress cover, an almost imperceptible smile reached the corner of Mike's mouth. Before his thoughts became a jumble of images, Mike realized that his girls now had a chance. His Plan B would protect them. He felt at peace. His job was over. Blackness overcame him.

Serena stared at the scene, detached from the reality of the situation. Only seconds passed before she understood that her body was going into shock. Instinctively, she pulled at the pen and yanked it away from her midsection. She felt a warm flow over her fingers. In a moment of uncluttered, cognitive thinking, she pressed a hand firmly against the small hole in her stomach.

Serena's mind was starting to communicate that her survival was in serious jeopardy.

Her only hope was an attempt to get Chris's attention on the Tiara. She turned away from the bloody scene on the V-berth and clambered up the steps and outside into the cockpit of the Sea Ray.

Her vision narrowing, Serena swiveled her head and scanned the ocean for any sign of the Tiara. She saw nothing. She screamed, "Chris!" But what came out of her mouth was only a harsh whisper. Serena pivoted around and glanced at the throttle quadrant. She staggered toward the helm. Maybe she could start the engines and motor toward the Tiara.

In an attempt to catch her balance, Serena reached forward to grasp the helm. The chrome wheel rotated away from her grip, the momentum carrying her toward the side rail. With her strength waning and her body responding in slow motion to her brain's commands, she could do nothing to keep from falling over the side. She struggled, flailing with her arms and legs in an attempt to attach herself to any part of the boat. Her efforts were in vain.

Serena slipped into the waters of the Atlantic Ocean with a feathery splash. If someone had been in the vicinity, it might have sounded like a fish jumping out of the water, attempting to escape an unseen predator.

06:30 EDT

The whole operation was getting messy. Chris hadn't expected casualties, certainly not with his girls. He had grown fond of Amber. He never considered her his girlfriend exactly, but the occasional romp in the sack was always on her agenda. She loved to screw. And now she was gone. Unfortunately, he had no choice but to give her a burial at sea. Amber's body would have been a liability, evidence of a crime.

Hopefully, Serena had extracted the information from that fucking pilot. Chris hated to admit it, but that skinny, dick-sucker had balls. But how did the guy find them in the first place? How did he even know that his daughters were being held on a boat?

The girls had supposedly taken the cell phones away from the daughters. But something was tracking them. And if something were tracking them it would only be a matter of time before law enforcement could do the same. What type of tracking device and where was it?

The realization that the entire mission could be in

jeopardy hit Chris like a ton of bricks. He had to find the tracking device, destroy it, and then get the hell out of the area. What made the most sense is that one or both of the daughters had it in their possession. But watching them on the video monitors in the salon revealed nothing. Nor did their conversations. They were just scared little kids.

Shit! Where the hell was Serena? She should have brought that old Sea Ray back and been tied up alongside the Tiara by now. Chris reached for the cell phone in the front pocket of his cargo shorts. He found the speed dial listing for Serena and pressed the Talk button. The display indicated a call was in progress. He immediately got Serena's sultry voice but it was her voice-mail greeting. He pressed the redial button. Voice mail. He tried again. Still voice mail.

Crap! Chris's only hope to contact Serena was via the radio on Channel 16. And who was to say that the pilot had left the radio on in that old tub anyhow. It didn't matter. The radio was too dangerous. The Coast Guard and the Marine Patrol monitored that frequency, notwithstanding the fact that those transmissions most likely could be recorded.

Chris glanced at the dark, red smear on the deck where Amber had fallen. He'd have to clean up that mess, too. The whole boat would need a good scrubbing. He puffed out a long breath. But for now, his priority was finding the source of the tracking information. He could start a search for the Sea Ray and Serena later.

And what was that noise? Was that screaming Chris was hearing from down below? Great. He hadn't envisioned his job description to include babysitting. Maybe the older one discovered a cracked fingernail. He rolled his eyes. He had never really been comfortable around kids. The Iraq War hadn't helped. Chris had watched a young girl, clothed in a typical black burka, walk out onto a dusty street, pull out a semiautomatic handgun and start firing randomly at anyone dressed in U.S. soldier camo. Fortunately, the girl had only managed to wound one private first class in the shoulder before she was shot with about twenty-five rounds from an M60. The girl couldn't have been any older than fifteen.

The screaming from below continued. Chris turned to face the locked door of the salon. Terrified teenage girls. Just what he needed.

06:35 EDT

"Ash, you can't freak out on me now!" Kim said with a loud whisper.

"Why do I have to be the one to scream?" Ashley said with wide eyes.

"Because you're the best at it."

"I've heard you. You're not so bad yourself."

"Really, Ash? You're going to argue with me now about this?" Kim rolled her eyes and let out an exasperated sigh. "You've got a higher-pitched scream."

"I think technically that my scream is more of a shriek."

"Ash!!" Kim exclaimed using a restrained volume level. She glared.

"Okay. Okay. I'm just not sure I can be realistic under the circumstances."

"I've got an idea. Why don't you imagine that you only got a 'B' in calculus?"

"Funny. Maybe you should imagine that Forever 21 moved out of the mall."

Kim grit her teeth, "Ash! You're killing me!"

Ashley's upper lip quivered. She looked at her sister with soulful, brown eyes and said, "I'm scared."

"I know. I am too." Kim walked over to Ashley, brushed her sister's hair back away from her cheeks, and hugged. The two rocked slowly on their heels in a firm embrace. "We're going to make it, Ash. I promise." Kim surprised herself for uttering the statement with such conviction. "We've got to take this opportunity now. It's only the bald guy that we have to deal with. I'm fairly positive that the blonde bitch is with Dad on the Sea Ray." Ashley nodded.

"And remember, Dad taught us those defensive tactics. Anything can be used as a weapon," Kim added.

The two separated. Kim moved toward the aft berth, away from the line of sight of the steps. Ashley resumed her position in front of the galley stove. A silver coffee pot resting on a flat top, glass burner coughed out wisps of white steam.

Kim took a deep breath, looked at her sister, and asked, "Ready?"

Ashley looked down at the tiled floor for a moment and then at the salon door. She pursed her lips and then opened them wide. The blood-curdling shriek that came out of her mouth startled Kim despite the fact she had been expecting it. When her breath was exhausted, Ashley sucked in a gulp of air and began an encore.

It wasn't long before the girls heard the familiar clack of the salon door latch. Within seconds, the thump of footsteps accompanied the swish of the door opening. Moments later, the hulking, bald guy thudded into the salon. His expression was annoyance mixed in with a good dose of anger.

"What the hell!?" Chris shouted. "Can't you little, spoiled brats take care of yourselves?"

With her shrieking task complete, Ashley cried out in mock distress, "I was making tea and burned myself...bad." Ashley reached for the steaming coffee pot, grabbed the handle, and tossed the contents directly into the bald man's face. He emitted a dog's guttural yell while attempting to wipe the scalding water from his face.

As the man staggered, his eyes crunched closed in agony,

Ashley swung back the coffee pot with the strength of a professional batter. Rocketing her arm forward, she struck him across the forehead. Beads of moisture flew like bullets from his reddened skin. Ashley moved away, still wielding the coffee pot as though it were part of her arm.

With the big man wobbling, Kim jumped in front of him. She held a fire extinguisher up above her chest and aimed the nozzle. She gritted her teeth and squeezed the trigger. A spray of chemical retardant doused Chris, completely enveloping his bald head in gooey, white foam. Clawing at his face, he tried desperately to clear the foam from his mouth and eyes.

Still holding the red fire extinguisher, Kim jumped up onto the dining table. Towering above the teetering bald man, she swung the canister and thrust it hard against the side of his head. The strike made the squishy sound of a wet tree branch cracking. Droplets of red dots splattered Kim's face and her T-shirt. The tile floor beaded with red dots.

For a split second he remained rigid, and then he dropped to his knees like a marionette that had lost its strings. He collapsed face forward onto the floor. He didn't move. Ashley stared at the grisly sight for a brief moment, and then in a flurry, repeatedly struck the giant in the head with the coffee pot.

"Ash! Stop! It's over!"

Kim jumped off the dining table and began to pull her sister away from the motionless figure on the floor. She pried the coffee pot from Ashley's frozen grip. Rivulets of water started to flow in torrents down Ashley's face. She began to sob, her chest heaving in irregular movements.

Gripping Ashley firmly by the shoulders and staring into her eyes, Kim said, "It's okay. It's okay. You did great! You're the bravest little geek I've ever seen. Kim tried to smile through the tears that were forming in her own eyes. "I thought you were going to kill Shrek with just your shriek."

For effect, she emphasized the "sh" in both words. "If fish had earwax, it would all be gone by now after that performance."

With her sobbing beginning to subside, Ashley tried to laugh, only managing a quick squeak. Kim grabbed her sister's wrist and led her away from the carnage on the floor. They climbed up the salon stairs and into the cockpit. They paused for a moment, breathing in the sea air. The rising sun bathed the water with an orange glow.

If only the circumstances were different, the girls could have appreciated the moment. Memories of such scenes shared with their parents had been etched in their minds. But they were in survival mode. What now?

Ashley curled up her blouse, dabbed at her eyes with the material, looked at Kim, and asked, "Dad?"

Kim nodded and began to scan the horizon. Ashley joined in the search. She stepped to a corner of the deck and peered into the distance. Minutes passed.

Placing her hands on her hips in frustration, Kim said, "I've got nothing."

"Me either," Ashley said with a sigh. "We need to call 911."

"Good idea. Where's your phone?"

Ashley gestured at the open salon door, shook her head, and turned away.

"You don't have to go down there, Ash. I will." Ashley nodded.

Pivoting on her bare feet, Kim took a few cautious steps toward the salon. She began to climb down, disappearing for less than a minute. She rematerialized back to the cockpit in a flurry. Kim held Ashley's phone in a hand while she frantically mashed a thumb on the display. Her expression held a look of despair.

"What's the matter, Kim?"

"Your phone...it must have been on the galley counter.

It fell on the tile floor. The display is cracked. Water got into it…and foam…and…" Kim shook her head, still staring at the phone. "Shit!"

"I'm sorry," Ashley said with a faint whimper.

"It's not your fault."

A minute passed in silence.

Ashley glanced at the open salon door and then looked at her sister. She asked, "Can we lock the door, please?"

Hesitating for a brief moment, Kim opened her mouth to speak. She stared at Ashley, noting the fear still residing in her sister's eyes. The bald man was dead, but it didn't matter. Kim nodded, walked over to the door, slid it close with a thwack, and turned the key that was still stuck in the latch.

"Thanks," Ashley said with an expression that could barely be interpreted as a smile. She scanned the spacious outside sitting area of the lower salon. "Got any ideas?"

"Actually, yeah. Just thought of it now." Kim gestured at the cockpit helm station. "Let's start this bitch up and go home!"

"Seriously?"

Ashley pointed at the VHF radio and asked, "What about Channel 16? We could call the Coast Guard."

"And wait for them to come to our rescue? We could be home by then."

"Do you think we can drive this thing?"

"Ash, it's simpler than the Sea Ray." Kim pointed at the throttles. "There's no transmission levers, just forward and back."

"We don't even know where we are."

Kim took a step toward Ashley and grabbed her hand, guiding her sister toward the transom. Kim pointed at the faint outline of the shore. She said, "I'm pretty sure that's Hillsboro Inlet." A momentary flash appeared. "That's gotta be the lighthouse." Kim swept a finger in a slightly different direction. “And the red and green lights are the buoys that mark the entrance.”

“And what about Dad?”

Glancing down at the deck with a sigh, Kim said, “If we can’t find him now, it might become a wild goose chase. And it might be dangerous if that blond bitch is with Dad. Let’s hope for the best and give the Coast Guard a call when we get home.”

“Kim, we were kidnapped. We were witnesses to a murder at our school. The world is looking for us. Cops. FBI. Mom. I don’t think we’re going to have to call anybody.”

“You’re right, Ash. Then, all the better. When we come sailing into our canal with a fifty-foot Tiara, we’ll be the heroes of the day! Shit, we’ll be the heroes of the month!”

Ashley shook her head and said, “I don’t feel like a hero right now.”

“Tell you what. Let’s at least get to the inlet. Then we’ll call the Coast Guard. That won’t be much of delay to start the search for Dad. I don’t want them trying to stop us. Okay?”

“Okay,” Ashley whispered.

Kim put an arm around her sister’s shoulder. She squeezed. “I understand how you feel, Ash. We’ll be okay. And Dad will be okay too. He’d want us to be safe.”

Something deep in the pit of Kim’s stomach was becoming unsettled. She didn’t want to ponder any further thoughts. She just wanted to get them home. Nothing else mattered.

CHAPTER SIXTEEN

Sunday
08:55 EDT

The doors to the elevator opened with a Starship Enterprise swoosh. Hart stepped out onto the third floor and nodded a greeting to three uniformed pilots dragging their rolling bags behind them. He exhaled a deep breath and glanced down the hall at the glass door that led to Operations and the Miami chief pilot's office.

The office was open on a Sunday. Funny stuff. Rod Moretti had instituted a weekend policy in response to complaints that the administrative staff was never around during the odd hours of typical pilot schedules. It was a skeleton staff of employees that volunteered to come in on a weekend and then have the benefit of choosing a day off during the normal work week.

With the NTSB press conference complete in record time, Hart had been able to catch the first flight back to Miami. He had called the flight office to alert Rod that he would stop by.

Although his encounter with Rod the other day was cordial, Hart couldn't shake off his anxiety. Once again, this next exchange would be a professional matter. No reason to expect anything other than a business conversation.

Hart had promised Rod a briefing on Flight 63. Sammy had condoned the briefing, not only to maintain an open line of communication between the union and management, but for the fact he was aware that Rod and Hart had history.

Ordinarily, chief pilots were briefed via company sources. Despite Rod's management status, Hart knew that his old friend was still a pilot's pilot, and he wanted the story from a perspective he could both relate and trust.

As he strode into the office, Hart exchanged broad smiles with Donna, the senior staff administrator. Still smiling, Donna shook her head and rose from the swivel chair behind her cubicle.

"Captain Lindy, don't even think that you can walk past my desk without giving me a hug!"

A buxom woman with chocolate skin, wispy highlights of gray hair smattered among black strands, and an ivory smile took a step toward Hart.

"The thought never crossed my mind," Hart said in a matter-of-fact tone.

The two embraced and applied mutual pecks on each other's cheeks.

As Hart relaxed his arms, he said, "If you had squeezed any harder, I would have filed a pilot abuse complaint with HR."

Donna snickered and replied, "No worries. I've got HR on speed dial. Besides, it was probably the best hug you're going to get all day with your clothes on."

Hart grinned. "How are things?"

Donna said, "Living my dream, Captain Lindy, just like you."

"So that must mean you found another job?"

Donna snorted, tilted her head toward an open office door, and said with a slightly higher volume level, "Fat chance. Besides, if it weren't for me, the new boss would be a bowl of Jell-O."

From the open office door a familiar voice bellowed, "I'm lucky that you know how to use the electric pencil sharpener!"

"At least I know which end of the pencil to insert!" Donna said with a smirk. She grinned at Hart. "I miss my two favorite check airmen." She rolled her eyes and looked at the open office door. "I still haven't got used to the other half of the old team crossing over to the dark side."

"Most of us figure the decision was made when he was off his meds," Hart said with a smile. The banter was helping to relieve his tension.

Rod Moretti appeared in the door frame, his head shaking as he glanced at Donna. He waved Hart over and said, "Don't you have something better to do, like jam the printer?"

Donna snickered, "Already did that."

"I'm not surprised. Well, the only remaining task is to let the phones ring and not answer them."

"In progress."

Rod chuckled as Hart entered the office. He grinned at Donna and closed the door. "Love that woman. She keeps this place sane. Don't know what I'd do without her."

Hart nodded and sat down on the office chair opposite Rod's desk. The chief pilot shuffled a few manila folders toward the corner of the desk, leaned back in his chair, and clasped his hands behind his neck.

"Where do you want me to start?" Hart asked. He could feel the tension ooze into the room. He felt awkward. How should he treat an estranged friend that he had known for almost thirty years?

Rod cleared his throat. "Well…start with the important stuff. How is my crew doing?"

Hart said, "The worst situation is the captain. I'm sure you've got the report. Cracked ribs. Bad concussion. A lot of bruises. A few cuts."

"I'm aware of his physical status." Rod tapped his temple with an exaggerated motion. "Tell me about what's going on inside his head."

Rod genuinely gave a shit. He had a natural ability to separate the wheat from the chaff. Hart nodded and said, "I don't know for certain about his mental state. The peer support guys did their kumbaya magic. It's all supposed to be confidential stuff. I don't get the details."

"Don't need the details. I get it. Just give me your opinion. When our captain gets out of the hospital, will he be able to wrap his head around the whole event, or will he be kissing the dog and kicking the wife?"

"Can't say for sure, but it appears that despite a morphine addiction that he blames on the Bermuda hospital staff, he's managed to harass the head nurse on a regular basis. Perhaps that's a reflection of his mental health." Hart's expression remained deadpan. "In all seriousness, I think our captain will be okay. He and Sully will be competing for media air time as the two greatest aviation heroes of the twenty-first century."

Rod smiled and said, "Good." He glanced at an open folder and looked back at Hart. "I'm concerned about the copilot. He's got a lot on his plate. The accident. Daughters kidnapped. I offered him a ride home. Our conversation was brief. Not sure how I would react under the same stress, but we need to monitor his situation."

"Agreed." Hart rested an elbow on the arm of his chair and cupped his chin in a contemplative gesture. Should he give Rod all the information? Could he trust his old friend? Probably. But he would have to keep it brief.

Noting the silence after Hart's response, Rod asked, "Is there more to Mike Townsend's story?"

Hart sighed. His eyes narrowed. "It could get ugly with Mike Townsend."

"From what standpoint?"

"I saw security footage of the walk-around in Port of Spain. Without getting into details, Mike is seen…"

The conversation was interrupted by the *Airport* movie theme. Hart leaned to his side and pulled the vibrating iPhone from his pocket. His pulse started to quicken as he viewed the caller ID.

"Sorry, I've got to get this," Hart said, glancing back at Rod. "It's Maureen Blackford, the IIC of the investigation."

Rod nodded and rose from his chair. He pointed a finger at himself and then the door. It was an offer to have the conversation in private.

Hart shook his head and motioned for Rod to sit back down, saying, "This should only take a minute." Hart touched the Talk button and put the phone to his ear. Rod began to re-shuffle papers on his desk.

"Hello, Ms. Blackford, how can I help?"

On the other end of the line, Maureen responded, "Ms. Blackford? Really? What's with the formality?" Two seconds of silence passed. "Whoops. I get it. You're with someone. I won't make it any more uncomfortable."

"It's not what you think, Maureen."

"No worries. Just wanted to make you aware that the team is transporting most of the significant pieces from the airplane to Washington. We'll continue with some further analysis under the supervision of the FBI, of course. The cockpit voice recorder and the digital flight data recorder will be transcribed. I have a feeling this will progress quickly, so we should have a preliminary report within a month."

"That's good news," Hart said, briefly glancing at Rod.

"We would like to have one of your team members come to Washington and help identify crew member voices and other various sounds picked up by the cockpit area mic. I wouldn't ask but it is my understanding that the flight's captain and copilot are still unavailable. Perhaps you would consider accompanying the individual you choose?"

"Not sure I can work out a trip to D.C., but I'll initiate a search for a 767 pilot familiar with the crew's voices."

"Are you turning down the investigator-in-charge, Captain Lindy?" Maureen said with a horsey, sarcastic whisper.

Hart squirmed in his seat and said, "No. I'm just not sure that I could provide any useful services in that area of the investigation."

"Witty response, Captain Lindy. I'm thinking of a useful service you could provide right now."

Hart ignored the innuendo and said, "Well, let me know your timeline and maybe I can reconsider."

Maureen offered a breathy chuckle and said, "I will, Captain Lindy. I will."

The connection went silent. Hart looked back up at Rod with an uncomfortable smile that barely moved the corners of his lips.

Hart said, "The NTSB will be analyzing pertinent airplane pieces along with transcribing the CVR and the DFDR. The FBI still has their hands deep in the mud on this one. It sounds like the investigation process will be moving quicker than normal, however."

Rod's expression became drawn. His eyes narrowed. He remarked, "Good stuff." His positive words did not reflect the negative tone in his voice.

Sensing a darkening mood, Hart cleared his throat and said, "Well, back to Mike Townsend. It seems that he has aroused some suspicion. As soon as I have something more definitive, I'll let you know. The big picture at this point is that the engine didn't come apart on its own. Terrorism. Sabotage. Everything is still on the table."

Hart grasped the arms of his chair, started to leverage himself up, and said, "Anything else?"

An awkward, thick silence permeated the room. Rod stared at Hart for a moment and then shook his head. An expression of disgust had painted itself onto Rod's face.

"You haven't changed, Captain Lindy, have you?"

Hart considered responding, but words that would be considered full sentences weren't making it to his lips. Instead, he just sighed, sensing that a hammer was about to fall.

"Tell me something," Rod began. "When you took that phone call, were you looking for bragging rights or were you thinking that your clever conversation was so well disguised that I'm enough of an idiot I wouldn't think you and the IIC are boning each other?"

Opening his mouth, Hart got out, "Look, I thought this was going to be a civil and professional meeting…"

Rod dismissed Hart with a wave of his hand. "It might have remained professional. But you brought this on yourself!" Rod pointed at the cell phone still gripped in Hart's hand. "I offered to leave the room. I thought you were smarter than that."

"Look, I came here as a fucking courtesy!" Hart said with a volume level that was barely restrained. "Just when did you and Dr. Ruth partner up to give me advice?"

With no attempt at hiding a facetious tone, Rod said, "Thanks for coming. I appreciate your efforts." He paused. "But I happen to be very fond of that woman who tolerates your total disregard for anything that doesn't involve Hart Lindy. And now you're at it again. At least you're broadening your horizons beyond cocktail waitress. Too bad that Cathy hasn't broadened her horizons."

"Thanks for your instant analysis, Dr. Phil." Hart could feel his pulse quicken. He wasn't going to lose control, but he couldn't resist twisting the knife. "And I suppose your ex-wife is a great reflection on your own relationship skills?"

"Well, it seems that you would have a better understanding of that attribute," Rod spat out. "After all, you broadened her horizons!"

"Do we need to go over that again?"

"Well, explain how you thought it was okay to be boinking your best friend's wife?"

"We've been down this road. It happened one hundred years ago before you were married…and you already know that."

"Sorry. You're right." Rod rolled his eyes and shook his head. "I'm supposed to accept the fact that it was okay for you to have maintained a cloak of secrecy until I had to hear about the whole sordid story through my divorce attorney." He paused. "And you were testifying as a character witness. Now that's almost comical."

"I was the one that had to live with my conscience."

"Yup, once again, it was all about you."

Hart took a deep breath and said, "Look, if you want to discuss this topic in a civil manner, and perhaps attempt an understanding from my vantage point, just let me know. I promise to be a grown-up if you will. But at this point…" Hart said, standing and waving his arms around the office, "…and in this venue, I'm done."

Nodding with a final glare directed at Rod, Hart reached for the door.

Rod said, "Just a minute, Captain Lindy. Before you leave in a huff, I have one more piece of professional business."

Hart held a hand on the doorknob and turned back to face Rod.

"The VP of Ops has requested a meeting concerning the investigation. I would appreciate if you would accommodate him, although you're under no obligation. We can have the meeting in the conference room." Rod smirked. "No guns are allowed. His secretary will contact you directly to coordinate."

Hart asked, "Do you have any idea of his agenda?"

"Not really. Reading between the lines of our brief conversation, it seems he'd like your perspective on the investigation."

"You do understand that some information is confidential, even for the VP of Ops."

"He is aware." A moment of silence passed.

"Is that it?" Hart asked.

Rod sighed and replied, "Yeah, that's it."

"Nice chatting with you, Captain Moretti."

Hart began to twist the doorknob and then stopped. He turned back to face Rod and asked, "What happened with my request for your golfing buddy to watch Cathy?"

"I called him as promised. He said that he was working on a case and it might occupy his weekend, but he'd pass through Cathy's neighborhood when he got a chance. Why?"

"Thanks. That was a big help." Hart rolled his eyes. "He couldn't have called a patrol cop to keep an eye on her?"

Rod opened the palm of his hands and said, "What happened?"

"Some creepy asshole followed her for part of the day. He may be connected to this whole investigation."

"I'm sorry," Rod replied with a tone of resignation.

Shaking his head, Hart walked out of Rod's office. He exchanged glances with Donna as he passed her cubicle. Her face was solemn, her eyes sad.

"That went well," Hart said, making no effort at disguising a phony smile.

09:05 EDT

The investigation had too many loose ends. Alvarez was starting to consider the need for further assistance. Soon, it would be mostly out of his hands anyhow. Every agency was involved. Broward County Sheriff. Marine Patrol. Coast

Guard. FBI. He wouldn't be surprised if the FAA eventually got their finger in the pie for whatever reason.

The round-faced detective put his hands on his hips. He glanced at the chalky, white Sea Ray tied up at that Coast Guard dock and then stared back at Tony Cusmano. The Italian guy was still seated on BSO's Marine Patrol boat. The three white outboard engines sparkled in the morning sun. Cusmano had his arms folded against his chest, his elbows resting on top of an expansive belly. It had been a long night for everyone.

Alvarez shook his head and walked toward the Marine Patrol boat. He sat down on the dock and slid onto the deck, nodding at the uniformed BSO cop. The cop took a couple of steps back and leaned against the center console helm station. Tony Cusmano peered up at Alvarez with bloodshot eyes.

With a sigh, Alvarez said, "Mr. Cusmano, I'd like to believe the story that your encounter with the airline pilot's boat was all just a coincidence. And that you were being a maritime good Samaritan."

"It's the fucking truth, Detective," Tony said. His voice was gravelly with fatigue.

Nodding, Alvarez said, "Unfortunately, your prior encounter with the now mutilated boyfriend doesn't work in your favor. In that regard, I have you potentially involved with two crime scenes." Alvarez gestured at the Sea Ray. "And at the current crime scene, it appears that we have prints that indicate your buddy was holding the murder weapon."

Tony shook his head and said, "I already told you earlier, man. Frankie just picked up the gun for only a second, right after he got on board."

"A lot of coincidences, Mr. Cusmano."

"Did you check with Blue Water at Bimini? The black dudes at the marina would remember me."

"We're working on that, Mr. Cusmano. It would help if you had some receipts with a time stamp."

"I bring cash over there. The Bahamians love cash. I don't get receipts." Tony said, his voice raising an octave.

"You had to buy fuel, didn't you?"

"No, it's too expensive over there. And the Donzi can make the round trip with no problem."

"An alibi for Bimini doesn't help you with the murdered bartender boyfriend on Los Olas. What about that?"

"I don't know when the guy was murdered, but I avoid that fucking area. Too many tourists."

"I'd love for all this to be a big mistake, Mr. Cusmano." Alvarez cleared his throat. "But you've got a good motive."

Squirming on the bench seat, Tony asked, "What fucking motive?" His voice held a measure of despair with a good dose of annoyance starting to seep through.

"Maybe after you murdered the bartender, the pilot boyfriend showed up at the wrong place and the wrong time. He could identify both you and Frankie, so you forced him at gunpoint to drive his boat offshore. Your buddy shot him on board, and then you guys continued on to Bimini in your Donzi. And then on your return home, you were surprised when you found the boat still adrift on the way into Port Everglades. Rather than leave anything to chance, you towed the boat into Port Everglades."

"Why would we do a dumb-ass thing like that?"

"The classic case of returning to the scene of the crime, Mr. Cusmano."

Tony felt a rumbling in his stomach. He cupped his hands and buried his head for a moment. Tony shook his head, rubbed his eyes, and stared back at the brown detective. He waved his arms, palms up and said, "I think it's time for me to lawyer up."

"That's fine, Mr. Cusmano, but I'm not arresting you at

the moment."

"Really?" Tony replied with wide eyes. "Then we're free to go?"

"You've been watching too many cop shows." Alvarez gestured his head at the Donzi tied up nearby. "Sure, you can get back on your boat and go home. But if you continue to cooperate, the outcome might be more positive."

Hesitating for a moment, Tony looked down at the deck, took a deep breath, and then stared back at the big detective. "Yeah…fine…okay"

Alvarez nodded at Tony and said, "Good." The detective noticed that Tom, his impromptu uniformed cop assistant, had reappeared on the Coast Guard dock. He was beckoning Alvarez over to his position. Alvarez said, "I'll be back shortly, Mr. Cusmano."

After hoisting himself off the Marine Patrol boat with a bit of a struggle, Alvarez waddled over to Tom. He wiped his brow with the back of his hand, grinned at the uniformed cop, patted his round belly, and asked, "Jenny Craig or a personal trainer…or both?"

Tom smiled and said, "Start with Jenny Craig. At least you get to eat."

"Good thinking." Alvarez clasped his hands in front of his stomach. "Whatcha got for me?"

"I've been staying after class, so to speak. Had nothing going on this weekend, so I've been keeping an off-duty eye on our high school vice principal."

"A little overachieving. Very nice," Alvarez said with a grin.

"Ms. Abbott lives in a condo just off Atlantic Boulevard in Pompano. I'm making unverified assumptions, but apparently, she shares the residence with an unidentified brunette woman. Before Ms. Abbott exited the condo, she engaged the brunette woman in a kiss at the front entrance."

Tom watched an egret flap its wings and then dive into the water off a nearby piling. He continued. "Ms. Abbott made two separate trips to a canal home off Bayview Drive in Fort Lauderdale. I think you know the neighborhood. Let's just say that you don't find too many Hyundai station wagons in the driveways."

Alvarez nodded.

Tom said, "Ms. Abbott rang the doorbell at the canal home. No one answered. She did this numerous times. The more she rang the doorbell, the more exasperated she appeared to be. She left with a very frustrated expression."

"And she's done this routine twice this weekend?"

"Yup." Tom pulled a small notepad from his pocket and flipped open to a page scribbled with blue writing. "I checked the city records. The house is owned by a law firm with a mailing address listed in New York City."

"Interesting. This just gets better and better. If you are correct about Ms. Abbott's sexual orientation, perhaps her friendship with Robin Townsend may have ulterior motives."

Alvarez glanced over at Tony Cusmano. He was standing up against the side railing and drinking a bottle of water that one of the Marine Patrol cops had given him. "Honestly, my gut tells me that those two morons didn't have anything to do with the murders. I made the Cusmano guy squirm with a cockamamie motive story just to gauge his reaction. They might have some peripheral participation in this whole mess, but I don't know what it could be. Sooner or later, we'll get some blood tests back from the boat and the Los Olas crime scene. The ballistic tests on the Glock found in the Sea Ray are in progress. I only hope that the forensics doesn't add more confusion to this investigation."

"This story has a lot of legs," Tom said.

"It does. But nice work, Tom. Thanks." Alvarez sighed and brought his arms across his chest. "And chances are good that Mr. Cusmano will have an alibi of sorts when we hear back from Bimini."

"So what are you going to do with your good Samaritans?"

"Until I get back some forensic information, those guys are all I've got. Maybe they'll come up with some useful information." Alvarez sighed. "Mr. Cusmano has threatened to lawyer up. If he does it again, I'll probably throw them both in a patrol unit and bring them in for an official interview with their attorney present. I've got enough circumstantial evidence to arrest them."

Tom nodded and said, "I agree. It sounds like a reasonable strategy."

The two men began to walk toward the Marine Patrol boat. But before they had reached the boat, a petty officer, third class, with an alabaster complexion jogged toward them, waving a hand. His physique was such that the officer's uniform seemed to be wearing him rather than him wearing the uniform.

"What's up?" Alvarez asked.

The petty officer darted his eyes from one cop to the other and said, "I think you'll want to hear this, sirs." He gestured at the main building. "Please come with me."

The young man turned and began a crisp walk down the perimeter dock. Tom and Alvarez exchanged curious glances and followed, attempting to match the petty officer's pace. They were led inside a building that housed a control room. An array of computer monitors, communication equipment, and console desks were scattered about the room in a pattern of organization that only the officers seated about the area probably understood. The control room was relatively quiet except for the occasional murmur of conversation and the low-pitched hum of electronic cooling fans.

The petty officer walked over to a uniformed man seated in front of a console. The uniformed man was speaking into a flexible boom microphone.

"Say again your position, Tiara?"

"Just south of Hillsboro Inlet, continuing southbound on the Intercoastal," a squeaky, female voice replied from a speaker on the console.

"Are you injured?"

Alvarez raised his eyebrows. Was that the voice of one of the abducted daughters? He stared at the black speaker as if he could see an image of the young girl.

"No. We're okay." A few seconds passed. "But there is a dead guy down below in the salon."

Taking a deep breath, Alvarez tapped the shoulder of the Coast Guard officer that was using the mic. He asked the officer, "Have you identified the communication as one of the Townsend sisters that was abducted?"

Still facing his console, the Coast Guard officer nodded.

"How the hell did they end up on a boat?" Alvarez asked, thinking out loud.

The Coast Guard officer shrugged. He keyed his mic again and asked, "Can you shut down the boat, Tiara? We will have Marine Patrol at your position in ten minutes. They will transport you home."

"Negative. We are continuing to our house on Southeast Fourteenth Street," a more assertive female voice answered.

"Are you able to dock the boat, ma'am?"

"If you let me get off this radio, I can."

Alvarez chuckled. To the Coast Guard officer he said, "Please tell the young lady that's fine. Call Marine Patrol and have them provide an escort. I'll get a couple of BSO patrol cars and an EMT unit to meet me at the Townsend residence."

The squeaky female voice was back on the radio. She said, "You need to search for a 1984 Sea Ray express cruiser. The name of the boat is 'Fearless Flyer.' Our dad, Mike Townsend, should be on board. He tried to rescue us. He disappeared last night just south of Commercial Boulevard, off shore."

The Coast Guard officer on the radio swiveled his chair to face Alvarez. He looked at the detective with a sad, inquisitive expression.

Although the old Sea Ray was hidden from view, Alvarez turned his head toward where the boat was tied up at the dock. He sighed and said to the radio officer, "Tell them that we're looking for her dad's boat. Just leave it at that."

The officer nodded in resignation and swiveled back toward his mic.

Turning to Tom, Alvarez said, "Now is not the time." He shook his head. "At least we are dealing with some resourceful teenagers. I wish this story had a completely happy ending." Alvarez glanced away from the console.

Tom shrugged. "You'd better get over to the Townsend residence before the media storm descends on the property."

Turning his attention toward a TV monitor hung in the corner of the control room, Alvarez rolled his eyes. A muted screen tuned to CNN displayed a block letter caption that read, "Abducted girls escape aboard yacht." An aerial view above the yacht was following its progress as it motored down the Intercoastal Waterway.

"Too late," Alvarez said, gesturing at the TV monitor. "How the hell did they get eyes on the scene already?"

Tom said, "Somebody was monitoring Channel 16 and got a drone airborne most likely. Want somebody to shoot it down?"

Alvarez replied, "I'm really starting to hate those things. Didn't the FAA announce a new mandate for flying drones? Yeah, shoot it down. Just don't hurt my girls." He smiled and added, "Nice yacht. Do you think the department will let me borrow it for a few days?"

"Good luck with that, sir," Tom replied with a snort.

CHAPTER SEVENTEEN

Sunday
09:30 EDT

A passing rain shower that occurred sometime during Hart's absence had smeared the red paintball dye that peppered his truck on I-95. Although the addition of water only made the appearance more of a calamity, at least it gave hope that a good wash and wax would clear the mess. Maybe a little brainless chore was what he needed to clear his mind.

Unfortunately, the call from the VP of Ops's secretary had disturbed Hart's attempt at a homeopathic mental health strategy. He had barely left the employee parking lot when his cell phone rang and, with clenched teeth, Hart had agreed to return to Miami International Airport.

Assuming that the meeting would be brief, he had afforded himself the luxury of using the short-term parking garage. He rolled into a miraculously open space on the ground level just across from the terminal entrance that led to the Patriot Airlines administration offices. Hart closed the door of the truck, pressed the lock button of his key fob, and stepped out from behind. His peripheral vision momentarily caught a glimpse of a black vehicle. The vehicle was stopped, about ten cars away.

Within a fraction of a second, Hart heard the motor race as it accelerated toward him. He didn't waste time assessing the black car's movement. Hart leaped onto the rear bumper of his truck and catapulted into the open pickup bed. The car sped by within inches, the driver hidden behind the opaqueness of tinted windows. As quickly as it had come, the black car was gone.

Collecting his thoughts, Hart stood up in the truck bed and brushed himself off. Another warning? Seriously, how often was he going to be an actor in a bad spy movie? Should he report this incident? What good would it do? He hadn't memorized a license plate number let alone been quick enough to identify the type of vehicle. Maybe the Miami/ Dade cops could review security footage, but by the time a positive ID was made, the car would be history. And chances were good that the plate, or the car itself, was stolen anyhow.

Was this just another scare tactic or had it been a bona fide attempt at keeping him quiet permanently? The fact that he was questioning the motivation behind a hit and run was unsettling enough.

Hart took a few deep breaths, jumped down from his truck, and strode uneasily toward the terminal. He crossed the pedestrian walkway, looking both ways with an abundance of trepidation. What the hell was next?

As he walked through the doors of the chief pilot's office for the second time that day, Hart felt his chest constrict with tension. Crap. Apparently the angst leftover from his conversation with Rod still lingered.

Donna peered over the top of her cubicle and said, "I'd like to believe that you couldn't manage another moment without me, but I'd probably be disappointed."

Hart managed a smile.

Pointing at the conference room on the other side of the office, Donna said, "They're waiting for you."

"Thanks," Hart said with a nod.

It had been over two years since Hart had seen Bob Redmond. The crow's feet embedded in his tan face did more to accent his affable demeanor than to reveal his age.

His perfectly combed brown hair didn't even offer a hint of grey. He wore a sport jacket over a crisp, open collar, blue shirt. Not a wrinkle in sight. Why did Redmond remind Hart of the manager that sat behind the glass windows of a used car dealership while pretending to agonize over a piece of paper that a salesman had just presented from a negotiation with a customer?

As Hart approached, the VP of Ops grinned with a mouthful of perfectly aligned teeth. Towering over Hart, he reached out a hand and shook with a firm grip.

"It's been a while, Captain Lindy."

"I'm guessing the last time was at a standardization meeting with all of us ace-of-the-base check airmen," Hart said with a hint of factiousness. "I think you were discussing the financial impact of our line captains requesting additional fuel when statistically it didn't appear necessary."

"If I recall, my speech went over like the proverbial lead balloon."

"Well, yeah. Anything involving captain's authority is received with a heavy dose of resistance. It's a little like maneuvering a Carnival Cruise ship. It's hard to overcome inertia. But we did eventually increase awareness among our line pilots."

"But you left the cadre of intrepid check airman?" Bob asked.

"I did. It was time. My union called. I thought it was better to sacrifice without pay rather than to sacrifice with pay. I've never been very smart."

Bob Redmond chuckled. "You were one of the good guys. Sorry you left."

Standing off to the side of the conference table, Rod Moretti took a step forward and said, "Gentlemen, now that the pleasantries are complete, I don't think you need my assistance." Rod walked toward the door and smiled.

"Please make yourselves comfortable. I have some knives to sharpen and some pilot beatings to schedule."

The VP of Ops and Hart nodded in unison, watching as Rod exited. Hart felt relieved that his former friend would not be a participant in this informal meeting. Bob Redmond waved an upturned palm at a chair. They seated themselves at the far end of the long conference table.

Bob leaned back in his chair and said, "Thanks for coming, Hart. I know it's been a long couple of days."

"No worries. How can I help?"

"Can you offer some insight into where this investigation is going?"

"How much have you been briefed?"

"Well, I've got the basic facts. But your perspective would be appreciated," Bob said with a polite smile.

Hart took in a deep breath. He began a narrative of the investigation in chronological order of discovery. He ended with the last press conference briefing, offering details in the areas he was most familiar. Hart excluded the ramp security footage in Port of Spain.

The expression of the VP of Ops remained impassive throughout Hart's entire dissertation. He would not want to bet a poker hand against the man. It left Hart feeling uncomfortable.

"Has the FBI indicated a terrorist organization has claimed responsibility?" Redmond asked.

"Not that I'm aware of," Hart replied.

"Why would a terrorist place an explosive device in an engine versus placing one in a cargo hold?"

"Perhaps a terrorist might have theorized that destruction of the engine would also result in destruction of the airplane. Maybe it was simpler to access the engine than the cargo bays. A new terrorist innovation, perhaps."

"Perhaps," Redmond said while tapping his fingers on

the conference table. "Got anything else?"

"Nope. That's it." Hart found it difficult to look Redmond directly in the eye. No doubt, the man suspected Hart was withholding information.

The VP of Ops stared at Hart for a few moments and said, "Well, I'd appreciate if you'd pass on any further developments." Redmond reached inside his sport jacket, pulled out a business card, and slid it across the table toward Hart. "Please feel free to call me directly"

Both men rose to their feet and shook hands.

Redmond said, "Have a safe drive home, Captain Lindy." He began to exit the conference room, but turned back to face Hart. "I know that your accident crew probably won't have any issues, but if they do…in regard to potential civil lawsuits from the victims' families perhaps…the company will provide legal assistance at no expense to the union or the pilots."

"I am aware that our crews are indemnified for the responsible performance of their duties, but I appreciate that, Bob."

Nodding, the VP of Ops said, "We retain a good law firm in New York for such things…Horton and Carty." Redmond flashed a smile and strode out the door.

Hart took in a deep breath and then slowly exhaled. Holy shit. The same law firm? It now was even more compelling to conduct a little snooping in New York. He would take the first flight out of Miami to LaGuardia the following morning. And at some point, he'd have to call Special Agent Fredricks.

09:35 EDT

The golden rays of the sun were slicing through the edges of the cotton clouds that dotted the hazy, blue sky. The rays stabbed at the dark, green water of the canal, flashing with an almost painful brilliance into Kim's eyes. Kim had decided it was a better vantage point to steer the boat from the upper fly bridge. Besides, it was just way cool.

Scanning the view from the port side of the fly bridge, Ashley asked her sister, "Are you sure you know what you're doing?"

"A little late in asking that question now, don't you think?"

"I suppose." Ashley pondered. "You *have* whacked our boat a few times trying to dock at the house. Remember that Saturday you went for a joy ride with your crazy girlfriends when Mom and Dad left for that weekend getaway in New York? Didn't Dad have to spend megabucks to have the side rail fixed? How long were you grounded for…like…until you turned thirty?" Ashley gestured at the Marine Patrol boat that had been escorting them for the last twenty minutes. "I'm sure those guys wouldn't mind helping."

"Ash, give it a rest. We just survived a kidnapping." Kim pointed an index finger at the deck below. "And we killed a giant…a freak. Just maybe we can live through my docking skills."

As the mundane, yellow ranch house on the corner of their neighborhood canal slid into view, Kim slithered the two throttle levers aft. The wake behind the stern of the Tiara began to flatten and uncurl as the boat slowed. Even before the girls got a view of their house, a display of blue and red flashing lights was making an appearance.

With raised eyebrows, Ashley said, "I have a feeling they're expecting us."

"That's an understatement," Kim snickered.

"I think I see a satellite dish. You sure you want to embarrass yourself on national TV?"

"Ash!"

"Just sayin'." Ashley shrugged her shoulders. "I'm looking out for my big sister."

"You can look out for your big sister by climbing down below and finding a few lines to tie up this beast, thank you very much!" Kim pointed at the bow and then the stern. "Attach the lines to the port-side cleats, please."

"Aye, aye, Captain!" Ashley said with a twinge of sarcasm. She climbed down the teak steps that led to the lower deck.

Almost the entire south side of their neighborhood canal was dotted with people. Uniforms. Suits. Ties. Skirts. Cameras. Megaphones. Guns. Badges. A small swath of concrete that defined the Townsends' dock had been cleared. The girls' mom stood, with one arm tucked underneath the opposite elbow, wiping tears from her eyes with the other hand. A big, round man stood next to her.

Fortunately for Kim, the wind and the tide cooperated with limited resistance. She docked the boat with only the slightest of bumps, kissing the wooden pilings with a satisfying squeak. Uniformed cops reached for the lines and began to tie up the Tiara. With only a moment to bask in the glory, Kim surveyed the crowd of faces. She turned the ignition keys off with two assertive clicks. The diesel engines ceased their throaty rumble.

As Kim climbed down from the fly bridge, she could hear the clattering of applause. She grinned and locked eyes with her sister. She took a few steps toward Ashley, and they embraced. A flood poured from the girls' eyes as they began to weep, and laugh, and sob. The sisters dropped slowly to their knees, still locked in a hug. Shutters clicked. Pinpoints of white light flashed. It was a moment that was captured and rebroadcast by every TV network across the county.

Not wasting a second, Robin Townsend rushed past the uniforms scattered around the perimeter of the dock and leapt onto the aft end of the Tiara. With outstretched arms, she knelt down and grabbed her daughters around the shoulders and squeezed. They laughed uncontrollably. They wept uncontrollably. No words were spoken.

10:05 EDT

He turned into the driveway and rolled the truck to a stop behind Cathy's car. One of the doors of the old Volvo was open. Hart turned the ignition off and stepped out of his truck. Two reusable cloth sacks stuffed with groceries sat on the back seat of the Volvo. The cloth bags made him smile. While he wouldn't think twice about accepting plastic bags for his purchases, Cathy was a recycling fanatic. He reached in and grabbed the bags. As Hart backed out of the car, he turned to find Cathy behind him, staring at his truck.

Startled, Hart said, "Yikes, you snuck up on me! I haven't taken my pills today."

Cathy was staring at the driver's side of Hart's truck. Her eyes scanned the paintball mess, assessing the damage. Without looking away, she said, "That's too much of a contrast. I would have gone for a lighter color."

"Sorry, I'll consult with you for the next time," Hart said with a feeble smile.

"When did you take up paintball?" Cathy asked, her expression impassive.

"It wasn't my idea."

"Hmmm…" Cathy turned, took a step toward Hart, and gave him a peck on the lips. "Exactly what aren't you telling me this time?"

Exhaling, Hart said, "It's probably something we should discuss over a bottle of wine." He shifted the grocery bags in his arms and gestured at the house. "Can we talk inside?"

Nodding, Cathy walked toward the front door.

Once inside, Hart deposited the grocery bags on the kitchen counter. He took a few steps toward the metal wine rack at the other end of the counter and pulled out a bottle. In the elegant style of a waiter at a white tablecloth restaurant, he displayed the bottle.

"Might I recommend this vintage of pinot noir? The grapes were stomped just last week by a group of local monks that have taken a lifetime vow of nonbathing."

Shuffling items on the shelves of the open refrigerator, Cathy said, "It doesn't sound as delectable as last month's convenience store wine, but I suppose. And it *is* Sunday morning."

Smiling, Hart pulled a corkscrew opener from a drawer and plopped out the cork. He reached into an open cupboard and set two glasses down on the center island of the kitchen. He poured. The dark, red liquid swirled into the glass. Hart handed a drink to Cathy. They clinked glasses, looked into each other's eyes, and took a sip.

"Not bad for smelly monks," Cathy said, twisting the glass while examining the wine. She set the glass back down on the island and rotated the stem. She looked at Hart. "Talk to me, Captain Lindy."

"Where do you want me to start?"

Tilting her head toward the driveway, Cathy replied, "How about your new paintball hobby?"

With a sigh, Hart said, "Apparently there is an element that does not want this event in Bermuda to be investigated."An element?" Cathy's expression was scornful. "Seriously, Hart? Is this conversation going to be another exercise in pulling teeth?" Cathy's tone turned sour. "I'm already aware of that *element.* I met the jerk. Remember? Or did you forget because you were too busy with the investigation in your room when I called late last night."

"Okay, okay." Hart held up a hand in traffic cop style.

"I've received threatening phone calls. And on my drive to the airport, some psychopaths in a black Mercedes fired a paintball gun at the truck. It was another warning." He cleared his throat. "And just before a meeting in the flight office, a maniac attempted…or pretended an attempt…to run me down in the Dolphin parking garage."

"That's it? Or are you giving me the Reader's Digest version?" Cathy took another sip of wine and placed her hands on her hips.

"It's slightly abbreviated. But the details aren't going to add much to the whole picture."

"How about the details regarding the creepy guy that followed me around for part of the day?"

"I'm almost certain that your creepy guy is the same as my creepy guy. To be honest, Rod Moretti's cop friend and golf buddy was supposed to keep an eye on you while I was gone. Based on his reassurances, I felt reasonably confident that your safety was not in jeopardy before I left for Bermuda. Sorry about your experience. I'm really pissed."

Cathy took a deep breath and then had another sip of wine. She replied, "I'm okay. What's going on with this investigation?"

"I don't like where it could be going. Suffice it to say, this is not a typical accident. It seems likely that the airplane was sabotaged. But why? And by whom? While the NTSB continues their forensic research with the FBI, I have to do a little investigation of my own."

Squinting her eyes in an inquisitive expression, Cathy asked, "What does that mean?"

"I need to take a visit into Manhattan tomorrow. I'm sorry, hon, but it's better that I don't get into the specifics."

"You're not going to give me the, 'If I told you I'd have to kill you' line are you?"

"No, but it *is* for your protection."

"The creepy guy?"

"Maybe. But actually, I'm more concerned with the FBI. If you don't have knowledge of the investigation, then you don't have anything to hide."

Wrapping her arms across her chest, Cathy's gaze grew intense. She asked, "Do *you* have anything to hide?"

For a brief moment, Hart glanced down at his glass of wine. He looked back up into the radiant sparkle of Cathy's dark, brown eyes. He sighed. She always knew. Hart said nothing.

Moisture began to fill the corner of Cathy's eyes. With a whisper, she said, "I thought so." She picked up her glass and walked out of the kitchen and into the master bedroom. She closed the door with a quiet clack.

Grimacing, Hart looked down at the Mexican tile floor. He shook his head in resignation. Following Cathy into the bedroom at this moment would be futile. He had screwed up again…maybe for the last time.

10:15 EDT

As Alvarez drove away from the scene at the Townsend home, a deep heaviness began to settle in his chest. No matter how many times Alvarez had performed the solemn task of informing families that a loved one had died tragically, he had always found the grim responsibility awkward and uncomfortable. He had stopped using the words, "I'm sorry for your loss." The phrase seemed mechanical and ritualistic. Certainly someone's passing deserved a remark of greater meaning. Lately, he had found it more respectful to just remain silent after the announcement. He had done just that with the Townsend family.

As he had watched their eyes widen and lips begin to quiver, Alvarez felt a fond admiration for the stoic resolve of Robin Townsend. She had not reached for the support of the nearest piece of furniture nor crumpled to her knees. She had simply nodded in anguish even as her daughters broke down into inconsolable sobbing. Perhaps the woman had already accepted her husband's fate before it became official. Perhaps the discovery of her husband's secret life had become a form of death anyhow.

Predicting the reaction he would cause by announcing Mike Townsend's demise, Alvarez had strategically interviewed the daughters beforehand. He felt horrible, but he needed to build his case. After all, Alvarez had to connect the dots with the two abductions, and now…six related homicides. He visualized the names and faces in his head. The school security guard. The two hot bod girls. A monster of a bald guy. A gay pilot. And a gay pilot's boyfriend. Shit!

Somehow this killing spree had something to do with Mike Townsend. The daughters had been held hostage as an insurance policy, or some form of extortion. And the pilot was at the center of the mess. The airplane incident in Bermuda was certainly related. Crap! What the hell did a dumb-ass detective know about airplanes? Was this about drugs? Or was this about money? Or both?

The traffic on U.S.-1 was beginning to compress like a Slinky. A line of cars was funneling into the flippers of a giant pinball machine as they diverted around a road construction site dotted with fluorescent orange cones. Alvarez released a quiet groan, a frustrated resignation to the scene ahead of him. His mind wandered into thought fragments.

He had heard that the FBI was involved with the investigation in Bermuda. It was probably time to consult with them, perhaps a little quid pro quo?

For the moment, the most concrete form of evidence that the detective had was an ID on the big, bald guy. Chris DeFazio was a war vet. Actually he was a war hero. He was awarded a Silver Star for pulling two of his platoon buddies out of a burning Humvee after it had exploded from an IED while they were taking on automatic weapons fire from all sides on an Iraqi street. Apparently Chris had single-handedly neutralized the enemy enough to allow for additional ground troops to overtake the area. He was a modern-day Rambo.

But when he returned home from the desert, Chris must have begun to unravel. He had accumulated an arrest record of minor assaults, mostly bar fights. Except for a brief stint at his brother's insurance office, he had changed employers like some people changed clothes. Somehow he had become associated with the mystery guy who owned the yacht. Bodyguard, maybe?

Alvarez was still working on the identity of the yacht owner. So far it seemed that the guy was some type of high-powered lawyer. He was a partner in a Manhattan law firm. For the moment, the guy was nowhere to be found. Alvarez had the NYPD researching his background. In the meantime, the guy's house was under surveillance.

Feeling a vibration in the pocket of his khaki pants, Alvarez reached for his cell phone. He pulled the phone out and slapped it to his ear without looking at the caller ID.

"Alvarez here."

"Hey, Detective, it's Captain Gordon at the Fort Lauderdale Coast Guard station."

"Yes, sir?"

"Think we have something you'd be interested in. We just got done transferring two floaters off a charter boat from one of our local dive shops." The captain coughed and cleared his throat. "A newlywed couple rented two of those Seabob diving scooter devices and got more than they bargained for."

"What exactly do you mean, Captain?"

"The newlywed couple were operating their scooters

along the reef, looking for the standard array of fish, and literally bumped into two deceased white females within close proximity to each other. After calming his clients, the dive master recovered the bodies to the boat's swim platform. He called us on Channel 16."

"Lovely," Alvarez said.

"Not so much, Detective. But the females fit the description you indicated."

"Are you certain, Captain?"

"I'll let you folks complete your own forensic homework, but the dive master recognized the deceased. He frequents the hot bod contests. The women were regular contestants."

"How are the newlyweds doing?"

"Can't answer that question, sir. But I'm sure they have a honeymoon memory they would like to forget."

"True statement." Alvarez sighed. "Forensic homework aside, did you ID them with your data base?"

"Yessir. You have one Anita Cohen, aka Amber. And one Sarah Sorenson, aka Serena." A keyboard clicked in the background. "Ms. Cohen dropped out of pre-law at FSU to pursue a modeling career. Her dad is a district judge. Ms. Cohen's priors were an assault and a DUI. Interestingly enough, she listed her occupation as law clerk. The employer's address appears to be a residence on Bayview Drive in Fort Lauderdale."

Alvarez said, "She was probably not making Daddy happy." The detective watched a white BMW race through a red light as he released his foot off the brake at an intersection. He was glad his days as a patrol cop were gone. "And that address makes sense."

The captain continued, "Ms. Sorenson was also an FSU grad. Liberal arts degree. She listed her current occupation as executive secretary with the same employer address as Ms. Cohen. No priors. Her mother is a local charter boat captain;

I've personally seen her skipper on the Lady Windridge."

"That explains her daughter's boating skills according to the abducted Townsend sisters."

"Both women had extensive training at a local martial arts studio. And they both had concealed carry permits."

"Very nice. I would have bought Girl Scout cookies from them."

"Unofficially, for Ms. Cohen, it appears that the cause of death would be a gunshot wound to the chest. And for Ms. Sorenson, cause of death most likely was a penetration of her abdomen via some type of improvised projectile device."

"Perhaps our pilot retained some combat skills from the military. Sounds like he made an escape attempt of his own." Alvarez glanced at the traffic ahead. Cars were creeping past the intersection at a snail's pace. As always, the red light was decidedly longer than the green. "At the end of the day, Mike Townsend's rescue mission was successful."

"Agreed, Detective. But tragic nonetheless."

"Very unfortunate. Your assistance is much appreciated. I assume the coroner is en route along with a CSI team?"

"Yessir, that's my understanding."

"Thanks, Captain." Alvarez slid the phone from his ear and pressed the End button. "This could get more interesting," he said to the empty car seat to his right. He felt a sinking in his gut, a hollowness. Alvarez missed the banter with his partner. Abrasively funny, his partner would have talked through the situation, presenting the facts in perspective. But this time, Alvarez would have to work it all out on his own.

With the traffic finally beginning to flow, he looked at his speedometer: forty-five mph. His adrenalin applied more pressure to the gas pedal. Alvarez's increasing anxiety began to match his increasing speed. He needed to have a very serious conversation with Tracey Abbott.

CHAPTER EIGHTEEN

Sunday
10:30 EDT

The ringing of his cell phone jolted him like an electrical charge. After his drooped-shoulder departure from Cathy's house, Hart's trance hadn't been disturbed despite the wait at the Hillsboro Inlet drawbridge. He glanced at the caller ID. Diane Yellen. Seriously?

Diane was Hart's seventy-something next-door neighbor. Their first encounter shortly after Hart moved into the community became immediately adversarial. Before he had grunted the last box out of the U-Haul truck, a dispute erupted over a coconut palm tree that had been unceremoniously dumping its wares on Diane's property.

Not quite understanding that the issue was merely an awkward attempt at garnering attention and filling the hole in her life that Diane's deceased husband had left, Hart went on the defensive. It was not the neighborhood welcome he had envisioned.

The relationship remained contentious. But as almost fifteen years passed, and a handful of peace offerings in the form of Cathy and her famous chocolate chip cookies, time healed most of the wounds. Now Hart could maintain a conversation with his neighbor beyond a discussion of the week's weather. He realized that Diane was an intelligent woman with more on her mind than just displeasure at errant coconuts.

Even though Hart had given her his cell phone number in the event that she needed his assistance, she never called. Why now? His mood certainly wasn't conducive to a friendly chat.

Hart pressed the Talk button. "Uh…Hi, Diane. Are you okay?"

Diane's gravelly but articulate voice was edgy and tense. "I thought that maybe they had called you. But you don't know, do you?"

"Don't know what, Diane?"

"Oh my…" The elderly woman gasped. "I called the minute I saw the black smoke. I knew you weren't home."

"Diane…"

"Your house. It's on fire, Hart! They're here now! Fire trucks! Hoses everywhere! They're spraying! It's awful."

As Hart held the phone to his ear, the giant metal leaf of the drawbridge was descending. He stared into the distance, trying to process the information being conveyed by his neighbor. It was barely making sense. His thoughts were an unfinished jigsaw puzzle, pieces missing.

Hart managed to ask, "Is anybody hurt? How bad is the damage?"

"No. No one has been hurt. When I first saw it, the entire house was engulfed from within. Black smoke everywhere." Diane paused for a moment. Hart could hear the metallic clack of a screen door opening. His neighbor must have stepped outside to further survey the scene. "It looks the fire has penetrated the roof line over your kitchen."

The red and white traffic gates briefly formed an arch as they rose and separated to opposite sides of the road. The cars ahead of Hart began to move toward the grated surface of the lowered drawbridge. He shook his head and took his foot off the brake pedal. Hart unconsciously tightened his grip on the steering wheel as his truck rolled forward.

“Shit! That bastard!” Hart muttered through his teeth. He slapped the dashboard with the heel of his palm. “That creepy Middle Eastern guy or his associates had to be involved,” Hart thought.

“Excuse me?” his elderly neighbor asked.

“Sorry, Diane. I was expressing my frustration out loud. It wasn’t directed at you.”

“I understand, Hart. This is awful.”

“Thanks for the call, Diane. I’m just crossing the Hillsboro Bridge. Be there shortly.”

Hart ended the conversation abruptly. As he crossed over the inlet, he glanced up in the direction of his street. An ominous charcoal gray cloud billowed from above the shimmering green of the palm trees. The cloud formed a cluster of enormous cauliflower shapes. Hart pressed down on the gas pedal.

10:35 EDT

The click of the deadbolt was followed by the rotation of the bronze doorknob. The white door opened a small crack, restricted by the dangling chain from the inside latch. One eye, pink lips, and the sharp chin of Tracey Abbott’s face was all Alvarez could identify of the high school vice principal. The pupil widened as she began to blink in recognition of the detective.

“Ms. Abbott, may I come in?” Alvarez asked with a forced smile.

The vice principal’s eye scanned the detective. She said, “Have you come to tell me they found our girls? Thanks, I already know. It’s all over the news. I can’t tell you how elated I am!”

“No, Ms. Abbott. I have some additional questions. May I come in, please?”

"Can it wait? I'm expecting company and haven't even showered."

"Your assistance would really be appreciated," Alvarez said with a hint of impatience.

As Tracey Abbott shifted her weight to the opposite foot, the other eye became visible. The eye scanned above Alvarez's shoulder to the outside. From behind, Alvarez heard the quiet hiss of tires rolling across pavement. He turned.

A black Mercedes was gliding through the condo parking lot. The car slowed for a brief moment and then accelerated, exiting in a blur. Alvarez's reflexes weren't quite fast enough to glimpse the entire Florida license plate before the sedan disappeared from view.

"Damn it!" Alvarez exclaimed. He turned back toward the vice principal and the open door. "Ms. Abbott, I suppose that was the company you were expecting!?"

The eye blinked and looked away. The lips drew tight. Tracey Abbott remained silent.

Alvarez shook his head, making no attempt at hiding his disgust. He reached into a pocket and yanked out his cell phone. His finger tapped the display. Alvarez put the phone to his ear and glared at the face in the crack of the door.

After a short delay, Alvarez said, "Tom, need your assistance now. Find a late model, E-class Mercedes. Maybe 2016. Maybe 2017. I can never figure out the year of this luxury stuff. Can't afford the snotty-looking things anyhow. I wasn't fast enough to get the whole plate, but the last numbers are 8-7. Sorry, I'm not much help."

Alvarez stared at Tracey Abbott and continued talking with the patrol cop. "There's a good chance that it's the car in the high school security footage." The detective nodded, the phone pressed hard against his ear. "You're a prince, Tom. Thanks." He tapped a finger to the display and slipped the phone back into his pocket.

"I suggest that you open the door, Ms. Abbott. If you cooperate now, it may not get ugly later," Alvarez said with a stern, matter-of-fact tone.

After a few moments of hesitation, the crack of open door disappeared. The chain clacked across the latch and the door opened. The detective nodded and stepped across the weathered, wooden threshold. The vice principal stepped back, allowed the big man to pass, and waved a hand at a black leather couch. Alvarez sat, the material creasing and crunching under his weight.

With her Miami Dolphins T-shirt flopped loosely over a pair of white gym shorts, Tracey Abbott slithered reluctantly onto the opposite end of the couch. She curled her knees into her chest and hugged her legs together.

Before Alvarez could speak, a thirty-something woman with flowing brown hair, jaguar eyes, and red toenails glided across the tile floor. Hands on her hips, her slender bare arms exposed, the woman shifted her gaze rapidly between Alvarez and Tracey Abbott.

"Who might this be?" the woman asked with a Hispanic accent. She focused on Alvarez without looking at Tracey Abbott.

"He's a detective, Sondra," Tracey said.

"I do not like detectives," Sondra said, flipping a lock of hair away from her cheek.

Grinning, Alvarez introduced himself and said, "It's okay. There are some detectives I don't like either."

Sondra snorted. "What do you want with my Tracey?"

"I need her help with a case."

"Do you mean the girls that were kidnapped from school?" Sondra asked, her eyebrows arched in a perfect V.

"Yes." Alvarez said, looking at the caramel-skinned woman with the lanky legs. "Do you know anything about the case?"

"Only what Tracey has told me." Sondra gestured at the blank TV screen in front of the couch. "The Wolf with the gray beard on CNN said the two sisters escaped in a yacht. They are okay, yes?"

Alvarez nodded, chuckling to himself at the CNN reference, and said, "Yes, they are mostly okay. But there is more to the story."

"Like, what more?" Sondra asked in a challenging tone. She plopped down onto the arm of the couch next to Tracey.

"I could tell you, but Ms. Abbott indicated that you are expecting company." Alvarez glanced at Tracey. The vice principal squirmed. "I don't want to interrupt your plans."

"Company?" Sondra asked, gazing at Tracey. Tracey looked away. "Oh…you mean the thin man with the bad teeth and the strange accent who doesn't shave much?"

"Does he drive a Mercedes, Sondra?"

"Yes, very nice. Always clean and shiny."

"How often does he come to visit?"

"He not my friend. He's Tracey's friend from the high school. He only come here once or twice before."

"Do you enjoy his visits?" Alvarez asked with a smile.

"Visits? He stay for barely a minute. He gives Tracey an envelope and leaves."

"What's in the envelope?"

"Money."

"Money? Really?" Alvarez asked, raising an eyebrow and feigning curiosity.

"*Si*. Usually hundred-dollar bills. Sometimes twenties. The money goes to a charity for homeless people that is collected from the students and teachers every week." Sondra smiled and patted the vice principal on the shoulder. Tracey looked down and subtly shook her head. "My Tracey is in charge of the charity. The Mercedes man is the school bookkeeper. He counts the money and gives it to her. She *dis-tra-bute* directly to homeless shelters."

"That's very admirable," Alvarez said with a wry smile. "How long have you and Ms. Abbott lived together, Sondra?"

"Well, I move here from Nicaragua more than two years ago. So…*dos*…two years."

"Are you ladies married?"

Sondra presented a wide smile with glittering white teeth. She stroked the back of Tracey Abbott's hair and said gleefully, "*Si*. The day it became legal in *Floor-ee-da*, we were second in line at the courthouse!"

"Very nice. Congratulations."

"*Gracias,*" Sondra said with an assertive nod.

Glancing at the vice principal and then clearing his throat, Alvarez asked, "Are you also friends with Robin Townsend?"

"Who?"

"You may have heard the name on the news. Her daughters are the girls that were abducted at Ms. Abbott's school."

Sondra's eyebrows raised. She replied, "No. Why would I know her?"

The detective looked at the vice principal with narrowed eyes. Tracey Abbott's pupils widened. Alvarez grinned and said, "No reason. Just covering all my bases." Tracey's expression softened with relief.

Turning her head to look at the slinky brunette, Tracey said, "Sondra, the detective and I have more to discuss. You were a big help. Didn't you have some groceries to pick up?"

"*Si*. I did. I go now if you're okay." Sondra slid off the arm of the couch and pointed at Alvarez. "He's not so bad."

Alvarez smiled.

With a flourish, Sondra swooped up the sequined straps of a purse that had been lying on a coffee table. She positioned the straps on one shoulder, slid into a pair of leather flip-flops, and reached for the doorknob while blowing a kiss to Tracey. Sondra glided out the door, thwacking it closed behind her.

Staring at the closed door, Alvarez said, "I pictured you with a more mature model, Ms. Abbott, but she certainly is beautiful." He shook his head and chuckled. "Homeless charity? Very special. Nothing like a little subterfuge to keep the relationship strong." The detective turned to face the vice principal. His expression grew stern.

Tracey Abbott glared, her face a mixture of anxiety and anger. "There is no need for sarcasm, Detective. I'll tell you a very simple story."

Beckoning with the wave of his fingers from an open palm, Alvarez motioned for the vice principal to speak.

"In various ways, I was solicited by the man driving the Mercedes." Tracey sighed. Sondra was not a legal resident of the U.S. In addition, lesbians are not exactly embraced by the local school board. This man..." She gestured her head outside toward the parking lot. "I think he's of Middle Eastern descent, but I'm not sure...he threatened to expose both of these details unless I cooperated with his requests. Without getting into details, he demonstrated his resolve through different methods.

"As an example, he stuffed my mailbox with samples of potentially damaging letters addressed to key players on the school board and local politicians...pleasant stuff like that. He would periodically remind me with such things. As long as I complied with his requests, I would receive cash payments that normally amounted to around $1,000."

"Go on, Ms. Abbott," Alvarez said.

"Despite the rumors, school administrators aren't exactly on top of the food chain with salaries. And the money helped with attorney fees to expedite Sondra's citizenship status."

"Cops aren't on top of the food chain either, Ms. Abbott, but accepting bribes isn't exactly a good career move in the department."

"Call it a bribe if you wish, Detective, but my situation was more of an extortion."

"We can argue over semantics later. But you could have notified the police, Ms. Abbott. Please continue."

Taking a deep breath, Tracey said. "Calling the police wasn't an option. He threatened me with the same scenario of revealing my dirty, little secrets. And judging by the fact the creep seemed to know the brand of granola that I had for breakfast in the morning, I had no reason to doubt his convictions."

"I'll take that statement into consideration," Alvarez said with a stone-faced expression.

"I was asked to develop a relationship with Robin Townsend. It was easy. Her oldest daughter is challenging, oftentimes a disciplinary problem. For that reason, Robin was a frequent visitor to my office. My extortionist was probably aware of that fact. I was told to pass on any pertinent information concerning the Townsend sisters, Robin, and especially the airline pilot husband."

"Were you told why?" Alvarez asked.

"Really, Detective? You have to ask that question? No, I was never given an explanation." The vice principal shook her head. "When the situation developed in Bermuda regarding the accident flight with their father, I was asked to isolate the sisters immediately and then move them outside. Knowing that Robin was on her way to pick up the girls, I wasn't especially concerned. As per school policy, I had the girls escorted to the parking lot by our security officer. I stayed in the shadows, but had no idea of the consequences."

"Seriously, Ms. Abbott, you don't consider yourself complicit in the abduction? You accepted a payment on the day of the incident."

"How do you think I've felt over the last several hours, Detective Alvarez?"

"I'm not really sure, Ms. Abbott."

The vice principal shook her head and closed her eyes. She said, "That's the story, Detective Alvarez."

"I think you're missing one detail."

"I've told you everything."

"No. Not exactly," Alvarez stated. "Why did you make at least two visits to a residence on Bayview Drive?"

Tracey Abbott looked up at the ceiling and then back at the detective. She sighed and said, "It was the residence of my extortionist. With the Townsend sisters abducted and the security guard murdered, I wanted out. I fulfilled my obligations."

"Your motivation couldn't have possibly been a final payment, perhaps?" Alvarez asked with a sneer.

Folding her arms across her chest, Tracey Abbott said nothing.

"I hope your conscience makes your life miserable," Alvarez said at a low volume level.

"Comment all you want, Detective, but don't judge me until you've walked in my shoes."

"This might sound cliché but it's not my job to judge, Ms. Abbott. I'll leave that up to a jury."

"Are you arresting me?"

Alvarez smiled and said, "Not at the moment, but I suggest you don't stray too far from the neighborhood." The detective planted his hands into the plush couch and pushed himself to his feet. "We'll be in touch, Ms. Abbott." He took a few steps toward the door. "Thank you for the visit." Alvarez twisted the doorknob and walked out of the condo.

11:05 EDT

The sky outside Rod's office window had become the color of charcoal. Within the charcoal, a shade of mucus green blended itself in. The scene had an ominous quality. Clouds roiled above. Streaks of jagged orange crisscrossed the clouds, the lightning not quite ready to strike the ground. Just as predicted by the airline's weather experts, an evil line of thunderstorms produced by a well-defined cold front was about to strike MIA.

Sadly, Mother Nature's disruptive scene was a welcome distraction to the discussion that was taking place in his office. A flight attendant supervisor, a flight attendant, a flight attendant union rep, and a pilots union rep were arguing the merits of a decision made by a Miami-based captain just prior to a particular evening's 777 departure to Buenos Aires. Twirling a lock of her blond hair, the flight attendant growled, "The captain said that it was *his* airplane!"

"Well, technically, Ms. Kozinski, he *is* the pilot in command," Rod said. "You've been flying long enough to know that it's a colloquial expression, meaning he is in charge. Despite USA Today's rumors that we pay captains a million dollars a year, I am certain he had no illusions of ownership regarding a $250 million airplane."

The pilots union rep seemed to be clearing his throat, but Rod wasn't quite certain the sound from the man's throat hadn't just been an attempt at disguising a chuckle. The union rep also appeared to be fighting a smile. Rod peered at the man over the top of his glasses.

"Captain Moretti, do you honestly believe that your pilot in command has jurisdiction over the distribution of bottled water?" the flight attendant supervisor asked.

"The short answer is, yes," Rod replied. "Look…"

The pilots union rep raised a finger and said, "If I can interrupt, Captain Moretti?"

Rod nodded.

The union rep continued. "It was a reasonable request for the captain to make. If you've been following the news lately, Argentina has been dealing with occasional contaminated water supplies. He simply wanted Ms. Kozinski, the purser, to be certain that his crew would have bottled water for the layover."

"Despite the short supply on board? Our customers are the number one priority," the flight attendant supervisor said, crossing her arms.

The pilots union rep responded. "Our customers won't be able to fly if our pilots become ill."

"So, the solution was to remove our purser from the trip?"

"It was the captain's prerogative based on insubordination," the pilots union rep said in a matter-of-fact-tone.

"Insubordination? Really? Over bottled water?"

Rod raised his hands in traffic cop fashion and said, "All right. All right." He looked directly at the flight attendants union rep. "Your purser was still paid for the trip, correct?"

"Yes, but this is not a precedent we care to establish."

"I don't consider the matter a precedent, but certainly the captain could have exercised a few more drops of diplomacy," Rod said. He glanced at the pilots union rep and then looked back at the flight attendant supervisor. "Although our pilots union representative is not under any obligation, I am certain that as a professional standards committee member, he can discuss options with our captain that involve more tactful measures in the future."

The flight attendant slid forward in her chair and began to open her mouth. Her expression held an appearance of protest. Rod held up an index finger. "Trust me. This is an amicable compromise. I reviewed your file, Ms. Kozinski.

You seem to have a history of confrontation with the cockpit."

Darts of rain began to assault the glass of the office window. Outside, invisible currents of air began to strike at newly formed puddles on the ramp. A handful of unsecured baggage pallets began to creep across the white concrete.

The phone on Rod's desk warbled its electronic tone. An amber light blinked next to his direct line. And it seemed that all the other lines were blinking also. Rod raised his eyebrows. Normally, his calls were not routed to him during a meeting. "Saved by the bell," he thought. Rod snatched the handset off its cradle.

"Moretti."

"It's your favorite admin assistant, Captain Moretti," Donna said. Rod could hear the faint sound of her actual voice coming from the cubicle around the corner. "I was thinking that you could probably use a little comic relief."

"You're clairvoyant, Donna," Rod said, attempting not to grin.

"Yup. I've been reminded to use my psychic powers with caution. Unfortunately, I can't really offer comic relief. But what I have does merit an interruption. You need to turn on the news. Try Channel 7, as much as I know you love to hate that station. The office lines are overheating. It isn't good."

"What's up?"

"Trust me."

"Donna, I'm already aware that Mike Townsend's daughters are safe. Is that what this is about?"

"No. Different stuff. Get rid of your meeting."

Shaking his head, Rod plopped the handset back onto the cradle. He scanned the faces in his office and said, "Something urgent has developed. I'm sorry. I'd like to believe that we've reached an understanding on this matter. Can we all agree?" Heads nodded, some with a degree of reluctance. "Cool. Thank you all for your time." Rod stood from behind his desk and began shaking hands from left to right. The meeting participants walked out of his office in quiet procession.

Reaching for the remote control buried under a manila folder, Rod aimed at the TV and pressed the power button. He selected Channel 7 and was immediately presented with a recognizable image.

The screen displayed a photo of a younger Mike Townsend in uniform. The Patriot Airlines logo was in the background. Divided by a thin white line, a snapshot photo of a black-haired man wearing a clinging V-neck T-shirt was displayed next to the copilot's image. A caption beneath it read, "Jonathan Goodman."

Rod pressed the volume button. The afternoon news anchor was narrating.

"The copilot of Patriot Airlines Flight 63, who helped to land the crippled airliner, was found dead on board his boat…gunshot wound…attempted rescue of his abducted daughters…secret life…relationship with gay restaurant owner…owner brutally murdered at Los Olas home… contestants from hot bod circuit thought to be involved in abduction found floating over reef by honeymoon divers."

The intensity of his focus on the news prevented Rod from noticing that Donna had walked into his office. She stood beside him and turned to view the TV.

"It's awful, isn't it?" Donna said.

"This is right out of a Hollywood script." Rod looked back at the TV and exhaled a deep breath. "Get Sammy on the phone. He needs to get a trained union rep to the house. The family needs support from PAPA."

"Sam already called. They're on the case."

"Good. I should make a visit to the Townsend home."

"Do you want to wait for the dust to settle first?" Donna asked.

"The dust won't be settling for a long time. Mrs. Townsend and her daughters need to know now that this flight department will do everything in its power to assist in this crisis."

"You could be stepping into a quagmire. Be careful, Captain Moretti."

"Thanks, Donna. I'm aware of that. In that regard, get Bob Redmond on the phone please." Rod glanced out the window at the monsoon. "We need to work out a strategy."

"I've tried the VP of Ops numerous times. Office number. Cell phone. Texts. E-mails. No response. His secretary can't find him. It's a little unusual."

"He's probably holding his finger on the dam. He'll turn up."

Just as Rod was about to press the power button of the remote, the anchor announced, "On what might be a related story…"

"Shit, there's more?" Rod grunted.

The camera zoomed in on a residential street lined with manicured lawns and tiled driveways. As the live scene enlarged, charred and blackened wood that at one time framed a roof, smoldered. Wispy, white smoke rose from an unrecognizable pile of rubble. Off to the side, orange flames and a black cloud engulfed the remaining structure. It was somebody's nightmare.

And then Rod recognized a truck parked off to the side. A tall, lanky figure with short, straw-colored hair was leaning against the cab. His arms were drawn tight across his chest. His hair was becoming matted from the slanted rain that was beginning to fall, his shirt dotted with the drops. He seemed oblivious to the approaching storm. Was it? No. It couldn't be.

The news anchor's voice droned, "Hart Lindy, a Patriot Airlines captain and pilots union accident investigator involved with Flight 63 in Bermuda, arrived to his Lighthouse Point neighborhood today to find his home in flames. According to some sources, arson is suspected."

Donna stared at the screen and said, "Oh, shit."

"This has not been a good day for Captain Lindy," Rod said, shaking his head.

"At least you have an alibi, Captain Moretti."

Rolling his eyes at Donna, Rod said, "Very funny. Despite what you think, my heart pumps blood at a temperature of 98.6 degrees like everybody else."

"Sorry, I didn't mean it that way. I just hate to see you guys at each other's throats."

Momentarily locking soft eyes with Rod, Donna smiled and began to walk out of the office. Just before leaving, she turned back toward her boss and said, "Make the call. You guys were friends for a long time."

Donna closed the office door behind her.

11:35 EDT

The sun was attempting an appearance from behind the remnants of gray clouds left behind by the storm. Detached palm fronds were scattered about the grounds of the building and throughout the parking lot of the FBI's Miami field office. Pools of dark water splotched the pavement.

The little flight school airplanes from North Perry Airport were resuming their westbound departures like locusts escaping from the fields. As Ryan Fredricks looked out his fifth-floor office, he was certain that the day would come when one of the damn things would impale itself into the mirrored glass of the contemporary-style building. Pilots are all insane. He thought of Hart Lindy and his team.

Hart was not having a good day. Ryan had just got a tweet with a photo of the captain's charcoal-grilled house from a secretary. Twitter? That's how the Bureau was communicating? Gee whiz. Anyhow, he'd wait for the locals to complete the arson investigation. He was confident that it was all linked to Flight 63. He just had to connect the dots. And if Hart would just sit still for a minute, he could offer the guy some protection.

When he got the intel that the Flight 63 copilot had been murdered in what appeared to be a botched rescue attempt of his abducted daughters, Ryan's radar went on high alert. What was this gay airline pilot attempting to accomplish? Why would he sabotage his own airplane? No matter what Hart Lindy was trying to rationalize, the security footage at Port of Spain's Piarco Airport was undeniable--Mike Townsend had placed something in the engine nacelle.

Ryan's train of thought was interrupted with the buzzing of his cell phone vibrating itself across the wood veneer of the desk like the miniature players of the old electric football games. He glanced at the caller ID and raised his eyebrows. The number was from the Miami P.D. He placed the phone to his ear.

"Special Agent Ryan Fredricks."

"Agent Fredricks, Detective Rita Sanchez." The voice was sultry with no trace of a Hispanic accent.

"What can I do for you, Detective Sanchez?"

"Actually, I have some information for you. We have word that your field office is investigating the circumstances surrounding Patriot Airlines Flight 63."

"That is a true statement," Ryan said, his curiosity piqued.

"Well, it seems that Patriot Airlines is having a bad week. Don't know if this info is related, but we're investigating a fresh homicide." In the background, the static of a police radio crackled with the unemotional voice of a dispatcher responding to a disturbance call. "Wanted you to get the word before it was posted on Facebook."

"Apparently the Bureau prefers Twitter these days, but thanks."

"A Robert Redmond, white male, age 55, was found in his 5-series BMW in the parking lot of the Intercontinental Hotel, just south of Bayfront Park. Gunshot wound to the head. His title with the airline is VP of Operations, which is a big deal. He would have direct knowledge of the Flight 63 situation."

"Any suspects?"

"Possibly. We've traced one of the victim's calls to a burner phone that was found in a housekeeper's cleaning cart at the hotel. The housekeeper gave us a sketchy description of some scruffy guy with bad teeth and a strange accent that was on her floor when she discovered the phone among a pile of dirty towels."

Ryan glanced out the window and watched another airplane lurch skyward. "Security footage?"

"We're reviewing footage from inside the hotel and outside the hotel. The shooter must have known that the camera view was out of range in the section of the parking lot that Redmond was murdered."

"Of course," Ryan said with a sigh.

"We're working all the angles."

"Understood."

"One of the victim's other recent calls was to the direct line of an office in the Tobago Bank of Trinidad."

"Interesting."

"The last app the victim used on his iPhone was Notes. In addition to the phone number I just mentioned, Redmond had typed in 'N' as in November, 3-2-1-4, 'W' as in Whiskey. Not sure what that means, but you probably do."

"I'm fairly certain that's a registration number for a U.S.-registered airplane."

"Makes sense. I can secure-email all the info we have so

far if you'd like."

"Please. That would be great, Detective." Ryan paused. He thought of Hart Lindy's I-95 paintball encounter with a black Mercedes. "Do me a favor. Check the outside security footage again. If a black E-series Mercedes is in the vicinity at the time of the murder, let me know."

"Agent Fredricks, you do know that those things are like M&M's around here?"

"Humor me, Detective Sanchez."

Ryan slid the phone from his ear and pressed the End button.

Security footage? Why hadn't he thought of that earlier? If the copilot had sabotaged the airplane, it might stand to reason that he had planned the Bermuda diversion. And the security footage of Flight 63's arrival at the gate might have some clues. Had something of value been placed in the cargo hold? Would the cargo manifest have an answer?

Ryan glanced out the window for a moment. He picked up the half-smoked unlit cigar from an unused ashtray on his desk and then rolled it around in his mouth. He trotted over to the main secretary's desk.

Momentarily surprised by Agent Fredrick's stealthy appearance, the pepper-haired woman looked up from her computer screen and forced a smile.

"Please find me the manager of Bermuda's airport security police. Tell him it's urgent that he contact me ASAP. Also, contact the Patriot Airlines station manager with the same urgency." Ryan began to turn away and then pulled a scrap of notepaper from his pocket. He scanned the notepaper. "Call the Bureau's local contact with Air Traffic Control at the FAA. Have them locate an airplane with the registration number N3214W. Thanks."

The secretary nodded. Ryan walked back toward his desk. He wished he could light his damn Monte Cristo stogy in the environmentally controlled, smoke-free building. A cigar made him focus.

No matter. His gut told him that he was on the right track.

CHAPTER NINETEEN

Sunday
14:45 EDT

After speaking with the cops, the fire department, Diane Yellen, and the insurance company, he was as burned out as his charred house. Hart just wanted to disappear. Having planned on a visit to Manhattan anyhow, he hopped on the next available flight to New York.

For all intents and purposes, Hart was now homeless. On the flight up from MIA to LaGuardia, he had half-chuckled to himself that he was appropriately traveling to the homeless capital of the world. Maybe he could find a cardboard box and a bench with a view in Central Park.

The doors rattled open to the twenty-fifth floor of the Hudson Hotel. Hart stepped out into the darkened, euro-décor of the hallway. His concentration over the last several hours had been a jumbled mosaic of thoughts: Cathy. The pile of smoldering rubble that had been his home. Flight 63. Mike Townsend. Rod Moretti. His dad and the family airport. His career.

Hart stood for a moment, the elevator doors clanking closed behind him. So why would a law firm rent an office suite in a hotel on Fifty-Eighth Street near Columbus Circle anyhow? Hart walked down the corridor, noting the room numbers. He nodded a greeting to an Asian housekeeper who was scurrying about a wheeled cart full of towels, miniature shampoo bottles, and mops. He stopped in front of a door with a brass placard mounted off to the side of the jam. The placard read, "Horton and Carty, Attorneys."

Hearing the sound of a muted voice from behind the door, Hart rapped, twisted the decorative knob, and walked inside. A blonde, barely in her twenties, sat behind an ornate cherry wood desk. The handset of a console phone was pressed against an ear. The curly black cord of the handset that draped across her chest brought attention to an ample amount of cleavage, enhanced by an appropriately chosen push-up bra. Every other sentence from the woman's conversation seemed to end in a giggle. If she had been chewing gum, the young woman would have been a living cliché.

The woman smiled at Hart and said into the handset, "Gotta go. Someone just walked into the office. Hee-hee! Call you later." She clicked the phone down onto the console cradle. "How can I help you, sir?"

Smiling, with an attempt at remaining focused only on the blonde's eyes, Hart said, "I have an injury matter that I would like considered." He cleared his throat and continued with his rehearsed scenario. "Heard good things about this firm."

"Really? Hmm…well…their cases are all done through referrals. Were you referred by someone?"

"Uhh…I was. But I can't remember his name. Sorry."

Hart shuffled his feet and scanned the office. Except for a handful of small art deco paintings, the walls were bare. The office was void of the typical certificates, accolades, and award plaques. Not a file cabinet anywhere in sight.

"Were you given a business card?" The blonde asked, leaning over and exposing additional cleavage along with the white outlines that the sun hadn't quite reached. "Usually that's how I get things started." She twisted a finger into a lock of hair and giggled.

"Nope, sorry. No business card." Hart sighed. "Where

did you get the nice tan? Couldn't be here in New York."

"The boss has a really awesome home in Fort Lauderdale with a huge boat. I get to go every once in a while."

"Cool." Hart said with a half-serious attempt at sounding twenty-something. "So does your boss see clients in this office?"

"If he does, I don't know about them. I just answer the phones and take messages. Usually, Mr. Horton comes in by himself and closes his office door. He brings a leather briefcase and that's it. And then somebody else picks up the briefcase and leaves." The blonde giggled again. "It pays better than my cocktail waitress job. And I don't have to deal with creepy assholes."

"Got it," Hart said with a nod. "Well, guess I'd better get a business card from my friend and come back later."

"Sorry," the blonde said shrugging her shoulders.

"No problem." Hart turned and reached for the doorknob behind him. "Thanks for your help anyhow." He walked out of the office and back into the dark corridor.

Asking more questions of the quasi-Victoria's Secrets model behind the desk may have aroused suspicions, notwithstanding the real possibility of security cameras. Hart got the picture anyhow. A law firm that really wasn't. Great. So where were the union's mysterious wire transfers really going? And what was the source of the deposit money? And according to Bob Redmond, the airline was utilizing the same attorneys; that just seemed contrary to union common sense.

14:50 EDT

"Are you serious, Tom?" Alvarez asked. He pressed a thumb to a button on the steering wheel, raising the speaker volume.

"Positive, sir." Your E-Class Mercedes, license plate number India-Mike-Alpha-7-8-7, rolled into the very same Bayview Drive home that I observed our high school vice principal had visited the other day."

"And let me guess, the car is registered to an address in New York City that belongs to a law firm?"

"Yup. And the yacht that the Townsend sisters were abducted on belongs to the same law firm. It's a documented vessel. The Coast Guard did a search just after you left the base."

"Sit tight, Tom." Alvarez watched a man wearing ragged jeans and an oil-stained parka roll a rusty shopping cart full of aluminum cans through the intersection. "Are you in a BSO patrol car, today?"

"I am."

"Stay out of sight for the moment. I don't want to alert this guy. I'll let you know when I'm a couple minutes out. At the moment, I'm southbound on U.S. 1 at Atlantic."

"Roger."

Ending the call, Alvarez felt the familiar adrenalin rush. Maybe he would actually be able to catch a bad guy. The light turned green. The detective pressed down on the accelerator with a heavy foot.

Despite the construction traffic he encountered, Alvarez arrived sooner than anticipated. Before he could redial his patrol cop partner, he noticed Tom's patrol car parked in a strip mall just prior to the turn onto Bayview Drive. Smart man. Alvarez waved for him to follow. Within minutes, both cars rolled quietly onto a circular driveway in front of an impeccably maintained two-story home.

Tiny puddles, remnants of the storm, dotted the surface of the meticulously laid pavers in the driveway. The palm trees planted in the island at the center fluttered against a light breeze. The only sound that disturbed the tranquility was that of a distant yip from an over-indulged lap dog.

Both cops exited their cars simultaneously.

Alvarez asked in a restrained voice, gesturing at the house, "Ted Horton is the name of the owner?"

"It took some digging through county records, but yes," Tom answered. "That being said, I don't think the guy I've been following is Horton. I'm placing bets that it's the courier that handed off the cash payments to our school VP."

With a nod, Alvarez said, "Stay by your car, Tom." The detective turned and walked toward the ornate front door. The etched glass on the upper section of the door glinted a brief reflection of the sun.

Fishing for his credentials in a pocket with one hand, Alvarez raised the other to knock. His clenched knuckles never made contact with the door. With a quiet mechanical whir, the garage door of the house began to rise. Alvarez watched Tom bolt to attention. The patrol cop was sliding his hand to the top of his holstered .40 caliber Glock 22.

When the garage door was less than halfway up, both cops moved forward. The pant legs of a man and an open car door became visible. The legs stopped their movement for a split second. Alvarez and Tom remained motionless, poised like mountain lions espying their prey.

As the garage door reached its upward limit, a wiry man appeared. His Mediterranean complexion was further darkened by the shadow of beard stubble. His pupils were dark and wild.

Time seemed to progress in a series of photo frames, advancing like the old-time kinescopes in a penny arcade. The driver's side door of the Mercedes was open. Alvarez watched as the man began to swing an arm toward the opening of the garage door. A black object was silhouetted in the man's grip. A voice from somewhere within Alvarez's throat, heard him scream, "Police! Drop the weapon! Drop the weapon now!"

From nearby, the detective heard an ear-splitting crack followed immediately by an explosion of sound that vibrated the air surrounding him. His peripheral vision processed an instantaneous flash of tangerine light. In the next instant, the unshaven man was thrown into the open car door by an invisible force. He convulsed and then began to slump halfway onto the garage floor and halfway onto the driver's seat of the jet-black car.

The brief moment of silence that followed lasted an eternity. Alvarez swiveled his head toward Tom. The patrol cop was slowly lowering his extended two-handed grip on his service weapon. If not for Tom's wide-eyed expression, the Academy could have made his stance a recruitment poster.

With robotic movements, the patrol cop took a few steps toward the motionless man in the garage, his hands still gripping the Glock with stiffened arms. Alvarez followed, forgetting that he had unsnapped his holster and had drawn his own weapon.

Careful not to alarm Tom's adrenalin-infused body, Alvarez gently rested a hand on the man's shoulder. He said, "It's over, Officer. I'll take it from here. You did it by the book. Get on the radio and call this in with an ambulance request."

Tom stared into Alvarez's eyes, nodded, and with a deliberate effort began to holster his weapon. He straightened and began to walk toward his patrol car. Alvarez knew that there was no turning back from this day. The young police officer would keep this memory forever. The memory would define him.

14:55 EDT

It was therapeutic to sit in the lobby of the Hudson Hotel. If Hart wasn't staring into space, he was people-watching. The activities and expressions at the expansive front desk were curious and amusing all at the same time. Cathy would enjoy the whole scene. He was tempted to call her. But what would he say?

Hart's phone vibrated in his pocket. The white noise of footsteps and conversations prevented him from hearing the ring tone. He yanked the phone out and pushed it against an ear without looking at the caller ID. He plugged his other ear with a finger.

"Hey, it's Hart."

"Hart, it's Rod. Can you talk?"

A few moments of uncomfortable silence passed. Hart watched an elderly couple shuffle past, a dachshund skittering ahead of their feet. The dog was attached to a bejeweled leash held begrudgingly by the husband.

"What's this about? Is my sick time usage on your radar? Do you need a delay code for my last tardy departure?" Hart made no attempt at disguising his sarcasm.

Rod sighed and said, "Glad you've maintained that famous sense of humor. It sounds like you're going to need it."

"You caught me during a good minute. The next minute I could be manic depressive."

"I'm very sorry about your house. That had to suck." Rod glanced up at the TV in his office. The weatherman was waving his arms over a map of Florida; the spikes of a cold front were marching in animation across the screen.

"I've had better days," Hart said.

"Is there anything I can do?" Rod asked.

"You mean other than pay off my mortgage and find that Picasso painting that was hanging in the foyer?"

"Seriously, Hart."

"No. Thanks. I just have to work through this mess."

"I'm coding your pay as a special assignment for now. Take all the time off you need."

"Special assignment? Really? Why not just do the standard drill and give me some emergency days off? It will come out of my vacation allotment anyhow."

"You're working on an airline investigation, aren't you?"

"Well, yeah. But PAPA's got me covered. Paid union leave."

"No worries. We'll work it out from the flight office."

Hart exhaled a deep breath and said, "I'd rather not be in indebted to you at the moment. Honestly, I thought you would have been the one to show up at the house with marshmallows."

With a sigh, Rod said, "Look, we've both been shitty to each other."

"Yeah, I suppose that's true."

"I'd rather not have this discussion over the phone."

"Agreed," Hart said.

"When the dust settles, let's grab a beer and work this out. In the meantime, can we be civil to each other?"

"I'm on my meds. I don't see why not."

"Good. I hope you share pills." Rod paused. "In the interest of sharing, I've got some intel for you."

The elderly couple and the dachshund finished their business with the front desk. A bellhop pushing a brass-framed luggage cart nodded and directed the couple toward the elevators. The dachshund poked its nose nervously at Hart's shoes as it trotted by accompanying the procession of humans. Hotel patrons greeted the sausage-shaped animal with affectionate smiles.

"What's up?" Hart asked.

"You may be getting a call from the Miami P.D. It isn't good. I hope you're sitting down."

"Great."

"Bob Redmond was murdered a couple of hours ago. He was found in his car. And you were one of the last people to talk with him."

"Holy shit," Hart exclaimed.

"I know. This is getting ugly."

"Are they looking at me as a suspect?"

"No. I don't think so. I didn't get that feeling. The Miami detective that just showed up here in the flight office is aware that you're part of the Flight 63 investigation. They're connecting the dots. And you may be able to provide some insight."

Exhaling, Hart said, "Crap. OK. Thanks. I'm hoping that they hold off for a bit. I'm juggling a few balls of my own."

"Do you want to tell me?"

"It's better that you don't know for the moment," Hart said in a softer tone.

"Understood."

Rod glanced outside his office window. A 757 was taxiing out the main ramp, its winglets flexing as it rolled. He said, "Try to keep in touch. If I can help, let me know."

"Will do," Hart said. "Gotta run." After pressing the End Call icon, Hart shoved the phone back into his pocket. He walked out the hotel exit and hailed a cab.

Mend fences with Rod? The thought relaxed him. The investigation of Flight 63 was taking a bizarre turn. Hart needed time to think. In the meantime, he owed his father a visit. Maybe a road trip to upstate New York would be his best therapy. He could handle the new developments long-distance…at least for the moment.

15:05 EDT

Seated with her legs laid out across the long couch, a half-full glass of pinot noir clutched in one hand, the remote in the other, Robin Townsend stared at the TV. Images flashed across the screen. Nothing was comprehensible. It was just noise for the eyes and the ears, a way to fill the void.

A CNN correspondent, microphone in hand, appeared on the sidewalk in front of an art deco building. The camera panned over the anchor's shoulder and to a second floor window. The caption, "Breaking News," was displayed at the bottom of the TV screen. With a crown of wavy black hair subtly flowing in the breeze, the correspondent began speaking.

"In the latest development surrounding the accident of Flight 63 in Bermuda, it appears that the copilot had a relationship with the murdered owner of a local restaurant frequented by gay clientele." The correspondent turned toward the building and then back toward the camera. "The restaurant owner lived in this Fort Lauderdale condominium building. He was brutally murdered, and then his body parts were found in a nearby dumpster."

"The police have not yet found a specific motive for this homicide. Through questioning of restaurant employees, it appears they have one suspect. And some of our sources are indicating that the suspect may have been killed himself."

With her eyes still focused on the TV, Robin felt the gentle touch of two hands on her shoulders. Kim had walked into the living room and had sat down on the arm of the couch. Robin patted Kim's hands and offered a feeble smile. They stared intently at the screen.

"The murder is thought to have occurred within hours of the emergency landing in Bermuda. And as we have previously reported, the copilot was found shot and adrift in his boat just a few miles offshore from the Port Everglades inlet."

Kim's eyes began to fill with tears. She was tempted to

turn away from the TV but continued to watch. A side-by-side photo of her dad and the restaurant owner appeared in the corner of the screen.

"Sources close to this story are telling CNN there is an indication that the copilot, Mike Townsend, may have been involved with some type of scheme embezzling union funds from the Patriot Airlines Pilots Association. We are working to confirm this information."

Interrupting the report with a press of the pause button on the remote control, Robin turned toward Kim. She looked into her daughter's eyes and said, "Don't believe everything you hear, especially if it's on the news."

"I know, Mom," Kim said with a quivering lip.

"Your dad was not that kind of person."

Nodding, Kim rose from the couch. She smiled and then walked down the hallway toward her room. She passed her dad's office and then stopped in the doorway. Manila folders and papers sat in an organized pile on the desk. A coffee cup half-filled with brown liquid was perched on top of the pile. Placed to one corner of the wood veneer surface, a magazine sat open to an article. A pen with the airline logo rested in the open binder of the magazine. The scene looked normal, as if any minute Dad would walk in and sit down.

Kim lowered her head, once again attempting to fight the tears forming in her eyes. The only item that seemed to be missing was Dad's MacPro. The forensic cops had taken the laptop, along with an assortment of paperwork. Had they already found evidence that Dad was stealing money?

And the note that she found in the glove compartment of her VW Bug in Dad's handwriting…What exactly did that mean? "Check your computer. Everything is there. Everything is taken care of. I love all of you." At the bottom of the sticky note were the capital letters, "N-I-B-O-R-M-I-K-Y-E-L-H-S-A."

Should she get Ashley involved? Something told her that it was best not to bring it to Mom's attention…and certainly not the cops'…at least for now.

15:30 EDT

Glancing down at the digital display of his speed, Hart read the number "74." He peered into the rearview mirror. The lights were flashing on top of the ominous black police interceptor five hundred yards behind him. Seriously? The speed limit on this section of I-81 was sixty-five mph. Hart had already been passed in a blur by at least ten lunatics traveling at the speed of stupid. So why him? It was par for the course. He clicked off the cruise control and allowed the rental car to coast to a stop on the shoulder. Hart waited for the cop to roll up behind him.

A quick warble of a siren announced the New York state trooper's arrival. Was that really necessary? Hart pulled the driver's license from his wallet, snatched the Hertz rental agreement from the glove compartment, and carefully placed his hands on the steering wheel at the 12 o'clock position. Maybe the cop wouldn't shoot him.

Looking into the side view mirror, Hart watched as the long, grey-uniformed figure walked toward the open window of the rental car. The man's face was made of stone. Crap. Just what he needed--a speeding ticket. Guess it was time to put on the charm and beg for mercy.

As the trooper leaned into the window, Hart said, "You got me fair and square, Officer. Thought the cruise control had kept me at a reasonable speed, but it's my fault for not monitoring."

A long moment of silence passed. The officer said, "License and registration, please."

"Yessir," Hart said as he passed the documentation

through the open window. He watched as the expressionless man with the fresh Marine haircut examined Hart's license. He was doomed.

"Mr. Lindy, I need you to follow me, sir."

"Uh…are you arresting me, Officer?"

"I have not been instructed to arrest you at this time. I will be escorting you to the State Police barracks."

"For what purpose?"

"I am unable to say, sir. Those are my only instructions."

"Great. And if I don't comply?"

"Then I am instructed to arrest you."

Hart grinned and said, "I'm not seeing a lot of choices here, Officer."

The trooper's thin lips lifted at the corner of his mouth forming a facsimile of a grin for only a fraction of a second. He said, "I will retain possession of your driver's license, Mr. Lindy. Please follow me."

Shaking his head, Hart said, "Checkmate."

As Hart maintained a reasonably safe distance from the state trooper's interceptor, he glanced at his speed: sixty-five. Hart chuckled. He was following a Boy Scout with a gun and no sense of humor. Nice. Hart could only imagine the scene when he arrived at the barracks. Handcuffs. Fingerprints. Phone calls. Lawyers. Was this episode the work of that Middle Eastern asshole? Could he and whatever organization he belonged to have connections with law enforcement?

The police barracks was a small austere building in the middle of mostly nowhere. Adobe paint. Two flag poles. A parking lot with two patrol cars and a Ford pickup truck. It was a testament to the budget constraints of New York state taxpayers. Nobody would find Hart's body.

The state trooper parked directly in front of the building and got out of his car. Hart parked one space over and followed the cop inside. Another state trooper, with three chevron stripes sewn to the shoulders of his uniform, looked up from his desk and smiled as Hart approached.

"Mr. Lindy, we've been expecting you." Hart raised his eyebrows and said nothing as the state trooper rose from his chair and reached out a meaty hand. "I'm Sergeant Jack Mulvihill." Hart shook. As expected, the man's hand was made of iron. The sergeant gestured toward a back room. "You'll have privacy in that office. There is a secure computer on the desk. Special Agent Fredricks indicated that he wanted you to view some video footage. I'll call him now and then leave you alone."

"Special Agent Ryan Fredricks?" Hart replied, not able to utter any other words.

"Yes, sir," the sergeant said with a grin. "The FBI works in mysterious ways." He picked up the handset from a console phone that was propped on the desk and pressed some numbers while looking at a notepad through a pair of bifocals resting on his nose. The sergeant handed the phone to Hart and waved an arm at the desk chair. "Have a seat."

Hart nodded, lowered himself to the worn fabric cushion, and put the phone to his ear. A familiar voice answered on the second ring.

"Ahh…my favorite airline pilot. It's about time, Captain Lindy," Ryan Fredricks said.

"My favorite G-man," Hart said with a sullen tone. "Has the FBI ever heard of cell phone technology? Or does your protocol require the theatrics I just experienced?"

"You should feel privileged, Captain. Only the governor gets a State Police escort."

"The governor has a choice."

"I tried to call actually…went right to voice mail. Anyhow, I've been tracking your movements. You make it very easy, by the way. Oh…and I'm very sorry about your house."

"That almost sounds sincere," Hart said with a good dose of sarcasm.

"Honestly, it is." Ryan cleared his throat. "I can only imagine how that must feel. The arson investigators will find the culprit. Anyhow, I need to move onto more serious business. The Miami P.D. is not happy with you."

"Why?"

"Well, that's the reason I saw urgency in contacting you. Does the name Bob Redmond mean anything?" Ryan didn't wait for a response. "Of course it does. You could be considered an accessory to a homicide since you skipped town. But don't worry, I put the brakes on."

"I owe you a box of Monte Cristos."

"Thanks, but it won't make up for your escapade in Manhattan. Since when is conducting a criminal investigation part of your job description?"

"But I *am* conducting an investigation."

"Don't piss me off, Captain. You get my drift. Besides, I cut you some slack in regard to your copilot on Flight 63."

"I appreciate the consideration. Do you want to know what I found in Manhattan?"

"Go ahead," Ryan said with a hint of annoyance.

"Absolutely nothing…as in the law practice doesn't seem to really be a law practice."

Hart described the office and the conversation he had with the secretary at the Hudson Hotel.

Ryan said, "I'm not surprised. We're doing some forensic research on our end. The results so far are leading us down an ugly path."

"What kind of ugly path?"

"For starters, money laundering," Ryan replied. "But let's forget that for the moment. I need you to watch about fifteen minutes of an Academy Award performance. The good sergeant should have the secure website set up on the computer in front of you. Watch it, and I'll call you back."

The phone connection went quiet. Hart set the handset back on the cradle and shuffled the computer mouse resting on a pad in front of him from side to side. The screen illuminated with a grainy, frozen image. He moved the cursor over the Play arrow and then clicked the mouse button.

The video was of a 767 parked at a gate taken from in front of the nose at an elevation slightly higher than the top of the fuselage. Hart leaned forward, closer to the screen. He recognized the soot and gnarled pieces of the compressor blades on the damaged right engine. It was Flight 63.

Men wearing asbestos suits and reflective gear were scattered about the perimeter of the airplane. The airline's ground handlers were scurrying around the cargo compartments, baggage equipment mated to the airplane. A handful of passengers were deplaning down the portable air stairs from the L1 entry door.

From behind the nosewheel, a slim man wearing a white shirt with three stripes on the shoulders and a pilot's hat appeared. It was Mike Townsend. He was surveying the destruction. A minute later, Mike Townsend could be seen with a cell phone to his ear. More time passed and the captain joined his copilot, both men pointing at various damaged sections of the airplane.

At nearly the end of the video clip, Hart observed an armored vehicle park next to the bulk cargo compartment at the aft end of the airplane. A uniformed man exited the truck, had a brief conversation with the baggage crew chief, and was handed a package wrapped in clear plastic the size of a small file cabinet. The armored car drove off the ramp and out of view of the camera. The video ended.

Hart stared at the computer screen. He tried to process the video. What were the implications?

The console phone chirped an electronic ring. The sound

briefly startled Hart. A light was blinking. He looked up at Sergeant Mulvihill seated back at his desk. The state trooper motioned for him to pick up the handset. Hart snatched the phone off the cradle and slid the phone over his ear.

"What did you observe, Captain?" Ryan asked.

"Not really sure. But it doesn't seem YouTube worthy. Do you want to tell me?"

"Did you see your copilot place a phone call?"

"I did."

"How about the armored car arrival? Did you notice that?"

"I did."

"Well, we traced the phone call that Mike Townsend made."

"And?"

"The phone call was made to the dispatcher of the armored car company." The connection remained silent for a few moments. "Are you still there, Captain?" the FBI agent asked.

"Yeah, I'm still here," Hart, answered with a deep sigh.

"And here's the kicker. I hope you're sitting down. The cargo manifest listed the recipient of that armored car freight as Horton and Carty, Attorneys, New York City. But as we know, the shipment remained in Bermuda."

Hart stared at the grainy image still paused on the computer screen. He shook his head. "Shit…"

CHAPTER TWENTY

Sunday
15:35 EDT

Alvarez had no doubt that the quiet, BMW/white Cadillac neighborhood, wasn't accustomed to the army of police vehicles that arrived at the canal community off Bayview Drive. The only visitations from police were the occasional house security alarm investigation. And, most likely, no burglary was ever in progress, just a drunk husband or a housekeeping service that forgot to enter the appropriate code.

After the CSI team had examined the body of the victim, Tom had draped it with a gray blanket from his patrol car. The unshaven, dark-skinned man was still slumped halfway out of the Mercedes parked in the garage, his legs splayed out from underneath the blanket at an unnatural angle. The patrol cop had felt compelled to cover the man, perhaps as a gesture of respect.

Alvarez understood. The first time he had pulled the trigger of his service weapon in the line of duty was at an eighteen-year-old kid who had just robbed a liquor store. The kid had bludgeoned the Polish immigrant owner with a bottle of Chivas Regal and then used his gun to shoot a reluctant cash register. Alvarez's decision to fire was instantaneous once he saw the kid brandish his weapon.

Six rounds were discharged according to the Internal Affairs investigation, but it didn't matter. In the midst of his adrenalin rush, Alvarez hadn't a clue whether it was six or sixteen rounds. Besides, a child's life had ended for idiotic reasons. Despite the insistence of the detectives that he leave the scene, Alvarez had hovered over the body. The realization that he was responsible for taking a human life was more than he was capable of processing at the time.

And now Alvarez watched as Tom paced around his patrol car, the performance a thinly veiled attempt at normal behavior. Behind the patrol car, a glossy black Ford F-150 with sparkling chrome running boards rolled to a stop and parked. The truck body was raised high above its black, knobby tires like a panther ready to strike.

A stocky man wearing an open neck Tommy Bahama shirt, covered by a blue windbreaker, climbed down from the cab and strutted toward the detective. The man clenched a stubby, chocolate-colored cigar between his teeth, a puff of smoke billowing from his mouth like the exhaust of an old fashioned locomotive.

As the stocky man approached, Alvarez noticed the white letters "F-B-I" emblazoned on the jacket.

"Seriously?" Alvarez thought. *"Where did Quantico get this guy?"*

The stocky man stepped within two feet of the detective and asked, "Where do I find Detective Alvarez?"

Grinning, Alvarez said, "You might just be looking at him." He scanned the cigar-smoking man and pointed at the F-B-I letters. "I'll need you to badge me, Special Agent. Sorry, I haven't seen many like you." Alvarez gestured at the black truck. "Especially a fed that drives that thing. What happened to the Crown Vic, the gold cuff links and the pretentious initials embroidered on the sleeve?"

Expressionless, the FBI man reached into a back pocket and pulled out a black leather wallet. He flipped the wallet open, displayed his credentials and reached out a hand.

"Detective Alvarez, I'm Special Agent Ryan Fredricks." The two men exchanged firm grips. "I damaged my cuff links along with the embroidered shirt at my last gunfight in a Miami Starbucks. They wouldn't serve me a caramel macchiato. As for the Ford, it was my favorite ride as a kid. You know the lyrics to the Don McLean song, '…a pink carnation and a pickup truck…the day the music died.' I figure when the music does die, I can mount a nice Browning .50 caliber M2 in the bed and wait out the Apocalypse in true Mad Max style."

Alvarez smirked and wrapped his arms across his chest.

Ryan said, "If it wasn't for my vivacious personality and my Batman costume, the Bureau would probably move me to a file clerk position." Ryan remained stone-faced. He puffed on his cigar, the red embers glowing brighter.

"How can I help, Special Agent Fredricks?"

"Well, I think we can help each other. We're operating in parallel universes."

"I kind of figured. My investigation started with a high school homicide and abduction. Yours probably started with an airplane."

Ryan nodded, and said, "Yup, I did some research on your investigation. But would you mind bringing me up to speed with your pieces of the jigsaw puzzle?"

In cryptic fashion with typical police jargon, and a sprinkling of dark humor, Alvarez discussed his case. Ryan listened in silence, hands clasped behind his back and feet spread apart in a wide stance. The FBI man acknowledged various facts with the appropriate nods.

Ryan asked, "Did you arrest or detain the high school VP?"

"No, sir. I don't have enough evidence to charge her with anything at the moment. And she could be a more useful asset outside of police custody, especially if she feels pressure enough to lawyer up. I put her on notice to remain in the neighborhood."

"Nicaraguan wife? She could be a flight risk," Ryan said, rolling the cigar around in his mouth.

"Agreed. I have that covered with Customs. Her passport and her wife's passport are tagged. And I believe you guys also have a pony in that show."

Ryan nodded.

"Okay, Special Agent Fredricks, what do you have for me?'

"Well, it would seem that all of your homicides are connected directly to a New York attorney that owns this property." Ryan pointed a finger at the house behind Alvarez. "And he also owns that yacht the daughters were abducted on."

"Is Ted Horton the lawyer?"

"You've done your homework, Detective. Yes."

"Then who is my dead guy in the Mercedes?" Alvarez asked, turning toward the buzz of police activity still occurring in the open garage. "At the moment, the only thing we've got is a false ID that was traced to some recently deceased elderly gentleman in Manhattan."

"Your dead guy is Sayid Abdul-Qadir. He is a resident of the UK. However, he has ties to Syria. Mr. Abdul-Qadir has a finance background from the University of London."

Alvarez frowned and said, "Wait. Don't tell me. ISIS?"

"We think so."

"Wonderful."

"I've got our financial analysts at the Bureau connecting the dots, but it seems at first glance that the law firm is laundering money for not-so-nice purposes in the Middle East."

"And how is my deceased airline pilot connected to this mess?" Alvarez asked.

"Not sure just yet, but it appears that he and the pilots union were complicit in laundering money for this Manhattan law firm. We're working with the bank in Trinidad. They became cooperative when we started to connect the dots to Syria for them. It just wouldn't help their business if word got out to the Wall Street Journal."

"It's always about the money."

Ryan sighed and said, "I think your airline pilot got more than he bargained for. The emergency landing in Bermuda was most likely sabotage, a plot he devised on his own. A large sum of cash was in the cargo bay of the airplane. It was removed by an armored car to a Bermuda Bank through his direction."

"Yikes. Copilot Townsend was getting crafty."

"I think our lawyer, Ted Horton, suspected this occurred, and used his army of thugs and beach beauties to abduct the Townsend daughters as leverage."

"Makes sense."

"The airline pilot botched the rescue attempt as you know. But I assume that you have firsthand accounts from the daughters."

"I do," Alvarez said with a nod. "And with reference to the dead bald guy on the yacht, he was probably attempting to garner intel from Townsend's boyfriend. Once the big, bald guy had confirmation of what the airline pilot was plotting, the boyfriend became a liability and was murdered."

"That would be my guess," Ryan said. The FBI agent scanned the bustle of activity around the house. Police vehicles were backing out of the circular driveway. Two paramedics were rolling a stretcher with a body bag into the garage. "And the bathing suit beauties died in the line of duty, so to speak?"

"It would appear the women had no real criminal record. I would imagine they were well compensated…in many ways." Alvarez released a long breath. "Have you guys located this Ted Horton guy?"

"Not yet. But I think we found his Global Express corporate jet. It was tracked on a departure from Opa Locka Airport on a flight plan to the Caribbean."

"Mystery and intrigue. Very nice." Alvarez sighed. "Well, let's stay in touch. Hopefully your loose ends can tie up my loose ends."

"I've got one loose end that's really puzzling."

"What would that be?" Alvarez asked.

"Robert Redmond, the VP of Ops at Patriot Airlines was found murdered in his car at the Intercontinental Hotel's parking lot. When you work out the forensics on your crime scene, I'm willing to bet that the round in Redmond's head will match the gun found on Abdul-Qadir."

"Okay, sounds plausible. What's the puzzling part?"

"I'm confident that Miami P.D. will have security footage that will confirm Abdul-Qadir's presence at the hotel at the time of the murder. The puzzling part is that Redmond called Abdul-Qadir's burner phone. And he called the Bank in Trinidad, all within minutes of his murder."

Alvarez frowned and said, "This gets better."

"So, all the more reason for us to play well in the sandbox."

"Agreed."

The two men exchanged business cards.

Ryan glanced over at the patrol car nearest their position on the street. He gestured his chin at the uniformed officer leaning against the driver's side door and said, "That cop has been running laps around his vehicle ever since we started this conversation. The man's expression looks as though he just put his kid's dog to sleep." Ryan sighed. "He shot Abdul-Qadir didn't he?"

Alvarez nodded and said, "He's been assisting with my

investigation. Really good guy."

"It was his first, wasn't it?"

"It was."

"About one hundred years ago I put a textbook, center of mass shot through the chest of a Wells Fargo robbery suspect that had taken hostages and murdered an elderly man. When it was over, the Bureau gave me all the official pats on the back. I replayed the shooting in my dreams every night for almost two years. I can still remember the day like it happened last week."

"We're on the same page, Special Agent Fredricks."

"Make sure he gets some help," Ryan said, his eyes softening.

18:35 EDT

As Hart turned off Route 41 onto Route 174, a flash of childhood memories flooded his thoughts in a jumble of images. Nearby Otisco Lake was where he had first learned to water-ski. Older friends had coached him both on the art of water-skiing and on the art of consuming Pabst Blue Ribbon. Apparently, neither was mutually exclusive. Hart excelled at water-skiing. But beer consumption required a few more lessons.

Hart winced, recalling the chunks of the ham and cheese sandwich that had speckled the water and the side of the boat. Laughably, PBR was now considered a craft beer. Till this day he can't even look at a blue and white can without his stomach turning.

Above the tree line in the distance, Hart caught glimpse of a small low-wing airplane. A dagger of sunlight flashed off the white wings. It looked to be a Cherokee that had just departed the west runway at Otisco, his dad's airport. The nose was angled in a climb. But as a quickly as the airplane appeared, it began to vanish below the trees tops.

"Crap!" Hart said out loud. "Why today?" He pressed down on the gas pedal of the rental car. He knew exactly where to drive.

Arriving at the west end of the airport perimeter fence, Hart rolled onto the tall grass, parked the car, jumped out, and ran toward the locked gate. Peering through the crisscrossed mosaic of the fence, he caught sight of the Cherokee. The airplane had skidded off the paved runway surface and was cocked sideways to the grass overrun area, the nose partially embedded into the brown earth. The propeller tips were mangled, curled back at the tips like ribbon candy.

A woman with flowing blond hair, strands separated in clumps, was exiting the airplane. The only door, located on the passenger side, had been flung open. Despite her frantic movements, she attempted to gracefully step down the nonskid surface of the wing in her platform shoes.

In a flurry, Hart pressed the numbers of the gate code into the mechanical lock. With the gate open, he jogged toward the crippled airplane. As he drew closer, Hart heard a familiar chug-chug in the distance. His dad was driving the "Tank," an old Korean War vintage tug, down from the main hangar. Most likely, Dad was hoping to tow the airplane away from the departure end of the runway once the FAA had an opportunity to investigate. But the airplane didn't look towable. Hart was certain the nosewheel had collapsed.

"Are you okay?" Hart yelled out to the blonde as he approached the front of the airplane.

"I'm fine," the woman responded in a feeble voice. Moisture filled her eyes. "But my boyfriend may be hurt. He's bleeding bad. I think his forehead struck the dashboard."

Grimacing at hearing the woman's terminology for the airplane's glareshield, Hart glanced through the tinted windscreen and into the cockpit. The boyfriend was sliding himself off the pilot's seat and over to the door. A couple streaks of crimson had streaked the man's forehead. Hart wasn't terribly concerned, aware that head wounds appeared more dramatic than they were serious.

As he circled around the left wing toward the back of the airplane, Hart caught a glimpse of the red, rotating beacon on top of the tail. It was flashing. Shit! The electrical system was still energized! He sniffed the air. No fuel smell. Good. Regardless, the power had to be shut down. He reached the back of the right wing at the same moment the boyfriend was staggering out the open door.

Hart stretched out a hand and said, "Take your time."

The thirty-something boyfriend grasped Hart's forearm and tentatively began to step down the wing until he reached the soft grass with a final awkward hop. Gently grabbing his waist, Hart guided the man away from the airplane toward his girlfriend, who was now standing fifty feet off to the side of the right wingtip, arms clutched tightly across her chest. She was biting her lower lip, her forehead wrinkled in anguish.

Sirens began to whine in the distance, the sound becoming louder with each wail. The boyfriend began to mumble.

"Engine just quit. Couldn't get the nose down fast enough…"

Hart said, "Take some deep breaths. Sit down. You've got some nasty cuts on your forehead, but you'll be fine."

Hart guided the boyfriend to a seated position on the ground. The man spread out his legs and moved his arms behind him to support his torso. The girlfriend sat down beside him and began to hug his shoulders.

Hart strode back toward the airplane, climbed up the nonskid walkway of the wing, and slid into the cockpit. He reached for the red mixture control and pulled it back, ensuring fuel was no longer flowing to the engine. He clicked the red rocker switch of the electrical system to the off position.

Just before exiting the cockpit, Hart glanced at the fuel selector switch. The selector was positioned to the right fuel tank. Hart thought for a moment. No fuel smell? Interesting. He climbed back out of the airplane and circled around to the leading edge of the right wing. Hart twisted the fuel cap open and peered into the tank. He could clearly see the silvery bottom. Barely a drop remained.

Bending down onto his knees, Hart looked under the wing. Spotting the fuel drain valve, he examined the position of the petcock. The petcock was stuck in the open position. Not good. Hart shook his head.

Glancing through the canopy of trees that lined the airport road, Hart caught streaks of red vehicles moving at a rapid pace. The squawking of sirens was becoming louder by the second. Hart walked back toward the perimeter fence and swung both sides of the gates open. He had just finished when a cherry red fire truck rumbled its way onto the grass, rolling slowly toward the crippled airplane. The EMT truck followed moments later.

Men wearing heavy, straw-colored overalls, the bright yellow bands of reflective striping around their sleeves and midsections, clambered out. Fire hoses were unwrapped. Walkie-talkies held to ears. Anonymous unemotional voices were heard stating matter-of-fact circumstances, the digital beep of their completed radio transmissions punctuating their reports.

A familiar face, his fireman's helmet cocked to one side with the straps dangling loose, grinned at Hart. The fireman nodded and walked toward him. Hart was still standing by an open gate. The man removed the thick glove from his hand and held it out, grasping Hart's outstretched hand.

Hart smiled and said, "Chief O'Brien, I thought you'd

have bought that Irish bar by now and you were done rescuing Siamese cats from trees."

The fireman said, "Nah, I realized it's much easier to just drink at an Irish bar. Besides, I thought about the potential for stolen inventory. I'd have to fire myself." The chief shook his head. "It's good to see you, Hart. It's about time you graced us with your presence."

"Good to see you, Frank," Hart said. He pointed at the crumpled airplane. "Your crash site is secured. Electrical system is off. Fuel is off with no leaks noted. Doesn't appear to be any imminent danger of explosion." Hart gestured at the couple sitting on the ground. "Other than a nice gash on the pilot's forehead, injuries seem minor. Understandably, they're both shaken."

"Thanks, Hart." The chief waved at the fireman about to walk on the wing. He drew a hand across his throat and keyed the mic on his portable radio. "According to our expert airline captain here on scene, the airplane is secured. Please walk around the aircraft and make an assessment. For the moment you can all stand down."

Both men watched as two paramedics scrambled over to the couple sitting on the ground, utility boxes in hand. Hart's dad had just parked the Tank off to the side of the crash site and was dismounting the tug.

The chief said, "Your timing is impeccable, Captain. Are you sure that you didn't cause this little disaster?"

"The way the last few days have been going, you may be right, Frank."

The chief nodded with a smirk, shook his head at the airplane, and said, "Just what your dad needs. It's one of his rentals, isn't it?"

"Yup, afraid so. Airplane has been in the fleet since before I left for college. It takes a licking and keeps on ticking. This isn't the first rodeo. The last time it was in this kind of shape, one of our students had taken it on his first trip after getting his private pilot's license. He landed hard and fast and ran it off the end of the runway in Saratoga Springs. So much for betting on the ponies."

"Actually, I have fond memories of this airplane. Shortly after you got me my license, I joined the mile-high club with Mary Ellen."

"I trained you well. Wasn't she a homecoming queen?"

"Yup. Only way a greaser like me could get a date was if I took her up flying. You changed my life, man."

Hart smiled and asked, "You still current?"

"I wish." The fire chief sighed. "Kids. Mortgage. College. Maybe someday when the dust settles."

With a slight shuffle, Hart's father had begun to walk around the perimeter of the Cherokee. His face was expressionless. His eyes wandered about the nooks and crannies of the stricken airplane. The oversized plaid cotton shirt and the loose-fitting jeans made Hart's dad appear thinner than usual. His tall frame that was normally straight and rigid was angled at the shoulders.

The fire chief said, "Giant John has got the same old stoic Lindy face."

"He does," Hart replied. The two men walked over to the older man.

"Sorry about your airplane, John. The good news is that nobody got badly hurt," The fire chief said. He reached out and shook hands with Hart's dad.

John Lindy seemed to ponder the statement for a moment and then said, "I agree, Frank. Although, it's probably going to be me that gets hurt after I make the phone call to the insurance company. Thanks for coming with your boys." He turned, scanned his son, and smiled. "Nice to see you, Captain."

Father and son took a step toward each other and

embraced in an awkward hug. They patted each other's back and then stood apart.

"Sorry about your machine, Dad."

"We'll get her fixed." John Lindy let out a deep breath. "I saw from the office that you got on scene right after it happened. Any ideas on probable cause, Mr. Crash Investigator?"

"Yeah, I've got a pretty good idea."

With raised eyebrows, John Lindy said, "Speak."

"Dad, not that I don't trust our esteemed fire chief…," Hart smiled at O'Brien, "…but what he doesn't know won't hurt him for the moment. Can we discuss this in your office? Hart pointed at his rental car. "Leave the Tank here. I'll drive us back down the taxiway to the hangar."

Holding out his hand, Hart said, "Nice to see you, Frank. Maybe we can toss a couple back before I leave. We'll catch up. I'll leave you here to play with the FAA. Tell the nice inspector to come see Dad and me before he leaves if you wouldn't mind." Both men shook knowing that it would probably be another few years before they would see each other again.

Softly grabbing his dad by the shoulder, Hart led him toward the rental car. Father and son opened their respective doors and plopped into their seats. Hart drove off down the quiet taxiway toward the main hangar and his dad's office.

As Hart parked the car, he noticed not much had changed since his last visit a few months ago. Wiry, green and yellow weeds were sprouting up in the cracks of the oil-stained, black pavement of the ramp. The chlorine blue of the corrugated aluminum hangars and office had faded another shade. A broken gutter hung at an angle, steady drops of moisture plopping to a puddle on the ground near the corner of the building.

They walked through the open hangar door of the

maintenance shop. A Cessna 172 was parked in a far corner, its cowl removed, the engine exposed, the prop removed. A mechanic's towering, red toolbox and a shelved cart surrounded the airplane. In another corner of the hangar, the skeleton of an Aeronca Champ sat on its haunches, naked to the world. Hart had lost count on the years that had passed with that Champ in the same condition.

As they entered the office, Hart scanned the room. Certainly nothing had changed here either. The same marred and scratched monster oak desk, its surface condition a mystery because of the paper chaos strewn on every inch, was still anchored in the middle. The same scratchy, olive green fabric sofa, the cushions indented with years of rear ends sitting in the same spots, was still jammed in a corner. And the same framed photos, mostly black-and-whites, hung in a random pattern on all four walls. The photo that Hart had sent as a gag with him wearing his airline uniform superimposed between Charles Lindbergh and Amelia Earhart was displayed proudly on a corner of his dad's desk.

John Lindy squeezed behind the desk and sat down on the black, leather high back office chair, the only valuable piece of furniture in the room. Hart plopped onto the sofa. A thin cloud of dust rose into the air.

Hart chuckled and said, "Did you fire the housekeeper again, Dad?"

"Funny," said his dad with a tiny grin.

"How are you feeling these days?"

"I'm peeing a lot more."

"Good to know, Dad. What about the radiation treatments?"

"They say it's shrinking the tumor, but I get the feeling that it's not aggressive enough for their taste."

"Well, let's hope slow and steady wins the race."

"Slow and steady takes a lot of visits to the clinic. I don't have the time for that shit."

Hart sighed and said, "Dad, it's prostate cancer. It's got a high survival rate. The problem was that it was diagnosed late. I kept bugging you to get regular check-ups."

"I'm not dealing with I-told-you-so's today."

"Sorry, Dad. I just wanted to keep you around for a while. I was hoping to pick out your old folks home. We could argue about which facility had the best Jell-O."

"That was never happening anyhow. You were going to push me out of an airplane, remember?"

Hart grinned and said, "All right, let's talk about this some other time." He angled a thumb in the direction of the crashed Cherokee 180. "You want to discuss your accident airplane?"

John Lindy held his palms open in a gesture of curiosity.

"It's simple. Apparently, it didn't register on your renter that the right tank was low. Why no one balanced it from the previous flight, I'll never know. But the boyfriend didn't complete a proper preflight. Anyhow, he probably did the usual and sampled the fuel with the tester. But he never noticed that the petcock on the fuel drain valve remained open after it was tested. So, whatever was left in the right tank drained with just enough fuel to taxi, complete a run-up, and a takeoff to about two hundred feet. Had he at least positioned the fuel selector to the left tank prior to his departure roll, as per procedure, the engine would never have quit. End of story."

"End of stupidity, you mean."

"Dad, who checked this guy out anyhow?"

"No one. He showed me that he had Cherokee 180 time in his logbook. It looked legitimate. None of my kid instructors were around. I didn't have time to check him out."

"Dad, really?"

"All right, I'm an idiot."

Hart sighed and said, “Maybe it’s time to sell this place, Dad. The accident could have been a lot worse and you know it. The FAA. Attorneys. Lawsuits.”

“I get it.” John Lindy exhaled. “Who’s gonna buy this dump, Hart?”

“Well, I’ll give you a hand fixing it up.”

“And then what?”

“You sell the airport and slurp down rum-runners on the beach in Sarasota like all the other people your age.”

“I hate rum. I hate Florida. And I hate people my age.”

“It was a thought, Dad.”

“This is all I’ve got, son. Take this away and you might just as well push me out of an airplane.”

“I’m just exploring options, Dad.”

Glancing out the office window for a brief moment, John Lindy asked, “How’s Cathy doing?”

“She’s good, Dad.”

“Really? There wasn’t a lot of conviction behind that statement. And you didn’t look me in the eye, Hart. What’s going on?”

“We’re having some difficulty at the moment.”

“You screwed around on her again, didn’t you?”

Hart let out a deep breath, opened his mouth to speak, but then just stared at an old photo on the wall.

“You can’t keep doing that shit and expect her to stick around, Hart”

Looking into his dad’s, brown eyes, hints of dark circles underneath the wrinkles, Hart said, “Mom didn’t set a good example, I guess. I hated what she did to you.”

“So you’re going to punish Cathy for your mom’s infidelity?”

“I guess not,” Hart said with an unconvincing degree of resignation.

“Do you think your mom did what she did in a vacuum?”

"No, but how am I going to be certain that any woman remains committed to me?"

"Hart, I wasn't committed to your mother." John Lindy spread his arms and waved them around the room. "I was committed to this airport."

"And that warranted Mom's drinking?"

"Of course not, but that was one of her coping mechanisms. And she had a disease. Only now is she finally getting help for it. I knew she had issues with alcohol before you were born, son."

"Is that the reason I was an only child?"

"Partially."

John Lindy rubbed his eyes, glanced out the window for a moment, locked eyes with Hart, and said, "You're not an only child."

Stunned, attempting to process his father's words, Hart's jaw grew slack. He said nothing for a few long seconds and then asked, "What do you mean, Dad?"

"Do you think your Dad was without his own faults?" Hart said nothing. John Lindy continued. "It became a vicious circle. I wasn't there for your mother. She turned to alcohol and other men. And then she wasn't there for me. Out of the blue, a woman came into my life when things were really miserable. It just happened. And then it was over."

"Who was she, Dad?"

"It's not important." John Lindy sighed. "But you have a half brother about fifteen years younger."

"Where is he?"

"I don't know, Hart. I gave her some money to survive, and that's all she asked from me. I never heard from her again."

"When were you going to spring this on me? On your deathbed? Very cliché." Hart's voice began to take on a sharp and sarcastic tone. "Great. You have another son. I have a brother. No big deal."

"I guess I was trying to protect you, son. It was probably the wrong thing to do. But as the years passed, it got harder to tell you and easier to keep it quiet. After I divorced your mother, it didn't seem to matter."

Hart quietly shook his head and stared out the window at the activity still occurring at the far end of the runway. The red fire truck had been repositioned off the grass and onto a portion of the taxiway. The paramedics were escorting the boyfriend and girlfriend into the back of their vehicle. A New York State Patrol car had joined the entourage.

Closing his eyes for a moment, Hart reviewed the last two days. The Bermuda accident investigation. Pilot sabotage. Union involvement. Murder. A relationship on the rocks. His house up in smoke. His dad's health. The airport. And a half brother.

It just couldn't get any better…

CHAPTER TWENTY ONE

Sunday
18:40 EDT

The two pilots union volunteers who had arrived at the Townsend home were pleasant enough, but their uniform attire was too soon a reminder that Ashley and Kim would never again see their dad trudge through the door after a trip with his tie loosened around his neck, the three-stripe jacket hung over an arm, and a hand clutching the worn handle of a battered, black leather flight bag.

Perhaps the visual reminder of their dad as an airline pilot was why the girls gravitated more toward his boss from the flight office. Captain Moretti had a sincere smile, his manner inviting without awkwardness. The chief pilot was wearing khakis and a blazer with an open-collar shirt. He had shown up at their house with four boxes of pizzas. His brief speech to all three of them was simple and to the point, completely void of phony pretentions.

Their mom sat with the union pilots at the kitchen table. The conversation was solemn and stiff. The sisters had slipped away, feeling uncomfortable with the atmosphere. Even the friends and neighbors who had filtered through the house became bothersome. Although well intended, most of them struggled to find the appropriate words.

With a whispered exchange, Kim and Ashley had mutually decided it was best to reveal their discovery to Captain Moretti. For whatever reason, he just seemed trustworthy in the eyes of two teenage girls. They had ushered him into their dad's office, offering him a seat behind the desk.

Kim said, "I found a note from Dad in the console of my VW Bug. The note contained a group of weird letters. My sister figured out the letters were a website password. The password actually spelled out our first names backwards."

Rod raised his eyebrows, smiled, and then asked, "Why are you telling me this, ladies?"

"Because we're certain this is important, but didn't want the police to get involved just yet," Kim said.

Kim and Ashley nodded in unison.

"I'm flattered that you two consulted with me, but how can I help?"

Clutching a laptop in her arms, Ashley set the computer on the desk in front of Rod. She turned on the screen and said, "This is Kim's computer."

Ashley stepped over to Rod's side of the desk and began to tap on the keyboard. A website appeared on the display. The website was from a bank in Bermuda. Ashley typed a password into the login box. An account displayed with Mike Townsend's name. A few clicks on the touchpad and a series of numbers appeared opposite various lines of investment names.

The amounts of the investment balances were a blur to Rod. He blinked. The dollar values were staggering, many worth tens of millions. The figure he viewed at the bottom of the page was his last point of focus. $152,543,654.32. He drew in a deep breath and shook his head. He really shouldn't be viewing this information.

Rod looked up from the screen and said, "You've got to report this to the police, ladies. There is no way around it."

"Does this mean our dad was embezzling money from the union?" Ashley asked.

"Frankly, I don't know what it means."

"Our dad will be considered a criminal. He'll be disgraced," Ashley said.

"Not necessarily."

Kim responded in a stern and sarcastic tone, "Really? A gay airline pilot? An elected officer that embezzled money from the union? We'll all be abused."

Rod lowered his head and massaged his temples. He said, "Your dad was clever. It appears that all the transactions were performed on Kim's computer."

"I wish Dad was clever enough to still be alive," Ashley said, wiping her damp eyes.

19:05 EDT

It had taken four of the firefighters and Hart to lift the nose of the damaged airplane off its position embedded in the dirt. The divot that remained looked as though a small meteor had impacted the spot. Although Hart had resisted the plan, a local tow truck was being used to transport the Cherokee back to the maintenance hangar. It was a messy operation. Hart feared additional damage to the airplane, preferring the more expensive method of using the combination of a crane and flatbed truck. Rather than argue with his dad, Hart had just shrugged his shoulders.

While the recovery operation was being organized, Hart had received a phone call from Rod. The information he conveyed was disturbing. The investigation would only get worse for the copilot and his family. After the discussion with Rod was over, Hart had immediately dialed the union president, leaving him a voice-mail message to call ASAP.

In addition, Hart had called Maureen Blackford. It was another tense and awkward phone call, but eventually they were able to discuss business. The forensic evidence of the engine parts that were being gathered in Washington at NTSB headquarters indicated overwhelmingly that an explosive device had been used. Detonation had occurred via a satellite phone signal

As the tow truck winch began to drag the airplane onto its ramp, Hart felt his phone vibrate. He waved one of the firefighters over to where he was holding the right wing tip. The firefighter nodded and walked over, exchanging positions with Hart.

Glancing at the caller ID, Hart took a deep breath. He pressed the Talk button. "Isn't it way past cocktail hour, Sammy?"

"I would have preferred to skip cocktail hour actually. I was involved with an anger management candidate in the form of a domicile chairman who had one too many vodka tonics. It was a pleasant finger-pointing discussion involving my failure to reduce the list of presidential grievances not yet scheduled for arbitration." The union president sighed. "So this better be good."

"I'm afraid that what I have to say will seem like waterboarding compared to your finger pointing session."

"Wonderful."

"Sam, you need to organize people you trust for damage control. I hope PAPA's attorneys are on speed dial."

"You've got my attention, Hart. Can we do without the melodrama?"

"Sorry. I'll make it simple. Mike Townsend, our recently deceased secretary-treasurer, has been transferring funds from PAPA accounts to a bank in Trinidad. The funds were coming into our accounts via deposits from an unknown source. It appears that First Officer Townsend arranged to have these funds physically moved from Trinidad via Flight 63."

"But Flight 63 diverted to Bermuda and never arrived in New York."

"Sammy, are you connecting the dots yet?"

A few moments of silence passed.

Sam said, "Oh, shit. He blew up the engine and caused the diversion!"

"Correct. According to the latest info I got from the NTSB and the FAA, Townsend used a sat phone to send a signal to a sat receiver that was connected to a detonator hidden in the engine cowl. They're not quite sure if the signal originated from a source outside the airplane or from within the cockpit. If it originated outside of the airplane, then Townsend had at least one accomplice."

"And he attempted to steal the funds once they landed in Bermuda?" Sammy asked.

The cable on the tow truck had now grown taught under the weight of the wounded airplane as it slowly rolled onto the beginning of the ramp. Hart heard a metallic scraping sound as part of the belly began to drag. With his phone pressed against an ear, he looked at his father and gestured at the Cherokee. Hart's dad nodded, moving his thumb and finger to shape an OK sign. Apparently, his dad had already planned on repairing the underside of the fuselage.

Hart said, "Mike Townsend had already set up an account in Bermuda for a funds transfer. He was seen on security footage making a call. According to cell phone records obtained by the FBI, the call was made to an armored car company for them to pick up the physical cash."

"But why not just steal the cash when Flight 63 arrived in New York?"

"Good question. Maybe he wanted the funds unencumbered by U.S. law. Considering that New York and Miami are our only destinations out of Trinidad, the island of Bermuda was the best diversion choice along the route. I can't think of any other Caribbean islands that would have been more armored-car friendly."

"This is great stuff, Hart. Just the kind of discourse the union needed. It's bad enough that the company's finances look bleak and we've been negotiating a contract for five years. Now we get the opportunity to air our dirty laundry in public. The membership is going to love this new development."

"I know, Sam. It sucks."

"Are you sure about everything?"

"There may be more to the story."

"Keep me in the loop, Hart."

"Will do."

Hart's screen displayed "End call." He slipped the phone back into his jeans pocket and shook his head. The apocalypse was near. What was next? In a way, it was comforting to be in his hometown with Dad. Maybe he could stay out of the line of fire. Probably not.

19:15 EDT

The ride over to the Townsend home was mostly quiet. Alvarez had thought it best to let Tom talk whenever he felt the need rather than attempt idle conversation. The effects of the shooting had subsided for the moment. Tom's face was a sober mixture of numbness and solemnity. The detective had asked the patrol cop to accompany him in his car. Aside from his general support, Tom had developed a rapport with Robin Townsend. In addition, a uniformed cop added an element of official police business to the visit.

Expecting to be greeted by Robin Townsend, Alvarez instead was met at the door by a pepper-haired man. The man introduced himself as Rod Moretti, the Miami-based chief pilot for Patriot Airlines. Moretti ushered both cops into the house, leading them into Mike Townsend's office. The two daughters and Robin Townsend stood anxiously around the desk. Pleasantries were exchanged and handshakes extended.

Alvarez asked, "So, you have something on a computer to show me?"

Rod Moretti pointed at the swivel chair behind the desk and said, "Please, Detective. Have a seat." Alvarez nodded, sat down, and looked at a laptop screen. "As Ms. Townsend explained over the phone when she called you, Kim and Ashley brought all of this to my attention. You're looking at Kim's computer. Apparently, Mr. Townsend utilized his daughter's laptop to transact bank business without her knowledge."

Alvarez studied the screen and without looking away, said, "Interesting. I suppose that explains why we found virtually nothing on Mr. Townsend's MacPro." The detective looked at Kim. "And you had absolutely no part in this, young lady?"

Ashley interjected before Kim could speak, and said, "She only knows how to use Facebook and Google."

Kim stuck out her tongue in mock disgust and rolled her eyes. Kim said, "No, Officer. I didn't have a clue that Dad was using my laptop. I mostly use my phone and my iPad anyhow."

Standing in the office doorway, the corner of Tom's lips turned up ever so slightly. It was the first smile Alvarez had seen on the patrol cop in the last twenty-four hours.

"So, how did you get the password for this bank account, Kim?"

"Dad left me a note in the center console of my VW Bug," Kim said, handing the big detective a yellow sticky note.

More explanations and speculations were discussed. The balances in the account were stated with subdued amazement. Robin Townsend remained silent, her expression unreadable. In the midst of the conversation, the gong of the doorbell sounded.

Tom said, “I’ll be glad to get the door.”

Alvarez nodded and watched the patrol cop walk out of the office.

Standing under the portico on the front step was the same stocky man wearing the same sailfish jumping, Tommy Bahama shirt and FBI windbreaker that Tom had seen at the Bayview Drive house. A stubby cigar protruded from the side of his mouth.

“Special Agent Fredricks, I believe?” Tom asked.

“Yes, Officer. May I come in?”

“Can you lose the cigar, sir?”

“It’s not lit, Officer.”

Tom stared at the FBI man for a few seconds without saying a word.

“All right, I get the point,” Ryan Fredricks said, shoving the cigar into a pocket of the windbreaker. “Nobody appreciates a good Romeo and Juileta these days.” He grinned.

“Detective Alvarez is in Mr. Townsend’s office. Please follow me.”

The two men walked down the corridor, nodding to a handful of people that had straggled in earlier to support the family. Tom gestured a hand at the open doorway of the office. Ryan trotted in.

Alvarez stood up from behind the desk and introduced the FBI man to the Townsend family and Rod Moretti. A couple of handshakes. A handful of somber nods. A lot of anxious expressions. A lot of feet shuffled.

“What do you have for me, Detective?” Ryan asked.

Sliding away from the desk, Alvarez motioned for Ryan to sit in the chair he had just vacated. The FBI man nodded, sat down, and studied the laptop screen.

“As per our phone conversation, Special Agent Fredricks,

the Bermuda account is in Mike Townsend's name. For the moment, the laptop is not critical to my investigation. Am I to assume the FBI would like to take custody?"

Still scanning the screen, Ryan said, "I would appreciate that, Detective."

Reaching over to a corner of the desk, Alvarez picked up the sticky note given to him by Kim Townsend. He handed the note to Ryan and said, "You'll need this too. It has the password for the account."

Ryan nodded and abruptly closed the lid of the laptop. He shoved the computer under an arm, stood up, glanced around the room, and said, "Thank you, everybody. If I have any questions, I'll be in touch."

With barely a flurry, Ryan disappeared from the office. Before anyone could comment, the front door clacked. The FBI agent was gone.

Shaking his head, Rod Moretti said, "Interesting man. 'Verbose' is probably not an apt description of his personality."

Alvarez grinned and said, "Agreed. Most likely, the bank account information was self-explanatory. There wasn't much to say."

But judging by Ryan's expression, the detective was certain that the laptop had connected a lot of dots. The federal investigation was becoming more complicated.

19:30 EDT

The shouting and clanking from the maintenance hangar had subsided. The accident airplane had been slid off the tow truck ramp and rolled toward the west wall. The Cherokee had a lost and forlorn appearance, as though it were crying for attention. The two A&P mechanics scoured the damage, mentally assessing their repair strategy. The FAA inspector continued to take notes on a clipboard.

Hart said that he would lock up, dismissing his dad's protests of paperwork to complete. In the midst of all the activity, he hadn't quite decided whether to be angry with his old man or just plain sad. How should he react knowing that he now had a brother?

For the moment, Hart was content to tilt back the chair in his dad's office and sling his feet up on the desk. He soaked in the silence and scanned the photos on the walls. He was surrounded by memories. For the first time in days, he felt a sense of calm.

Hart had just glanced out the window to catch a glimpse of the orange glow left by the setting sun, when a tall figure suddenly appeared as a silhouette in the open door frame. Surprised by the unexpected intrusion, Hart instinctively sat up and slid his feet off the desk and onto the floor. The figure was smiling, white teeth contrasting against the fading light. Hart heard a recognizable, deep-throated chuckle.

The man took a step forward and said, "Sorry, Captain. I didn't mean to surprise you, especially at your age." His smile broadened, the white handlebar mustache widening across a creased, brown face. He reached out a leathery hand and extended it to Hart.

Rising to his feet, grasping the man's hand, Hart grinned and said, "Captain Don Peters, you still have the ability to materialize out of thin air. Only you and the childhood monster of my nightmares can take credit for that talent."

"Are you calling me a ghost?" Don chided.

"Well, you haven't aged since the day you soloed me."

"No need to suck up, Hart. Even my copilots at the airline weren't that blatant before I retired."

"I'm completely serious."

Snorting out a laugh, Don Peters said, "I watched you for a moment before I walked in. It looks like you have the weight of a 747 on your shoulders."

"I wish our airline flew those airplanes."

Hart pointed an upturned palm at the couch, motioning for Don to sit. Don nodded and sunk slowly onto the worn fabric.

Don said, "I've been following you vicariously through your father's reports. The 767 accident in Bermuda. Your dad's health. Your house. And maybe that beautiful woman in your life. Sounds like you've got a lot on your plate."

"No more than anybody else, Captain Peters."

"I see. It's best if you internalize everything. Just like your dad. He taught you well," Don said with a frown.

"Maybe I shouldn't have become an airline pilot. I would have been happier just running the airport with Dad. Fixing airplanes. Fueling them on days when my hands were cold enough to go painfully numb. Screaming at flight instructors for leaving the master switch on. Chasing rich people down for hangar rent. But, no, you got me into the airline mess."

"You're full of shit, Hart. I had nothing to do with it. You went to the airline because it was a goal ever since you were a kid. You were motivated and you persevered. And your dad wanted the same for you. He's proud of his son. All I did was sign my name to a recommendation letter."

"Don, you're full of shit, too." Hart sighed. "You did more than you realize. You were always around to kick me in the ass even when I thought my future would never go beyond Cherokee 140 flight instructor."

"True. And look at your sorry ass now," Don said with a wide grin. He ran his fingers through a cloud of wavy, white hair.

Over the next few minutes the two men discussed various subjects from airplanes to the latest town gossip.

"How's the Bonanza running these days?" Hart asked.

"Haven't been flying it much. It's not the same without

my copilot."

"Sorry, Don. How long has she been gone?"

"Five years now. I miss her every day."

"She was a wonderful woman."

"You should be so lucky, Hart. If you've got something special now, don't fuck it up."

"Guess you've been talking to Dad," Hart said with a wince.

"I just know you. The grass is always greener somewhere else."

"I'm mostly afraid that if I don't pay attention to the grass, it will grow weeds."

"Don't let your mother dictate your happiness, Hart."

Hart exhaled a long breath. He stared out the window at the darkening sky. "Can we change the subject? Whatever happened to the old Super Cub? I was thinking of buying it."

"I'm not sure. The last I heard some overpaid software executive bought it." Don Peters pointed at an old photo of Hart standing by the strut of the Super Cub. "You're pursuing a memory, Hart. It can be dangerous."

"What do you mean?"

"You'll figure it out someday. It's part of the grass-is-greener mentality," Don said with a wry smile.

As Hart was about to probe Don for further explanation, his cell phone warbled Roy Orbison's, "Pretty Woman." Cathy was calling. She hated that ringtone. It embarrassed her. He was surprised that she would call. Even simple arguments took a few days for both of them to cool. And this last argument went beyond simple.

Although Hart motioned for Don to remain, he shook his head and rose from the couch. The mustached man saluted and walked out of the office.

"Hi," Hart said, not knowing if he had used the appropriate amount of enthusiasm.

"Hi," Cathy responded. A moment of silence passed. "I just called to make sure that you were doing okay."

"Thanks. I'm good."

"Same old, Captain Lindy. Suppress the real emotions." Cathy sighed. "I'm very sorry about your house and the airline."

Raising his eyebrows, Hart asked, "What about the airline, Cathy?"

"Are you under a rock? It's all over the news."

"Yes, I am under a rock. I'm at Dad's airport in Otisco."

"Patriot Airlines went Chapter 11. They declared bankruptcy."

Slithering back down into his dad's chair, Hart shook his head. He rested an elbow on the desk, cupped his forehead in a hand, and said, "Shit."

"I'm sorry, Hart."

"I shouldn't be surprised. We all knew the assholes were looking for a way to circumvent any semblance of management skills. It's the best solution. Screw the creditors. Screw the stockholders. And screw the employees. Hopefully, their bonuses will remain intact. This had to be the plan all along."

"I'd be angry too, Hart."

"I can't wait to see how they decimate our pensions."

"Look, I hadn't intended on being the messenger of shitty news, Hart. I just wanted you to know that I cared."

"Thanks."

"Hart, I know you're going through a rough time at the moment, but I can't keep letting you fuck up this relationship. It's not healthy for you or me."

"You're right, Cath."

"Look, don't say anything right now because I don't know if it's the angry Hart Lindy talking or the sad Hart Lindy talking." Cathy exhaled. "Your parents' baggage dictates our relationship. It has to stop if we have any hope of a future together. And I'm not even sure that we have a future at this point."

The phone was silent for a long time.

Cathy asked, "Did any of that make sense?"

"Is it okay for me to talk now?"

"Don't be a jerk, Hart."

"Yes, it makes sense. But I need to think this all through. Does that make sense?"

"Yes, but this time is different. It goes beyond your screwing around and me forgiving you until the next bimbo comes along. You need to find the real Hart Lindy. And honestly, I may not like him."

"Well, you don't like him very much now."

"Hart, you know what I'm saying."

"I may spend some time up here in New York with Dad." Hart exhaled. "Rod said that he'd work out getting me some time off."

"Good idea. And you're talking with Rod again?"

"We're being polite. Nothing has been resolved at the moment. But we're working in that direction."

"That's a step, Hart. Maybe there *is* hope for you."

"I'm thinking I'll DVR a few episodes of 'Dr. Phil.' Maybe that will give me perspective on just how mentally deranged I really am."

"You're an idiot, Hart."

"That's the nicest thing anybody has said to me all day." Hart began to fiddle with a model airplane on the desk. He exhaled a large breath.

"The next call is yours to make, Hart. I'll give you some time."

The phone went quiet. Hart rose to his feet and walked out the office door. He snapped the light switch off. Bankruptcy. Great.

CHAPTER TWENTY-TWO

19:45 EDT

Ryan Fredricks cursed at himself for the decision to take I-95 after leaving the Townsend home. He had moved faster leaving the parking lot of the new Miami stadium after a Dolphins game. In a moment of exasperation, he deliberately bonked his forehead on the steering wheel. Maybe it *was* time to mount that M2 in the bed of his truck sooner than later. The demented thought helped him pass the time.

As Ryan fantasized about the first target he would shoot among the sea of cars ahead of him, his government issued cell phone rang through the speakers in the truck. Glancing at his display, the caller ID indicated an international number. He pressed the talk button on the steering wheel.

"Special Agent Fredricks here."

"Ryan, it's Frank in Port of Spain," a soft-spoken, monotone voice said.

"Hey, Frank. What's the word? Did you catch my globe-trotting attorney?"

"Do you want the good news or the bad news?"

"Crap, Frank. Did you lose the bastard?"

"The short answer is, yes."

"What happened?" Ryan asked with an annoyed tone.

"Before we got to the bank, he had already headed out to the airport and hopped in his jet. According to Piarco Center, the flight plan lists the destination as Manaus, Brazil."

"Manaus is in the middle of nowhere. Couldn't you have

just shot the airplane down?"

"As you know, the Bureau has been discouraging those tactics. It makes us look bad on CNN...and FoxNews for that matter. Don't worry. We'll catch up with Horton."

"And there's good news?" Ryan asked with a sigh. He shook his head at the crawling traffic.

"Well, apparently a meeting was arranged with the bank manager. Two other white males dressed in jackets and ties accompanied Horton to the meeting. The unidentified white males were also passengers from Opa Locka Airport on Horton's Global Express. According to the manager, the exchange was heated. The conversation was recorded on audio and also on video via the security cameras."

"Give me the Reader's Digest version," Ryan said tersely.

"Horton and the other two males were attempting to recover a large sum of cash that had been liquidated from an account--approximately $152 million. The liquidation occurred without their authorization."

"Let me guess. The cash was transported on Flight 63."

"That's why you get paid the big bucks, Ryan."

"So, please make my day and tell me that you identified the other two white males?"

"We did. Are you ready?"

"Frank...please...I hate suspense novels."

"Burt Cummins and Gary Allen. The CFO and CEO of Patriot Airlines."

"Holy shit," Ryan said with a voice that was barely audible.

"My sentiments, exactly."

"Where are these guys now? In your custody, I hope."

"Nope, we're sending them to you."

"Seriously?"

"We discovered that they had already booked reservations via their company travel system back to Miami. Why deal with extradition if they're already on their way back to the U.S.?"

"Cummins and Allen are not very good criminals," Ryan said with a snort.

"Alleged criminals."

"Text me the flight number and seat numbers. I'll assemble a team at MIA to greet the 'alleged criminals.'"

The cars in Ryan's lane began to move at a pace that could be considered actual driving speed. A few hundred yards ahead, he could see the flashing lights of a tow truck and a couple of patrol cars. The vehicle mess of the accident that had apparently caused the traffic jam was being reshuffled out of the travel lanes and onto the shoulder. Ryan caught sight of a crumpled hood and a mangled windshield facing opposite the flow of traffic.

The soft-spoken voice said, "And Ryan. I've got one more thing for you to munch on."

"I'm listening."

"When the bank manager left the office temporarily during the meeting with Horton, et al, the recorded conversation indicated that the bankruptcy filing for Patriot Airlines had already occurred prior to their departure from Opa Locka Airport."

"Interesting," Ryan replied. He thought of Hart Lindy and the other hundreds of employees that worked for the airline. This was going to be a miserable experience for those people and their families

"I thought you'd like to corroborate the bankruptcy filing with the forensic accounting geeks."

Ryan heard a beep over the truck's speakers. He glanced at his phone that was resting in a cup holder of the center console. The phone displayed a Broward County number. He was getting another call.

Ryan said, "Not bad work after all, Frank. If anything

else pertinent comes to your attention, you know where to find me. I'm getting another call. Talk to you soon."

"Will do, Ryan."

After mashing the Talk button on his steering wheel, Ryan answered, "Special Agent Fredricks."

A familiar voice asked, "I was wondering if you guys carried those laminated, give-me-immunity-from-prosecution cards these days?"

"It depends. Who is this?"

"It's Detective Alvarez. In the interest of cooperation and brotherly love, I've got a witness that you may just want to join me with in a nice chat."

"Who might that be?"

"The sister of the pilot's dead boyfriend and owner of the restaurant on Los Olas. She claims to have information regarding Mike Townsend's motives. And she wants immunity."

"You've got my attention."

"Thought so. Swing your monster truck on over to the crime scene at the restaurant on Los Olas. The sister will meet us there."

"On my way," Ryan said. He pressed the button on the steering wheel, ending the call.

Fortunately, the flow of cars on I-95 had continued to accelerate. Even with the multitude of traffic lights on Broward Boulevard and Los Olas, Ryan arrived at the restaurant in fifteen minutes. Despite the angry eyes of two patrol cops, he rolled a couple of tires up on the sidewalk and parked the truck just west of the crime scene at the far end of the yellow tape.

He grabbed an unlit cigar from his ashless ashtray, shoved it between his teeth, and climbed out of the truck. He flashed his credentials at the approaching cops who appeared anxious to unholster their weapons. Acknowledging his FBI status, the cops nodded with rolling eyes.

The restaurant had a small frontage with large, open-framed glass to one side of a cherry-stained wooden door. Both an American flag and a rainbow flag mounted above the door flapped quietly in the breeze. Ryan pulled on the door handle and walked into the restaurant.

When his eyes had adjusted to the dim light, Ryan spotted Alvarez and a round-faced brunette seated at a wooden table. Her elbows were perched on the tabletop. She was rubbing her forehead, the locks of her short hair in mild disarray. The woman had a bowling pin shape to her stout figure.

The big, brown detective waved Ryan over to the table. After introductions were made, Ryan sat opposite the woman. He pulled the cigar from his mouth and rolled it around between his fingers.

Nodding at the woman, Alvarez said, "Sharon Goodman has requested immunity from prosecution based on information she is willing to provide concerning her deceased brother and Mr. Townsend."

"What kind of information, Ms. Goodman?" Ryan asked in a serious tone. He locked eyes with the brunette.

"I am aware of the finance aspect regarding Mike Townsend's strategy and his motivation," Sharon responded in a matter of fact tone.

"Okay. And how would you have knowledge of such information?" Ryan asked.

"My brother and I were close. Our blue-collar father did not approve of Jonathan's lifestyle. He did his best to avoid contact with my brother except for the occasional holiday. And Mom did her best to avoid conflict with anybody. So in essence, I was really my brother's only family."

"I get the picture."

"You probably don't, Special Agent Fredricks, but it doesn't matter." The brunette sighed. "Jonathan loved Mike

Townsend. Mike had a glamorous occupation. He traveled the world. He was a type-A personality. And Mike's other life, the one with kids and two cats in the yard, added an element of mystery and even danger. But Mike's slow acceptance of his homosexuality made him vulnerable, an attractive quality to my brother."

"I appreciate the background insight, but I can't offer immunity based on your opinion."

"I have fairly specific information, Special Agent Fredricks."

"Ms. Goodman, I can't guarantee anything, because it's not completely up to me. But if you weren't directly involved with your brother's murder, or anyone else's for that matter, then immunity is a possibility."

The stout woman glanced around the restaurant for a brief moment. She clasped her hands together and placed them on the tabletop. She drew in a deep breath.

"I am a licensed financial advisor and a CPA. The information I disclose could jeopardize my career and/ or subject me to an SEC investigation. The fact that the FBI might criminally prosecute would seem minor in comparison."

Ryan nodded and held out his hands with palms up, beckoning her to continue.

"Before my brother and Mike Townsend developed their relationship, Mike had made a bad financial decision. He had dumped a major portion of his investments into a fund that financed rock concerts and other similar venues. The concert promoter promised an outrageous rate of return." The brunette shook her head. "I think you can predict the end of the story. The promoter declared personal bankruptcy and literally disappeared from the country.

"Apparently, during a break at a negotiating session with Patriot Airlines and the pilots union, Mike compared notes with one of the company executives. His name was Bob Redmond."

Alvarez raised his eyebrows and exchanged glances with Ryan. Simultaneously, they both drew their arms across their chests.

"Redmond had also lost a substantial amount of money investing in the same concert fund. Apparently, because the promoter was a former airline pilot, he was trusted. In any case, Redmond offered Mike an opportunity to recoup his losses simply by transferring funds from union accounts to an escrow account held by a New York law firm. He would collect a commission based on a percentage that was deposited and then transferred. Mike was PAPA's secretary/treasurer, so such transactions would be under his control."

"But why utilize the union's account?" Alvarez asked.

Ryan looked at Sharon and said, "Because if anything went wrong, it wouldn't be traced to a personal account. But if the transactions were discovered, the pilots union could be blamed. It would be a nice corruption scandal."

Sharon said, "Correct. Which is how the news media is portraying it anyhow. Mike accepted that risk for the reward. His straight family was never aware of the financial loss. His conscience was keeping him up at night. Although Mike never asked, he was fairly certain that the money was coming from executive stock bonuses."

"So what compelled him to steal the cash?" Ryan asked.

"Just before he was almost made whole from his concert fund losses, he received information that the company was going to declare bankruptcy. It was confirmation that the executive stock options that had been cashed out a little bit at a time were insurance that management paychecks wouldn't be in jeopardy.

"Mike wanted out. But Redmond refused to release him from his services. The bastard threatened to reveal Mike's homosexuality to his family. Gay pilots are not exactly accepted with open arms in the profession. In addition, Redmond threatened to reveal his concert fund loss and his money laundering activity. So Mike took matters into his own hands, and removed the funds from the bank in Trinidad as extortion to use as leverage so he could end his money laundering role."

Clearing his throat, Ryan asked, "And what was your role in this scheme?"

"I advised my brother on various aspects of transferring funds without drawing attention both domestically and internationally. And I advised Mike on an appropriate investment portfolio."

"Anything else, Ms. Goodman?" Alvarez asked.

"No, not that I can think of at the moment." The brunette exhaled. "I just wanted Jonathan and Mike's relationship to work out. Mike was setting the foundation to establish his family's financial independence without him. In colloquial terms, he was going to come out of the closet. But my brother knew better. He felt Mike was unrealistic. And the scheme to extort over $150 million was beyond his comprehension. In the end, my brother got caught in the middle. I miss him more than anything in the world."

A moment of silence permeated the group. The activity of a few detectives scurrying about, others snapping photos of various items surrounding the bar area, and hushed conversations of uniformed cops became more noticeable.

Slipping the cigar back in his mouth and rising from the table, Ryan said, "Thank you, Ms. Goodman. That was a riveting story. We'll be in touch. Please don't stray far from home." The FBI man nodded at Alvarez and then disappeared out the door.

CHAPTER TWENTY-THREE

Monday
07:55 EDT

It had been a fitful night's sleep for Hart. He had attempted to rid his mind of thoughts, but the exercise became a vicious circle. The harder he attempted, the more he focused on his thoughts. It didn't help matters that the mattress in his old room had developed a sag precisely in the geographic center. Nor did it help that Piper, Dad's elderly cat of twelve years and twenty pounds, was determined to share the exact same space.

Still groggy, Hart scanned the walls surrounding the bed. The room itself hadn't really changed since the day he had left for college. But over a period of time, Dad had made it a shrine to Hart's accomplishments. Photos of him wearing a cap and gown. His first 4-bar, captain's epaulets. Plaques. Trophies. Posters. More photos.

In the midst of Hart's fuzzy reminiscing, his cell phone vibrated. The phone rattled a shaky dance across the top of the marred nightstand. He looked at the caller ID. Crap. It was Ryan Fredricks. What had he done now?

Hart pressed the Talk button and said, "I told the front desk not to bother with a wake-up call."

"Well, you won't be getting room service either," Ryan said with a sneer in his tone.

"Good morning, Special Agent Fredricks. To what do I owe this displeasure?"

"When exactly were you going to tell me about the transactions Mike Townsend was making via union accounts?"

"Thought it was already common knowledge with you guys."

"Now it is. But we hadn't confirmed the transactions until a few hours ago."

"And?"

"You had knowledge of this information and failed to disclose it. That's obstruction of justice."

"I went to New York for the purpose of discovery with regard to Horton and Carty and the law firm's relationship to Mike Townsend, Bob Redmond, and the airline." Hart snapped a Kleenex from the nightstand and blew his nose. "I'll turn myself in to the local police."

Ryan exhaled a long and slow breath. He said, "I get it, Captain Lindy. You were attempting to protect your boy until you had more information. But now you give me pause for concern that you might be withholding additional intelligence."

"I've got nothing else, Ryan."

"Well, I'll be the judge of that later." Ryan paused. "Moving along, as opposed to your clandestine tactics, I have information to share. Are you sitting down?"

Adjusting the pillows against the backboard of the bed, Hart said, "Actually, I happen to be lying down. Go ahead."

Hart's dad poked his head in the door and pantomimed bringing a fork to his mouth. It was breakfast time. Hart nodded. Dad's favorite, scrambled eggs and cheese, were probably on the menu.

Ryan said, "Last night I had the pleasure of making the acquaintance of your CEO and CFO. My team and I met them on the jet bridge of your airline's flight arriving from Port of Spain, Trinidad. We fitted them for bracelets and brought them to our office."

"Excuse me?"

"We arrested them on suspicion of money laundering… at least to start."

"Holy shit."

"It appears that the bankruptcy filing was long ago their strategy. Aware of the possibility that a bankruptcy judge could potentially negate a previously arranged compensation package, the CEO, CFO, and VP of Ops conspired to transfer the proceeds from their stock bonuses. The stock sales were done over time in small amounts so as not to arouse suspicion with the SEC."

"Okay, so how did Mike Townsend and PAPA enter into the picture?" Hart asked.

"First Officer Townsend was a conduit. He deposited the stock bonus proceeds into your pilots union account and then transferred them to the law firm of Horton and Carty. He would then physically take the cash on his trips to Trinidad and deposit them in a Port of Spain bank."

"That sounds simple."

"It gets complicated. Horton and Carty laundered the money and then took their commission."

"Yikes."

"It gets better. Your Middle Eastern guy, now identified as Sayid Abdul-Qadir, was actually an accountant of sorts. He took part of the commission money from the law firm and transferred it to Syria. In exchange, Horton and Carty were paid financial advisory fees for managing certain accounts in Syria. We haven't quite figured out the routing, but our finance geeks are still working on the forensics."

"Terrorism? ISIS?" Hart asked.

"It would appear. But this whole plan blew up literally on the airplane when Mike Townsend physically moved the funds. That's why these guys flew down to Trinidad in

Ted Horton's private jet. They were hoping to recover at least some of the funds before the bankruptcy filing was announced."

"But why take the extra step of depositing money into our union account?"

"I'll get to that in a minute."

"So what happened to Bob Redmond? Was he getting greedy?"

"Reading between the lines of our interrogation process, it would seem Redmond was getting anxious. When he held a meeting with you, Abdul-Qadir probably saw the VP of Ops as a liability. We're still waiting on the autopsy, but it seems likely Redmond was murdered by Abdul-Qadir."

With a quiet rap on the bedroom door, John Lindy peered into the bedroom. He displayed a thumbs-up. Breakfast was ready.

Hart said, "Ryan, hang on a minute. My room service is at the door." John Lindy frowned with a curious smile. Hart pulled the phone away from his ear. "Sorry, Dad. This call may take a while longer. Can you keep my plate warm for a bit?" His dad nodded, shook his head, and shuffled down the hall toward the kitchen. "So how did Mike Townsend get involved with this financial intrigue?"

"Good question. Let me tell you a bedtime story. Well… it was a bedtime story for me last night."

With all the inflection of Ben Stein in his *Ferris Beuller* role, Ryan Fredricks provided a narrative of Mike Townsend's fall from grace. The explanation was presented like a business-as-usual event.

Deliberately imitating Ryan Fredricks, Hart asked in the tone of *Dragnet*'s Joe Friday, "And that's it?"

"I'm sure there are more pieces to the jigsaw puzzle, but, yes, that's it for now, Mr. Smart-ass Airline Pilot."

With a softened voice, Hart said, "You did good work

Special Agent Fredricks."

"Thanks." A moment of silence passed. "I'm sorry about your airline. Back when I was a kid, it was rough on my dad and our family when the machine shop declared bankruptcy and closed its doors."

"Well, I appreciate the sentiment, but airline bankruptcies are different. The flying public never sees a thing. It's just the employees, the creditors, and the stockholders that suffer the most wounds."

"Understood."

"Anything else, Special Agent Fredricks?"

"Not at the moment. If I need your expertise, I know how to find you. Nice working with you, Captain."

"Same."

The line went silent and the phone displayed "Call ended." Hart was just about to place the phone back onto the nightstand, when it vibrated again in his hand. He glanced at the display. This time it was an email alert. He tapped the email icon with a thumb, expecting to see the usual potpourri of Viagra deals and rental car specials, but one email caught his attention.

The email was from an individual. It was someone Hart didn't recognize. His curiosity aroused, he opened the message. It read:

To: Captain Hart Lindy
From: Tonya Gibson
Subject: Crash of TransGlobal Flight 4291

Hello Captain Lindy,

I am writing this note to ask for your assistance regarding the investigation of TransGlobal Flight 4291 that crashed on approach five years ago today while landing at JFK. My father, Tom Gibson, was the captain of that flight. As you know, there was only one survivor-- a flight attendant.

Through the findings of a toxicology report, my father was said to have alcohol in his bloodstream. The NTSB listed my father's impairment as a probable cause for the accident. The media reported my father to be a recovering alcoholic. This fact is true. However, Dad had been faithfully attending both AA meetings and the airline's addiction program for two years prior. He was clean and sober.

With all my heart, I believe that my father has been wrongfully accused and that another probable cause is the culprit for this tragedy. Beyond the lawsuits and the financial hardships that my family will endure, it is more important that I clear my father's name and reputation. He was a good man and a well-respected professional.

A captain from your airline spoke highly of your investigative skills. He thought that you might consider assisting my family and offered your email address. My apologies for invading your privacy, but it is my hope that you would come to our rescue. Our attorneys would be glad to discuss terms of a consulting contract.

Thank you for your time.

Sincerely,
Tonya Gibson

Shaking his head, Hart recalled the devastation of the accident. Fatalities on the airplane. Fatalities on the ground. The death of a popular country music star. It became a media firestorm. Drunk pilots. Drug and alcohol testing prior to every flight. Why would he want to get involved?

And then Hart thought for a moment. Maybe he *should* get involved. If indeed this captain was innocent of causing the horrible accident, then shouldn't the world know what really occurred? Perhaps this was a new way to give back, to pay it forward.

Hart took in a deep breath and slid off the squeaky bed. He put on a pair of oil-stained jeans and slipped the sweatshirt with the Piper Cub logo over his head. He ran a few fingers through his matted, dirty blonde hair and shuffled in his bare feet out his bedroom and into the kitchen.

Reading the paper and sipping his coffee, John Lindy sat at the round breakfast table. He glanced up at Hart and gestured his chin at the chipped dinner plate that was topped by an oversized pot cover. Hart nodded, sat down, and lifted the pot cover. He smiled at a steaming plate of mustard-yellow scrambled eggs covered in a swirl of cheddar cheese. A browned English muffin doused in butter rested off to the side.

"Thanks, Dad," Hart said.

His father muttered an unintelligible acknowledgement and continued to read the paper. Hart scooped a fork into his scrambled eggs and looked around the battered kitchen. The Formica countertop had knife wounds and stains. Cupboards had hinges attached by only one screw, the wood marred and faded. Dishes sat in a yellowed white tub of a sink. The gooseneck faucet percolated a drop of water once every few seconds.

"I'm reading about your airline," John Lindy said. "I'm sorry."

"Thanks. We'll see how this all plays out," Hart said, making his first attempt at sounding upbeat.

"Was that phone call about the accident in Bermuda?"

"It was."

"The newspaper is saying that the copilot was the criminal and the union laundered money for the airline."

"That's also what the phone call was about, Dad. It was the FBI agent that I worked with during the investigation. There's a lot more to the story. Hopefully the whole truth will be released soon. So don't believe everything you read."

"I never do." John Lindy dropped the paper onto the kitchen table and looked at Hart. "Are you going to be all right?"

"Yeah, Dad. I think so," Hart said with a thin smile.

John Lindy stared at his son for a moment and then rose from the table. He grabbed his empty plate, and walked toward the sink. He asked, "How about a cup of coffee?"

"Sure, Dad. That would be great."

Hart's father pulled the glass carafe from the ancient Mr. Coffee machine, walked back to the kitchen table, and poured the dark brown liquid into Hart's empty mug.

"I'm going to get some fresh air on the deck. Finish your eggs and meet me outside if you'd like," John Lindy said. He walked away from the table, opened the sliding glass door, and stepped outside.

Not realizing that he was famished, Hart finished his breakfast in a flurry. He dumped his plate in the sink and joined his dad, who was leaning on the outer railing of the deck. The wood planking was peeled and warped, the stain almost nonexistent.

Holding his cup of steaming coffee, Hart asked, "What if I stay here for a while, Dad? I could take some time off from the airline and help you run this place."

John Lindy turned to face his son and said, "You *have* gone insane."

"Seriously, Dad. I could use a break."

"Is this one of those help-the-poor-old-man sympathy things?"

"No. It's not. Well, maybe a little bit."

"Can I think about it?"

"Sure, Dad."

In the distance, the rumble of jet engines grew louder. The sound competed with the chirping birds and the rustle of the leaves. Instinctively, both men gazed up into the pale, blue sky. A twin-engine jetliner was silhouetted against the atmospheric canvas, its two contrails flowing behind in a billowing straight line of white.

Watching the airplane, Hart said, "You know, Dad, I think our wise, old buddy Captain Peters was right."

"How's that?"

"It's no longer the magic of the Bernoulli Principle that creates the lift to keep airplanes airborne. Greed keeps those airliners airborne. Those wings are made from paper. That's all they are. Just paper wings."

Hart shook his head. Maybe it was time to refocus his priorities. He had a lot to consider, perhaps a new life chapter. He put an arm around his dad's shoulder and smiled.

08:15 EDT

Wishing she could stop crying and feeling angry all at the same time, Robin Townsend crossed her arms and stared out through the glass sliding doors at the canal. A seagull perched on a piling flapped its wings and then launched skyward but not before depositing a splotch of white, the act an apropos reflection of her mood.

The Tiara that the girls had brought home after their abduction was still tied up at the dock. It was evidence, a crime scene. When the hell were they going to move that fucking yacht! The boat was a reminder of all that had gone wrong. It was a reminder of what she would never have.

How were they going to survive? Although $500,000 in insurance money sounded like a fortune, it would only last so long. She couldn't believe that was the only policy Mike had purchased. She should have paid closer attention to their finances. She should have paid closer attention to their marriage.

Robin heard a shuffling of feet and turned to see her daughters approaching. Ashley was holding her laptop, the lid open. The girls were smiling. Kim was pointing at the screen.

"Mom, we have something to show you," Ashley said.

Stepping behind the girls and looking over their shoulders at the laptop screen, Robin said, "Okay. I hope it's something funny. I could use a laugh today."

Kim said, "It depends upon your perspective, Mom." Kim pointed at a number on the screen. "This is Ashley's online investment account. Do you remember when Dad set us both up with college funds?"

"Yes, but I never paid much attention. My understanding from Dad was that you really weren't doing much except depositing some of your allowance."

"Mostly true, Mom," Ashley said. "But…do you see this balance?"

Squinting, Robin stared at a number. She read aloud, "Two million, two-hundred-three thousand, four-hundred eighty-two." Robin reflected for a moment. "Is that dollars?"

"Yes, Mom, it's dollars," Kim said with a smirk.

Clutching Ashley gently by the arm and whirling her around, Robin asked, "Where did that money come from, Ashley?"

"It came from Dad," Ashley said.

"Please explain."

Ashley pursed her lips and then opened her mouth. She said, "Dad told me that he was involved with an investment that was making us lots of money. He wanted to keep it a secret, so he periodically deposited the proceeds into my account."

"You're serious?" Robin asked with raised eyebrows. Her thoughts wandered. She remembered the months they had borrowed from a savings account to pay the bills.

"Dad got me interested in finance. I learned about investing. My portfolio did well. I almost doubled Dad's deposits."

"My little sister is a badass!" Kim exclaimed, raising a fist in the air. "And all this time I thought she was a Girl Scout!"

Robin plopped down onto the arm of the sofa and said, "And you kept this a secret?"

"I'm sorry, Mom. Daddy made me promise. And honestly it just seemed like a game to me." Ashley waved her hand across the laptop screen. "They were just numbers on the computer, not dollars."

"Who else knows about this, Ashley?" Robin asked.

"Just the three of us."

"It has to stay that way. Do you girls understand?" Robin said, staring into the wide eyes of both daughters. Kim and Ashley nodded in unison. Mentally crossing her fingers, Robin hoped the FBI wouldn't make a new discovery. The three of them just might be all right.

Robin began to smile for the first time in days. "Thanks for making me laugh, girls."

*

Thank you for reading Paper Wings. Reviews help authors reach readers. If you enjoyed the book the way I hope you did, then I would appreciate an honest review at:

http://wbp.bz/paperwingsa

You can sign up for advance notice of new releases at:

http://wildbluepress.com/AdvanceNotice

Thanks again for reading.